MW01463220

It's Not Dark Yet

SIMON PACK NOVEL # 3

John M. Vermillion

ISBN: **1543133592**
ISBN 13: **9781543133592**

Prologue

September

Cody Wilcox's watch sergeant that evening concluded his inspection with his standard admonition: "Obey the law. Follow your oath. Do your duty. Dismissed." The squad saluted smartly and moved out briskly.

The rookie patrolman took the keys to a cruiser numbered A102. This was a new number to him. When he found it, he was slightly disappointed, in that it was a slick top, one devoid of the standard mounted light bars. To effect a stop you had to reach outside the window to mount the magnetically attached twirling red light to the roof.

In Montana all cops, local and state, attend the same academy. Cody Wilcox was never a gifted athlete and even some in his family were dubious he could successfully complete the rigorous 26-week course. And even if he did make it, he wasn't guaranteed to get one of the few openings available. He drove himself harder than he had in any pursuit in his life, and graduated with honors. He reflected as he drove the Missoula streets that it was proper to feel pride in his unexpected accomplishment. He determined to distinguish himself again as a valued member of the force, maybe even rise a rank or three before his career wound down.

Wilcox cruised northwest along Business Loop 90, also known as Broadway, at 0234 hours on a Tuesday morning in Missoula. He constantly scanned for anything out of the ordinary that might put citizens or property in danger. It was that time of autumn when the overnight temperatures were demanding a change into winter clothing, and drivers were dialing up their vehicle heaters. The 19,000-acre city of 70,000 inhabitants was asleep. Even the college haunts were dead. As Wilcox approached the complex of buildings housing the Montana DOT and Highway Patrol on one side and the Missoula County Detention Center on the other, an ill-maintained Range Rover roared at high speed down Broadway in the opposite direction. Cody reckoned the man he glimpsed behind the wheel was doing 70, maybe 80, on this city street, with only his parking lights illuminated. Cody thought maybe he hadn't seen license plates either.

Cody Wilcox slapped on the red lollipop light, did a swift U-turn and sped in the direction of the Range Rover. The cruiser speedometer read sixty, then seventy, then seventy-five. As he called in the pursuit, he added, "He's slowing to a stop. I've got this." Wilcox could see the man in the Rover's passenger side mirror. He strode toward the offender deliberately, on the oblique. "Good evening, sir," Cody said, "Do you know why I've pulled you over?"

The occupant was a scruffy white man, of middle age, bearded, long hair sticking out of a University of Montana Griz baseball cap, looked to be 180 pounds or so. He did not reply. "Sir, do you understand why I stopped you?" Wilcox repeated. Still no response.

Cody had noted the decal on the rear window. It read, "Sovereign Citizens." The decal told Cody the fellow would likely be cranky, stubborn even, but not really a hardened criminal. A third time he asked the man to cooperate, but for a third time got no answer. That's when he began to think through the department mantra, which they called "ATM," for "Ask, Tell, Make." It's the way in which patrolmen were instructed to ramp up pressure on an offender. The next step therefore entailed ordering the offender to comply with his directions.

"Step out of your vehicle sir, now," Cody said authoritatively, his right hand now gripping the sidearm in his holster. "As you do, keep your hands up and away from your body where I can see them."

"No way, copper," the man said. "You have no power over me, no authority to make me comply with any instruction. I do not recognize the authority of any government agency, and that most damn especially includes your department."

Time to proceed to step three of ATM. As he stepped forward to open the driver's door, Cody's eyes widened as he saw the man whip up a Colt 1911. Before Officer Wilcox could get his sidearm out, he had taken a bullet squarely in his forehead. Red lollipop still flashing, the Range Rover pulled away, thumping slightly as it ran over Wilcox's splayed arm.

The dispatcher's voice rang through the night air: "Romeo Uniform 324, Romeo Uniform 324, SITREP, OVER."

♦ ♦ ♦

In the Deep Woods Along the Montana-Canada Border: Ng Trang sat in his four-wheeler in an overwatch position. Through his high-powered, fourth-generation night scope he could observe the handoff of the big booze shipment down below. His men didn't know for sure Trang was able to witness this operation, but they never took chances. Cross Trang, or imperil an operation through lack of precision, and you were a dead man, and that applied to women in his employ as well. Two eighteen-wheelers were transferring control of Canadian booze, mostly whiskey, which represented a profit to Trang of roughly $400,000 US. Most was being cached for the time being, but some was being transloaded onto smaller vehicles for shipment today. Ingress and egress routes had been carefully choreographed and the applicable authorities paid off to ensure safe passage. The concealed cache site would be emptied within two weeks, its contents delivered throughout America.

Trang was a smart guy, a leader in his SoCal high school, National Honor Society, recipient of a comprehensive academic scholarship to Berkeley. An omnivorous reader, Trang dropped out after a year in which he stumbled upon, through truant reading, a small mountain of information about early-20th-century bootleggers in Montana. Many of the stories he read were about women who, unable to rear their children on their meager incomes from sewing and canning and other matronly pursuits, took to brewing moonshine. They developed elaborate distribution strategies. After Washington state passed Prohibition in 1916, and Montana in 1918—preliminary to the Eighteenth Amendment establishing federal Prohibition in 1920—some of these ladies were raking in $2,500 clear every two weeks, an enormous sum in those days. One of these women, Birdie Brown, an African-American woman from Missouri who homesteaded in eastern Fergus County, Montana, allegedly produced the best home brew in the country. In some cases, they had contacts among the rail workers, and when the train stopped, the booze handoff occurred. Why not, Trang reasoned, update and expand upon the path these legends had followed?

It didn't take Trang long to implement his vision and turn his profits over, getting himself tied into gunrunning contacts on the coast of North America. Ng Trang found himself on top of an illicit empire, far out of reach of the Feds. Ng Trang: cautious, curious, lethal, a man who imposed his considerable intelligence upon every circumstance, a man ever on the lookout to enlarge his already-abundant basket of holdings.

♦ ♦ ♦

The Reverend wasn't sure how he had wound up in this hellish place. The wife was afraid to step outside with all the vicious animals skulking around, ready to pounce on a good serving of fat and protein. His church elders back in Georgia had told him this was a sterling opportunity. They painted it as a kind of "missionary" assignment. At first he had thought they were about to inform him they were posting him someplace exotic, like—what with the opening of relations with that country—to Cuba. So it was quite a shock when they told him he was heading to the Yaak Valley area of northwest Montana, and he wasn't immediately sure how to react. He was daggum certain he couldn't put his finger on Montana if given a blank map of the states.

"The National Conference has long wanted to take advantage of the unique opportunity that area presents, Dar," the Bishop stated solemnly. As he spoke he surveyed with pride the wood-paneled office, bookshelves brimming with heavy theological texts. He steepled his hands before proceeding. "They inquired as to whether I might identify a good man to fill this new position. Thus, I have, after much thought and prayer, decided you are the fit. Do you understand me? I said the fit. A lot of people are depending on you, Reverend Castor. Don't let us down." In point of brutal fact, the Bishop was lying shamelessly, even as he was feeling righteously imperious. This Protestant denomination didn't fire ministers, especially ones forty-eight years of age. They needed to put Reverend Dar someplace he could do the least damage until he reached the minimum retirement age of sixty-two. "You'll have a week to get your belongings together. We've covered the details of moving your household goods." Reverend Dar remained stuporous as the Bishop rose to shake hands in farewell. As Dar rose, the normally humorless Bishop stifled a guffaw. Dar was wearing a black dead man's suit his father had bought him. The coat was unbuttoned, and the sides and tail were tucked tightly into the seat of his trousers, waist size sixty. "New fashion, Reverend?" the Bishop asked with a vulpine smile that displayed flavescent teeth; Dar had clearly come directly from the toilet. The Bishop thinking, "This picture of Reverend Dar is the perfect metaphor for his ineptness as a man of the cloth." The Bishop failed to imagine his own line of prevarication was anything more than a venial sin.

Chapter One

At that hour, ere the morn was born, Montana Governor Simon Pack set about attacking the day in his usual vigorous fashion. His four-year term was nearing the termination point, and he had made a solemn pledge not to seek a follow-on term. Those four years back he had exchanged the uniform of a Marine three-star for the respectable civilian clothing of an elected leader of his state. In the Capitol office he donned suit and tie. When out among the people, he attired himself in a style he thought of as casual-respectable, relying chiefly on his durable stock of Duluth Trading Company and Carhartt.

Pack wasn't given to looking back. Nothing conscious, that's just how his mind worked. There was always plenty of work ahead, and time was too precious to spend congratulating oneself on accomplishments, or for dwelling on failures. And Pack did have much he could have congratulated himself for, and more than he liked to acknowledge that hadn't panned out as he wanted. A man did the best he could, confident his sense of right and wrong didn't fail him too often.

He had been the greatest college football lineman of his generation. After West Point, he followed his father, who was killed at Khe Sanh when Simon was but a lad, into the Marine Corps, where he became a much- and properly-decorated fighting man for numerous acts of heroism. He had followed one personal dictum more closely than any other: stay as close to the combat Marine as he could for as long as he could. Bureaucratic politics meant nothing to him beyond recognizing he would avoid those involved in it. After leaving the Corps as a three-star, a brilliant Army General named William Harris Green persuaded him to return to active duty as Superintendent of his Alma Mater. After one year at West Point, a year in which he resurrected pride of place and mission at the

Academy, he went toe-to-toe with the President, backing the latter down from a plan which effectively would have dismantled West Point. And not to be forgotten was his return to national prominence as the Heroic Hobo who took down the head of al-Qaeda America. After leaving the Superintendency, Pack toppled the leading financier of the President's campaign, a crony capitalist who had pledged $100 million for his re-election. More recently, as Governor, he had devoted much of his opening two years in office leading fellow governors in a convention of the states, the effect of which was to offset the extra-Constitutional excesses of the present Administration. Of all the three hundred-plus million people in America, the President regarded Pack as Enemy One. Simon Pack may have been loathed in Washington, DC, but to the citizens of his state he was the lucida of this constellation in which they resided.

This morning he was following his routine. Rise between 0400 and 0430, get coffee downstairs, stuff two breakfast sandwiches into his cargo pockets, and trek in the darkness the seven miles to his Capitol office. He eschewed being picked up by a state trooper each day, knowing that the short drive would shortchange him by eliminating this essential time to ruminate. This daily pre-dawn perambulation constituted his most coveted oasis of thought. Like an athlete watching through his mind's eye every detail of a blocking technique, or of his swing path on a breaking ball, Pack played the events of the coming day on his brain's video.

Once in his office, he would review the material his Lieutenant Governor, James Dahl, had stacked neatly in the center of his desk, make notes and interrogatories for return to staff, then shower and shave in his personal washroom. Today, as had been the case since roughly the start of year three, he would dress casually and by nine would be on the helipad for a day out among the people. He had always believed in management by walking around, and the helicopter gave him the ability to manage by flying around. Not much picture-taking with the Guv, at least in Helena, during Pack's tenure. This morning he would meet with a citizen's group in Browning, the Blackfoot tribal seat. The chopper Pack used was an old UH-1H, commonly called a Huey, one of five on loan from the US Forest Service as part of the Federal Excess Personal Property program. Until such time as the Forestry Service required the helicopters to fight fires, they were under the operational control of the Montana Department of Natural Resources and Conservation. This Huey had been adapted for firefighting, but Pack had secured permission to employ it as personal transport during no-fire periods. The manifest normally consisted of three people: the pilot, a distinguished former Army aviator named Paul Fardink; Tetu Palaita, Pack's bodyman and Man Friday; and Pack himself. Pack had flown in this type airframe so often he was reasonably confident he could, in an emergency, fly it by himself.

Paul Fardink was one of Pack's few close personal friends. He socialized more with Fardink than anyone in Helena excepting his female friend, Keeley Eliopoulos. Their admiration was mutual. Fardink had retired from the Army five years ago and returned to his hometown of Helena. A graduate of West Point himself, Fardink leapt at the chance to pilot the Governor. Paul performed the job for a pittance, explaining to his wife that he regarded it as a small way to repay Pack for what he had done to revive, and subsequently save, West Point.

♦ ♦ ♦

Tetu Palaita was a gigantic American Samoan who had linked up with Pack at a serendipitous meeting in an Allentown, Pennsylvania, diner less than four years ago. Tetu still called Pack "Matai," a term of great respect in his native land, roughly translatable as "honored chief." From wounds sustained in Afghanistan, Tetu had been medically retired as an Army sergeant. Tetu believed the Army had pulled the medical retirement trigger too quickly, and had from the start expressed confidence he could regain a condition approximating his pre-injury levels of strength and stamina. With Pack's encouragement and guidance, Tetu had recuperated, and even thrived. The Army's loss was Pack's gain. They had been through their own fights together, physical encounters, a few involving gunplay, with Tetu demonstrating repeatedly his dedication to Pack. Tetu was sounding board, advisor, helpmate. If Pack was Matai, Tetu was myrmidon.

Six months from leaving office, Pack began to query Tetu about his future, urging him to commence a job search. Pack felt a strong obligation to his loyal subordinate. Pack made clear to Tetu that he could stay in Pack's cabin in western Montana for however much time he needed to get a job and settle himself into his own place. During his time as Governor, Pack had spoken glowingly of Tetu to lots of people around the state, and knew many gladly would hire Tetu, a man of many talents. Tetu never replied to Pack other than to express thanks, and Pack believed he knew why. During the gubernatorial campaign Tetu had fallen into the company of a Native American girl, of the Blackfoot tribe, named Swan Threemoons.

"Remember, Tetu, back in Pennsylvania when you caught me looking at Keeley's contact info? You said I should just go ahead and call her?"

"Sure, Matai, I remember. Why are you thinking of that now?" Tetu asked.

"Because it's time for me to tell you I'm well aware you've been seeing Miss Threemoons lots of weekends, and it's OK. Listen up: your wanting to spend time with her doesn't mean you're being disloyal to me. I want you to be happy. And I've seen those times when you have a special bounce in your step, and it hasn't been hard to figure out what has just come before. You've either been talking with her or you've been visiting her. Mind if I ask a personal question?"

"Matai can ask any question, and I will answer if I have answer," Tetu said.

"Great," Pack said with a grin. "Have you been introduced to her family, and if so do they accept you?"

"Tetu has met them. *All* of them. There are many Threemoons, that I can say. They tell Tetu he seems like Blackfoot to them, even if he does not carry their blood. Our cultures are much alike. A Swan brother calls me Warrior, so it seems to Tetu that they accept him. Is Tetu wrong, Matai? Also, they much approve of Matai, and believe if Matai puts trust in Tetu, they will too."

"I'm deeply happy to hear that, Tetu. Really gratified. I guess you intend to marry her?"

Tetu had a patented Tetu answer ready, but Pack would have to wait for it. James Dahl—a former Marine Colonel who still addressed Pack as 'General' despite injunctions not to—stuck his head in to shoo them out to the pad, where Fardink was standing more or less at attention beside his aircraft.

♦ ♦ ♦

"A fine flying morning, General. Cloudless skies and mild breezes over and back," Fardink reported by way of greeting. "We shall have full meal service thrice," Paul added jokingly, "and I'm pleased to announce the wine steward will be at your disposal throughout. I told him wine's fine, but next flight we insist upon Scotch, bourbon, and cognac as well."

"Fardink," Pack glowered, "Tetu said on the way out here he's sick of you, and my man, I'm gonna second that dam emotion. How 'bout you just fly the plane an' git me whur I'm 'posed to be? Your nonsensical comments manage to subtract from the world's collective IQ. Good to see you, Paulie. Let's get strapped in."

Pre-flights done, Fardink checked the IC system with Pack and Tetu. "Destination's just about 100 air miles, 345 degree azimuth, which will take us over scenic Choteau. Otherwise, you'll see only the occasional rancher underneath us. Promises to be a pleasant flight. Any questions or comments?"

Tetu seldom spoke on such flights, now more than a hundred in number, and kept his record intact today. Pack's only comment was, "Look at the majesty of this state. People in every state generally love their birth states, and that's as it should be, but I believe our people understand down deep how special our Montana is. And I ain't speaking as no Guv'ner. Forget the politics...it is simply appropriate for ours to be called the Treasure State. I never weary of seeing where we live."

About 10 miles outside Browning, Paul Fardink descended to 150 feet. Recent rains had made the terrain below boggy. A slight crescent-shaped rise protruded just ahead, so Fardink pulled the Huey up to 220 feet, but began the descent again down to 150 on the other side.

Then...all hell broke loose. It was as if a battalion of infantry had trained all its weapons on Fardink's aircraft. He had not seen--nor would anyone except by good luck--a large flock of Canadian geese spooked in their marshy home by the noise above. In a blink the view through the windscreen turned black, and in an instant it exploded, birds later determined to weigh between six and twelve pounds hurtling through the cockpit at 53 times the force of a baseball thrown at 100 miles per hour. Pack was struck directly in the face, rendered unconscious. The goggles had probably saved his eyes. Fardink remained semi-conscious, and fought with all his will to control the pitch and roll of the damaged chopper. In those critical seconds he wasn't clear whether the impact had nullified the working of the cycle stick. He was operating purely on instinct, all his training and experience coming to the fore. Had he managed to stick the hard landing before or after darkness curtained his brain? He could not say.

Tetu had gotten his arms up in time to block the onslaught, and he felt as a major leaguer standing in the box would if struck simultaneously by 10 fastballs. He hurt, but surmised he would be fine. The normally mute Tetu got on the radio to summon the emergency vehicles that would arrive only minutes later.

Chapter Two

The calamitous collision with the geese had occurred yesterday. A few in-state political rivals had swiftly surfaced to excoriate the Governor for his reckless behavior; they saw no need for him to fly throughout the state with such regularity. The accident was a law of averages thing, as they saw it, clearly implying Pack got what he had coming. But most Montanans probably believed Pack was doing what a leader does. Because Pack made these tours so often, the people had grown to understand he was assembling the pieces of a jigsaw puzzle, their state, so that when he offered recommendations and made decisions, there was context to them, and a fuller understanding of their potential impacts. And they weren't larks: he wrote detailed trip reports about what he learned on every trip. What he was *not* doing was: traveling for the sake of travel; appearing in hope of local interviews; striving to raise personal popularity; seeking to draw large crowds. One of the reasons they voted for him to begin with was that they sensed his essential humility.

Now Pack and Fardink lay in Blackfeet Community Hospital, run by the Indian Health Service. The hospital looked from the outside more like a clinic in many small towns. It was a flat one-story building, absolutely unimposing, but if Pack had known in whose medical hands he had been placed, he would have been pleased. In an earlier visit he had learned a good deal about the capabilities of this hospital staff, as well as a good deal about their federally imposed limitations. He had bloodied a few noses in Washington and gotten them much-appreciated assistance. They were indeed taking good care of their governor.

Media headquartered in Washington and New York were decidedly unfriendly to Pack, but they had to report on the accident. Pack may have been from a lightly populated state, and one far away from the East

Coast to boot, but it was impossible to view him as just another governor. Leading the fight to uphold the US Constitution had put him front and center in a major political struggle that had required two years to resolve. Governors of states with twenty times Montana's population had unabashedly followed his lead, in part because they believed him when he said he had no future political aspirations. In the minds of many Americans, however, he was a future presidential candidate, despite his protestations.

A small army of people filled the area around the small medical facility, hoping for news about Pack and Fardink. State troopers had arrived to prevent illegitimate people from entering it. Tetu stood watch outside Pack's room, and everyone could be assured nobody was getting past the seven-foot, 365-pound man mountain who had been Pack's omnipresent companion for four years. Tetu's physical pain had dissipated nearly to zero, and he was ready for a fight.

At the White House, President Rozan couldn't suppress a smile when Senior Advisor Sharon Locke brought him up to date on the situation. "Am I a heel, Sharon?" Rozan asked, tongue in cheek. "What I think is that if there's a God in heaven, He has shown *Mister* Simon Pack the meaning of karmic justice. I hate Pack because he is evil, and God hates Pack. His victories, as I'm sure he thinks of what he's done, have come at a heavy price. Sharon, would you like to hear in plain language what the President of the United States really thinks about Pack's current condition?"

"As you wish, sir," Locke replied.

"It is this, dear advisor: Your President hopes the sonuvabitch dies a horribly agonizing death. Now, nothing more about the bastard until you announce his death, clear?"

"Clear, Mr. President," Locke answered, feeling pleased that she was as cold-blooded as her boss.

♦ ♦ ♦

Later that afternoon, four doctors appeared before microphones set up outside the hospital. The lead physician led off with, "As you know, the helicopter that went down yesterday roughly eight miles from this location carried three passengers. One of the Governor's aides, Mr. Tetu Palaita, was seated in the rear compartment for passengers and cargo. He suffered multiple contusions on his left arm, but was never hospitalized. He has no broken bones or internal injuries. Although we have released him, he remains by General Pack's side. The second man was the General's pilot, a retired Army officer who now resides in Montana. Mr. Fardink remains in our ICU. Although scans are inconclusive relative to internal injuries, Mr. Fardink does have substantial facial lacerations as well as six fractured ribs. Most seriously, he is still unconscious because we have induced a coma. His brain is swollen from the concussive effects of the large objects that struck his head at high velocity. As to the Governor... we have similarly induced a coma until the swelling in his brain subsides. In addition, he received facial lacerations and fractured two areas in his jaw and cheek. We are proud of what we've been able to do for these patients, but we think it wise to transfer them to the hospital in Helena where the more sophisticated technologies and treatment methods of a Level 1 Trauma Center are available. To that end, a trauma team from Helena has already arrived and is carefully preparing the patients for air evacuation to Helena today. We appreciate your concern and thank you for letting us do our jobs with minimal distraction. Thank you, ladies and gentlemen. I will be followed by a member of the governor's staff, who will update you on the status of the accident itself."

Most of what the staffer reported about the accident had originated with Tetu's observations. In those chaotic few seconds of 'aerial combat,' Tetu thought maybe three or four of the large geese had penetrated the windscreen, in the process disintegrating it. Preliminary investigation revealed scattered parts of three birds, though that figure might rise as the investigation continued, the spokesman said.

Not many hours later, the specially equipped air ambulance flew Pack and Fardink back to the south. Tetu had shared a brief visit with Swan Threemoons, but neither had gotten much out of it.

Chapter Three

State Capitol: There was work to be done, and James Dahl, Pack's heir apparent, dug in to do it. The best he could do for his boss was to apply himself more assiduously than ever. Nobody seemed to know when Pack might walk out of the hospital. He'd been in ICU six days, and Dahl had stopped in once a day, discouraged each time not to see the indomitable General taking charge of this situation as he had every other in his life. *He will prevail,* Dahl mouthed to himself. *Don't shed a tear for the straightest and most stalwart Marine I've ever known or known of. His longanimity will see him through this.* Dahl had seen a damaged Pack after a bloody fight with an al-Qaeda operative, yet his boss managed to show up, heavily bandaged, for the chapel service the following morning. Marines around the world had been sending messages, and if Pack were aware of them, he would cherish them more than those of any political potentate. Who knew how much Pack was driven by the personal mandate to uphold the honor of the Corps?

Dahl was not happy to be the *de facto* governor at this moment. Dahl had become lieutenant governor on 29 December last year. His predecessor, a competent woman with whom he had enjoyed a comfortable professional relationship, stepped down on 30 November last year because of a critical injury to her 14-year-old daughter. At that point Pack appointed his chief of staff Dahl to serve the remainder of the lieutenant governor's term, in accordance with Article VI, Section 6 of the state constitution, which states: "If the office of the lieutenant governor becomes vacant by his succession to the office of the governor, *or by his death, resignation, or disability as determined by law, the governor shall appoint a qualified person to serve in that office for the remainder of the term."*

Dahl walked over to the window to look outside. Signs of encouragement planted across the Capitol's grounds expressed hope and encouragement as the misty winter rain gradually turned them soggy. He couldn't care less that there had been no note of condolence from the nation's capital.

Helena Regional Medical Center: Perhaps no one held such depth of feeling for Pack as Tetu Palaita. Hospital staff seldom allowed him in to sit with Matai, but he had not been outside this hospital since Pack was admitted. He walked the hallways for hours on end, his singular appearance embedded in the memories of every last employee. Everyone gave him a wide berth, for his face said he did not want to talk. In the cafeteria he habitually wrote in a pocket notebook while eating. Then back to the nurse's station to wait....

Pack lay in bed, the machine doing his breathing for him. Constant checks for signs of infection, constant calibrating of the pharmaceuticals being pumped into him, constant monitoring of vitals. Perhaps some of the physicians took comfort in their vast understanding of what was happening to their patient, immensely pleased at the advances in their areas of expertise, confident in the brilliance they had shown to have reached their lofty levels of competence in the medical profession. And yet...there were other, wiser physicians among them who knew they were largely ignorant of the complex processes at work in the human brain, processes unimaginably complex, so intricate no computer could make sense of them, no machine could map beyond the snapshot.

For the time being, Pack's neuro-pathways were scrambled madly, electrical impulses racing in one direction, short-circuiting, colliding with competing impulses jolting maniacally, coming down the same pathway. Knowing what actually was going on under Pack's unmoving exterior was far, far beyond the ken of the best medicine men.

He was, quite plainly, thinking. On a wholly different plane than he had ever thought before. Simon Pack was having the time of his life. He had become a synesthete, a person capable of feeling colors and smelling sounds and seeing what lay beneath his skin. *I can see my skin growing colder and grayer. I think I am dying, and it is a marvelous sensation. The sun's going down on me. It's getting dark. This dying is not bad. I know with utter certitude that when the process of dying is done, I will continue to exist in a state of happiness in a place of inexpressible beauty. Just don't ask how I know, friend, but don't doubt me. 'Utter certitude,' I said, and I mean it. I can follow blood flowing through my veins. You people out there will laugh at my claims, but I do not care. Listen to me now: I know everything that has ever been known on this earth; it sits right now inside a cell near the tip of my finger, and I am able to tunnel my vision narrowly to watch it intently.*

This is a state of total mental clarity. Will everyone someday have a chance to experience this? I interrupt myself to study a particular molecular interaction under the skin of my forearm...wow, no firefight or fireworks display has ever rivaled the Technicolor brilliance of this activity.

Now I am speaking with the Creator, and find I am highly conscious of my grammatical constructions. I ask, "May I go?" Not "Can I go?" I don't think He was impressed. I explain that because this dying feels so good, and because I know this is not the end, and because I know "going" does not mean actually going anywhere, but that I will continue to be somewhere, I am ready to give up and roll on in this state. Forevermore I will understand death is not a state to contemplate with apprehension, but joy. I tell the Creator all this, and wait for His answer.

"You must answer that question for yourself, Simon. I gave you things to do, and people to tend. If you believe you still have work to finish, you can write it off as unfinished business if you want. I won't hold it against you if you choose to take the Westbound, as you have referred to your journey to the Great Beyond. You decide."

Pack is thinking a trillion thoughts at the same time, yet he's inexplicably able to process them discretely. He has reached his go-or-stay decision.

At that moment he feels a mighty jolt from head to toe, as if his heart has burst. The coursing of blood through his body's passageways is something he thinks he is able to see, as if he is tracking a single vehicle through a crowded thoroughfare...and then some unseen substance is released through the web of plastic lines and he fades again to black, wistfully bidding farewell to the Elysian Fields. He discerns the sound of voices near him, in the corporeal world, but he cannot yet make out their words.

♦ ♦ ♦

In order not to distract the nurse at her station just outside Pack's room, they talked softly among themselves. James Dahl was there. Tetu, of course, was there. Wilkie Buffer, theformer Secretary of Defense who now ran the state university system, was there. Dahl had decided on a limit of three. Dahl had received word that the intra-cranial swelling had diminished dramatically, and that the medical staff had deemed it proper to bring him out of the coma. That wouldn't happen instantaneously, but he would come out of it today, probably this morning. Tetu walked over and whispered something to the nurse. She nodded affirmatively, and he entered Pack's room alone, closing the door halfway. The giant was kneeling at the side of the bed, head bowed, holding Pack's arm at the only place he could find an opening. Voice hoarse and raspy from the intubation, Pack said with reasonable clarity, "Get up, Tetu, you want to pray, go to the chapel. There are a lot of people I think need prayers more than me." Pack frowned, which Tetu knew to be a Pack grin. "Would you get me some water, big man?" Pack mumbled.

"Matai, Matai, Tetu is bursting happy to see you," Tetu said as he scurried to pour a cup of water. He held it to Pack's lips, then spread something like Chapstick on them as he had seen the nurses do. "So glad…let me bring in the others."

"Wait, Tetu. I see you're walking, which makes me as happy as you are, but how is Paul, the pilot? Is he OK?" Pack noticed his inability to enunciate clearly.

"Tetu will let someone smarter explain, but Mr. Paul also lays down this hall, still recovering, I would say," Tetu answered.

Wilkie Buffer and James Dahl were just about to barge in to join Tetu when the nurse waved them back. "Sorry, fellows, the Governor's medical team is on the way up," she said, "and the Governor has to be left alone until they're finished examining him." She went in and grabbed her watchful friend Tetu by the sleeve and tugged him out too. Then she began her ministrations to Pack.

"Welcome back, Governor," the petite nurse said with a broad white smile. "The hospital will probably be glad to see you leave if only because we can't handle the traffic from well-wishers. But I won't be glad. I don't have a chance to serve many VIPs."

Mouthing the words, Pack said, "And you still haven't served a VIP, but thank you sincerely." Then he felt tired enough to close his eyes again. He hadn't stayed awake long enough for the nurse to say his vitals looked great. Pack was back.

♦ ♦ ♦

The surgical team had looked him over carefully and administered a number of preliminary neurological exams. The team chief told Pack they were highly satisfied with his condition, but before going further wondered if Pack would object to having the three people close to him come in to listen to the remainder. "We are aware of your close contact with these gentlemen," the surgeon said, "and frankly, they can help keep an eye on you for a little while."

"I'm aw foh it," Pack said with difficulty. "Bwing them in."

Dahl, Buffer, and Tetu knew they were only to listen as long as the team was with Pack. "OK," the surgeon began, "first you must know these were life-threatening injuries. Nothing I say will be mocked. As you would expect, my explanation could be extremely complex, riddled with abstruse medical terms, but my objective is to keep this to layman's language. You sustained head and facial injuries. Both are described as closed, meaning the skin was unbroken in both. Your head injury was not a concussion, but a contusion; it was a brain bruise, but one strong enough to cause a serious degree of swelling. Luckily, bleeding was not involved. Nonetheless, it was a TBI, traumatic brain injury, a condition you will recognize as serious. You had two facial injuries. One was a left maxillary fracture, that is to say a fracture of your left upper jaw, and it was a big one. The other was a somewhat smaller zygomatic fracture, meaning of your right cheekbone. Your bones are dense, a good thing in this case because there is commonly a crumbling and/or splintering along the fracture line, but we saw none of that in your case. Questions so far?" He turned to look at each person. No questions.

"As a momentary aside, you'll want to know your pilot remains in induced coma because although his TBI was similar to yours, his facial injuries were more extensive and did include the shattering effects I mentioned a moment ago. Still, his long-term prognosis is good.

"All right, when you were taken in at the Browning hospital, I personally flew up immediately to help determine the first steps of your care and treatment. It was clear that we needed to get you here ASAP so that we could repair those facial fractures. See, Governor, research indicates that that surgery should be performed as quickly after the event as possible. Yes, it was risky because you were comatose, but the fact is that chances of complications from the facial surgery increase a good deal with the passage of each day. Best we can determine, risk of complications of the surgery done as swiftly as we did it is only about 11%. On the other hand, you're a smart man with a good support structure around you, so I would peg the risks at much less than 11%. Just hold off on being a wild man for at least a year. That's not too much to ask. Your face will be sore for a while, but in short order your face will be harder to crack than it was before the injury, if you follow orders. You can thank the maxillo-facial surgeon for a marvelous job.

"The anesthesia will keep the pain at bay probably for the rest of this day. But then pain will set in...you'll have problems speaking, as you've already noticed; malocclusion is still a possibility; your face will be swollen for a week or so; and we'll expect you to follow a soft diet for several weeks. We'll give you a handout to explain all these things, but please hear them from me first. Because the breaks were clean, we didn't have to wire your mouth shut, and believe me that is a very uncomfortable situation, so you may be thankful on that count. We repaired the broken bones by making incisions on the inside of your mouth, and inserting small titanium plates and screws to bind them back together. The incisions were stitched up with dissolvable material. We'll have you walking soon to get your legs back, and you'll stay here two to three days as we follow your general state of recovery, but then, if all goes well, you can go home, where we expect you to rest for two weeks. Light duty after that, until your term expires. No alcohol for six weeks, and do the mouth-opening exercises we give you, even if they do produce headaches. I'll see you again in two weeks. The nurse will go over your med schedule with you. Are we all clear?"

"Thanks, Doctor Hinshaw, and ditto to each of you. Except for a crappy throat, I feel pretty good," Pack rasped.

"We're done. Best wishes, Governor," Hinshaw said as he nodded for his crew to exit.

Pack plodded through the next few days, experiencing the same desire to return to familiar work surroundings as every person has who has ever been laid up in a hospital. He visited the still-unresponsive Paul Fardink several times a day, doing nothing more than sitting with his friend, hoping he knew Pack was there. Pack had not forgotten the dreams he had had during the coma. Thing is, he knew they weren't dreams. Of that he was sure in the absolute. He pondered if Paul Fardink were having a similar experience, the power and wonder of which he may never be able to express to another person.

His decision had been to come back to the world. The Creator had left it to him to decide, and he figured he did have unfinished business, and did owe big debts. He needed to clear his accounts. His daughters had come right away...no debts there. He wanted to be the one responsible for his final State of the State; only decision there was manner of presentation—he wanted to deliver it in person to the legislature, and thus the people, but that would depend on how well he could speak...

his first three had been written only. Then he remembered he'd lost track of time...the next State of the State would be the responsibility of his successor. He was actually thinking of a Farewell Address, or should it be in writing? He wanted to help, as discreetly as he could, Tetu get established in a new line of work, and Paul Fardink seen through to full recovery. He wanted his closest colleague, James Dahl, to replace him as Governor. Didn't want to get in Dahl's way, but wanted him to know he was there as a kitchen cabinet advisor if his advice were sought. Further, he intended to organize a transition at least as thorough as his predecessor had organized for him. His penultimate wish was to return to his cabin in the mountainous western area of the state and do the manual labor he enjoyed, as well as hike, camp, and flyfish more than he had in the past.

His mind returned to Tetu. Pack's dog, Chesty, had been under Tetu's care for—Pack had to admit—most of the time he had held office. Chesty had arguably saved one or both their lives on two occasions. Almost every dog owner has a tight relationship with his animal, but Tetu's connection with Chesty was manifestly different, almost mystical. Maybe he ought to give his beloved dog to Tetu when, as was overwhelmingly likely, they moved apart just months from now. He had once asked Tetu about the peculiar Tetu-Chesty bond, and the reply shone brighter light on who Tetu is, a mammoth man who had no problem clashing violently with evil men, but whose heart at its base was as gentle as any person he had met.

"Matai," Tetu had commenced, "in Samoa dogs are a subject of much talk. First, Tetu must tell you he loves Samoa and most people there. Beautiful country, mostly beautiful people. They are loving people, but a few hate dogs. Dogs affect our main industry of tourism. See, dogs are everywhere, and at night they 'pack up.' Sometimes in day too. We have well-known foot races, you know, the 10-, 20-, 50-kilometer kind intended for best runners in world, but when runners get bitten by dogs on race route they won't return to Samoa. Half injuries reported in hospitals are dog bites. Tourists cancel trips to Samoa because they hear about mean dogs. Why so many dogs? Because vets are few and cost much, so only rich get their animals de-sexed. Some of my poor people are known to bury unwanted female puppies alive and abandon males of litter. Still, too many dogs in countryside and towns. Tourists afraid to walk anywhere, most carry stones in pocket or umbrellas to fight off. I am enemy of countrymen who are cruel to dogs. Some go dog hunting in cars, have mission to run over many as they can. Other guys hunt with machetes, cut their heads off. You see dog guts on side of roads. Now these bad among Samoans speak about profiting from export of dog food, made of ground dog bodies. Tetu got sick of this cruelty, and ashamed of those with bloodlust against animal who did not make problem. Problem is people who do not care for them in proper ways. Tetu sees Chesty, and wants to be sure no harm comes to him." His voice rising and eyes slitting, Tetu finishes with, "Tetu's mind sees someone trying to murder friend Chesty, and he **will not** allow it."

Pack's biggest personal desire was to firmly establish the nature of his relationship with Keeley Eliopoulos. He met her in a national park in Pennsylvania enroute to Montana from West Point. They spoke by phone a few times, finding they enjoyed talking. When Pack ran for Governor, she contacted his campaign manager, Wilkie Buffer, and got herself an unpaid job as Volunteer Coordinator. She moved to Montana without consulting Pack. He was flattered, but unsure how he felt about that. He couldn't make her any promises, but then she hadn't asked for any. She seemed content to see Simon only occasionally. He actually knew very little about her beyond the fact that her family still resided in Greece. He was aware she had held a professorship at a name university, but was reluctant to explain her reasons for leaving it. She was in her own fashion as private a woman as Pack was private a man.

The day before Pack's recent injury, he received a hastily scrawled letter from Keeley. She didn't say she loved him (nor had he said those words to her), but did dwell on how much she liked him, how much she admired and respected him and all he had done for her adopted country. She waxed eloquent about the pride she felt when others praised him for the qualities she saw in him. Now, however, she had to return to Greece on the first flight out, at the behest of her mother, who related that her father appeared to be in the throes of death. She hoped to return to Montana, but as a rare only child in her native land, she would surely have to sort through a formidable array of administrative and financial concerns. Because she faced so many unknowns, she could not accurately ascertain the length of her stay. If this were going to take months, she invited Pack to visit her in Greece. She concluded with, "My heart is broken, Simon, that I will be unable to keep a close eye on you. I hope you will not forget me."

Pack had no way to know her father was a man of wealth, great wealth. He was leaving her a woman who would be described on any continent as mega-rich.

Pack had forced Tetu to back off a little, but just a little, from his bedside vigil. He had to admit Tetu's was a comforting presence, and he liked seeing his outsized friend stoop to clear the doorway every time he came in. They were battle buddies, he and Tetu Palaita.

Chapter Four

Pack was in his basement office in the Governor's residence, at the moment peering intently at a few of the Native American fetishes various tribes had presented him. Fetishes are Native American symbols of animals, and typically are carved from organic materials such as stone, antlers, bones, shells, or wood. They represent characteristics associated with animals, and putatively impart to the bearer of the fetish the particular power the tribal members believe they possess.

"To have created this required skill of a high order," Pack was thinking to himself. This one was less than an inch tall, yet it was intricately detailed, perfectly proportioned. It was of a turtle, signifying long life. Another was of a bear, meant to suggest the bearer had been, or would be granted, unusually great strength. He found the one he was searching for. It was the raven, known for its healing powers. He needed a strong dose of healing right now. So he put it in his pocket. He had experienced bad headaches, and his jawlines had alternately felt numb or tingled and itched. He frequently felt sleepy, and occasionally napped, something he wasn't accustomed to doing. Chewing wasn't easy, but Tetu had taken pains to put Pack's food through a blender to puree it. As Pack was thinking of his debt to Tetu, Tetu appeared in the flesh.

"Sorry, Matai, for interruption, but you need anything?" Tetu asked. "I got wood neatly stacked, and all loose brush organized. Found a larch not doing good, maybe needs knocked down. Tetu can do, or want me to wait till you look over?"

"Come on in and have a seat, Tetu. I'm sure the man or woman who crafted these small beautiful fetishes would enjoy having them studied every now and then. Who knows the time it took to make the one I have in my hand? It's an owl, signifying patience and wisdom. And now I want to present it to you, as a small way of telling you I see you as a patient and wise man. Yes, you are, my friend, and yes, some people think the same as I. On the other hand, you're a quiet, reserved man and most I guess never get past your physical stature, and don't know the extent of your knowledge and understanding. And don't tell me you don't care, because I know you don't." He handed the delicate amulet to Tetu in military style, left hand to left hand followed by a handshake.

Tetu sat, and Pack opened: "Look, Tetu, you're a son to me. Your second father. A grown son who is now free to tell his father—respectfully, of course--he has crossed a line into his personal life into which the father shouldn't intrude. Before we took that flight to Browning, I began to ask about your future plans. You're on the payroll until I pass the baton, and if Colonel Dahl wins, as I expect he will, you can remain in his employ if you want. If, however, you want to take a different direction, I'd like to know so that I might have the pleasure of helping you toward your objective. Am I getting overly personal?"

"Of course no," Tetu said in his style of speaking English. "First, Matai, you have made Tetu very proud with this gift. You will never find me without it. Second, I would like to say you what I am thinking. It is not you, but Tetu, you may say is going too far, but please do not.

"Miss Swan Threemoons is excellent woman. She would be good for Tetu. But she must wait, and we will see if she is willing to wait, even she says she is. I reached decision when you were not moving, not speaking, in hospital bed. I said my first duty now is to Matai. Has been since Tetu met Matai, and will always be so. When you go back to cabin, I will not stay there if you are better, but I also cannot be far away. I cannot be as far away as Blackfeet Reservation. Within two hours by car is limit. There is lodge for sale in Yaak, 15 rooms, also restaurant attached, with good price, I think. Rooms occupied near full most days, mostly hunters and fishers, but sometimes other rough men too. Owner now is scared of rough crowd, says time to leave, maybe go back to lower California. Tetu has no fear of rough crowd, can handle them. Maybe I can get loan, maybe not. If Matai needs Tetu, he will come quickly, and is not so far from cabin. If I succeed after six months, Tetu will ask Miss Swan to join him in marriage, and she will come or not. Tetu is prepared either way. Now Tetu will hear what Matai says."

Pack was thinking the most important part of what Tetu said had to do with securing a business loan. He could help, but he couldn't admit it to Tetu. No, if he could find out who the banker Tetu was or would be dealing with, Pack could and would back Tetu up, but only surreptitiously. Instead, Pack said, "Fine, your decision is yours alone, and it's not for me to question. I'd like to see this place in Yaak. Sounds interesting, and I'm sure you've plotted out how to handle the housekeeping, cleaning, and maintenance jobs. And, Tetu, making the deal could take some time to be final, so I am counting on you to stay in my cabin until then. OK?"

"Tetu would be happy to do that. Thank you, Matai. But you will be busy when you return to Governor job, so maybe no time to go to Yaak."

"Hey, man, I'm supposed to be resting these two weeks. I can rest in a car, can't I? Get the maps and let me see how long a drive we'd have," Pack said, now warming to the idea of getting out of the residence. He constitutionally could not abide immuration.

"Tetu has made the trip, Matai. No map needed. It's six-hour drive, 320 miles. Shortest route is state road 83 north and US 2 west through Kalispell and Libby."

"What are you waiting for then, you big tub of margarine?" Pack said jocularly. "Call the owner and see if he can find a room or two for his potential buyer. If he can, we'll go tomorrow and stay for the night, get a good look around. Next doc appointment is four days away. You drive, I sleep, got that, big man?" Pack was being facetious again, as he was inclined to do when happy. He went on in the same vein, acting serious but being foolish, telling Tetu as he stood up to go make the phone call, "Mr. Tetu Palaita, your ponderosity is exceeded only by your generosity, or is it that your stupidity is exceeded only by your cupidity? And my insanity is exceeded only by my inanity, my pedantic exceeded only by my puritanic."

All the talking had got his jaw to aching, and his head too. He just nodded OK when Tetu came back a few minutes later to say he had gotten the single room with two beds. Even in this discomfort, he mused he and Tetu were two offbeat old boys, each trying in his own way to get to heaven before He closed the door.

The meds were still getting to Pack. He did indeed nod off more than once in the Jeep even as he wanted to keep Tetu company. "Sorry, Tetu, I'm doing my best to stay alert to be a good traveling partner, but guess I can't yet shake off these meds. This never happened on our trip from back east, did it? Anyway, where are we?"

"Not a problem, Matai. Tetu is well awake, excited to see Matai out again. We not far from Libby, passed turnoff at Kalispell a while back."

From this point on, Pack knew there wasn't much commerce of any type. Funny, because north of here was fine trout fishing, yet there were few fly shops, only a couple, in fact. One of those was renowned among flyfishermen, and it lay about 10 miles ahead. Pack had never been there, but instructed Tetu to stop when he saw it. They were past before Pack spotted it on the west side of the road. They did a U and returned to it. Pack was astonished that this place had a reputation. It was an add-on to a simple wood-frame house, and no customers were present, although this was a prime business hour. There was a sidewalk leading to a locked reinforced screen door with a buzzer to request entry. The inner door was open. Presently a pleasant-looking middle-aged white man came to the door and let them in.

"Welcome, fellows, come on in." He did a double-take and amended his greeting to, "By gosh, it's Governor Pack and Mr. Tetu. Honored to have you in my little establishment. How are you gentlemen?"

It was, as the man said, quite a small place, no larger than 30' by 20'. Pack was bowled over, in that based on what he'd read he had anticipated a much larger place teeming with customers. "I've had good doctors and am recovering quickly, thank you, sir. It'll be a while before I can get out on the Clark Fork or the Blackfoot, but I'm hoping to be out in the Spring, for sure. Just wanted to see today where I ought to stop to check on river conditions and what flies you'd recommend before I head up to the deep Yaak."

"Well, Governor, I'd like to say you're welcome to stop back here in the Spring, but frankly, I'm not sure I'll be here at that time. If I can sell, I will. If not, I may just close up."

"Business that bad?" Pack asked.

"It is not that bad. Right now, nobody's here but you, granted, but most of the time we do a good business. I personally tie most of the flies, as well as build most of the other gear you see in here. It's very high-quality stuff. Costs more than you'd pay in the big stores, but in my humble opinion, it'll catch more fish and keep you more comfortable on the water and last a lot longer than the big-store stuff," the man said. "I'm the manufacturer, the sales clerk, the phone answerer, the shipper, the owner, a one-man operation, and have been more than 20 years."

"Then why would you consider giving up a business you've carefully built up?" Pack asked.

"In my early working days, I had a good job mining silver and copper around here. They pretty much shut down for reasons I don't need to explain to you, even though there are supposedly 12 million ounces of silver still below this ground. Minority rule, the way I see it. So I tried to make a go of my passion for all things related to flyfishing. I've had a fun run, been recognized by numerous fishing groups. But I'm telling you, Governor, this whole Yaak Valley has gotten weird. There are some bad hombres running the road just outside. People who when you look 'em straight on would as soon kill ya as speak to ya. Don't know who they are or what they're up to, but they give me the willies, I can tell you that."

Pack was thinking fast, a bit embarrassed that as Governor he was having unmasked before him a failure of leadership. At the same time, he was thinking of what Tetu had told him about the lodge owner wanting to flee the Yaak. Yesterday, he had supposed the lodge proprietor was just a wuss who couldn't take the rigors of this part of the country. Today, he was considering other possibilities. What he said to the man was, "Let's hope conditions change and you'll be right here when spring arrives. In the meantime, you've given me something to think about. Thanks for your time, sir."

Failure was an alien concept to Pack. He had succeeded at just about everything in his life. Individual exploits aside, he had demonstrated virtually peerless talent as leader and manager at tactical, operational, and strategic levels. He had a solid grasp on how to lead organizations small to large. Now the idea gnawed at him that in some important, fundamental fashion he was seeing a fissure in his reputation. It wasn't like him to question his competence as he was now. It didn't feel good. He considered that the recent injuries were the cause of this sudden malaise, but quickly tossed off that notion as mere excuse. Another possibility was that he was misreading the evidence, such as it existed. What proof was there, really, that a large slice of Montana, in terms of geographic extent, was in poor health? A shop owner had made a facile comment and maybe a lodge owner had as well. Too early to draw conclusions from what may turn out to have been offhand talk.

Tetu turned his head toward the back seat to check a snoring Chesty. He started to speak to the dog before deciding not to break up the deep sleep. Then he turned toward Pack. "You OK, Matai?" Tetu asked, interrupting Pack's reverie.

Pack smiled, trying to conceal the onset of angst. "Yeah, fine, just thinking our talk with this lodge guy could be very interesting."

Chapter Five

It may be averred safely that much of America knows little or nothing about the Yaak River Valley. It sits in the extreme northwestern sector of Montana. The community of Yaak, population under 250, is the northwestern anchor of the state. The valley itself rests mostly inside the Kootenai National Forest. It spreads to more than one million acres. More than 180,000 of those acres are roadless, wild habitat. Its weather is influenced by the Pacific Northwest and Rocky Mountain climates. Summers are hot and humid and winters are cold, sometimes in the extreme. 98% of the valley is government-owned, and most of that belongs to the National Forest Service. In warm weather, the valley is a spray of vivid colors, the seahorse-shaped Indian pipe flowers blossoming beside pastures of Oregon grape and breathtaking Western cedar, and in the fall the aspen groves are overtaken by the brilliant yellow of the quaking aspen leaves. The one-half million-acre upper section reportedly has a year-round population of about 150, which means its density is about .03 people per square mile. Compare that with the Los Angeles-Long Beach-Anaheim corridor, which is estimated at 7,000 per square mile. That said, there are many itinerants, typically non-Montanans, who today roam those vast expanses, hidden under a thick veil of trees and in the countless creases in the land formed by glacial lacerations from ages too deep in the past for humans to recall. The purposes of the people who slink furtively in the penumbral isolation of this land are more often than not iniquitous, nefarious, villainous. It is the most inviting locale in the Lower 48 to evade the law.

For thousands of years Indians flowed across this terrain following the migratory patterns of large game and in-season crops in their quest for survival. They swept down from Canada and across into what is now

Wyoming and Colorado. Then the flow would reverse and they would migrate back into Canada. Native tribes many of whose names are lost to us populated the Yaak. The Kootenai tribe named the place Yaak, which in their language means 'arrow'.

The Yaak, as the valley is known, remains a cornucopia of wildlife, the most biologically diverse ecosystem in America. Beaver, otter, muskrat, rare birds, the grizzly bear, wolverine, mountain lion, pronghorn, bull trout, and so many more do battle in the endless cycle of life in the broken and uneven surfaces of this country. Indeed, the people of the Yaak refer to this wild place as 'this country' as if they are speaking of an authentically different country, as if it is a nation unto itself.

Tucked here and there around the million acres were a few mountain men and women, followers of a Montana tradition that goes back to the 18th century. These people typically are without political predispositions, Thoreauesque in their aspirations. They are minimalists, people who live off the grid truly, people who make do with what the earth they live in provides. Reality TV, as it is inappropriately denominated, has tried to open some of these lives to us, but their production and writing teams have gotten too much in the way for them to be convincing. Nonetheless, the point is that some mountain people do live out there in the Yaak. A few out there today are close kin to people of the past like rugged Jim Bridger, who took two arrows in the back but left one in for three years. Like Jeremiah "Liver-Eater" Johnston, who slew dozens of Crow warriors, then ate their livers. Like "Stagecoach" Mary Fields, an African-American woman who distinguished herself as an original pioneer outdoorswoman, and the beaver trapper Jedediah Smith. And like John Colter, a multi-talented man like Captain Meriwether Lewis, the head of the Corps of Discovery into which he enlisted. And like another Montana mountain man who also became a member of Lewis's Corps of Discovery, George Drouillard, mortally wounded in an Indian ambush. All these men and women had their time in the Yaak.

Craig Wood and his woman Judith Buck live out there at this moment, living the lives of the Montana predecessors about whose lives they are conversant. They took up this life 50 years ago, settling on a 1 ½-acre plot that remains out of sight of all but the accidental trekker. They craft traditional buckskin moccasins, pants, shirts and jackets. They make durable, bone-handled knives. They braintan—a skill learned from Native Americans--wild game hides. They use no machines for any purpose. They live in a yurt, a great round tent with a domed top. They built the roof ribs and tension bands with natural materials, and fashioned the sides with animal hides, even devising a means of radiant insulation. They are a part of the Yaak story.

Draw a line diagonally across America from the Yaak and you find the Everglades at the opposite end. The 1.5 million-acre "river of grass" wetlands is almost diametrically opposite the Yaak geographically and climatically. High ground versus low ground. But there are similarities: both have Native American tribes on them. Few people reside in each area. But in one other key respect they are similar—each has an army of people at loggerheads with regard to how the land ought to be treated. Those who want to afford greater public access. Those who want to designate it formally as Wilderness Area, and thus to put the public at further remove. The conflict in the Yaak was more pointedly hostile than in the Everglades. The multiple interests clashing here constituted one of Governor Pack's thorniest problems.

Fourteen months ago, in August, lightning kicked off an inferno in the southern sector of the Yaak. Turned out, that year was the most damaging for wildlife ever recorded. Fire scientists claim 10% of wildfires have their origin in lightning. Such fires are a naturally occurring part of the environment. All sides in the conflict accept this as fact. What's at issue, then, is what can be done to limit the damage. We will always have fires, but each side rejects the other's answer concerning retardation measures.

The lead voice on the 'environmentalist' side was a man named Kjell Johnson. Kjell had an advantage because, in Pack's way of thinking, he possessed a trained voice, one that could command an audience a rough rancher was unable to draw. He was a writer of some renown, and he had made his bones by writing lyrically about the Yaak. Most of the residents of Montana were familiar with Kjell, and the literati on the coasts were as well. For decades he had waxed poetic about the land he cherished, and at first that was the extent of it. Then he took notice of his growing fame, and as he did his voice grew more strident. He thought of himself as the lone voice defending the Yaak. He sometimes felt he was the only force standing between total destruction of the land and a healthy valley. He saw himself most days as an updated, more effective protector of the environment than Rachel Carson.

Pack had an innate skepticism about Kjell Johnson, believing anyone so much in love with himself was to be taken with a modicum of doubt. Pack also objected to the label 'environmentalist' Johnson had appropriated. Couldn't a rancher be just as much an environmentalist as a writer? On the other hand, Kjell Johnson had introduced some strong points into the discussion, so he was not to be dismissed wholly. Although he had a love-hate relationship with the Forest Service, he argued that its stupidity showed through in the case of District Managers receiving bonuses for the leases they let on their land. He frequently claimed the USFS was the largest road builder in America, citing the fact that the roads it built exceeded the total mileage of the interstate highway system. So, he liked to use the example of the Manager who issues $2,000,000 in logging leases, only to pay for the construction of roads for those loggers in an amount that far exceeded the $2,000,000. His point was the Manager actually lost taxpayer money, yet he got rewarded for it.

Mr. Kjell Johnson argued that fires burned hotter these days because when loggers clearcut, the USFS replaced trees that had fire-resistant properties with a random selection of other types of trees that were in essence adding fuel to the fire. How much the USFS replaced larch and cedar with fir and lodgepole pine is open to debate, but where this is true Mr. Johnson had a point.

On the other hand, a consortium of ranch foremen and stewards had countered with the sensible notion that they themselves were expert tenders of the land who were every bit as concerned about preserving natural resources as Johnson. "He has no monopoly on 'environmentalist'," one said heatedly. "Every rancher and farmer I know is the biggest environmentalist in the world. If the Forest Service let us partner with them in a meaningful way, we would make the forests safe for elk, deer, sage grouse, and all the rest. Instead of a 200,000-acre fire, you'd have a 2-acre fire." To Johnson directly, this foreman said, "When you've lost all your cows to a fire, seen deer and elk and cattle still alive with the hooves burnt off, seen countless geese dead from smoke inhalation, and some animals literally cooked from the inside out, as a rancher you think first of the misery unnecessarily inflicted upon these innocent creatures and a distant second about lost revenue. It's heartbreaking, it really is. God has entrusted us to take care of those animals."

All this took place at a meeting Pack arranged for all key parties concerned. Only now was he seeing what a failure he had been. A second rancher had spoken more crudely but no less passionately: "Logging and grazing, properly done, have kept our forests thriving for more than 160 years. Contrary to all you hear, the damn loggers do care about preservation about as much as we do. But the federal government belittles what we do and know by throwing red tape in our way, and the 'environmentalists' like Mr. Johnson do too with their endless lawsuits. They want every logging road closed, and to a great extent they've got what they want. See, they close the roads by digging trenches, what you as a former military man would recognize as a tank trap, throughout the system. So what happens? When there's a fire, the firefighting trucks can't get to where they need to go. It's lunacy! Also, we ranchers have asked the USFS to let us man—on a voluntary basis—the lookout towers they've abandoned. If we could spot an infant fire, as they did in the old days, the odds of suppressing it quickly rise greatly. These geniuses from Washington put 80,000 acres of the forest off limits to all human activity to save the spotted owl. Save the spotted owl habitat, they crowed. But what happened was the spotted owl was destroyed anyway because it couldn't compete with the horned owl.

"They tell us when they let us have a stake in the forests, they observe a lack of timber management. Really? It's just the opposite. When our animals graze on the forest land, they minimize the amount of forage on the ground. That understory, untrimmed, is a tremendous fuel-loading vehicle. And I'm just getting started...."

Simon Pack had won most battles with Washington, but it hurt him, badly, that he hadn't won that one. And now he was learning he may have let the Yaak down in other ways as well. His headache was intensifying.

Chapter Six

The nails of Mr. Ng Trang's little fingers were long enough to scour the grouting on a kitchen floor. Trang honed them to razor sharpness, working them over every few days. Twice, he had plucked out the eyeballs of an underling who had crossed him. Witnessing human pain was a fact of his job, as he saw it, and elicited from him no shudder, no flinch, no emotion discernible to the eye. It was this *sangfroid* that made his people fear him.

Trang coveted the Yaak. The politics of the place meant nothing to him, and he didn't care to familiarize himself with positions taken by any of the parties who believed themselves aggrieved. All he wanted was for it to be left alone, a giant wilderness in which he could continue to orchestrate his illicit operations unnoticed. At the moment it looked like someone was making a damn movie inside its boundaries. It was looking like all of Hollywood was moving in to make some Cecil B. DeMille epic. Busloads of people and officious directors yelling into loudspeakers and tow trucks and wreckers...what a goatscrew. He learned that all those crews were there at the behest of that famous author, Kjell Johnson. Seemed to Trang what Kjell was most interested in was becoming a national hero before he croaked. Selling more books too, he supposed, but mainly to see his image on magazine covers and television screens all over the country. Trang thought, with a touch of smugness of his own, that Johnson and he were the antipodes, polar opposites. Where Trang needed anonymity, Johnson wanted adoration. He couldn't think of even one Vietnamese-American in the American spotlight. Vietnamese were patient and inner-directed, Trang believed, and average Americans were frantic and crowd puppets. What Trang wasn't up to speed on was that Kjell Johnson, the man who lobbied incessantly for the banishing of all human footprints from the Yaak, was the man directing the movements of the filmmakers.

Trang for a moment or two toyed with the idea of ambushing some of those assholes. Pick off one or two and see how fast the rats scurried out! Or blow up one of their buses...but, no, he never really gave that serious consideration because that would only bring greater attention to the place. Maybe they won't be here long.

Trang had meth labs in the Yaak. They were mobile, but not very, given the complexity and sensitivity of the manufacturing equipment and the difficulty of moving on that terrain. This Kjell guy and his posse had busted into the territory of one of his labs, so disrupting the cook underway that Trang had lost product worth hundreds of thousands, maybe more.

Trang assigned a woman to follow Johnson. He told her to report back when she had an idea for bringing harmony back to the valley. Whatever it took.

Trang had found it helpful to have a graceful, exotic woman on the payroll. Her beauty, intelligence, social sense, and charm could get her through doors as no man could. Even her alliterative name, A'nh Tran, was soothing to the ear of an Anglophone. American men especially lowered their guard around her.

At the same moment Pack and Tetu were knocking on the door of the Sportsman's Lodge in Yaak, A'nh Tran was rapping gently on the door of Reverend Dar Castor's hut. When Dar opened the door, he wished his wife, Moms, weren't inside. "Wow," he thought, "she's a stunner. Have I ever seen a woman this beautiful?"

"Can I help you, ma'am?" Dar asked. "It's pretty cold out there, so I guess you should come on inside. I'm Reverend Dar Castor. You sure you're looking for me or Moms?" Dar wore a fur-lined aviator hat with the chinstrap buckled, adding to his already-odd appearance. He also had on a Michelin Man coat that emphasized his impressive girth. He stood a shade over six feet, she estimated, but who knew his weight? His 'beard' appeared to consist of cotton balls glued onto his face with blank spots inexplicably arrayed throughout.

A'nh Tran found it a challenge not to allow her visage to betray the revulsion she actually felt at this man whose own visage fairly screamed *lack of discipline!* She was offput further by the alliaceous odor emanating from his breath. Aromas of unpleasant body odors and garlic permeated the overheated room. Stacks of Rubbermaid containers sat propped high against the sidewalls and blankets littered the floor. Two chairs provided all the available seating. The old swivel chair had to have been Dar's, given that the center cushion's springs had been crushed and the cushion itself sagged nearly to the floor. A modest recliner was the other, the one in which A'nh supposed she was to deposit her slender frame. Nonetheless, she accepted the challenge of the confined quarters to smile broadly: "Well, as you know better than I, this mountain country is big and if you're looking for someone, it could take an eternity, especially with the rutted dirt roads and absence of signs. I see your house and I stop to ask if you can help, maybe get me to the person I am searching for. His name is Mr. Kjell Johnson. Have you heard of him and do you know his whereabouts?"

Dar liked this woman, yessir, he liked her looks very much indeed, and would like to salivate upon her a little longer, so he yelled toward a back room, "Moms, can you rustle up a couple coffees? We got a visitor!

"Turns out, Miss Train," he said, without her correcting him, "I am acquainted with Mr. Johnson. He was the first guest in my humble home. He is quite concerned about maintaining the health of this valley. He says he has lots of opponents, although he called them enemies."

"This is news to me," Tran said. "I know nothing of the gentleman. My purpose is to advise him that a wealthy friend of the environment has bequeathed to him a handsome sum to help him carry on the fight against those who seek to destroy this lovely place. Perhaps it would help me if you could tell me more about him. You know, so that when I do finally reach him I can hold up my end of the conversation."

A loud snort erupted from the back room. Moms apparently remained abed, not having heard the plea for coffee. Dar thought that was just as well. He could leer at the toothsome Miss Tran away from the beady eyes of his stout wife. He ditched the coffee idea. Apropos of nothing, the Rev asked, "Are you from the Orient?"

"My family is of Asian ancestry, if that's what you mean. But I've lived all my life in America. Why do you ask?"

"Oh, I dunno, I guess because I didn't see many Orients in the parts of Georgia I come from," Dar said.

"Reverend, don't be offended, but I suppose you've heard that today we call American Indians 'Native Americans,' right?"

"Of course I have," Dar answered, not wanting to show he felt she had just stung him.

"Well, with respect, Reverend," A'nh continued, "people like me are usually called Asian-Americans today."

"What's wrong with Orient?" Castor asked. "Seems to me if a person's from the Orient, he or she is Oriental, am I right?"

A'nh Tran had no good answer for that, so she said, "It's not a big deal, really. If you want to call me Oriental, go ahead."

Dar Castor brightened at that, believing he had bested her on that point. In fact, she just wanted to move on and get this over with, get these noxious smells out of her nostrils. So A'nh said, "So, Reverend, you were telling me about Mr. Johnson."

"Yeah, he's a writer, a bigshot writer at that, based on what he told me. Says he has the ear of lots of politicians in Washington, too. And lots of important magazines have written about him, and he's been on the TV a lot. Left me four or five of his books. Told him I can't wait to read them, but truth is, I'm not much of a reader. By the way, how much is this mystery man giving him?"

She ignored the question about the lie concerning the monetary gift. "So, what does he want with you?" Tran asked, before realizing maybe that sounded dismissive of Reverend Dar. "What I mean is, I'm sure he sees you as an asset in his fight, so in what way is he expecting you to assist?"

"He said he views me as 'connective tissue.' He knows I'm a minister, and in my flock are Indians...Native Americans...and also others peppered around this valley, and they trust me as a man of both faith and good faith. He wants me to form a council of concerned citizens and lead them over to his side. Mr. Johnson says it's a job calling for a real strong man, but what he's heard is I'm the logical choice, maybe, as he said, the only choice. Nobody around here has my moral power, he says, and what the hey, he might be right." In the effort to prop himself up in this comely lady's opinion, he added, "I haven't been here long, but already you can see the great results my expanding ministry's getting. If you're going to be around, I'd like you to attend one of my Sunday services."

"You can be sure I'll do my best to get there, Reverend Dar," A'nh Tran said. "I'll find your church. Now I have to be going. Thank you."

As she left to get into her Range Rover, A'nh summarized her report to Trang. One, the Rev Dar Castor is a sloppy man, as evidenced by the clutter in the hut, the clothes he wore, and the language he employed. He was altogether an artless, uncultivated man. Two, he had a wife he called Moms, but she never appeared; she was, however, heard. Three, no domestic animals were in sight. Four, Kjell Johnson's intellectual attainments impressed him. Five, he had a church, but she hadn't seen it. Dangit, she thought, and returned to Castor's door to ask for directions to it. Knowing Trang, the church itself could become a target if the Reverend got out of control.

She didn't go back inside the hut this time, just took down the directions and departed. Dar was real excited to see her again. Another note: he melted in the presence of a pretty woman. And her final note was: *the wily Kjell Johnson is setting up the slow-witted minister to take the fall for a meeting that was bound to stir up passions and create trouble.* If she knew Trang, he wouldn't permit the meeting to take place.

Pack and Tetu arrived for their meet with Rex Carnes, owner of the Sportsman's Lodge in Yaak. The lodge had no designated parking lot. An acre of grass lay to the front and patrons were expected to leave enough space between their vehicles so everyone could maneuver as necessary to get in and out. It was a Scandinavian-looking establishment with a tall stone chimney dominating the kitchen and dining room, which sat at the front of the place. A branch of the Yaak River was down the hill in back of the lodge about a hundred meters; some guidebooks designated the stream as blue ribbon, but someone might have paid for that accolade. In any case, there was access to better waters not far away.

Pack had passed by this lodge a few times, but never stopped to see it up close. Tetu had phoned the owner back in Libby, where cell connection was possible, saying he and Pack would arrive between noon and one p.m. They arrived in the center of that window, and found the man waiting. He escorted them to his office, where he had a lunch tray brought in for each of them. After exchanging pleasantries and kind inquiries about the governor's health, they got down to the reason for the trip.

The man didn't match the description he imagined. Pack figured the fellow for frail, meek, pusillanimous, but instead he found a man in good shape at about 215 pounds. He'd let Tetu do the talking; moving his mouth too much was still damn uncomfortable.

"Look here, gentlemen," the proprietor began in earnest, "I'm the type guy who when he goes to buy a vehicle makes a fair offer immediately, an offer both buyer and seller know is fair, and I want them to accept or reject. If they reject, I'm gone, no hard feelings. I'm not a BSer, and I've never wanted to be around those who are. What I'm saying is, I'm gonna tell you the truth about my experience here, and if it repels you, so be it. No sugarcoating.

"This is a lovely setting, to me it's as lovely in winter as in any other season. I love the animals and the trees, and I love the hard work it takes to keep the place running. I'm a good handyman, and anybody who takes my place better be too, or he'll run out of money pretty quick. This place sits at the end of a long supply line, don't need to tell you that. You ain't hopping in the truck and running five minutes to a Home Depot or Lowe's up here. You have to plan well to know roughly what you'll need when, spare parts here and there. And then there are times you'll need someone more qualified to fix, say, a broken oven or freezer. Whatever. I'm a busy man, if you don't mind my saying. But I love it, headaches and all, I really do.

"I thought I knew what I was getting into. On the work required to make the operation hum, I did and I do. But what I didn't understand was that my clientele, my guests, would change. I got the class of guests I anticipated up until about a year or three ago. Instead of sportsmen and their ladies, I began to get more and more very rough fellows who have no interest in outdoor activities. It's as if there's a head bad guy somewhere who sent out a memo that this is the best place to stay to do business up here. And the truth is it's about the only place, unless you're camping." The proprietor paused to sip from a glass of water; he looked at the table, not appearing to be concerned about gauging Tetu's reaction.

"You have not caused Tetu to walk away yet, sir," Tetu said. "Do you know who these people are? Are they half of who stays here, or more or less?"

"Thank you, Mr. Palaita...hope I pronounced your name close to right."

"Close enough," Tetu said. "Easy way is just call me Tetu."

"OK, Tetu it is. Who are these people, you ask? Almost all men, but some have women with them, probably not their wives. I'd say half my rooms now hold these guys. At first, there were a few, then more, and at this rate they'll occupy three-quarters of the rooms within a couple years. Sportsmen they're not. They're driving the sportsmen away."

"So, do you know who they work for?" Tetu asked.

"Well, every now and then we get the FTRA crowd. That stands for Freight Train Riders of America, wear black bandannas, most have forearm tats. I've done a little research on them, and some writers say they like to beat up, even murder, fellow rail riders. Supposedly carry contraband across state lines. What they're doing up here I don't know. A good percentage of the other questionables we get are motorcycle gang guys with Washington state plates. Mostly I see them when Sturgis is about to open, so I guess they're on the way there. Then there's others I can't tell who they are except they ain't sportsmen for sure.

"Up the road a mile there's a bar, the biggest one for many miles around. The owner's a nice fellow, and he hires quite a few bouncers for special occasions, but they can't compete with these outsiders we're talking about.

"Don't want to go off on a tangent, but till recently that bar, Montana's Armpit as they call it, was owned by a minister. He actually had two churches, one down in Troy and the other in Libby, he supposedly tended to, at the same time he owned this bar. He was a pretty regular drinker at the bar, I understand. Anyway, the reason he was in Montana was his church back East sent him here to get rid of him. Accused of child molestation, he got off on a fine legal point, so he went back to his church. Rather than fire him, they sent him to this part of the world, far away as they could throw him. Last year, new facts came to light in his case and he was extradited back to the state he came from...I forget if it was Maryland or Connecticut or wherever, doesn't matter. In his early 80s at the time, he got a 15-year sentence. Six years that man owned the bar, and it seemed during that time it went from a peaceful local watering hole to a hellraising fun center where he came up with some kind of special event ever damn month. He just made up names for the events, you know, like 'Madness in the Mountains' weekend, BS like that. Lots of fighting, lots of public sex, cars parked along the roads for miles. The summer months, you find people in various states of undress layin' all over the place the next morning. I guess the preacher must've got rich, but a lotta good it did him, huh?"

"So, is it still that bad, the bar, I mean?" Tetu asked.

Mr. Proprietor paused, thinking, eyes shifting around the office. "Good question, Tetu, because you remind me I should draw a distinction that could be important. OK, let's go back in time to when the preacher took over Montana's Armpit. For most of that time, his ownership I'm speaking of, seems to me the behavior of his patrons could be called rowdy. Adult-style rowdiness, yeah, but still just rowdiness. It lacked the element of meanness, I think it's fair to say. Then something happened. Did criminal types find this area because of Montana's Armpit, or were they already here? I don't know the answer. I do know the conduct of the bar patrons and of my patrons changed from rowdy to criminal at some point during those years. Not long ago, a guy in the bar was stabbed six times and dragged out to the roadside, where he died. No idea who did it, and I don't think anyone's been charged. When bikers beat common folks, local people, with chains, a line's been crossed."

"Don't you have law enforcement help?" Tetu asked.

"You're right, Tetu, this area with few people **is** part of a county, but the seat is 40 rugged miles away, and it takes a while in bad weather, a couple hours in fact, to get from Libby to here. I've heard cops say—with my own ears—they never come up in just one vehicle. They travel in pairs if they come up at all. They recognize the lawless nature of this place. And I'm not putting all the blame on them. A lot of the mountain people here around don't want anything to do with the law, or most anything to do with the government in general. Quite a few belong to Sovereign Citizens and a couple other groups similar. Poor cops can't have much desire to help people who hate them. Also gotta consider they probably got better things to do than break up a bar fight that's two hours away. And if they were called to every fight up at Montana's Armpit, they'd be there more or less permanently.

"Once upon a time, not that many years ago, Lincoln County was part of the county sitting to the east, Flathead, and policing was better. Then the dudes in Troy and Eureka and Libby petitioned to have their own county, and they carried the day, so this is what we got. 19,000 folks in the gigantic county, almost all of them in those three towns, and we suck hind teat. But, hey, as I said, I'm in the minority, no doubt about it. Most of my fellow Yaakers like things just as they are."

Tetu just nodded his head, soberly and silently. Pack looked lost in his thoughts, continuing to remain mute. Then Tetu said, "When you tell Tetu the bad news?"

That broke the ice. The proprietor laughed a real laugh, so stunned was he by the big man's reaction. "Are you serious, Tetu? I haven't convinced you yet not to buy the lodge?"

"Tetu is very serious. They will need more than knives and chains to stop him," Tetu said with finality. "Matai Pack would be ashamed if Tetu could not handle such a situation." He was also thinking he wanted Miss Swan Threemoons to feel proud of her warrior.

Chapter Seven

At the moment, Moms was still asleep in the back room. Sleeping was her favorite activity, such as it was, and Dar was particularly grateful for that right now. He was mulling over his wretched life, its causes and continuance, and yes, he recognized he had led a wretched life. He wasn't such a fool that he could fool himself. *Wherefore this, my life?* he thought. *How did I wind up in this Montana gulag?*

All my life I have existed in a state of fear. As a child in a small town, D'Artagnan Castor had avoided the other boys who played Army and sports. He supposed that because his mother was afraid he would get hurt playing the typical boy games he ought to stay away from them, and he had. So he himself grew phobic about playing with them. Instead, he found a couple of other milquetoast lads, brothers, the sons of a doctor, whose ages were a year on either side of his own. They spent much of those growing-up years sitting in the brothers' tree house, not doing much of anything except speculating on the horrors of the world at large. The three milquetoasts would call on the phone and say their code phrase, 'Let's *rendezvous*', which they cheerily drew out to *RAHN-DAY-VOOOOO.* They were members of the Nerd Club, that had always been clear to him.

His mama and daddy drove a long way to North Carolina to pick him up at the adoption center. He was a handsome blondish two-year old. It took them a year-and-a-half to complete the process. The name he carried there was Mason Headley Richards, but they changed the name immediately. After watching the movie version of *The Three Musketeers*, his mama grew attached to the name D'Artagnan. It sounded important and exotic and smart to her unlettered ear, so that was the name she gave him. Teachers took to calling him Dart in favor of getting hung up in the full name, only he was anything but swift. He tended more toward the limacine, as he did to this day.

Daddy was a good man who worked for a railroad company in hard manual labor. His bosses loved him, and maybe because of that, gave him more overtime work opportunities than anyone else. He earned a nice paycheck and, since mama was tightfisted, he banked most of it. Daddy thought he loved his adopted son, but was never comfortable being a daddy. Mama was domineering, and he just pretty much left the rearing to her. The one area she didn't fret about spending on was Dar. She wanted her little man well-dressed and well-fed. So well did she feed the boy that by pre-pubescence his corpulence began to show.

High school band practice was the closest he came to strenuous exercise. Still, the band director was incessantly calling him out for not lifting his knees high enough. "It's called marching, Mr. Castor, not shambling. Lift those knees, son!"

Although the military draft was formally ended in January 1973, Dar lived in mortal fear of being conscripted. Some athletes at the school pushed him against a locker and told him their fathers knew members of the draft board and they were going to see to it that his saggy ass got called up. He figured they might be able to do it, and he thought gloomily of the prospect every day. He didn't even like the sight of guns, for goodness sakes. He knew he wouldn't survive two days of boot camp. His weight pegged somewhere between 270 and 300 at the time, and his knees were already giving him trouble.

He graduated high school wholly without distinction. His marginal grades were sufficient to get him into a community college a mile from the house. After two years, he transferred to a nearby four-year school of the commuter variety. Mama and daddy understood no more about college than they did about Euclidian geometry, so they acceded to his repeated requests to drop one course and pick up another. He scraped by for a full eight years, at the conclusion of which his fears reached the boiling point. The idea of being cast into the workaday world terrified Dar. What could he do? He possessed no banausic talents. He looked at everyone he saw, in every walk of life, asking himself if he could perform their work, and knew the answer was negative. By this point he was closer to 30 than 22, and in his heart he saw himself for the parasite he was. Meanwhile, his hard-laboring daddy and clueless mama went through their lives apparently unaware it took anyone this long to negotiate college studies. They paid his bills without concern.

D'Artagnan's parents had always attended Sunday School and the 11 o'clock service. Daddy sleepwalked through most of the church goings-on, including his scheduled collection plate duties, but mama said she liked the 'fellowship', an oft-employed word at the church. With routine ill-directed comments, however, she kept many of the church ladies in a state of high dudgeon. They weren't as keen on Teodora's fellowship. Teodora seemed to be missing a social-sense gene, in that she never apprehended the effect of her words; she was a blurter who obeyed the code *speak now, think later.* Her standard reply to anyone who registered offense was, "Why, I dunno, huuuuneee. What on earth are you tawkin' about?" These words she would chirp as she walked away with a smile. It is fair to aver that Teodora Castor regarded herself as the linchpin of the church, and she imagined the other congregants did as well.

So, with Teodora's abiding interest in her church, she was elated when, after Dar's extended schooling, he stated after the graduation ceremony, "Mama, I wanna be a minister. I've heard the calling!"

"Oh, hunnee, I'm sa proud ah you. Give your mama a big hug... How much's it gonna cost?" Teodora was unacquainted with the concept of students working their way through school. "That's fine, just fine, D'Artagnan, it don't matter the cost, we're a sending you just as fore as you can go. I was thinkin' you'd probly go into computers or some such, whur you'd make big money. And I 'member you sayin' sumthin like that once or twice." Truth was, today's average three-year-old was more computer literate, but mama would never know that because she had never used one.

Dar had arrived at the clergy solution logically. He couldn't think of a more comforting safe space, a place free of micro-aggressions and the hurly-burly of the real world. He had visions of being called 'The Right Reverend Doctor Castor.' He would sit in solitary splendor in a wood-paneled study crafting sermons his parishioners would rave about, and tell him, while shaking hands on the way out, "Reverend Castor, that was just about the finest sermon I ever did hear." And he would maintain his earnest regal bearing and reply humbly, "Why, thank you, Eunice, but that was the Spirit speaking through me, so don't give me too much credit."

What he also thought was, "hey, a lot of the big-time preachers have their full file of sermons on the Internet, and I can honor them by passing them off as my own. If I don't have much energy some weeks, I can just read them."

And the fact was he did like to preach within his milquetoast circle of friends. He was Lord Chesterfield writing out practical advice to his son about how to conduct oneself in various social situations. He told them which party to vote for, always citing the mantra, "it's the government's duty to care for the lesser among us." He said this with an eye toward the possibility the government might be providing for him one day soon. Yes, he could dispense advice with the best of them, even if he couldn't march words across a page to produce a standard grammatically correct English sentence.

D'Artagnan Castor had settled the matter: he would become a churchman. Most of his fears would be eradicated. No military threat to loom over him any longer. But first he had to get into a seminary, and any seminary would do. His perfect record of attendance at the local church might come in handy, considering the minister there would probably be inclined to support him with a letter of recommendation. Dar was reluctant to query the minister on the matter, but Teodora relished the chance to approach Reverend Steele with the good news.

"Doc-ter Steele," Teodora began, much aware of the man's preference for the scholarly 'Doctor' over the pedestrian 'Reverend,' "my boy D'Artagnan wants to preach, like you, and hopes to get a letter from you to, you know, a fine minister school, and if anybody knows a fine one, I'm sure it's you. He'd appreciate it soon as you can get to write it. Just call the house and we'll be over to pick it up right away. Thanks for your help." Although Teodora had severe limits to her social skills, she did in the instant situation have a fine intuitive sense that appealing to her minister would call for drawing attention to the exclusive spiritual pedigree he perceived he possessed.

Doctor Steele hadn't known the subject of the visit, but supposed it was the usual request for counseling following a domestic dispute. This jolted him a bit. First things first, he was thinking: do I know how much they put in the plate each week? Second, do I even know her boy? "Tell me a little more about your son, Teodora. And why do you think he's suited to my calling?"

"Cause he told us he's been called. And I don't think he'd say that after—whatever it is—eight or ten years of hard college unlest that'es the case. He's a smart boy, never been no problem atall. No run-ins with the law or nothing like that. You probly remember him as the trombonist in our band, and he never missed a Sunday here all the time he'es growin' up. I guess he's liked all the preachers we ever had here."

"But if he has been at college all those years, I wouldn't have known him, and I'm due to rotate to a new pastoral position in six months," the preacher pointed out saliently. Couldn't this woman see the discomfort this matter was causing him? "My point, Teodora, is that I cannot in good conscience write a letter of recommendation for someone I don't even know."

A thundercloud came over Teodora's visage, as she confronted him angrily. "So you're sayin' you won't do it, is that what I'm hearin', after all me and my husband done for this church for forty years? Ever time they's been a funeral, too many of 'em to count, I've brung over a large mushroom hamburger casserole, and all of them families sure was grateful, I can tell you that. In my own way, I've done as much bereavement counselin' as you." She folded her arms, scowled, and trained her eyes on her shoes.

The minister felt good and properly upbraided, so he changed tack and said, "I'm sorry, Teodora, for sounding uncharitable. Please send your son over to talk with me, and we'll see what I can do for him. Refresh me on his name, please."

So Dar met with the minister, and the minister saw nothing to make him believe Dar could cut the mustard in the pulpit. At the same time, he would be moving on soon, so he threw caution to the wind, and wrote a statement on Dar's behalf that anyone, except maybe Dar himself, could see was a halfhearted endorsement. Weak college transcript notwithstanding, Dar was admitted to a theological school, the first of a half-dozen in as many states. D'Artagnan Castor finally was ordained.

His Conference assigned him as an Associate Pastor at several backwater churches where he seldom got a chance to take the pulpit. Dar, however, felt secure in these obscure country churches. Terrorists he heard so much about did not lurk in these bucolic settings. His accommodations weren't much, but he was safe and members gave him hams and turkeys and the fruits of their crops, and his daddy kept him in clothes and a car.

After a few years, the denomination felt sorry for him and finally assigned him a series of churches of his own. He did not stay at any longer than a year. At one such church, he had thirteen members, about five of which regularly attended his service. But Dar felt no shame in his inability to attract a larger audience. He felt safe, tucked away in villatic places where few were aware of his existence.

"Time I became a man," Dar mouthed to himself. He wondered what Miss A'nh Tran thought of him, and was surprised he actually cared. Maybe it was because the last time Moms had praised him had been the end of World War II. "Here I sit in my Michelin Man coat in a 600 square foot hut, afraid to step outside lest a damn mountain lion rip my heart out. And Moms says she is a prisoner here. How long will she stand by me? All she'll do is scurry as rapidly as her squatty body will allow to the safety of the car, which luckily is an aging 4 by 4 daddy passed on to me when he was done with it."

He and Moms were unable to have children, which seemed a good thing given their present circumstances. They had once taken in two foster children, a brother and sister, as potential adoptees, but after ten days reneged on the agreement and took them back. "Too much trouble," Dar and Moms agreed.

The Kootenai Indians had given him the hut and a place for services. Not a church in any normal sense, but a good-sized wooden structure, heated by an overtaxed wood stove, that in a pinch could accommodate fifty worshippers. So far eighteen had been the most he'd had in there at once, but he was suddenly optimistic he could fill it one day soon. The Kootenai were the key; many of them had a foot in two doors, covering their bases—they followed many of the rituals and beliefs of their native culture, but simultaneously sought refuge in the Christian faith—just in case.

Dar thought of the opening words to the great gospel hymn, "Amazing Grace," hoping against hope he might yet redeem his miserable life:

Amazing grace, how sweet the sound
That saved a wretch like me
I once was lost, but now am found
Was blind, but now I see

'Twas grace that taught my heart to fear
And grace my fears relieved
How precious did that grace appear
The hour I first believed

Chapter Eight

The election was just weeks away, and although Jim Dahl did not assume victory, he always charted branches and sequels to every plan. If, therefore, he won the gubernatorial election, he would have to deliver a State of the State Address in January. Seemed a little odd to him, but then Montana itself was peculiar. Just ask any restaurant owner who had attempted to secure an alcohol license—a man had to be MENSA certified to understand that byzantine law, and changing it definitely wasn't near the head of his priority list. So, what would he say to the joint session of legislature and the PBS cameras that would broadcast it live, given he would have been in office just two months?

Well, one topic for inclusion that seemed right and fitting was one that Pack himself had brushed off: what Pack and his team, of which Dahl had been part, had done for the country with respect to the Constitutional Convention. It was a gargantuan task, but Pack had stayed on it like wild dogs on a freshly downed wildebeest. Dahl was sure no other person in America possessed the powers of moral suasion and communications skills Pack had demonstrated in getting the job to completion. Pack had seemed tireless; to have bagged five hours of sleep in 24 was a rare blessing. There had been so many moving parts in the project, of people placing demands on Pack's schedule: Constitutional scholars; state legislative leaders; state governors; myriad potent interest groups; news organizations; the DNC; the RNC, and numerous others. Throughout, Pack had remained unflappable, strong, steady, with eyes fixed upon the principles that guided him. But Dahl made a note to include the vital point that Pack had been driven to undertake the Convention idea first and foremost because it was in the long-term interest of his own state. Simon Pack never sought human praise, Dahl ruminated, and that alone makes him very different from almost everyone else. His present boss had had much life experience that had required him to make decisions in treacherous circumstances, and they had been as uniformly correct as any human can be. "If you are a spiritually and intellectually mature person," Pack had said once, "you do what is right, and the rest will fall into place." Pack had said this at the end of a long week at West Point, where Pack was Superintendent and Dahl his Chief of Staff. They were alone, holding glasses with three fingers of Knob Creek in their hands, kicked back in the chairs of Pack's study in Quarters 100, his on-Post residence. Dahl recalled with difficulty Pack's brilliant explanation of what constitutes intellectual and spiritual discernment, as well as the trademarks of their opposites. What he remembered with no difficulty—indeed, with precision—were Pack's next words, which he seemed to have been saying to himself as much as to Dahl: "Do not be tossed and blown by every wind of new teaching. We will not be influenced when people try to trick us with lies so clever they sound like the truth. Light cannot live with darkness, Jim. Turgid arguments from self-anointed intellectuals can be seductive, but we will not be charmed. Break down their overblown language and what you get—their vapid, puerile, inane arguments--can be confuted with good sense, assuming your moral bases are sound." Pack was sound of mind, sound of body, a Marine warrior, but he was also in his own way a spiritual leader, almost monkish is his slavery to right action. Yes, Simon Pack was a man of few words, a humble man, but when he spoke only the fool did not listen. Dahl often reflected that Pack's most lasting achievement lay in the line of distinguished leaders who had witnessed, then followed, his example.

Dahl himself had been a remarkably talented Marine Colonel, and getting Dahl as Chief at West Point had been one of only two demands Pack had made when the Pentagon lured him out of retirement to take the West Point Superintendency. Dahl himself had the star of a General Officer coming before he was ambushed and beaten badly by thugs in the employ of a billionaire trying to send Pack a message. Healthy again, Dahl was confident he had the ability and background to serve as Governor with an order of distinction similar to the Pack administration.

Jim Dahl laid his pencil down and fantasized about a few things he just might say to an incredulous legislature: first, he would erect signs prominently at every border entry point, including air and rail terminals. They would say, “YOU ARE ENTERING LAWFUL MONTANA: Do Not Test It!” Law and order would be a main, perhaps *the* theme, of his address. He would tell the legislature, “I am POBAR about the lawlessness and corruption from one end of America to the other, and I am determined it will not take root in this state. We’ll respect every man and woman’s rights to privacy and public dissent, but we will not tolerate those who in the process of dissent damage other people’s property or imperil others’ physical security.” The ruggedly-clad rancher men and women might cheer such words, but the suited legislators would be aghast, left with tongues lolling.

He picked up the pencil again and jotted notes on ideas he believed in. Whether they would make it into the address was for further consideration, but at this moment they sounded good to Dahl. He would adjure Montana citizens to:

- Post the Ten Commandments in and on all Montana State Government Buildings
- Restrict media access to State Government. I speak to the media, and only when I want to.
- Stop illegal immigration in this state. Comply with current laws. Absolutely no ‘sanctuary cities.’
- Protect our right to bear arms.
- Pledge of Allegiance (with ‘Under God’) is back.
- Protect our elections from fraud and abuse. Montana National Guard monitors polls.
- Maintain a budget surplus.
- Fund fully and expand the Montana National Guard.

Boy, when the Professors and the journalists got a load of this list, Dahl mused, amused, they will wish Simon Pack were back in office. Before I finish the address, there'll be electrifying headlines out there exclaiming against this right-wing wacko bellicose crankcase we've put into office. Well, he thought further, guess I ought to wait until the ship of state sets sail before giving the enemy U-Boats the torpedoes to sink it. Calm down, Jimmy, calm down. "Even if I do tone it down a notch, I am resolved to crush lawlessness and corruption, so I have a main theme settled, and that's a good start as an organizing principle," he soliloquized.

Dahl knew himself, well aware he could appear jocular and serious simultaneously. His serious side right now had him thinking about the Founders, that elite assemblage of early Americans to whose ideas Pack regularly paid homage. When they wrote of obedience to 'the Laws of Nature and of Nature's God' in the Declaration of Independence, they were recognizing how future generations would have to guard against the erosion of public morality. Apropos of the present, they were providing the serious underpinning of the notes he had just penciled in. The Founders wanted it clearly understood that every right has a corresponding obligation. Society—in the form of its elected government—would have the right, indeed the duty, to proscribe any behavior that lent itself to the destruction of the public good, even if it conduced to the individual's private or perceived pleasures. In some states not far from this one, Dahl thought, it is manifestly the individual's right that is satisfied first, at the expense of the public good, and I cannot be true to the vision of the Founders and permit that. He ended this train of thought with the notion that today's politicians had scant understanding of what the Founders described as *rational liberty* and *rational happiness*.

Now back to giving Pack his due. Yes, thick reams of newsprint had contained explanations of what Pack had accomplished with the Constitutional Amendments, but not so much here in his home state. Dahl would rectify that shortcoming.

Pack hadn't gotten everything he sought, such as rolling back the voting age from 18 to 21, but the changes he wrought were momentous. Dahl wanted to stay out of the weeds, just hit the high points. Some of the Amendments, as written, were long and tortuous. The people needed reminding of the effects only. Montanans had lives, and if they wanted to get down to the legalisms, a little research would take them there.

One: a balanced budget to limit federal spending and taxing.

Two: Term limits of 12 years for members of both House and Senate.

Three: State legislatures, as originally intended, shall choose United States Senators. Further, a Senator may be removed from office by 2/3 vote of the state legislature from which he or she came.

Four: A super-majority of state legislatures can overturn a majority opinion of the US Supreme Court. Such action must be done within 24 months of the majority opinion.

Five: There shall be term limits for US Supreme Court Justices.

Six: In accordance with scales based on the total US population, the size of the federal bureaucracy will have a ceiling.

Taken as a whole, Pack's efforts and speeches in leading and convening a Convention of the States had led to a populist revival in the United States. The American people stood up to be heard, loud and proud, willing and able to throw off the chains their government had shackled them with. Pack, one man on a mission to elevate and extol average American citizens of all colors and social standings, had certainly caused the earth to shake. There was no question in Dahl's mind that what Pack had done was pave the way for a like-minded populist to dethrone the American Emperor, President Rozan. Dahl had on his desk an article written about the President-Elect that could have been a paean to Pack. It read: "Galt was a pragmatic choice. First, on matters of public policy the Rozan Administration is out of step with the people. We believe a country without borders is not a country. We believe immigration should cease until assimilation occurs. We believe if you elect not to assimilate, you are not an American and have no claim to the fruits of our country. We are appalled and alarmed at our number one national security risk, a debt in the inconceivable amount of $20 trillion. It sickens us that our generation is so selfish it is willing to saddle future generations with an economic burden so onerous their prospects from birth will be dim.

We loathe inferior trade deals that relegate America to a one-dimensional, service-based economy. We want a country that makes things again, and that challenges the Tigers of East Asia. We want the good jobs that will come from making steel in Birmingham and Pittsburgh and Mobile, and from a genuine all-of-the-above energy policy that Rozan promised but did not deliver. We want clean coal and oil that will free us forever from being hostage to the Emirs and Kings of the Arab Gulf states.

We find the regulation-makers without faces repugnant and stifling, and we hate a Government that abets this kind of oppression.

We mourn education standards that have gotten lost, and we mock a president who crows about the highest percentage of high school graduates in decades. What value is in a diploma if it is worth no more than an eighth-grade education 60 years ago? We loathe a Kakistocrat party that thrives on perpetuating a permanent underclass in order to pack its voter rolls, but is otherwise detached from American minorities. We believe *every* American has talent, and we want to realize that talent to build an America in which *every* citizen has a stake in its success and prosperity, especially including inner-city minorities.

We have grown weary of a Kakistocrat party that has two primary constituents: the mega-rich, and the very poor who pay no taxes. Each of those groups benefits in a different way from Kakistocrats. But the group left out of their calculations is all those between the very top and the very bottom, to wit, the middle class that itself is in danger of extinction. I watched BRM, the last Kakistocrat candidate, closely in his final two weeks, and he hardly acknowledged the existence of the last-mentioned group.

The foregoing said, this presidential election produced a predictable result for one reason that eclipses all others, in my opinion: millions upon millions of Galt voters are **angry** at being told what to think, what to eat, what kind of vehicle to drive, what energy to consume—government has intruded too far, too deep, too much into our lives. And who is doing the dictating? Coastal elites for the most part, people showing just how much the Kakistocrat party has devolved into a regional political caste.

Throw in Illinois if you want. Average people in Kansas and Oklahoma and Tennessee and most other states are tired of dictates from big-city dwellers and entertainers and athletes. Here is how I describe it, in a nutshell: there's a big raucous party going on on one side of the vast picture window. Champagne flows. Mickey P and Uptown and Lady Scream and Keith Rozan and BRM are inside whooping it up. Loudspeakers outside inform the common people out there to tighten their belts and just be compliant, because we know what's best for you people. The common people have had their noses pressed against the glass for too long, looking in upon the hypocrites putatively in charge. The people have decided they do not reside in an ancient feudal state in which the moronic lord of the manor keeps them underfoot. And that is that."

Many believed the President-elect owed a good deal to Simon Pack. Pack's emergence as a leader of the Constitutional Convention prepared the way for the new President. Pack had argued that the people were being trampled underfoot by their government, and showed them ways to reassert their own voices. He began the populist uprising that led to Galt's election.

Chapter Nine

Pack stepped outside their room at the Sportsman's Lodge into the chilly night air. He hadn't said much to Tetu after their session with the current owner, Rex Carnes. Tetu seemed set on mortgaging his future on this place. Yes, it was nice, and the price seemed more than fair, but so many things could blow up in Tetu's face. An increased presence of undesirables could drive true sportsmen away for good, once the word spread—and the Internet guaranteed it would—and his protégé would go from holding a basket of flowers to a bucket of feces.

It was fully dark now, but Simon began a slow-paced trek down the slope toward the river. He stopped to urinate, recalling for the nth time how much more relieving it was to take a leak in the open air versus any indoor facility. In the stillness he could hear the music and loud voices from the Montana's Armpit Bar a mile away. From what Rex Carnes had related, there surely seemed to be a nexus between that bar and this lodge. At some point, he would get back up here and explore some options with the bar owner.

He had seen on the lodge man's desk an envelope bearing the name of the bank Tetu was dealing with. Before he knew as much as he did now about this place, he had been eager to help Tetu secure the loan. At this moment, he wasn't sure how he felt about that. He wanted Tetu to know he had his back, but just as important, he didn't want Tetu to make a big mistake. The best course of action, he decided, was to continue in the vein he had all day today. Think it over more, not showing his hand, let Tetu take the reins.

But this lodge, and the ground upon which it rested, was only a cloud covering what was really disturbing him at a deeper level: Simon Pack was feeling like a failure. He wasn't himself, he thought, but just as quickly, he thought, "Yes, it is me. I can't pretend otherwise. A lot of stuff is going on up here in the Yaak, and I don't understand much of it. But my sense is that the pot is about to blow...just as I'm leaving office. I'll be leaving Dahl with a mess, and I'll be seen not to have done my job. The people who stand to be hurt are the permanent residents of this valley." It was no consolation that most residents of Montana had never set foot in the Yaak. It was remote to everyone. But he was the Governor, and he was responsible for the *entire* state, not just the parts tourists took pictures of. He had let down the permanent citizens of this valley, and the thought weighed liked a cannonball on his brain.

He had to think through how to handle this with great care. Jim Dahl had enough on his mind right now; Pack didn't want to paint a fuzzy picture for Dahl, then expect him to deal with it. Pack wanted his tenure to be over right this minute, because he wanted to delve deeper into the strange happenings in the Yaak. Nope, he wasn't going to dump on Dahl. He would devise some sort of plan that would enable him to define the problem, then perhaps recommend a course of action to fix it—unless he could handle it himself.

Some ten miles distant from the Sportsman's Lodge, Ng Trang was distrait. He directed his mistress, A'nh Tran, to fetch him a Bloody Mary. Just the two of them were aboard his luxurious RV in camping slot thirteen of the Pete Creek Campground. These federal campgrounds permitted seven-day stays, so when he was in the Yaak for a prolonged period, he moved from one to another up and down the fifty-mile stretch of highway. Slot thirteen was the most secluded and deepest of the fifteen in the small park. Trang liked this campground the best because the camp host seldom walked past, and wasn't nosey in the least. Long as the camper adhered to the cardinal rule, 'Pack it in, Pack it out,' he was satisfied.

Trang was distracted because he had a queasy feeling about this biker crew he had an arrangement with. Their honcho was always complaining, never satisfied with what they were paying for the high-grade meth. Hollow as Trang supposed the threat was, the biker boss had once threatened to blow the cover of the operation. Confident though he was that the man's threats were just noise, he still had to be cautious with these guys. On the other hand, he could just as easily cut them off, go with another group of motorcycle movers.

A'nh brought him the drink, slithering toward him with one of those Viagra looks. Trang pushed her away, ordering her to bring another before he took the first sip of this one. He downed both in a few gulps. He kept two dirt bikes on a carrier attached to the RV. "Let's take a ride," he said to A'nh. It was early morning of a glorious day.

He radioed ahead to alert his men he was coming in. A'nh marveled at her man's pathfinding skills. Even if she had been here a dozen times, she supposed she couldn't locate this remote hideout, and she a smart woman at that. Trang turned off fire roads onto game trails, then emerged back onto other fire roads, and along river banks, riding fast without hesitation until finally they arrived. This latest meth cook had finished last night, and the buyers were due to make the pickup right about now. Trang's men covered these biker buyers. His guys occupied defilade positions the full 360 degrees around the cook site. Even Trang had not spied them, but he knew they were there.

Trang had three cooks on this job, and as he pulled in he surveyed the scene. Five bikers, all five carrying iron, as they always did. Four were readying their bikes. The one presumably in charge had Trang's lead cook pinned against a tree. "Is there a problem here?" Trang asked stonily, softly, menacingly.

"You Trang?" muttered the Barbarian banger as he loosened his grip on the cook.

"I ask the questions, Babar, you answer, capisce?"

The fat Barbarian didn't reply.

"My question is to my man," Trang said, turning to his moneyman. "Has this tub of grease paid up, in full?"

"Yes, Mr. Trang."

"Well then," Trang said to the lead biker. "Perhaps I misunderstand the situation here. Do you have a problem with our product? No hard feelings if you do. I aim to please our customers, and will take any criticism under advisement."

The biker was emboldened by his size advantage over the slight Ng Trang, the biker thinking, "I don't care if he knows Tai Kwan Wooptiedoo, every damn martial art in the book, I can plow right through that lightweight little shitnoise." To throw Trang off balance, he said, leering at A'nh Tran, "Fine piece of Asian ass right there." Then to A'nh, the bearded fellow said, "You lookin' for a real man, I'm guessin', right honey?"

Tranh just smiled, saying, "That's why she's with me and not you, hyena face."

The biker lunged for Tranh, but the whippet-quick Trang violently plunged his sharpened little fingernail expertly into the man's jugular, blood spurting instantly and furiously. The larger man fell to his knees, grasping at his neck, trying futilely to staunch the rush of red onto the ochre dirt. None of his mates moved. Before long he was white, bled out.

A'nh had signaled the overwatch element to come down from their positions, but they hadn't needed her signal. They were there to put an end to more violence.

The remaining four Barbarians were cool with what had just transpired. They made no move to retaliate. Trang addressed them: "Nice doing business with you, gentlemen. Being a gentleman is important to me. I won't tolerate rudeness in a man, and I'd like you to keep that in mind. Tell your boss we're still cool. Tell him I approve of you who conducted yourselves like gentlemen. See, I care about you men. You could say I have a real interest is seeing to it you make money. When you make money you'll come back and see me again, and we'll all be happy. Now you boys take our product and load it up securely, and bon voyage. Enjoy all that money that's waiting for you on the other end. Don't worry, we'll clean up what's left behind here."

To show his fearlessness, Trang waved the overwatch guys back into their positions and stayed around to watch the bikers pack their loads.

Everyone involved in this trade knew what had just occurred was part of the business. If you didn't want to make big money, you got out, so he doubted he would ever hear of this incident again. These guys were professionals, probably had moved coke, meth, PCP, LSD much of their lives. They stowed it inside the point cover, in false bottoms of saddle-bags, inside the many concealed pockets of the biker jackets…they knew what they were doing. And you could be sure the ID numbers on any parts of the bikes had been altered.

Taking the huge bundle of cash from the moneyman, Trang said. "I'll save you the trip today, Davie. Good job. Clean up every last molecule of this place and get out of here. We'll be in touch."

With a nod to A'nh Tran, they cranked up the dirt bikes and were gone. Once back at the RV, Trang peeled the rubber bands from the bills he could cup in two hands, then strewed them across the bed, upon which they let their carnal passions explode.

Chapter Ten

Pack's exit from the Governor's seat was, for those who knew the man, expectedly low-key. There was no farewell tour, no parties, none of the silly roasts. He went out to visit individual members of the legislature and of his staff to thank them for their diligent efforts. He spent as much time as he could over at Paul Fardink's home, joking with him, making sure he was all covered on the medical front, encouraging him in every way he could, and threatening him with a State Police visit if he didn't get well enough soon to drive over for a visit to his cabin. Pack's health was much improved. He wasn't fully recovered, but the headaches came less and less, and he could eat solid food and enunciate his words better.

For the citizens of Montana he wrote a personal message thanking them for the chance to serve them; he listed no accomplishments, took no personal credit, but did re-live memorable moments from his trips across the state. There was the rancher who tried to gift him with several hundred pounds of elk meat for the trip back to Helena. Another rancher who, while conversing with his governor, choked on his tobacco chaw and had to be whisked to the hospital—the Heimlich was shown not to work so well with chewing tobacco. A Native American so honored to be speaking with Pack he drew out a huge blade to make them blood brothers on the spot. A farmer who got Pack into a horrifically expensive piece of machinery, a combine harvester, he was proud to have recently purchased. Once he got the Guv up in the cab, the farmer barked instructions to crank it up and drive it a little ways...Pack might as well have been strapped to a Stegosaurus, so poorly did he pilot the huge vehicle, bucking and lunging as if to throw him off. He might have employed a hundred such stories, but his love for all things Montana shone through on the few he chose. His staff forwarded his farewell message to newspapers, radio, and TV for broadcast as they saw fit. And that was it for Pack the Governor. Now it was just simple Simon Pack and sidekick Tetu boarding his black Wrangler Unlimited, with no more belongings than they had entered Helena with, hitting the road again, bound for his cabin in western Montana. Simon Pack had no need to look at the figures in a bankbook to know how rich he was.

Although not by the margin of Pack's landslide gubernatorial victory, James Dahl also won convincingly over a solid opponent. Pack's endorsement and frequent mentions of Dahl's talents over the full course of his term had helped propel him into office, no question about it. Dahl had assembled a good team, he thought, but one with less military flavor than Pack's.

His Lieutenant Governor, May Lawson, was a medical doctor general practitioner from Bozeman. He believed she would be a good teammate, although frankly her knowledge of social and business affairs in the state would require considerable fleshing out. He intended to introduce her to state government by assigning her specific duties that probably lay outside her areas of expertise at this point.

Like Pack, he wanted to immunize his administration against groupthink by appointing a number of freethinkers to key positions. First among these was his chief of staff, an extraordinarily bright young man who had voluntarily left the Army as a Major in his early 30s. Following that, he held a variety of jobs with both private companies and the CIA in active combat zones overseas. Dahl had great faith in the people who had recommended this fellow Jack Schnee. They claimed it was impossible to overwork the super-energetic Schnee. Still, picking Schnee to a job so crucial was risky--he had to be sure he could tolerate the idiosyncrasies of a person he would be closer to than anyone else. His supporters said Schnee had a caustic humor, sharp wit, and acerbic tongue, all qualities Dahl actually appreciated. Outweighing all comments, though, was the weight they placed on his decisiveness and loyalty.

Following Pack's helicopter crash, the Forest Service had withdrawn their offer to provide a chopper for the Governor's use. For the time being, Dahl would need surface transportation to move around the state. In any event, finding a replacement airframe wasn't important to Dahl right now. He was just eager to get to work, to map plans, to develop a four-year blueprint, grateful Pack had left the state on a sound footing.

Pack's usual reason for wanting to see the cabin again was the joy he found in the familiar surroundings of his basement office, all those wonderful tools he operated to make furniture and repair little things around the place (sometimes the only person who could see this or that needing repair was Pack himself, most likely because he found pleasure in the work), and the chair with the excellent standing lamp that made for good reading. He also loved the seclusion the cabin afforded. Seldom did anyone stop in, and just as seldom did he receive a phone call. Only his closest friends had his home number, and nobody he knew of had his new smartphone number. He had zero social media presence. If someone with clout in the Pentagon wanted to reach him, they of course still could, as could Dahl or select members of his staff. As a general proposition, however, Simon Pack was off limits in this place.

He and Tetu had talked a lot on the way across the state, but they had kept it light. Pack was back behind the wheel, Tetu liking his old shotgun seat, from which he could occasionally reach back and rub Chesty. The nearest they had come to serious conversation was when Pack said, "Tetu, neither of us knows how long you'll be at the cabin, but however long it turns out is OK with me. Chesty is our dog, an iron link between us, but I want you to begin to take full responsibility for him. Look at his vet records, make appointments as necessary. When his food supply gets low, you top it off. Most important, when you go to the Yaak, I want him to be with you. I'm sure you can find uses for the old boy up there. He's a good watchdog, a good attack dog, a good varmint chaser, and a great companion. I don't want any more discussion about it." During Tetu's momentary silence, Pack added a little lie: "See, I'd like freedom of movement once you're gone...let's say I want to drive to Helena to see aviator Paul for a weekend, I can't take a dog into his house, and I sure don't intend to board him. The right place for him to be is with you."

Sensing Pack's resolution, Tetu acceded without objection. "You know I will care for him well, Matai, and you can see Chesty anytime you please. Matai will always be present with me in Chesty."

Pack had continued to stay out of Tetu's plans to purchase the lodge, and that included the particular of vouching for Tetu with the banker. Reservations remained, but he swallowed them. Tetu had chosen a tough way to build a new life for himself and Swan Threemoons, but Pack knew it was time to let go.

Pack had shared with no one, including Tetu, his preoccupation with the unrest in the Yaak. He felt compelled to find a way to help the people of the Upper Yaak.

Not many days after Pack's return to the cabin, a police vehicle pulled up his gravel driveway. It was around 0600 hours, still dark, Pack visible by the garage's overhead lighting. At the moment Sheriff Mollison caught sight of Pack, he was holding up a length of PVC pipe studying it for some purpose Mollison could not fathom. Pack instantly dropped the pipe and moved toward his old friend Mollison. Mollison ambled toward Pack, grinning. Mollison was deliberate in everything he did, never appearing rushed, always under control. He was the strong, silent sheriff the movies had popularized.

"So, what am I supposed to call you now?" the Sheriff asked. "You hammered me for calling you General, so I stopped. Is Governor OK with you? Can't get too close to you, ya' know, 'cause the force of your illumination would blind me."

"Nope, it ain't OK, Sheriff. You're old, you're dumb, you're insensitive, and you're damn disrespectful, you old goat," Pack said, in high good humor. Seeing Mollison raised his spirits, allowed him to set aside his compulsively focused attention on the Yaak for a few minutes. "You're also trespassing, so I might call the Sheriff's office to have you arrested."

He thrust out his hand, and pulled in his friend for a manhug. "How you doin', Joe?"

"Good to have you back, Simon, damn sure is. I'll feel even better if you'll haul your old lineman's ass into my vehicle and we go on down to the Sundance for breakfast. I'll buy, you get the heapingest plate they got, with a barrel of coffee to wash it down, how 'bout it?"

"Done deal, friend. Give me a sec' to grab a jacket and tell Tetu where I'm going, and I'll be right out."

Snow had come to northwestern Montana. The motor pool people had attached the chains to the Sheriff's SUV, so the drive into town presented no difficulty.

The Sundance was crowded with the usual breakfast crowd, but they always had a place for the Sheriff. The hostess was keenly attuned to Mollison's mannerisms, and this time she knew his look meant 'give the Governor his space.' One guest called out a "Welcome back, Governor Pack," which elicited applause from most of the others. Pack smiled and waved back to them weakly.

They took their booth seats and began to chat. "I see you're going mountain man—growing your beard for a reason? Never saw you with one before. Got a secret mission in the works?"

Pack started to answer, then caught his tongue. "Can't talk yet," he thought. In fact, Pack was going to let his facial and head hair grow out, and he might even color it when it got long enough. He wanted to be unrecognizable when he went back up in the Yaak. For now, he just said to his friend, "No, Joe, no secret missions I'm aware of."

"Well, OK then, but I know you, Simon, and I think something's up. But I won't press you....So, you say Tetu's staying with you?"

"Yeah, he's trying to purchase a lodge up around Yaak, so until the deal goes through, he's staying with me."

"Will he be able to pull it off?" the Sheriff asked.

"Financially, odds are yes. He has been a frugal man all his life, and I believe he'll get the loan. But whether he can make the business work, pay off, once he owns it I'll admit does give me pause," Pack said.

"Not enough business experience, you think?"

"That's not it, Joe. Tetu's a quick study, a close observer, and he understands exactly what's required to turn a profit. In a purely business sense, he's more than adequate to the task. It's a lot of poorly-defined, tangential stuff that bothers me," Pack offered.

The Sheriff went quiet; he knew something was heavy on Pack's mind, and he also knew it was more than just Tetu getting his lodge, or whatever it was. He knew the former Governor and General sitting across from him was a strategic, panoramic thinker. He was a man who, when he saw a problem, asked himself whether it was actually a *class of problem. If you have a systemic problem, you fix the system.* Mollison himself was no slouch. He was smart enough to have discerned right away that Pack was concerned about bigger problems in the Yaak. Out of respect for Pack, Mollison resolved to treat the subject discreetly.

Casually, Sheriff Mollison said, "Did you know Lincoln County used to be rolled up into Flathead County?" Mollison was the Sheriff of Flathead County.

"To be honest, Sheriff, I didn't know that until quite recently. But someone did indeed explain to me how the present Lincoln came to separate from yours. What did you think about that?"

"I want to be careful here, Simon, to avoid giving you the impression my opinion is parochial. You have an idea what my pay is, I'm sure. Fact is, I never got paid much, but that's never been a problem for me. I get enough, let's just leave it there. I'm happy, period. So let me lay that on the table. We good on this point?" the Sheriff asked.

"C'mon, Sheriff. From the beginning of our relationship, I've respected you, admired you, loved you. You don't need to convince me you're telling me anything but the truth. No preliminaries necessary, friend," Pack replied.

"Thanks for saying that....Anyway, it's true I got paid quite a bit more when the geography of this county was much greater. I had a much larger force, too. At the same time, Flathead's population was half of what it is today, so there's that. That said, the number of calls we got from the upper Yaak relative to the totality of the county was amazing. Always had problems up there, and I went up a lot myself, just to spend time with them, hoping to persuade them we weren't the enemy. My force maintains good comms with them today, I'm proud to say." He took time to refresh the two coffee cups, and looked at Pack to see if this line of talk was registering. It was, Mollison decided. He paused to offer Pack a chance to intervene.

"OK, Sheriff, if you're tied into Lincoln County pretty well, how much do you know about what's happening over there in the present?" Pack asked.

"Right," the Sheriff answered. "Let's start with a look from 50,000 feet. You have a million acres of wilderness, with most of the small population living in the southern half. The northern half is even wilder country than down south. More large mammals capable of eviscerating a man, more vast tracts with no people at all, more spectacular landscapes. To people like Kjell Johnson, hero to many and devil to many others, the upper Yaak is Heaven, a sacred place in which no human being has the right to tread. To thousands of average people, it's just like any other unprotected, undesignated wilderness area in America, a place they can ride their ATVs, their snowmobiles, and their dirt bikes and bicycles. Then you have the loggers, who see an opportunity to employ people in harvesting the good wood found there. There are the millworkers, who process that lumber. Then you can throw in the rebels, mostly good people who believe they've found a place in which they can live the simple, uncomplicated life out of reach of a government they perceive wants to control every facet of their lives. Last, you have ranchers who believe they should have the right to help protect the forests by permitting their herds controlled access to the undergrowth. For the sake of making my point, I need to exaggerate just a little: if you draw little circles containing the names of these various groups on a blank sheet of paper and project from each vectors of hatred so many lines would cross you'd be hard pressed to count them. I'm not finished, but let me visit the restroom to offload this coffee before I'm done."

Mollison rose and left. Pack took the time to process the Sheriff's input. He knew most of this stuff Mollison had told him, but hadn't taken the time to integrate it into an understandable whole. The Sheriff returned.

"Be honest. Should I go on? Maybe I'm not giving you anything of value," the Sheriff said.

"I *will* be honest: this isn't making me feel good, but it's what I need to hear. Please go on," Pack said.

"All right. A couple more things. First, I might've said 'hate vectors' when 'animosity vectors' would've been more appropriate. Second, there's another category of people who hang out up there I'll call outlaws. You've got your run-of-the-mill moonshiners, yes, 1950s-style guys who're breaking the law, but they aren't generally the evil hard-baked criminals; they're common 'scofflaws.' In addition, you have a mostly itinerant crowd that litters itself in the most hard-to-get-to places. What law agency has the manpower to track these people down unless it's got solid evidence they've committed a specific crime? I doubt even drones would help much when you're looking at a half-million acres in the upper Yaak. At various times we used to get reliable information about high-volume drug runners, white slave operators handing off their chattel, murderers on the lam, rival bikers using it as a battleground, weapons dealers, and so on.

"Finally, it might help to look at that situation this way: Lincoln's population is puny. It's a poor county, one without much of a tax base. The Sheriff over there has trouble buying copy paper and paper clips, and most of the time thinks he's tilting at windmills. I'd like this kept confidential, but he admitted that his little crew is damned apprehensive—he said 'scared'—to be seen in a cop car up there. Most Yaakers hate the law, see themselves as living in a place apart from America, and the Lincoln PD just refuse to go there unless they have at least two vehicles together. That, Simon, is kinda my ugly picture of life in the Yaak in the twenty-first century."

They were both serious eaters, now plowing through their small mountains of food, almost down to the point where they aggregated and consumed small clotlike masses one after another until the plates were barren. After wiping their mouths almost simultaneously with the back of their hands, they sat contentedly drinking the little left of their coffee. Simon finally said, "Good breakfast, good talk. You're pretty darned shrewd, Sheriff." They both took his meaning without openly acknowledging it.

"One question more, though" Pack said. "Why no mention of a Forest Ranger or Game Warden? Those people are normally real tuned in to everything that happens in their territories. Didn't you ever exchange intel with them?"

"I did. You bet I did. Common sense tells you they can be valuable resources for other law agencies. How much Sheriff Hackman over in Lincoln deals with them I don't know. I have an idea how much, but I won't express it. Not my place to rat out colleagues. Maybe my vague answer is a lead you can pursue," Mollison said.

Mollison drove Pack back to the cabin, Pack thinking it was time to make sure his Jeep was wholly prepared for the winter weather.

Chapter Eleven

***KEELEY*:** Keeley Eliopoulous was depressed. She had proved to herself, as if she needed proof, that money was no cure for love. She was still on the beautiful island in Greece, still mourning her father, whom they had lovingly settled into the soil two weeks ago. Her mother had always been strong, but never more than now. She was an exemplar of dignity and strength to all in her circle. Keeley only wished she possessed the strength she observed in her mother.

Keeley was rethinking her life. She sat alone in a beach chair facing out onto the sparkling blue and aqua of the Aegean. This, her father's resplendent beachfront estate, was evidence of her privileged upbringing. She had attended the finest private schools in Greece. She learned to speak flawless English, and she could travel anywhere in Europe and converse using the local colloquialisms. She attended Yale University, as had her father, and stayed on to earn a doctorate. The median time to earn a degree in her field of immunobiology was 6.4 years, but she did it in four. Of about 40 students total in the program, the university awarded only 8-10 doctorates each year. She approached schoolwork with the same intensity and exuberance she did everything. Most summers several Yale classmates went to Greece with her to enjoy life aboard her father's yacht.

Keeley was a classic Mediterranean beauty, olive-complected, abundant dark hair, exceptional of figure and face, clear of eye and skin. Attracting boys was effortless; repelling them required constant effort. Handsome males did not especially beguile her. She had, after all, grown up among countless of those the world knows as 'Greek gods.' She didn't enjoy the company of males who had never been called on to be men, and likely never would be. They were unaccustomed to hard work and to making difficult decisions. They honed their bodies and were careful about their hair, but most would grow into sloths, the types of men who lounged in the hammock of state assistance programs, the very types who had brought her fabled country to bankruptcy.

She was hopeful that at Yale she would encounter the Captain Call of *Lonesome Dove* or the Clint Eastwood of *The Outlaw Josey Wales*. She hoped to meet a real *man*. What she found was a large male metrosexual population, and another large population of males who were being persuaded to join the metrosexual group. After a while in New Haven, she therefore devoted herself to gnawing into the meat of the renowned university's academic offerings. Her circle of friends was overwhelmingly female.

Her dissertation director pushed his affections on her with unremitting pressure. She could and should have requested a replacement director, she knew, but she hadn't. It was a small department, and he would have poisoned the well against her. Well before he spoke of her beauty and his love for her, he showered praise on her intelligence. He dressed most of the time in the professorial uniform, the key feature of which was button-up cashmere sweater with elbow pads. When she looked back, she saw that he tried too hard to be professorial. He was actually an older version of the metrosexual male student. He was a good friend of any surface that reflected his visage. She thought she had shaken him off once she attained her degree, but he continued his pursuit, until finally weary of his advances, she consented to marry him. She joined him on the Yale faculty upon graduation, thanks in part to his intense lobbying for her, but after a year of torment, during which he found a new student to seduce, she divorced him. The image of his slender body and pudgy little midsection was such that she saw him as androgynous. He repulsed her. How could she have ever consented to fall into the arms of such an essentially effeminate man, she asked herself. Her marriage, she thought momentarily, was a mirage. Except that her firing had not been a mirage—the Dean believed the scurrilous falsehoods the most promising young man in the department, her quondam husband, passed around about the manifold ways in which Keeley had betrayed him. He claimed to have been the ghost author of her most respected publications. Rather than fight the charges, she looked at the Dean and saw her husband in 20 years, deciding then this community wasn't for her.

The Dean had summoned Keeley to tell her she was finished. She said, "Hey Dean, did you hear about the university president whose school declared bankruptcy?"

The man had expected Keeley to be nervous, maybe a little frightened, but here she was throwing up some infantile joke...he merely opened his mouth in surprise and shook his head side to side. "Well, what he said... keep in mind he was a big shot like you...was 'I've lost all my faculties!' And hey Dean, that's what I think too, all of you primrose professors have lost your faculties. Don't tell me to leave, 'cause I'm on my way. Here's my parting comment to you: you have excellent brains for an important field of study. People here have an awful lot to contribute to helping people in dire circumstances. Quit playing academic parlor games and apply yourselves to your field. See you. Bye-bye."

Miss Keeley Eliopoulous cast off the ex-husband's name and set out to discover America. Without knowing it, she had embarked on the same sort of journey Simon Pack had when he retired from the USMC the first time. Pack had first taken up the homebuilding trades at $15 an hour, then turned to the wandering life of the hobo, riding the rails until two self-defense killings on the tracks earned him a cease and desist order from assorted law agencies. Following his second retirement, he and Tetu intersected with her in a Pennsylvania National Park. She followed the news, and was sharply aware of General Simon Pack, a national hero whose photos appeared regularly in every form of media. *Now there,* she thought, *is a man. Darkness and light are not as far apart as Simon Pack and the epicene figure to whom I was betrothed. His face does not meet the standard definition of handsome, yet I find him extraordinarily so. He is so much a man of character, a man who has experienced hard times and made hard choices, a cosmos removed from the Greek gods of the beaches. I have fallen hard for a man I don't even know. I think I am in love with Simon Pack.*

He finally did phone her, after she had nudged him slightly by presenting him with an array of contact information. He had stumbled and fumbled for words, appearing unsure of himself, yet she found that even more endearing. The word seduction wasn't in his repertoire of words.

Then word leaked nationwide that the redoubtable Pack had been persuaded to run for Governor, and the main force behind it was the sitting Governor of Montana. Pack hastily assembled an A-Team of three or four people, led by his campaign manager, a very recently-resigned Secretary of Defense, Wilkie Buffer. Pack was a popular figure in Montana, and it showed in the election results...Pack in a landslide. One of the members of that campaign team was Miss Keeley Eliopoulous, who appropriated to herself the essential mission of enlisting and tasking volunteers. Had her former colleagues at Yale known what she had done, unbidden, they would have accused her of self-abasement. Running after a man would be how they saw it, and that was unseemly. And a man with his martial instincts...oh, my! Keeley didn't care. She was committed to Pack in some strong way she could not define. He saw her occasionally as she worked on the campaign, thanking her and showing sincere respect. He made her feel she had in no way abased herself.

After he won, he requested he be permitted to escort her to the Inaugural party, and she consented. He asked when she would return home, to which she replied she loved Montana and would stay in place for a while. Pack told her that made him happy. He bought her small 'thought gifts', but never discussed the possibility of a permanent arrangement.

Pack had dinner with her several nights a week, and occasionally stayed until bedtime, but he never went to her bed, nor did she to his.

Now she was in Greece, finalizing her father's estate, but she could return to the US anytime she wished as an American citizen. She was miserable. She wanted to be with Simon Pack, her best friend, if not yet her lover. She loved just talking with him, on a thousand topics, and she found him a more cogent thinker, on a broader variety of subjects, than anyone she had met at Yale. But what was wrong with him, she mused, almost angrily? Does he not want me? Do I not mean as much to him? Shall I return on the pretense of selling my home? Why doesn't he call for me? Do we even have a relationship, or is it just my imagining? What would he think of me were I to return? I've never been to his cabin, but believe I would like it there. *I do love Simon Pack.*

Here is a man whose accomplishments are off the scale, yet around me he acts like a high school kid on his first date. Beyond a polite peck on the cheek he will not go. Here, I say again, is a man whose achievements on behalf of his country will be written of glowingly in the honest historical records, yet he cannot bring himself to kiss me properly. He actually seems afraid of me. *I do love Simon Pack.*

From the start I knew he liked me a lot. Around men he kidded around with what he calls 'opposite talk.' If he told someone he was a loser, he meant he was a winner, and the person he was talking with always knew his true meaning. So it has been with me. He's full of foolish hypocorisms...over the time he's known me, he has called me maybe twenty names, the most recent of which is Possum Face. He is bursting inside to say more, I think, but just can't go the extra step. *I do love Simon Pack.*

He has never questioned the source of my funds to buy the house or do whatever I please. Knowing the money I have at my disposal might really drive this man away from me, so different from most men is he. He is whatever the opposite of gold-digger is. Because of this fear of turning him away, I bought a modest house and drive a modest car. Whenever in my life would I have considered doing such things? That says something, doesn't it, about each of us? I think I would be willing to give away everything to be with him. *Oh, yes, I do love Simon Pack. I love to speak aloud the words...Simon Pack.*

Simon: Pack was thinking: Give me a problem to deal with that doesn't involve me directly and I'm fine with it. I'm a good problem-solver and decision maker, able swiftly to sort a matter into main constituent elements for further breakdown into a manageable action plan. I'm comfortable and competent leading a complex combat operation or directing a staff or even fighting hand-to-hand. But with matters involving me directly, personally, I'm a dud, or close to it. I'm uncomfortable handling matters of my own heart. Case in point is Keeley Eliopoulous. She's a fine woman, I think too fine for me. What could she see in me? She's silky smooth; I'm lava rock rough. She's beautiful, I'm in no wise her counterpart as a man. For better or worse, the woman has ensorcelled me. She has a luminous mind that I love to see at work. She seems to have liked me so far, but I'd argue she hasn't seen enough of me. When she sees me in the bright light of common day, so to speak, she'll change her mind. I'm not much of a prize, a fact I've always owned up to.

And I'm back here in my cabin, a place I love, but would she appreciate it? I have my doubts. On the other hand, I probably should offer her the option, bring her here and let her decide. But who says she wants to come back to Montana at all? Maybe she has decided to remain in Greece by her mother's side. At some point, though, she probably will come back to Helena to sell her house. Then what? What happens after she becomes home-less in Montana? The decent thing, I suppose, would be to offer her a room here until she settles elsewhere.

What would Gioia make of this relationship with Keeley? Would my romantic connection with Keeley dishonor Gioia's memory? I suppose every widower has these same thoughts, but I don't have the answer. I loved Gioia, and I want to love Keeley. They are different women. I was the pursuer with Gioia, seems to me, though I could be wrong about that...I lost so much perspective after her death.

My biggest problem might be that for the next few months—could be longer--I won't be able to spread my attention much beyond the Yaak Project, as I've taken to calling it in my head. Do I expect her to hole up in this less-than-hospitable environment waiting for me to come back?

Why does a man want a wife? To be a helpmate, to share both joy and pain, and to keep his bed warm. That sounds nice, but really that's what a college student would reply...or a college professor. The real answer, for me, is that he wants to know he loves someone until the end of time, and to be so loved.

Final thoughts: I've botched this thing with Keeley, whatever it's called. Have I treated her with the respect she's due? Probably not. Guess I ought to rectify that by getting in touch with her and repeating these issues I've unsuccessfully wrestled with. That she would reject me is a horrible prospect.

Chapter Twelve

Pack divulged to Tetu the bare essentials regarding his solo day trip over to Lincoln County. Said it was a social call on an acquaintance of Sheriff Joe Mollison over there. Where Pack was headed was Libby. To get all the way up to the hamlet of Yaak, the route from Pack's cabin would look something like the mirror image of the letter J. The route to Libby, however, looked a lot more like the letter U.

Pack had gotten an early start and eaten a couple peanut butter and banana sandwiches along the way. His appointment with Sheriff Hackman was 10 a.m. He had been to Lincoln County many times, but never met Hackman. When he went to towns as Governor, he saw the people who turned out to talk with him, and that didn't necessarily include the local big shots.

The people in the county courthouse had probably been instructed to continue with their normal routines, Pack figured, but many stopped what they were doing to gawk at him when the black Jeep pulled up outside. It might've been the first time a Governor, sitting or out of office, had stepped inside their courthouse. Someone had clearly signaled the Sheriff that Pack had arrived, because he came hustling down the hallway tucking his uniform shirt over a broad gut with one hand and jamming the Smokey Bear hat onto his head with the other. "Sheriff Bob Hackman, Governor, happily at your service," Hackman pronounced with enthusiasm. "Can we get you a coffee, water, soda?"

"Water would be fine, Sheriff, thanks."

Hackman's office was decorated with diplomas and certifications and public service recognitions on two walls. A broad-shouldered elk was mounted on another. "What can this little old county sheriff do for an important man like you, Governor?"

"If you don't mind, Bob, I'd like you to call me Simon. I don't carry titles with me forever. I'm here as a private citizen who's lucky you made time for him. I suppose you can say I'm just here to satisfy a deep-seated curiosity," Pack said.

"OK, Simon, but I gotta say I feel a little uncomfortable callin' you by name." Pause, looking down. "No problem, I'll get over it in a moment. So what are you curious about?"

Pack drew a pocket notebook from his jacket. He ripped out a blank sheet. Bending over to place the paper on Hackman's desk he began to sketch a reasonable facsimile of the outline of Lincoln County. "This is your county." He made a mark down near the bottom. "This is Libby, where we sit now. Libby sits on relatively flat ground. This is the entrance to the great Yaak River Valley. If we step outside and look north, we see the ground rising steadily all the way up to the deep forests and high elevations. There aren't many people up there, but there are some." He stopped to look at Hackman. The Sheriff's expression said he didn't get what Pack was driving at.

"What strikes me, Sheriff, is how unbalanced the picture is. Your force is way down here, out in the open, yet you're responsible for a huge tract of mountainous terrain—and the people in it—who are far away. I can't think of another county in the state with such imbalance."

Pack noticed that a patrolman stood outside the open door of the Sheriff's office, at parade rest, presumably to keep the noise down and to keep others out.

Hackman replied, "What can I do? Libby is where it is, and the county commissioners designated Libby as the county seat. I have what I've been given, and there doesn't happen to be anything I can do about it. Am I missing something? Is somebody accusing me of something? I must say, Simon, this discussion is peculiar enough that I'm actually wondering if I need a lawyer."

Pack smiled, trying to set Hackman at ease. "Listen, Sheriff, as I said, I'm just a curious private citizen. Nobody sent me here. In fact, my temporary cabin mate is the only person who even knows I came here. On the other hand, I can see why you're concerned. Don't be. I guess what I would like to know is how you manage to adequately police this out-of-balance territory you're responsible for."

Hackman looked relieved, as manifested by a great exhale and a virtual fall back into his chair. His frown disappeared. "Oh, I see. OK...OK. Well, then, let me explain. I've got four main departments: Animal Control, Investigation, Patrol, and Drug Task Force. If you were just a regular civilian I'd describe the duties of each department, but as a recent Governor I expect you understand all that. Still, I'd be happy to if you'd like."

Pack said no, he was aware of their responsibilities, but that a more general approach might be helpful.

"I can tell you this, Simon. I've got a tight grip on this county. The people have elected me five times. They like that I keep them safe. The criminal element doesn't test me much either. My detention center—the mayor wants me to call it that, but I like to go with 'jail'--holds 29 people, but I usually have no more than five or six inmates back there. They're mostly in for public drunkenness, and those with the occasional outstanding warrant we discover when we pick up someone for a traffic violation. Not a damn bank robbery since I've worn this badge, not much burglary or car theft. I've got a great reputation to protect, and I work like hell to keep it intact. I sit heavy on lawbreakers."

Pack observed a lot of "I's" but nothing about the members of the force. He could also see this Sheriff had a low boil point. He was getting worked up again.

Hackman was about to say something sharp, about how he didn't appreciate a *former* Governor coming into his office full of insinuations. About to, that is, until he recalled that Pack was so close to the new Governor he might as well still be in office.

"Look, Governor, sorry if it looked like I was flarin' up. Feelin' sorry for myself, I reckon. Get paid peanuts, but citizens don't give a damn about that; all they care about is me savin' their asses when bad comes around."

Pack himself wasn't a man to be trifled with, or from whom to expect pity. "I told you I came to talk civilly, to ask a civil servant a few questions.

You've reared up on your hind legs so high, maybe I will think something's going on over here. I have no pity for you, Hackman. Lots of soldiers and marines make half your pay, some of them with their lives and limbs in danger almost daily. Be careful, awfully careful, who you try to bully. Your act won't play with me. Am I clear?"

Hackman turned a deep tint of red, as if he were experiencing a niacin flush. It would be impossible for him to defeat Pack either physically or intellectually. He backed down, and grew contrite. "Guess I'll be content to apologize for the second and last time. Shouldn't have got hot under the collar. I'll stand by my belief that I'm a good law officer."

"OK," Pack said. "We're square. I accused you of nothing, so keep that in mind. Now, when you were explaining about violators of the law, were you speaking exclusively of the Lower Yaak?"

"Absolutely not," Hackman said. "Truth is, not much goes on up there. We don't even get many calls from those folks. They mostly wanna be left alone, and I see no wrong in accommodating them, long as we don't get murders and such like."

"So, just to be sure I got the story right," Pack said, "if I asked what's your biggest headache as Sheriff, you wouldn't say the Upper Yaak?"

"No way, Governor. Bunch of hardheads up there, but that's as far as it goes. Wanna know the type of cases I get called to up there?"

"Sure, that's why I asked," Pack responded.

"OK, it's tough to relate this with a straight face. A 90-year-old codger lives alone, calls us to investigate a robbery. Claims a prostitute stole a woman's necklace from him. So we went on up, spoke to the old fella, told him that unfortunately for him we'll have to arrest him for soliciting prostitution, bring him back down here to jail. There was nobody to post bail for him, so he would have to sit in the cell for three or four days. We explained all this to him. His reply was priceless but not unusual for Yaakers. Understand this tells you how they think. He says, 'I don't give a shit. I'm 90 year old, bro.' By the way, my investigators did retrieve the necklace from a pawn shop, so everything turned out well for him in the end."

Pack believed the story about the old man, but not that it represented what was actually happening in the Yaak. He simply replied, "Great. Appreciate your time, and thanks for the coffee. I'll be on my way. May I call you if I think of other questions I'd like to ask?"

"Any time, Governor Pack. As I said when you came in, I'm happily at your service."

Pack began his exit down the hallway before realizing there was indeed one more question he'd prefer to have answered now. "Bob, I've thought of a hallway question, you don't mind."

"Shoot," Hackman said.

"Do you have a working relationship with the Game Warden up there? It's District 75, the last numbered one in the state, as I recall."

"Sure do. Name's Bill Strang. I'd say it's a real close relationship, 'cause he's a reserve deputy on my staff, works on and off here year round, but especially when his workload's off peak."

"Goes without saying, I suppose, you think highly of him or you wouldn't keep him on your force," Pack said.

"That's right. He's an unusual bird. Smart as hell. High school valedictorian, started out at Montana State in mining engineering, then switched majors to whatever it is opens the door for Fish, Wildlife, and Parks. Good cop, I can vouch for that."

"That's all I need to hear, Sheriff. Thanks again." Pack shook hands with Hackman and this time made it all the way out the door.

The Sheriff beckoned for the patrolman who had been posted outside his door to step into his office. "Tom, I want you to follow him to the county line. Nothing obvious. I don't want him snoopin' around. He asked too many questions. Get on it."

Patrol Officer Tom Wilson had three years' time on the force. He was quiet, attentive, and thorough in carrying out assigned duties.

Wilson thought he understood Pack. He knew his accomplishments in the military and as Governor. As he drove behind Pack, southbound, he decided to put his faith in Pack.

About 15 miles down the road he turned on siren and overheads. Pack pulled his Jeep over onto a broad shoulder. Wilson raised his hands high to show the Governor there was no cause for alarm. "Governor, I'm Officer Tom Wilson and I wonder if we could talk for a minute or two? This isn't a good spot, so if you would follow me a short distance, I'd appreciate it."

Less than a half-mile down the road, Wilson turned right onto an unplowed dirt road covered with six inches or so of snow that led to a small picnic area that was empty and also topped with snow. He got out and waited for Pack to join him at a picnic table.

"What's up, Officer?" Pack asked.

"I know you've heard salty language before, sir, but still, pardon me for saying my ass is hanging way out here. I have no intention of betraying my boss, but I made the snap decision while following you...as I was instructed to do...to fill in a few blanks from your talk with the Sheriff. In case you didn't notice, I was standing outside the room, but I could hear everything that was said."

"Whatever you tell me stays with me, Officer," Pack said. "I won't take it as betrayal."

"OK. It seemed to me you were interested in the Upper Yaak. The fact is, the Sheriff keeps us away from there. Yeah, we'll go up once in a while to collect rowdies from Montana's Armpit, but that's always at the request of the owner, and he doesn't call that much because he has his own bouncers who take care of most of the trouble. About a year after I joined the force, some real hard cases began to appear up there, guys I'm dead solid certain wouldn't have a problem murdering anyone in cop clothing. They're not native Yaakers, I can tell you that, because they'll greet you with a grin, and begin by asking questions like 'How's the wife Mary?' and 'Are Johnny and Billy getting along good over at Miss Watson's Daycare?' They're actually standing there reading off cards, letting you know they've done their research on your family. They're threatening people, and for most of the guys on the force it's frightening. Letting us know if we go too far, as they see it, we'll need to worry about the safety of our families.

They know all of us. If you stop one man on a motorcycle, four more will appear instantly and surround the cop. Might be fantasy, I don't know, but locals claim some of the bikers have gun ports concealed in their handlebars, which they can control by hand or feet or maybe either. That's why we never go up there alone."

"Who are they?" Pack asked.

"Don't know, Governor. They're a fluid bunch. You see a guy one day, you might never see him again, but there will be others just like him. Don't know what they do, where they operate out of, where they bed down, nothing much at all."

"OK, so what I hear is that things have changed up there. Conditions today aren't the same as two years ago. There are new, unknown elements of the equation, is that right?" Pack asked.

"That's it, sir. It's not the Upper Yaak of a couple years ago."

"And your department has no action plan to deal with it?" Pack asked again.

"I can't speak for Sheriff Hackman, sir, but as far as I know, the answer is no. But I'm just in the Patrol Department, and as he explained, we do have an Investigations Department, so it could be they have a plan and I'm just not in the need-to-know loop. That's a real possibility," Wilson said.

Pack tore another sheet from his pocket notebook and gave Wilson a phone number. "Don't let anyone else get hold of that number. No one. This is pretty important to me, son. I'm interested in any intel you think might help me. At this moment, I have nobody else in *my* loop, as I told the Sheriff. I was the Governor of the good citizens up there, and I believe I let them down. I want to make the situation right. Simple as that."

Wilson looked intently at the number, took out a lighter and burned it in front of Pack. "I'm good with mnemonic devices, sir. Have one for that number I won't forget, so no one will see it."

On the open stretch of snow-packed Montana highway Pack felt a frisson of fervor jolting through his physical being. He interpreted it as the signal that the meds had entirely left his system, that his spirit was rejuvenating, and that he was going to solve this puzzle. Only this wouldn't be the old man sitting in his easy chair scratching numbers to find the Sudoku solution. It might be a blood sport, and he was ready for it, physicians' cautions be damned. Earlier, someone else had said 'Pack is Back.' Now he could rightly and truly say of himself, 'Pack is Back.' Smiling at himself in the rearview, he thought, "I'll use a hot pack or a cold pack or a mud pack, whatever the hell is required." He listened approvingly on his Pandora channel to Bob Dylan singing "Things Have Changed."

Chapter Thirteen

Pack could see Tetu had shoveled a helluva lot of snow: up the last section of hill, then the gravel drive. The man must've worked the whole time I've been gone, Pack ascertained, from the volume of snow moved. Chesty sprinted from the garage as quickly as he heard the distinctive rumble of the Jeep's engine. He intercepted the Jeep a good way from the cabin. Pack got out and opened the passenger door for a Chesty that seemed frantic to see him. Pack let the animal—by commitment, now Tetu's--lick his face as he called him foul names, his expression of affection for this dog. "Thanks for tracking up my spitshined interior with the wet snow, el ricky bastardo, you ugly cur," Pack said as kindly as he could. He was smiling, and he figured Chesty could see the smile and sort it all out.

Pack got home, threw a manhug on Tetu, and gave the big fellow directions to make a big heavy meal, because by damn, he was back on his game, and had finished tiptoeing around a host of issues. "Seriously, Tetu, I haven't eaten a thing since breakfast and I'm hungry, and I want to get to the basement desk to make a few notes before we eat, so if you wouldn't mind, rustle up a big special meal."

He began making notes on a few next steps. He would decide later in which sequence to address them. Write a long letter to Keeley. Tell her vaguely about the crash, and that I was in a coma when her note got to me. When I regained consciousness, I was, illogically, miffed that she had abandoned me. Invite her to take a room here in the cabin for a while. Let her know the value I place on her friendship. Be honest in explaining I'll be gone now and then. Explain Tetu's present situation. If she couldn't reach him or Tetu, here's info for my good friend Sheriff Mollison. He can set you up in the cabin real well. Tell her I simply must solve a problem I should've identified and solved before. Just hope she understands. Most of all, tell her I want her to come; I miss her. And say I think she'll like it here.

Take care of the Helena business: close out my medical appointments up there, and transfer the records to the local hospital; go with Tetu to get a progress report from his banker; make the scheduled office call with Jim Dahl now that he's settled in. Grow a beard if you want, but not as a disguise. Do not try to conceal your identity in any way. Learn more about Bill Strang, the Game Warden. Try to get a better read on Sheriff Bob Hackman. Decide whether to take Tetu on the initial foray into the Yaak. Get his gear in good order. Talk with Tetu about progress on the lodge purchase. Decide when or if to speak with Dahl about this Yaak development.

Once he got his thoughts on paper, he went upstairs to sit at the table as Tetu fixed the meal. Tetu was first to speak: "Matai is like Tetu hasn't seen him since crash. He has spirit back. Good to see. Trip to Libby must have been good."

"Interesting comment, Tetu. I definitely did not get good news, but I got purpose. I have a broad outline of what I need to do. Don't know in enough detail to explain step by step what needs to be done, 'cause I'm still working it out. Understand, please, I'm not trying to hide anything from you. When I'm able to explain myself, you'll be the first to know. I can tell you, though, that I'm thinking of a winter trip to the Upper Yaak, and at this point I think it might be a good idea for you and Chesty to go too. The polite thing for me to do would be to leave you here, wingman, but that would deprive you of the chance to get more familiar with your future home. On the other hand, big fella, I know you're from Samoa, and maybe you can't handle the cold, maybe you'll suddenly decide to take a trip home to join your little playmates on the beach. So forget I even mentioned the possibility of your going with me. Chesty and I will take care of it ourselves. In fact, I'm wondering right about now why I even allow you inside my cabin."

Tetu was smiling. "You are back, Matai. Happy to see you are...what was word you taught me...ludic again. Tetu will go with you. What can Matai do without Tetu? Nothing, right?"

"You got me, Tetu. Now, what have you got for us to eat?"

The meal wasn't something that would be featured on the Food Channel, but it was special and it was superb: large slabs of elk, eggs, mashed potatoes, sourdough bread, carrots, and cranberry sauce, complete with side salad, iced tea, and Tetu's homemade apple pie a la mode. Pack's jaw was bothering him not at all. They watched through the window as a new coating of snow began falling outside.

On this frigid snowy day in the Yaak, Ng Trang was himself deciding on his own next steps. Here he was, a relatively young man, who already had an international reputation among covert figures of a certain type. His connections ran from Vancouver and Thunder Bay and Toronto and Montreal to Sarajevo to most of the Arab Gulf states to Indonesia. The chiefs of operations in those distant places didn't know how Trang worked his magic, nor did they particularly care, but he had done enough big jobs that by now they trusted him. If they wanted arms, he delivered. Women, he delivered. Drugs, he delivered. Always he delivered on time. He had the big North American brains under his thumb, seemed to them. In Trang's lines of work, logistics was as important as production, and to this point he had demonstrated mastery of both. This was an extremely organized and iron-fisted boss not known to make mistakes.

They were in the RV about ten miles south of the Pete Creek Campground. "Baby," Tranh said, "how much money you think we have?"

"A lifetime's worth, sweetie," A'nh answered.

"Wrong answer. It's all relative. We have a load compared to the average family in suburbia, but we don't have a lot compared to Gates and Bezos. I want what they have and more. Ng Trang wants to be second to no one, you understand?"

"Yes, baby, whatever you want, but greed has brought many people down, it might be good to remember," A'nh said.

"I've built this business, and it hasn't gone unnoticed. There are multi-billionaires whose names I don't yet know who recognize the quality work I do, and now they're coming to me. I'm on the cusp of moving into a different financial realm. I'll be able to look back on this shithole as a blip on my resume. I can leave this place behind, build a palace on a balmy island, and make endless love with you. Never have to look over my shoulder again, never have to herd cats again. How would you like that?"

"Sounds exciting, baby, but what will you have to do for that kind of money? Nobody gives it away."

"Can't tell anyone, even you, yet. There'll be a lot of organizing once a deal is done. Now, baby, I need you to get me new passports, say nine. Use the contact in San Fran. I'll have a man pick you up here tomorrow. Make it quick. I have places to go and people to see."

"How long will you be gone, and where do you want me to go?" A'nh asked.

"You'll stay right here, moving from one campsite to another as required. I want them to see you around, and let them think I'm here too if they show interest. Might be gone a week, maybe two, hard to say. Have to make sure the contracts are ironclad," Tranh said.

"And what about that Reverend you sent me to?"

"Who? Oh, for now forget him. I say let there be peace in the valley," Tranh replied.

The minister was just winding up a service. Nine people came today. That number, he thought thankfully, did not include him and Moms. He liked to feature a cappella solos in each service. Today it was "How Great Thou Art." He did possess a booming baritone, of which he was indescribably proud. One who knew him well would call it overweening pride, the type of pride not suited to a true Christian.

The congregants, five Native Americans and four whites, filed dully out following the short invocation for divine help, guidance, and blessing at the conclusion of the worship service. One of the four whites was Lucas Lincoln. Lincoln was a passing celebrity. He was the butt of jokes on late night shows and at the end of regular news shows. AP, UPI, and Reuters had been sure to circulate the titillating news across their panoply of platforms. Thing was, old Lucas wasn't wired in and seldom saw anyone other than the one lady on duty at the only place to buy groceries in the Upper Yaak, a tiny wooden structure that sat opposite Montana's

Armpit. Old Lucas, therefore, was absolutely unaware of his celebrity status as the unapologetic prostitute solicitor.

The plainspoken old gent remained back to have a word with Reverend D'Artagnan. He minced no words, getting to his point straightaway. "The lady down the grocery told me they's a new preacher up hyere, so I figgered I could use some uv what he's givin', so hyere I am. You innerested in seein' me agin?" Lucas asked.

"Why, yes, sir, thank you so much for coming, and I sure do hope you'll come again," the minister said.

"OK. Lissen at me, then. That was the sappiest, crappiest, shittiest, no-point sermon I ever did hear. You're either lazy or you don't know nothin' 'bout the Bible. Makes me wonder are you a real preacher. You think people with spiritual thirst come in hyere to hear about you? Lemme clue you in, they don't. You tellin' 'bout how you're a survivor. A survivor of what ezackly? Frum the looks a you, you're a survivor of yer own bad habits, gluttony among 'em. Was you a sojer? A cop? What ezackly did you survive? What wars was you in? Truth is, we don't really give a shit. The handful of folks come in today got spiritual needs, me top among 'em, and you ain't done nuthin to fill 'em. I'll give you one more chance, but that's it. My main message is, take yourself outta the pitcher, and preach the Bible. Another thing, you want people to hear you sing, go on to New York or Nashville. I bleeve King David wrote psalms for people to sing. Singin's 'posed to be part of a real worship service, singin' by all the people. We got voices, ya know?" Lucas Lincoln didn't wait for a response. He just staggered out, a lonely spavined figure walking the long distance back to his shanty.

Reverend Dar, now more dejected than ever, sent Moms packing back up the hill to his little house. He sat himself down in a church seat, and took to heart the old man's criticism—no, it was damnation. If I'm honest with myself, Dar reckoned, he's right. I'm not at all sure I can overcome the deficiencies so thoroughly ingrained in my character, but maybe I can try. What indeed am I a survivor of? It's true, I haven't been a good son to my adoptive parents, have never shown them the recognition they deserve for endless years of schools that came close to draining their bank accounts. I didn't visit my father when he fell off a 30-foot I-beam and landed on another beam on the ground, a fall that nearly killed him, back busted up, compound fractures in one arm. I gave the excuse that the Bishop demanded my presence at an off-site. And it was an excuse, because the Bishop would've understood my dad had to come first in that instance. Then there were the times I said I would come home if they sent me payment for the trip. I guess the lowest point I descended to was when I claimed one of my parishioners needed money, $1,200, for an emergency situation, but that parishioner was me. And to this day I haven't told them the truth. The old man was right—I am a shitstick, phony as a three-dollar bill.

And he's right about the other thing, saying I'm lazy or don't know the Bible. Truth is, I stopped studying the Bible once I left school. As for sermons, not having the wi-fi cut me off from the sermons I was intending to copy. And, oh yeah, the old man caught me...I'm lazy and haven't put much effort into these sermons. Didn't think it'd make much difference with these simple people.

It's past time that I should stop feeling sorry for myself. Will I ever change?

Chapter Fourteen

The first thing on their Helena agenda was a half-day visit to Paul Fardink, so they went up a day before their own scheduled appointments. Both Pack and Tetu were happy to find their pilot not only sounded strong (Pack had already ascertained that through phone conversations) but also looked wholesome if not robust. But everyone present, including Paul's wife Cheryl, was quite aware that with a serious head injury outward appearances could be deceptive. The medicine men would have to follow him carefully for months longer.

Pack had decided at the last minute to drop off Tetu at the bank while he went to the hospital to see his team. "Thanks to each of you," he said after going through their battery of exams, "I'm whole again. You can read your films and tell me how you evaluate my responses to various stimuli, but I'm telling you I feel great. You were right in alerting me that I'd go through a rough initial 6-8 weeks, but that time's over and I feel at least as well as I did before the accident. I respect your expertise. Now it's time to use your talents on others who need it more. I especially ask that you bring Paul Fardink back to the shape I'm now in, and I know you're determined to do that. I'll stay on him to assure that he'll be the model patient who follows your every direction. Finally, I'm requesting you to transfer all my records to my local hospital, which you'll agree has the best facilities and doctors in western Montana." Simon Pack saw no need to tell them he had no intention of ever following up at the marvelous hospital in his area.

After convincing himself he had seen the last of the Helena hospital, Pack picked up Tetu at the bank. "Mine went well," Pack said, "so you don't need to ask me. What'd your man have to report?"

"He told Tetu next decision point is two weeks, when board of directors meet to decide if they think Tetu is good security risk. Also, he wants to send a man up to look at the property to judge if price is fair. Sorry,

Matai, but seems to Tetu process moves slowly, which means more time Tetu spends with you. But I can move out if you want," Tetu said.

"I told you, you mushbrained soldier, you stay with me until the lodge is yours, however long it takes, and that's the way it will be," Pack said. "No problem at all, and you know it. You're a big help around the cabin, and you were invaluable in seeing me through that post-op period. Nobody could've helped me more. My question to you is whether you'd like me to talk with your banker. Not sure what good that would do, but there's a slight chance it might speed up the process."

"No, Matai, please do not be involved. I must be able one day to tell Swan Threemoons Tetu did this on his own."

"I respect that Tetu," Pack said, "and I'll stay out of it for now. But if things get real sticky, you know I'm here wanting to help."

It was homecoming at the Capitol. Most working there were holdovers from his Administration, so they wanted to shake his hand and ask how he was doing after the crash. And they all loved Tetu, so they hugged him endlessly. They finally reached the Chief of Staff's office, which sat outside the Governor's. The new Chief, a youngish fellow named Jack Schnee, jumped to his feet when Pack entered. Dahl had admitted he was taking a risk with the sharp-tongued Schnee, but Pack's first reaction was that this man looked just fine. He couldn't conceal his native intelligence; he just looked to Pack to be a quick, mentally agile person who cut through crap swiftly to make smart decisions. He was rather short and lean with close-cropped jet black hair, but he was nonetheless imposing, the kind of man who appeared he wouldn't back down from anyone. Pack instinctively liked him. "If I may say, Governor," Schnee said, "I don't think I've ever known one man to openly admire another as Governor Dahl does you. He's...." Dahl scrambled out of his office to hug Pack at that moment.

"Sorry, Jack, my turn now," Dahl said. "Both of you," he said, motioning to Tetu, "come on in and let's do some palavering."

They made it through a short set of small talk, the inquiries about health, the questioning about whether Dahl thought he had made a mistake in delaying his return to the farm in Minnesota.

Eventually they settled down to discuss more serious matters. "So tell me, Jim, what's going on?" Pack said.

"I'm having to figure out a different way of working with Jack Schnee. He's a good man, by my reckoning, but it's a far different relationship from what you and I had. I won't forget you once said we were in one another's minds, the way Field Marshal Berthier was in his Emperor Napoleon's mind. And while I don't equate myself to Berthier, I think your point was accurate. So for things to be right between Schnee and myself, the relationship must mature, and it will, I'm confident. The Lieutenant Governor's going to do well, also, but she'll have to grow into her job. There's just a lot she doesn't know right now. That's the big picture.

"As to what's filling my plate at the moment, the biggest issue is an inmate whose story I don't think has gotten out yet. He's in for life, murdered two kids. Contracted cancer of the penis while confined. It, the penis that is, had to be weed-whacked. Now his counsel has petitioned the state to fund a penile replacement. Surgery's only been performed successfully once, in Boston. I'm joking about that being my top concern, of course. You can imagine how I'll have the state reply to his counsel.

"As you know better than I, we do deal with issues of a more far-reaching nature as well. The first I'll mention involves a visit from DEA, who say we have a burgeoning drug problem in the state. Haven't pinpointed the source, but big shipments of meth and opioids are flooding into two places in particular. The first is Helena and the second is more unusual, at least to me. That would be Phillipsburg."

Pack paid close attention to this information, thinking of a possible link to the Yaak, but said nothing for now.

"The second, General...and I do think that from my present position I've earned the right to call you General," he said with a grin, "is this." He leaned down to pull out a grainy photograph from a desk drawer. "Any idea what this is? This is what began my day." He passed the photograph to Pack for inspection.

"This has the look of real bad news...it looks here like a clam, but I don't think it is. The FWP discussed this with me a couple years back. I believe this is what stuck with me as *Mollusca Bivalvia*, or a name close to that. Specifically, it's a type of mussel, am I right?"

"I'm impressed, General," Dahl said, "that you remember a point that obscure. You're right, of the several categories of destructive mussels, this is the zebra mussel. Right now we might as well just call it the massive headache. They've been discovered in both the Tiber and Canyon Ferry Reservoirs, and you will recall how fast they proliferate. They upset the entire marine ecosystem, plus produce the lethal algae blooms. Fish die by the shiploads. Your efforts have paid off till now. We're the last state not to have its freshwaters infected. The FWP fisheries manager has done a fabulous job, but now he has to run careful tests on all the waters throughout the state to see if we've gotten hit elsewhere.

"Our boat inspection stations have been good investments, but I have no doubt a lot of boats, especially the ones from out of state, simply bypass them and go ahead with their launch. I'm pretty sure there are some responsible boaters who see the signs announcing the inspection stations but don't understand stopping at them is mandatory. The wardens can't check every boat entering every body of water, and that's a problem. As you know the specialists have long thought the infestation source is mostly boat hulls. Those same specialists also claim once the quagga and zebra mussels get a foothold, so to speak, they're almost impossible to root out."

"OK, Jim," Pack said, his decision-making juices flowing, "let's review what we have here. I remember like it was this morning the figures that used to be thrown out in all the briefings having to do with these mussels. I remember because the economic impact is stupendous, and you know what? I trusted their numbers. They told me that in just two western counties, out near my cabin, the losses would amount to $1.6 billion in nature-based tourism and $6-8 billion in shoreline property values. We also know of the deleterious influence on water clarity, a diminution of water quality, and notable reduction in fish population. Multiply those numbers to cover the entire state, and the numbers are mind numbing. You're right, this is a crisis situation...want me to shut up yet?"

"Nope, this is better than a cabinet meeting, I want to hear your ideas," Dahl said.

"As soon as this gets out, you'll have every environmental lobbying group in the world on your ass constantly. As an advisor of Governor Dahl, I would say you should ignore them. Do what you can within the limitations of your budget. You need two general courses of action, one short-term and one long-term. Get the wheels rolling on the short-term course today. Get me out of here and get on it. Use the energy of that new Chief out there to start issuing directives to state agencies in your name. Get all the facts today and meet with the press as soon as possible. You and only you talk to them. Take responsibility and let them know you're on top of this cataclysm.

"Figure out how many more boat inspection stations you need, and tell them you need the money yesterday. Speaking of which, Jim, this will cost some money, and you'll have to cut some other programs to get what you need. You'll also need an aggressive public information campaign to make every man jack in the state understand how big a problem this is. The legislature has to be caused to understand this is an exigent circumstance. We presently spend $1 million a year on such programs, but Idaho spends $10 million. Wilkie Buffer maybe can help out with finding marine biologists who'll volunteer to conduct inspections in waters prioritized by potential for infestation. With respect to long-term needs, I'd look at having the professionals draft an Aquatic Invasive Species Act for your review, a vehicle that will permit you and future governors and legislatures to budget rationally and predictably. I know, Jim, that we are of the same mind on all this brainstorming, at least that's my guess, but we can't underestimate the magnitude of this threat. We're different from most states, in that our waters are our chief tourist draw. Ten million people a year come here yearly just to fish, most of them to flyfish. That's ten times the population of the state. Failure to act decisively will be tantamount to cutting our own throats. Now, if you please, I want to do two things: one, leave you to important work; and two, to ask your Chief, in your stead, for a little question I'd like answered."

"And I have two comments," Dahl said. "One, you couldn't have arrived at a better time. I appreciate your thoughts. Nobody could've offered sounder advice. And two, why can't I answer your question?"

"Thanks, Jim, but it's not a big urgent question. I'm sure Schnee can get the information I'm requesting. Has to do with a game warden, that's all. The man probably is doing his job well."

Dahl hesitated, thinking about delving further into the reason for Pack's question, but instead said, "OK, then, it was great to see you. Give me a day's notice, and you can come on in whenever you like, and I'd be the beneficiary."

Back in Jack Schnee's office, Pack said, "Chief, I told the Governor I wanted to ask you a question about a game warden, and he gave the OK. Please approach it discreetly, because I don't know the man, and he's probably great at his job. His name is Bill Strang, and he's based in the Yaak, District 75. Maybe you could ask around, to his Warden Sergeant or Captain, for example, what kind of fellow he is, and if he has a strong record. Low key, all right?"

"Already on it, Governor. When will you need an answer?" Schnee said.

"Three or four days would be nice. Main thing is for the information to be solid. However long it takes is a better answer," Pack replied.

Enroute to the cabin once more, Pack wondered if the potential problems in the Yaak were genuinely serious, now that there was a point of comparison with the mussels infestation.

Chapter Fifteen

Lincoln County Sheriff's Office. Saturday morning in Lincoln County is customarily tame. Friday nights may see some rowdiness at honky-tonks and card games, but Saturday morning is usually tomblike in its stillness. Patrolman Tom Wilson had completed an early morning circuit ride through Troy checking storefronts and locks for evidence of breaking and entering. He had been back for a few minutes and now sat at a small metal table in the force's kitchenette drinking a cup of hot chocolate and thumbing through a flimsy newspaper. Two of his colleagues were waiting beside the ancient burbling coffeemaker for a fresh brew of coffee. One said softly to another, "Strang's back this weekend. Exactly what does he do? You ever seen him answer a call?"

The second officer said, "Never. He's in the Chief's office reading a book, as always. What did he do to become our part-time boss? Pretty sweet gig he has, seems to me. Game warden five days, Sheriff two days. Wonder if he gets full pay the days he works here—or doesn't work here? Got nothin' against the man, but hey, least he could do is pretend he gives a shit about this department. You ever sat down to have a real conversation with him?"

"Nope," said the first, "we've spoken a couple times…no, quite a few more than that to be honest…but usually when he comes in here to get a coffee. Doesn't seem unfriendly, but not friendly either. Just stays in a place that's comfortable to him, you know, and does his own thing. I do see him in there poring over papers a lot, but who knows what they are. How long has he had this second job?"

"A couple years, I think. Wilson, do you know?"

"Long as I've been here, which is around three years, is all I know," Wilson answered.

"Oh well," number one whispered, "no skin off my ass, I reckon. Alls I can do is my job, and forget about everything else. Back up your buddies who're answering the calls is the best policy, and if it ain't the best policy, it's the only thing can be done."

Bob Hackman dropped in the office this same Saturday morning. He wore his uniform. Once a month, when Strang was on duty, Hackman would stop by. Their routine was the same one they followed today: "Mornin', Billy," Hackman said cheerfully. "What say we go for a ride?" It was clear Hackman didn't wish to hang around the stationhouse any longer than necessary. No stopping to chat with the employees, just signal for Strang and out the door.

They mounted the sheriff's heavy SUV, Hackman behind the wheel. "How's it going up there?" Hackman asked Strang.

"Before handing me the envelope, Trang told me he personally killed a biker gangbanger the other day, right there in the woods," Strang said. "Letting me know what he's capable of, and also depending on me to get the message to you. Said he's depending on me not to get transferred. 'Your family's life is hanging delicately in the balance,' he said. Also got very cordial and said maybe you could use another $20,000 for your campaign fund. The man's most likely committed other murders in the Yaak, but for some reason he told me this time. What's your opinion of why he did that?"

"Sounds to me he's just protecting his assets," Hackman said. "Making sure we maintain the distance we have to this point. And your thinking, is it any different?"

Strang didn't answer right away. "I don't know. Trang's an enigma, a very smart guy. He knows a lot of forces are competing for hegemony up there..."

Hackman interrupted. "Hegemony, what the hell does that mean?"

"Means say-so, control, like that," Strang said. "Anyway, his interest is in maintaining the status quo. Lately, the writer Kjell Johnson has been rooting around all the various groups pleading for them to form a council to bring peace among all the factions. He's hit on a preacher named—ready for this—D'Artagnan Castor, trying to get him to act as the middleman to bring the parties together. I don't think that's Johnson's agenda at all. I think he wants to create tensions that may erupt into violence. See, Johnson's a crafty fellow, or so he thinks, and he wants more national attention on himself. He wants to be the big authority, the famous author of all things Yaak, who acts as the spokesman for his causes, as well as the interpreter for the big news people. The way he gains more attention is by the press glomming on to conflict in the Yaak. I think Trang sees things the same way, and could be he's telling you and me he wants us to make damn sure things don't reach a boiling point, or in any way spin out of control."

Hackman wanted not to appear unsettled, like this news was no big deal, but inside his stomach roiled. "Billy boy, we've had everything under control, and going forward will be no different. Let me think on how to keep the lid on things up there. You got any ideas, you let me know, hear? Now, give me my envelope." He pulled in to a food market lot and put his hand out. Strang handed him a brown manila folder stuffed with cash. "I like you Billy, I do, but if I ever discover you're holding back some of what's rightly mine, I might have to arrest you. Think about it, and you'll see you're lucky I permit this to be a 50-50 arrangement."

Strang wanted to strangle Hackman. "Now *you* listen, *Bobby.* I am a meticulous record keeper. I cover my bases in great detail. I can never go down without having you go down right beside me. You let that sink in."

Hackman re-ignited his SUV and the two of them drove back to Libby in total silence. The Sheriff saw new challenges ahead.

Reverend Dar was deep in a state of confusion, rethinking his brutal assessment of his own life. In a short span of time a famous writer had placed high confidence in his judgment, asking him to mediate groups in the Yaak he hadn't yet even become acquainted with. He spoke glowingly of Dar's moral clout. Then he had this oleaginous, smelly old man get in his face and essentially call him a fake. What the hell was the truth, Dar wondered.

Let's review, he thought. Here I am, pretty much cut off from the civilized world. I have a wife who hates this place, these four wooden walls and frozen water pipes and a Warm Morning stove that went out of style in the 1950s. As retaliation, she stays in bed most of the time, saying it's her only way to stay warm. I talk more to the squirrels on the way to the church—chapel maybe is a better descriptor—than I do to Moms. Wouldn't be surprised she asked for a divorce sometime soon. And to be honest, I'm finding this "Yaak" a dang dumb place myself. Also it's a dumb-sounding place. I know I'm gonna get kidney stones, on account of all the bouncing and jouncing just to get down to the dirt road to carry me to the nearest county road. Gotta stop a couple times to pee; I can see the damage all that hammerin's doin' to my guts. Moms is almost afraid to make her best attempt at a sprint from this damn hut to the car. Always sayin' she feels like a turkey the week before Thanksgiving. There's a good part of bein' here, though: since I can barely find my way outta these thick woods, drivin' a hundred miles to do Christmas shopping at a convenience store or some such is outta the question. Sorry, Moms, might have to make do with a homemade laurel wreath this year. Thing is, yeah, I was at rural churches before, but they were genuine homespun country people raised up to look after the preacher. The people who didn't show up for services were sometimes the biggest givers, because both parties knew they felt guilty. Christmas, oh boy, we got a ton of pies and cakes and casseroles and knitted sweaters. But Moms and me'll have nothin' comin' our way this year, that's for damn sure. I gotta say, these people around here, I just am not clear what they are. They might live in the country, but they aren't country people. These people from what I can see have hard hearts, stone cold hearts. Puttin' fifty cents in the plate is a huge donation for them. Scrooges, you might say, describes these folks. These American Indians, the four or five of them, who come in to the service, might as well be the Cigar Store Indians you see at the novelty stores. I swear, they give no feedback through their body language. Hell, I'd be fired up if I saw even an eye blink. It's like somebody forced them to the church on pain of death. Might as well be preachin' in a morgue—hey, there's an idea, maybe I can get the Bishop to send me to an actual town, a place that has a morgue. The bodies there would listen to me as much as these yahoos in this godawful pisshole.

See, now I'm back where I started. I'm supposed to be a Christ-like man, willing to endure privation and suffering and to have a generous giving spirit, but I'm not that, am I? I'm a quitter and a complainer. It's like old smelly—there I go again, being hypercritical of my fellow human beings—Lucas Lincoln accusing me of not being a survivor. The man is right, I guess. I've been a consumer of oxygen and space, but haven't actually left a mark of any value. On the other hand, relative to these people, I'm highly educated and I consider myself a scholar of the Bible. Could it be I'm a better man than I think I am? That's probably it, I'm just my own worst critic. I have nothing to be ashamed of, if I think how the ministers I knew from the South would've fared if they were put in the position I've been put in up in these woods. Take them out of their beautiful churches all decorated with holly and trees and garlands of flowers in this season, and with a staff and a personal secretary, and warm cheery parsonages, and throw them into this wasteland, and just watch how they'd handle it. It wouldn't be pretty, that I can tell you. But here I sit, handling it mighty darned well, if you ask me. Not to be overly modest, but in a lot of ways I'm the example they strive to be.

Just then Dar had an unsettling apparition. At least a week had passed since he had started the four-wheeler his Dad had given him. He had trouble distinguishing a spark plug from a tire, and what a creek he was up if it wouldn't start! It was his lifeline to civilization, and if it went on the fritz his goose was supremely cooked. Not many people ever stopped by this remote speck of land. A frisson of fear ran through him. As with all the mechanical and manly arts his Dad had tried to teach him, Dar had not paid attention. To change the oil called for skill well beyond his ken. Indeed, his Dad had once said in frustration, "Son, you just don't know how to take care of nothin'". Actually, what had prompted that particular paternal objurgation was not a vehicular mechanical deficiency, but approximately 10 cubic feet of fast food wrappers littering the interior. "Son," his father said, anger morphing into disappointment, "think about how I feel, can you? I give you a vee-hikel ever few years, but you don't show no respect for it. It just ain't right, and I'd like you to think about that. Show it and me a little bit of respect, can ya do that?" This had happened not more than four years earlier, but Dar had failed to understand what all the fuss was about. What he said to his father was, "Anger gives a foothold to the devil, Dad." As Moms had stood up to tell every congregation they'd ever had, on one occasion or another, "Ya caint stop a preacher from uh preachin."

As he was beginning to panic at the thought of being stranded here like a character in a Stephen King novel, he heard another vehicle struggling up the hillside, its engine whining loudly as it sought purchase on the snow-packed earth. Dar, already fully clothed in his Michelin-man garb, stepped out onto the tiny porch. Seeing this official-looking vehicle seemed to be an unspoken prayer answered. Someone, he imagined, had arrived to see to it that his SUV started. A large man stepped out. Clearly, he was a Native American, probably Kootenai, but his racial identity was thrown into question by the uniform he wore. Until the man drew closer, Dar couldn't tell his official affiliation.

The large Kootenai fellow, for that is what he was, wore the uniform of the US Forest Service. Dar was happy, given his thoughts of moments earlier, to see the man, any man, driving a powerful vehicle. "I was just thinking of whether my car will start up," Dar said, "and up you drive. I am happy to see you."

The long-maned visitor said, "I am not AAA." Like his tribe who came to church, this man was devoid of expression.

"Well, excuse me, then," Dar said, "how can I help you?"

"I don't know," the Forest Service man said.

"Then, may I ask who you are and why you are here? Usually people do not reach this place by accident," Dar said.

"Ranklin Shiningfish, US Forest Service. I want to see who you are."

Shiningfish stood in the snow and gazed straight at the preacher, unblinking, still without expression or enthusiasm. Reverend Dar was uncomfortable trying to generate a conversation with this monosyllabic robot, so to fill the dead air, he said, "That's good, sir. I am Reverend Dar Castor, and I attend to the spiritual needs of this community. I have a church donated by the Kootenai Tribe that is a ways up the mountain. Some members of the tribe, as well as a cluster of whites, attend my services." Dar correctly guesstimated this man was Kootenai, and heck, nothing wrong with exaggerating a wee bit in order to ingratiate himself with Mr. Shiningfish. Except he was quickly ascertaining this man was not subject to ingratiation.

"Your name comes up in many quarters. People say you are organizing a council. Is that true?" Ranklin asked.

"I suppose it is. I have been asked to do so, and I probably will, but haven't put my head into it yet," Dar said. He was thinking that even if he performed the task Kjell Johnson had requested, he didn't know how to go about getting the word out. Plus, he didn't know the identities of the various parties he was to invite.

"Word of advice, Preacher. Could be dangerous assignment," Shiningfish said.

Dar Castor was shaken. Danger? He thought he was to bring peace to the valley, the same peace Roseanne Cash sang about:

Oh well, I'm tired and so weary
But I must go alone
Till the Lord comes and calls, calls me away, oh yes
Well the morning's so bright
And the lamp is alight
And the night, night is as black as the sea, oh yes
There will be peace in the valley for me, some day
There will be peace in the valley for me, oh Lord I pray
There'll be no sadness, no sorrow
No trouble, trouble I see
There will be peace in the valley for me, for me
Well the bear will be gentle
And the wolves will be tame

And the lion shall lay down by the lamb, oh yes
And the beasts from the wild
Shall be lit by a child
And I'll be changed, changed from this creature that I
am, oh yes
There will be peace in the valley for me, some day
There will be peace in the valley for me, oh Lord I pray
There'll be no sadness, no sorrow
No trouble, trouble I see
There will be peace in the valley for me, for me

"And what is this danger you're telling me about, Mr. Shiningman?" Dar asked.

"Name is Shiningfish, Preacher. You figure it out. Now I have seen you and will go."

"Hey, wait just a minute...." Dar implored shakily, but Shiningfish was already behind the wheel and moving out.

Chapter Sixteen

Tetu and Pack were wrapping up their low country affairs before heading up to the Yaak. Pack spoke with Sheriff Mollison, explaining that he might be gone just a few days in phase one, or it could stretch out to weeks, depending on the information he could piece together. He continued to be vague about his interest in the Upper Yaak. No problem, the Sheriff assured him, he would check the security of the cabin daily for whatever period Pack was gone. Pack informed Mollison he could be reached at one of the five campgrounds up there.

The black Wrangler Unlimited was packed tight, a load that included Chesty's food and water and bedding; a Napier tent extension tailor made for this vehicle; weapons and ammunition, just cleaned; books; sleeping bags with a thermal rating of -20 degrees Farenheit; Kindle; freeze-dried food, and the usual lamps and cooking gear. He also made sure to pack his personal choice of firestarter--a bag of lint saved from a month's worth of laundry dryer pickings and a jar of petroleum jelly to knead through it.

Pack had given over several hours early this morning to writing the long-pondered letter to Keeley Eliopoulous. He was satisfied he had said what he wanted, and now was eager to get it out of his hands and into the postal system. From this point, what would be, would be. No reply from Keeley he would take as her reply.

Pack had also considered it good fortune that Dahl had called him before he drifted into the land of extremely limited cell coverage. Pack was mum about the upcoming expedition. When Dahl dropped the news that Jack Schnee intended to phone shortly after he, Dahl, hung up, Pack knew he would remain at the cabin until Schnee called.

Dahl's chief purpose was to thank Pack for the advice to use Wilkie Buffer--former Secretary of Defense, autodidact, prolific and luculent author on a multitude of topics, and now Chancellor of the Montana University system—as a resource in luring marine scientists to investigate and ultimately combat the scourge of the mussel infestation. Buffer understood the ways in which these people could turn such a task to their own benefit. Within a couple of days Buffer's clarion call had a small army of scientists preparing to close on Helena to coordinate assignments and areas of responsibility. No state had ever assembled such a cadre of professionals to root out a freshwater threat. Dahl was hopeful the mussels issue might not become as devastating as first envisaged, thanks to the influence of Buffer's intellectual sophistication and moral clarity.

Dahl also used a few minutes to praise Buffer for deracinating the deadwood from Montana's professorial class. The state's news media had been behind Buffer. From the beginning Buffer went around the professors and directly to the people, explaining in his inimitably crafted logic the need for graduates to possess the intellectual and emotional maturity to acquit themselves admirably in a real-world workplace. And the need for the graduates to be able simply to do their jobs with their hands as well as their minds. He stressed that there were no Ivy League universities in Montana, and he had no desire for there to be. He wanted his system to produce solid citizens who understood the US Constitution and who lead the league year after year in giving back to their communities, good stewards of the magnificent environment in which Montanans are privileged to live. But he also told the citizens of the state that he wanted no 'safe spaces' and 'snowflakes' that have burgeoned on campuses in other parts of the country. He demanded intellectual rigor, and a reasonable balance of conservative and liberal thought. Wilkie Buffer, whom the President had on one occasion labeled "the black Pack", was simply fed up with undemanding teachers producing an ignorant crop of students who actually believed the PayPal-eolithic Era was an archeological period. The state was behind the formidable Wilkie Buffer, a man who simply would not tolerate the mediocre. Be mediocre and be gone, he warned his assembled professoriat. He had proved to be that rarity, a genuine change agent.

Meanwhile, Tetu was taking care of vital business of his own. He had had an ear-fatiguing lengthy phone conversation with Miss Swan Threemoons. He told her the loan was now almost a certainty; only technicalities remained. She told Tetu she would come to him, regardless of whether the loan went through. Assuming he got it, she had big news. When she had had her say, Tetu's heart was on fire with love for his lovely Swan. He could not believe she thought he might not want her after hearing her story.

Swan's story went like this: "Tetu, you are my warrior, the most goodness ever seen in a man. I think I know what you want from me when we move to Yaak. You want me beside you all the time. You want me there as your friend and lover and partner at the lodge. I tell you wherever I am I am always beside you. I will always love you, night and day for all time. I am your friend, now and forever. I want to be your wife, if you will take me after I say what I believe I must do if I am in Yaak. You see, Tetu, there is a pain I have carried with me since before I grew into the woman you know. You have said you want me to be proud of you; I am already. I hope you make me prouder still by giving me freedom to work on behalf of a cause that calls me.

"It is shameful, I imagine, I have not discussed this with you before. Accept my apology, husband-to-be. I love my family, and I love my tribe, in the general manner of speaking. I am blessed to have come from a family of good men. But there are many bad men among Native American tribes in total, and among the Blackfeet in particular. Your friend Matai understands the reason this is true, and he did many good things for us, but the problems, whatever the causes, will be with us for several generations at least. Robbed of dignity for a century and a half, our men turned to the bottle and traveled as far from our ancestral men as we can imagine. They lie about and drink and have no ambition and leave school, too many of them, and they turn their anger on our women. They assault the women, scar them for life, rape them, drive them into depression and despair. I have looked into this, Tetu, and have facts to back me up. A year ago, the Department of Justice studied 2,000 women on tribal lands. The study reports that *84%* of our women have experienced violence; 56% have experienced sexual violence. Tribal women are *two-and-a-half times more likely* to be sexually assaulted and raped than any other ethnic group in the United States. Would you not agree this is deplorable? And I, one of the few to receive a college education, thanks again to an exceptional family, what is my duty? I think it is to improve that situation, if it is somehow possible. I cannot bear to see children and young women destroyed as I stand on the side and watch.

"It is a complex problem that is too big for me. For example, if a woman calls the reservation police, they do not come in many cases, or if they do it is far too late to stop the beating or the rape. The tribal criminal justice system is poorly funded, and for jurisdictional reasons they cannot get much support from local non-tribal police. Last, the tribes get hardly any funding from Federal law enforcement agencies. It is an ugly picture, Tetu. But little Swan Threemoons can start small and help some of these forsaken women directly. Yes, I hope to do this with the Kootenai women in Yaak. Will you permit me to unburden my heart by helping in such a way? I am sure I can find support for this project, and I will do it by myself. I want you to make the lodge a success."

Tetu was moved by Swan's speech. "We will find a way, dear Swan, and you will do wonders."

Governor Dahl must have told his Chief of Staff, Jack Schnee, that he was off the line with Pack, because just moments after hanging up from Dahl's call, Schnee rang in. "Good morning, General," Schnee commenced. "I have an *interim* report. I'll need a few extra days to give you a more thorough report. How would that work?"

"That'll work. I might not be here when you call back, so on the machine just leave a good time to reach you. My mobile will most likely also be out of range, but it's worth a shot," Pack said.

"WILCO, sir," former Army Major Schnee replied. "Trust me, I'll get more, but for now it's vanilla ice cream—most people like him, some don't, and nobody on either side seems to be able to give a reason why.

His file is bland, he does his job not great, but not poor. He writes citations as he's supposed to, but apparently's never been involved in a real eye-catching case. His boss's ringing endorsement amounts to 'he's never given me a reason to try to dismiss him.' Once or twice a year he'll be called on to fill in for a fellow ranger in another district, which he's always done without complaint or, for that matter, distinction. As you know, different animals are in season in different parts of the state at different periods, so cross-pollination is a necessary fact of ranger life. So, General, what I have for you right now amounts to a bowl of vomit, you might say. But I want to do the job you asked for thoroughly, so I have a couple other avenues to pursue. He has an intern, and interestingly no one I've spoken with questions why he's the only ranger out of the 75 who apparently has one permanently. A young guy gets assigned to Strang, Strang keeps him longer than is normal, then when that intern leaves he gets another right away. No other district, I'm told, has a ranger with a more or less permanent intern. That strikes me as abnormal, and I'd like to get to the bottom of it. I've come up with a hokey reason this present intern needs to come to Helena for a physical examination. His channels are passing that info to him, not me. Once he has checked in for the physical, I'm going to call him in for a friendly chat, you know, Governor Dahl just wants to keep his finger on the pulse of people in the FWP. We'll shoot the breeze, I'll throw in some real business talk, then we'll discuss Bill Strang. If I get anything useful from the intern, I might speak with some of the others who've worked with Strang. I've gotten interested in this fellow myself.

"He also works as a Deputy Sheriff most weekends down in Lincoln County," Schnee said. Pack gave no indication he already knew this. "Maybe the County Sheriff can tell us something we don't know, so I was thinking of querying him about Strang," Schnee added.

Pack thought about calling Schnee off that inquiry, but caught himself. If there were something not kosher going on between Hackman and Strang, maybe a call from Schnee would infuse Hackman with some uneasiness, and he would likely tell Strang.

"Going off topic a minute, General," Schnee said, "but speaking of Lincoln County, don't know if you've heard this morning that Missoula police arrested the man who gunned down their cop on the street. Man's tied in with Sovereign Citizens, they say, and he's a resident of Lincoln County."

Pack ignored the comment about the killer from Lincoln County, then said, "I like the way you're going about this, Chief. My only concern is that it'll hold you back from fully supporting Governor Dahl. He's your boss, not me."

"General, I promise you I'll drop this like a hot coal if I feel this little request is preventing me from doing anything Governor Dahl tasks me to do. May I have more time to answer your request?"

"For sure, Jack. I don't want information for the sake of wanting information. I want actionable information," Pack concluded.

Pack and Tetu were ready at last to set out for the gelid world of the Upper Yaak, where the present temp had plummeted to the double-digit negatives.

Chapter Seventeen

Pack knew how to handle the cold, but he wasn't entirely confident about Tetu. He stopped at a sportsman's emporium in Kalispell to outfit Tetu with a couple pairs of thermal underwear and socks. "You want to turn back, Tetu? I'll take you back to the cabin if you want."

"Matai doesn't know how tough Tetu is, even if he is from Samoa," Tetu countered. "Tetu is also going to the Yaak. If Chesty can survive, so can Tetu."

"OK," Pack said. "We might be there two days or four or twenty. There's a good chance we'll be there Christmas Day." Tetu said nothing, so Pack began to remember his Christmas Eve of four, or was it five, years ago. It had occurred—a bloody encounter—in the railroad tunnel running under Thayer Hall at West Point. In that hand-to-hand combat he had slain the leader of al-Qaeda America, a man with several aliases, but whom Pack knew best as Hard Travelin', but Pack himself had also been pretty badly lacerated by a cutoff rail spike, and emerged with a broken nose as well. He smiled as he recalled his trusty Chief of Staff, Jim Dahl, cleaning and bandaging him during the wee hours of Christmas Day.

As they pulled off the road to the northernmost campsite in the Upper Yaak, they expected to see few campers, and they were correct. There was a Subaru Outback with a teardrop camper behind it and several sites away sat a huge luxury RV. That was it. Probably four people max, Pack thought, excluding the camp host. Pack knocked on the door of the host's rig, paid the man, and asked about firewood. The host said that considering he didn't expect more than a third occupancy for the next week or two, Pack could purchase as much as he wanted. Pack told Tetu to remain in his seat. He stacked Tetu's lap forward to the dash and above to the roof.

Most of the volunteer camp hosts were from different parts of the country; most of them, Pack knew from many expeditions, liked the excitement and novelty of experiencing a wholly different clime. This gentleman's rig bore Alabama license plates. Presumably for this reason he did not recognize Simon Pack by name or sight.

They got the tent extension up and the camp established. Night was coming on. Pack got the fire going and the chairs set out beside it. Chesty lay between them. "Tates," Pack said, using a new name for Tetu, "I don't care what the temperature is, there's not much better in this life, is there, than sitting in the dark, staring into a fire, and getting your mind straight? Pretty close to heaven on earth, in my catalogue of beautiful things."

"Tetu agrees. I will find time, I hope, to do this with Swan."

The snowfall had stopped, the sky was clear, the heavens starry, appearing particularly so given the absence of ambient light in this part of the world. The forecast called for steady warming over the next week, maybe even a snowmelt.

"You going to see the lodge owner while we're here?" Pack asked.

"Don't think so, Matai. It is a process. Bank is running process now. Owner and me have no influence. Better that Tetu let process work itself out."

"OK, let me try to explain what we're doing here then. My explanation won't be perfect," Pack said, "because I'm not sure what I'm looking for. Maybe phase one will end when I do understand what I'm looking for. If that's the case, we might take our information back to the cabin and draw up a plan for phase two. We'll just have to sniff around and see what we find."

"What can Tetu do?" Tetu said.

"We have only the Jeep, so mostly we'll go together. But maybe we'll discover it's possible for one of us to drop the other off sometimes. Let's not concern ourselves about that right now. Instead, let me explain the big picture.

"Think of this area, the Upper Yaak, as consisting of nodes. One is made up of permanent residents, who might be broken down into people with permanent addresses, and the transients who move around the woods. A second is the criminal element, which can be further divided into bikers and hobos and drug dealers and smugglers of various illicit commodities. A third is the Native Americans, chiefly the Kootenai. A fourth is the ranching node, people whose animals depend in various ways on the wilderness lands. A fifth is the militant environmentalists for whom the Yaak is a cause. A sixth is the people with logging and timber interests. A seventh overlaps one or more of these nodes. They are the anti-government people, those who resent most forms of authority. One member of this class, or node, was the man arrested for the murder of the cop down in Missoula not long ago. He was a Sovereign Citizens member, it is believed. An eighth node consists of law enforcement generally, and I include in that group police, forest rangers, and game wardens. These are the groups I think of at present, but there might be more, who knows?"

Tetu broke in with, "And Matai sees trouble up here. He remembers what the man at the fly shop told us, and then he added what the lodge owner told us, and he thinks of the policeman shot in Missoula. Tetu believes Matai wants to take responsibility for the bad things going on here."

"I've said it before: you are a discerning man, Tetu. This is a large section of this state, and I want to bring it into line with the rest of the state, that is, as a place where the rule of law pertains, and where citizens can live in peace. I fear this area is the Wild West. Somewhere in my bones I'm being told worse times are coming to the Yaak unless I head it off."

"You are wrong, Matai. Correct saying is *unless we* head it off. I also cannot have bad influences and see my lodge succeed. Whatever there is to do, we will do as one. Where do we start?"

"I'm thinking we get a good night's sleep in our bags, taking care to keep Chesty warm between us. Rise early; chow down; disconnect our tent from the Jeep; get a little hiking in; see if we can catch the camp host when he checks our site, see what he knows; midmorning visit the person I'm told knows every manjack in this valley, the woman who runs the little store up the road; later in the afternoon visit Nick Surgeon, the man who owns Montana's Armpit. That's our spitbubble of a plan," Pack said decisively.

"Tetu always loved the spitbubble, Matai," Tetu said.

Chapter Eighteen

Tetu had not tasted coffee growing up, but it suited him fine these days. Pack had convinced his protégé that campfire coffee was a sublime pleasure, as it was at this moment shortly after rousting out of their sleeping bags.

"So this is what I want to hear, Mr. Palaita: that you slept soundly. Know why I want to hear that? Answer is because that monstrous bag of yours is probably the single bulkiest, heaviest item in the Jeep's inventory. Eight feet high, about the same wide, but has to be to get your oversized ass into it...and rated at about a hundred below. Could fit a dozen kids in that thing." Pack wasn't exaggerating by much—it did weigh 18 pounds and was the bulkiest sleeping bag Pack had ever seen.

"Tetu sees Matai cares for his welfare. Fact is it was such a good bag it was too hot inside and Tetu had to unzip it after few hours. Chesty was lying on outside of bag, but not directly on me, me feeling part of his body heat also. So there you have answer. Tetu's night was fine, and Chesty's the same."

"Nice of you to ask about me, too," Pack joshed with Tetu. "Damned self-centered, that's what you've always been and probably always will be." Tetu enjoyed this kind of ribbing, reminded him of how much Pack did appreciate him.

The fortyish lady in the tiny general store was called Georgann, and they immediately tagged her as a jewel, smiling and laughing and friendly. She recognized Pack immediately. Although not obsequious, she seemed sincerely pleased to meet him. Georgann had a landline and told them it was available any time they wanted. Even the yurt people, Craig Wood and Judith Buck, had a landline, she said, at least for the time being. "You think of anybody you want to call, we'll see if they're in the book," she said, holding up what was more brochure than book. In that this was the only place within 40 miles to get essentials, everybody in the valley came through there at one time or another, and she was on a first-name basis with each one of them. Except for a teenaged boy, probably the lady's son, Pack and Tetu were the only patrons at this hour.

Pack bought items they didn't need...just because. Running this little general store couldn't be a path to wealth, he surmised, and making the purchases just seemed the right thing to do. And in truth, she was as vital to everyone in this valley as a medical doctor or schoolteacher. Probably no such thing as a day off here.

A space heater in each corner barely broke the chill. The lady wore a pullover sweater and jeans, unbothered by the coolness. She had a high stool behind the counter, but pushed it away and took one of the rockers in the center of the room. She gestured for Pack and Tetu to join her. "These chairs are for sale, but I can go a year or two without selling one. In the meantime they're good for what we're doing now, chewing the cud in a little circle. It's almost Christmas, a time only the most hardcore hunters come up here. You after a big game animal?"

"No, ma'am," Pack answered. "Guess the way to explain it is that as Governor I was less familiar with this area than any in the state, and I now feel I have some catching up to do. You're surely thinking, 'OK, but why in the winter?' and I'll reply why not? My friend Tetu—who might, and probably will be, your near neighbor pretty soon—spent a long time in the military, and even if we're never going to love the cold and snow, we know how to deal with it. We have the Jeep, and it has a winch, so all in all we're just fine this time of year in this beautiful country."

Unsurprisingly, the lodge owner had already described the potential new owner and friend of Governor Pack.

Pack then ran through his 'nodes' speech with Georgann, the same one he had tried out on Tetu the night before. She didn't say much, but nodded often, letting him know she seemed to agree. Before Pack had quite finished, the yurt couple arrived with a shopping list. Georgann was sharp enough not to repeat anything Pack had said, but she did enthusiastically welcome each person who came in, and introduced them to her new acquaintances Pack and Tetu. She did mention once or twice that Tetu most likely would take over the Sportsmen Lodge down the road. Most invited Pack and Tetu to visit them. Pack used his pocket Moleskine to sketch the instructions to navigate to their woodland abodes. Although Pack was pleased to meet these people, he was also pleased to overhear the small talk they made with the store lady as they were settling accounts on their way out.

Presently Georgann said, "I think you want to talk. We keep being interrupted, and it'll be this way all day. I know my busy days, and this is one, I can promise you. So I have an idea. You're welcome to stay here long as you want today. Might be a good idea, if I read you right, to give you a chance to meet more of our people. But what I'm offering is a meal for you and Tetu. Make it about eight, an hour after I get off. My little place is right behind us about 50 yards. We could talk more without interruption. Interested?"

Tetu was as surprised as Georgann at Pack's abrupt answer. "Nope."

Georgann seemed just a little hurt. Pack smiled kindly then, saying, "We won't have you working more after leaving here. We'll pick you up whenever you say and take you to the Lodge for a meal, whatever you'd like. And bring your son, absolutely bring him too. My treat. I'd be honored."

Georgann saw he meant it, and said, "I'm going to be the guest of the Governor and also of my future neighbor Tetu? My son and I are also honored. Seven-thirty we'll be on the porch of the store."

The lady knew her business. The people came in as promised, and after another hour Pack knew he had met half the permanent residents of the Yaak River Valley. It had been a fine day so far.

Pack normally took care of the fire, Tetu the cooking and washing, Pack the drying and putting away. Tetu knew Pack, though, and sensed Matai would want quiet time in which to jot notes from information they'd gathered. So Tetu made the afternoon fire and set out the chairs.

Before making notes, Pack gazed straight into the fire, momentarily outside of space and time, wondering how it was so many fine women like Georgann had married men who one day just went away, leaving woman and child to cope in a hard place. She'd said, "Tom's daddy just thought he was too big for Yaak. Just stood there, arms hanging limp at his sides, saying he was going and wouldn't be back. No kiss, no hug, no emotion. Tom was five, didn't speak for six months after. 'Bout destroyed the boy."

Pack scribbled: "Gen store is hub of valley life. G-ann knows everyone, incl women and children, better than anyone. Her store immune to danger? all have interest in keeping open. It takes place of F-book for unplugged people.

"CW and JB were holding back. They're not opening up during a chance encounter. Will accept offer to visit them. Craig not afraid to tell truth. Man has kind eyes, but unafraid of hard circumstances. Judith's a frontier woman. Craig asked if Kjell Johnson still doing all his 'trading' down south, as if doesn't want to do with valley people.

"Lot of talk about Rev Dar. Whole valley will flood church Christmas Day. Must be there.

"New name popped: Shane Goodfellow, linchpin, stalwart cit. Must've passed store on 508.

"Was I wrong? Nothing said about crime. Back to cabin to develop f/u plan."

Tetu saw Pack tucking his Moleskine back into his coat pocket, so he said, "Does Matai have new plan?"

"A partial plan, Tetu. We'll dine with Georgann and son tonight. I expect we'll learn new stuff from her, but no problem if we don't. She's a resourceful woman, making ends meet with that little store. Her life isn't easy, and I admire how she handles it. A person just feels better being around someone as pleasant as she is, don't you agree?"

"Tetu agrees. Georgann is nice lady, and Tom is very good boy. Tetu likes Tom a lot."

Pack went on, "Your presence up here will calm my concerns for her safety. I know you and Swan will keep eye on her and the boy. OK, to continue, I see us returning to the cabin tomorrow, but enroute making two stops—one to Nick Surgeon, proprietor of Montana's Armpit, and the second to Shane Goodfellow, the hunter slash trapper slash taxidermist who runs a shop down on 508. Once we're at the cabin, you can do your thing with Swan—heck, even drive over to see her a day or two if you like—and I can tie a couple of loose ends, such as the one with Jack Schnee. Within four or five days at most we'll return here, then among other things I'll find Reverend Dar's church for the Christmas service. If Georgann's right, the entire valley will turn out to his church that day."

Georgann's son Tom was quiet and well mannered at dinner, the kind of kid Pack supposed he would be. He was used to looking at the cost of things, most of which he couldn't afford, so he was reluctant to order what Pack and Tetu regarded as a full and sufficient meal. "Tom," Pack said, "you'll hurt my feelings if you don't go home thinking this was one of the best meals you ever ate, outside of your mother's cooking, of course. Mr. Tetu and I aren't rich, but as the most recent Governor of the Treasure State, I invoke the authority invested in me to order you to buy anything and everything you like on this menu. Whatever you can't get down tonight, you take home with you. And if that threat doesn't work, Tetu will hold you upside down by your ankles, right here, right now, until you do as we say." Both Pack and Tetu saw something of themselves in this boy when they were his age. Poor, but not knowing it most of the time because they had a mother who loved them. His face and head were scrubbed clean, his hair combed neatly, his shabby clothes laundered and pressed. Tetu placed his huge paw on the boy's shoulder and nodded, as if to say 'better follow what Matai says.'

Georgann seemed touched by their respectful, caring treatment of her son. She reached over to clasp Tom's forearm, her eyes taking in Tetu and Pack with a gentle glow. "They're good men, Tom. We should be thankful we're able to be here tonight, don't you think?"

"Yes, ma'am," Tom said.

Tetu explained to Tom that he was in process of buying the Sportsman's Lodge, and that maybe, if Tom were interested, he could find some work for him. Then Tetu said, "You look capable of real work. When I get the lodge, just come down and we'll work something out."

Tom hadn't been around Tetu long, but he intuited that he much liked the big man, so he said, "I know how to work, and I'm good at lots of things, and I know where to go to get things you'll probably need, and anything I don't know Mr. Tetu could teach me. Thank you, Mr. Tetu." The ice had been broken. Young Tom was now comfortable at the table.

Pack turned to Georgann and asked if she felt safe. Her answer was what he expected: "Yes, we feel safe. I think a war would break out in the valley if anything happened to us. Almost everyone who buys from us treats us like family. We're their refrigerator and their larder. And most of the time the person who comes in will ask about others who live around but aren't seen much. I'm sort of the old-time telephone operator who plugs them into whoever they're trying to reach. You know the electrified fences some people have for dogs? It's like there's one around my store. Montana's Armpit is within a snowball's throw of the store, and there are fights there often, sometimes big ones, but they never cross over the road and spill onto my property. Doesn't feel to me like that's an accident."

"That's how I see it too," Pack said. Then, because he wished he hadn't asked this question in the boy's company, Pack added, looking at Tom, "Your mom's right. Nobody's safer than you two, because everyone's looking after you."

To compensate for a partial lapse in judgment, Pack and Tetu passed the rest of the meal engaging Georgann and Tom in banter and persiflage. They didn't get to the meaty subjects Pack had hoped they would, but that was OK, for he felt full in spirit when they broke up and went to their places of rest.

Before seeing Surgeon and Goodfellow, Tetu helped Pack break camp. They informed the host the evening before they'd be leaving today, so he said he'd inspect their campsite at 0830. He was prompt. "Only one big rule here, right guys? 'Pack it In, Pack it Out,' which a man named Pack should find easy. Place looks great, like you've done this before."

Pack looked at Tetu, then said to the host, "Yep, this man Tetu's done this a thousand times in combat zones, where leaving a dirty camp could bring death."

The host mouthed the obligatory and rather lame, "Well, then, sir, thank you for your service. Expect you'll return anytime soon?"

"Glad you asked. Tentatively, next Thursday or so. I presume you'll have openings?" Pack said.

"Oh, yeah, there'll be openings. I sure don't plan to be in Montana next December. Not many people coming here in December. Three women been here four days, the ones in that teardrop. Often wondered what they do every day in these conditions. Maybe they cross-country ski, who knows? Then there's that huge RV, parks here about a week a month. Like to take a tour through that one, but never been invited. Got all the comforts of a first-class home. When I go through the grounds making my checks, an Asian woman answers the door. Holy shit, she's one beautiful woman," the man said, his voice weakening, looking at the ground, as if talking to himself. "Gorgeous enough to make this grown man melt at the sight of her." Then he saw he was making a bit of a fool of himself, so he continued with, "Rarely see the man, a young Asian fellow, must've hit it big in high-tech or something. I know for a fact they've been permanent residents of the Yaak long as I've been here, which is since July. You're driving that monster and carrying that woman, and not working, from the looks of it, you've gotta have some serious simoleons. Checked with my compadres in the other fed campgrounds in the Yaak, and find out these people beat the seven-day stay policy by shifting from one to the other. They're no problem, though, so I've got nothing to complain about." This host seemed intrigued by the RV users.

Pack couldn't say why, but the Asians interested him as well. "Do they ever have visitors?"

"Before winter came in earnest, one or two leathered-up bikers came a few times. From the sound those bikes made, I could hear when they'd leave, which was a couple hours after they arrived," the man said.

"Mind if I ask the name of the RV man?" Pack asked.

"Privileged information. No can do," the host replied.

The gargantuan Tetu stepped forward, and said, "Mister, you're speaking with the Governor of this state until last month, and a highly-decorated Marine General. If he asks for information, it's for good purpose, for an official purpose. Now, you want to think again?"

"Damnation, I'm talking to the Governor? The General? Sorry, I didn't know. That puts a whole new light on matters."

The beleaguered camp host ceded all the scant information he held on Mr. Ng Trang.

Pack decided to hit Goodfellow's place first, thinking the bar might not open until the afternoon. So it was about 10 a.m. when they pulled into Goodfellow's four-car parking area. Sign on the porch said "Pet Friendly—ALL Pets, including Muskrats and Possums."

Tetu was happy to tell Chesty he could go in with them.

Shane Goodfellow was short of Tetu's seven feet by a few inches. Put these three men together and their weight would compete with any NFL team's interior linemen. Goodfellow was a highly skilled outdoorsman; he had been featured on many of the niche-viewer cable channels. In fact, he often teamed on these productions with his friend Craig Wood. Craig passed most of his taxidermy and tanning and carving products to Shane, who sold them either in his store or, because he had a website, to people in search of high-quality animal-goods worldwide. Shane and Craig earned a respectable living through their trapping, hunting, and fishing.

Pack was quickly learning that stores in these parts tended to disappoint in terms of their size. Goodfellow's was tiny, maybe 200-250 square feet. Every inch was used. Pelts hung from rafters, knives and jewelry were under glass. He had soap made of animal tallow, perfumes from native plants, dyes, shampoos, homemade bear repellent.

"I's about ready to close for the day, gentlemen, when you drive up and squash that idea," Goodfellow greeted them with a friendly grin. "See, my rule is, after five vehicles come in, I close up, don't matter time of day. And yer the sixth, Governor Pack." He thought this was funny, and laughed at his joke. "See, I don't wanta do this if it feels like work. Trapping and hunting is what I do, but at the same time I got bills to pay." Pointing toward a small brick house a short distance away, he said, "Just got me a wife last year, built that house for her, and I guess I'll be payin' on it 30 years. What can I do for ya?"

"Sorry to say, we aren't buyers at the moment. We'll be making our way back toward the Flathead later today, but we'll be back soon, looks like next week. Reason we're here is I've seen you on a few of the Montana-based shows, and figure if you're even a little like the figure on screen, you could help us."

"Well, Governor, it's like this: I'm a big fan of you as a man, as a Marine, and as a Governor. I might live in the boondocks and live an old-school life, but I do keep up with what's going on in the world, and I'm not stupid. You bet I'll help if I can," Goodfellow said.

"Thanks, man," Pack said. "What's bothering me is that I've lately heard things that cause me to think I didn't pay enough attention to this under-populated part of the state. Some say I did a lot in getting government off the backs of ordinary Americans wherever they live, and that could be true, but to me that's irrelevant and immaterial. See, Shane, you look like a competitor to me, a man who hates losing. I can take losing if it's a personal repudiation of me or what I represent, but if in losing I've brought harm to anyone else, I can't take it. In brief, I want to know what's really going on up here. Can you help me answer that?"

"You're a helluva man, Governor. You had battlefield sense, and you've got a sharp sense for your fellow Montanans, I'd guess mainly because you've bothered to get to know them. And your senses haven't let you down now either. Mark my words, there's gonna be some dyin' in this land soon. Too many little groups of people going out of their way to be abrasive toward other groups. So many little groups acting morally superior to other groups.

"But it's a good deal more than that. Let's take me and my TV, and real-life, buddy Craig Wood. We have all the permits, we follow all the regulations, and you better believe we don't like all of them. We're live-and-let-live people, just want to make a living doing what our ancestors did, and what we love. I could take you up here to a pool off the side of Watkins Creek, and where we've trapped ten beavers a year for decades now there are none. Know why? I don't have to be Sherlock Holmes to know some assholes have been in the area cooking meth, meth that will destroy their and other people's lives. They've contaminated the water in that area, and for some distance downstream. I see their tracks all around there. Word is out there's a criminal ring from the West Coast acts with impunity not just in their meth-making but also in bootlegging a variety of illicit commodities from Canada. I suppose some of that's not true, but I believe most of it is.

"You can find abandoned ATVs and snowmobiles here and there, people wrecking animal habitats, kids of the wealthy probably, just leave their rigs in place and hop on a friend's and say to hell with it, we've had fun, haven't we? One thing I can say about the moonshiners is they treat the land with respect, so I leave them out of this, however you might feel about what they're doing.

"I ain't afraid to stand up for this land I was born in, and I'll give you some evidence that's the truth. As you said, I've been a regular on four nature channels, but the big one, the one I 'star' on with Craig Wood, is the one I asked to let me help produce a series about what's really happening here. The suits don't think it has commercial appeal, though, so for now it's a no-go. Point is, though, if you checked, you'd find out I'm willing to let the bastards see me on the tube badmouthing them," Shane Goodfellow said. His hands had moved wildly in the telling of his story, indicative of his consternation. "Hell, I'd walk right into a biker camp to confront them, don't matter to me. New wife held up marrying me for years 'cause of my confrontational frame of mind. Afraid, she is, of these people hurting me or killing me."

Pack and Tetu could see Shane wasn't finished, so they stayed silent, letting him collect his emotions and thoughts.

"And you know who might be at the top of the asshole chain? Mr. high and mighty Kjell Johnson, and I'm sorry if he's a friend of yours. Big writer, knows people in high places, acts as if he's the mayor of all the Yaak, lord of all he surveys. Met him a couple times, he took one look at me, his expression telling me he doesn't think I'm capable of reading or understanding his highbrow books. Well, I've read them all, and I'm calling him out as a fake. Man doesn't even live in the Yaak most of the time. Know what I said to him? I said—and I was out of control, no doubt about it—'Kjell, old boy, know what pisses me off about you? It is, above all, that you think you have a corner on the market of esoteric concern. You think you have a bigger heart than us boors.' Then I spit on the ground and walked away.

"What I'm saying is, there are more weeds in the Yaak than ever, and most are toxic weeds killing off a lot of the good growth. Should I go on?" Goodfellow asked.

Pack nodded his assent, flinty eyes showing Goodfellow his desire to learn more. "Where there are weeds, General, you need the strongest herbicide you can buy. I've given thought, idle bar thought, to what it would take to clean this place up. I guess I'm not very imaginative, 'cause for me it always comes back to the same simple solution: enforcing the laws. And whose job is that? Cops and game wardens and forest rangers come to mind, but what do I know?"

"OK, let's stipulate for the moment it's as simple as that. Why aren't these agents doing the job now?" Pack asked.

"If you weren't an important man—and I do say that sincerely—I'd answer, 'You gotta be shittin' me, Guv.' See, Hackman and his guys might as well be Casper the Friendly Ghost. He takes care of the folks down south, but they got nothing to do with the Upper Yaak. He's vomit worthy, in my very damn humble opinion. Think about it: it's no wonder we got an anti-government crowd up here, 'cause what the hell's the guvmint ever done for them? Oh, yeah, they'll come after you for a late tax payment, but try calling them for a home invasion, when you might see a cop four days later, if you see him at all. I think they know about the infusion of hoodlums and druggies, but they don't want to take them on. From there, you ask why. Is money changing hands somewhere along the line?" Big

Shane Goodfellow began dry washing his hands in evident frustration. He ran a hand through beard and hair, saying, "Am I frustrated? Oh, yeah, but I listen to what I just said, and it amounts to a bushel basket of manure. I have no proof of anything wrong. But to end where I started, I'm sure you're going to start finding bodies around these woods. The pot's boiling over."

Nick Surgeon was up the road in his bar, Montana's Armpit, getting ready for the larger crowd he expected around six. Nick was a bit of a fop and dandy, and he knew it. He had a photo of the Italian actor Giulio Berruti taped up behind the bar, and most patrons assumed it was Nick himself, a notion he would never deny. Thing was, he believed he was hotter than the 30-year-old Berruti because he was twenty years senior. His wife worked at the bar alongside him, and she looked to be a ravishing high schooler. In truth, she was twenty-two. He might be handsome as hell, but he was a long way from metrosexual. Before getting this bar at a discount, owing to the minister's hasty departure, he had served in the 82d Airborne as an infantry paratrooper, worked as a timber cutter, as a bouncer in Vegas, and as a custom furniture maker. On top of it all, he had the wiles of a back-alley cat, a fluid tongue in conversation, and abundant good sense. Even a harsh critic would concede Nick Surgeon was a formidable package.

At this mid-afternoon hour, only four customers were in the bar, all at separate tables, none at the bar. Pack and Tetu had been told you could buy a plate of basic food from noon onward, same menu at all hours, all along the lines of hash and ravioli and nachos with cheese and salsa. The General and his partner took a seat at the bar, greeted immediately by the sunny Surgeon. Surgeon shook quickly with each of them, saying, "Nick Surgeon, nice to have you join us. Sorta been expecting you, and woulda been disappointed as hell if you hadn't stopped in, Governor Pack and Tetu. Georgann's telling everyone in the valley what great people you are."

Pack began with, "So, Nick, is your brother's name Lance? Or maybe Scalpel or Butcherman or Sawbones?"

The quick-witted Surgeon instantly liked Pack's silly humor, calling his girlish wife over to repeat what Pack had said. "What do you think, babe? Think we ought to serve them?"

She was as delightful as she was pretty, and without hesitation stuck her hand out for a shake with Pack and Tetu. She said, "We were hoping you'd come, maybe get a picture with a famous man, but now that you're here, it's a little embarrassing. I'm the cook, but our kitchen's broken, and the guy back there working on the problem says four more hours, which really means it'll probably be tomorrow before we can serve food. In the meantime, what can we get you to drink?"

Pack thrust his hand at Nick once again, this time to say, "We like your place, Nick, and this is my solemn pledge to return very soon to wassail with you guys, beer mugs in hand. With hours of driving away from the Yaak today, though, make it two Cokes."

Pack wanted Tetu to assume control of the talking, so he could listen with one ear and take in the surroundings with his eyes. He explained to Nick and wife Lucy that Tetu would soon be their neighbor. He was tired of talking today. Pack picked up that Tetu really liked Nick, and to Lucy, Tetu, jumping way ahead of actual events, got all out of control and said his fiancé Swan Threemoons would join him in some months, and maybe they could get to know one another also. Lucy seemed excited about that.

Pack knew he could ply Surgeon with the types of questions he had asked of others in these parts, but also knew the chance would arise again. He simply concluded with this: "Next big event you have here that employs bouncers, Tetu and I would like to be in on the planning session with them. Also like you to consider allowing us to volunteer as bouncers. Maybe your fellows could deputize us to become part of their team."

Chapter Nineteen

Tetu asked to drive home. Pack assented. They began by topping off their gas tank. Even though they had half a tank, they wanted to give the business to Georgann, whose two pumps were the only ones in Yaak. It gave them a chance to say goodbye to her and Tom, and to tell them again how much pleasure they found in the dinner of the evening before. Tom even wanted to give them a hug. Tetu asked Tom if he could bring Chesty in for a bowl of water before they got on the road. Tom's eyes lit up at the offer, and he was quick to fetch a bowl. Then he took Tom to the Jeep to show him the special setup for Chesty and let Tom rattle some kibble into Chesty's food box.

Eventually, Pack said, "OK, Tetu, you've heard the same things I have. What do you make of this place you're about to reside in?"

"Some cleaning up to do, Matai, but we can do. We met people here who want to fix, so if we have plan, we can do it. People wearing uniforms of law must also do their part."

"Yeah," Pack said, "problem's same since beginning of time. Find where they live, catch them in the act of wrongdoing, bust them. The people we're dealing with in this case are hedonists, I figure, and probably don't much enjoy spending time in this wilderness, even if they're here a week or two at a time. So when Surgeon has party time at his bar, they flock to it. Montana's Armpit is a honey pot for the bees. Did you see the signs announcing the New Year's Eve bash? We'll be there on duty, and we're going to make some inroads into the bad guy scene, I guarantee that. Be in fighting trim, OK?"

"Tetu doesn't say much, but Matai knows he wants to do damage. Tetu been quiet too long. Tetu wants to hurt bad people."

There is a time and a place for every thing under the sun, the Preacher had said. Pack pondered that a more rational man might be inclined to lay out a case for the appropriate law agencies to pursue in the instant matter, but he wasn't feeling so rational lately. If he had crooked lawmen running the show in the Upper Yaak, he would expose them also. What kind of man would he be, he reasoned, if he simply dumped a problem he created on Dahl's lap? Nope, the time called for him to get down and dirty to solve this problem. At least that's the direction he was inclined to go as he and Tetu Palaita worked their way southward slowly down the icy roads.

When the three of them marched back into the cabin, they looked around, happy to be back in the warm, comfortable place. Tetu went to work brewing coffee as Pack made off to his downstairs office. Chesty was frisky, claws scraping noisily across the wood floors, coming back to look at Tetu expectantly, wanting to go outside for a walk. "Hang on, boy," Tetu said, "Tetu must get coffee for him and Matai first, then we go out."

Pack had a machine message from Jack Schnee. He called Dahl's Chief of Staff right away. "Hey, Jack, Pack here. How's the mussels mess?" Pack wasn't normally this abrupt, but he knew Schnee was busy, so no sense taking time for the niceties.

"Well, this job's gotten so tough so suddenly I'd have to go outside and flatten my balls with a hammer to feel better.

"OK, General, here it is. Intern's name is Bill Damon. He was confounded as to why he'd be summoned all the way to the capital for a routine physical. Told him it's because I, on behalf of Governor Dahl, really want to get a read on what's happening in his department. Asked a bunch of nothing questions, gradually boring my way into his relationship with Strang. He says Strang keeps a tight leash on him, so tight that he's not able to learn much. The kid didn't seem concerned about throwing his nominal boss under the bus. Said he's unimpressed with the zeal Strang brings to his job. Went on to explain he could never picture himself as a game warden being as unaggressive as Strang. Said Strang knows where the easy places are to catch fishermen and hunters violating a relatively minor regulation or two, so he meets his personal quota, but doesn't go beyond that. Spends a lot of time reading novels. Doesn't seem to care about showing Damon the ropes. Damon said he has pleaded with Strang to let him go out on his own—it's pretty boring, he added, when you're being held back from doing what you're paid to do—to uncover serious crimes that common sense says are being committed, but the boss says, 'son, I'm the boss, and I say you're staying put.'

"Pretty unprofessional picture of Strang he paints. Also said the only person he seems tight with is Sheriff Hackman down in Libby. Seems he's a deputy down there most weekends, and once in a while Hackman comes up there, but when they're together it's always private. Damon thinks their relationship is odd, in that if it were about pursuing criminal matters, there should be follow-up on leads Hackman has offered, or vice versa, but that doesn't appear to be the case. When Strang's in Libby, he assigns paperwork for Damon to do in the District HQ, and calls there a couple times on some pretext, but Damon thinks the real reason is to make sure he's not poking around up in the woods. That's my report."

"You've done well, Jack. It'd please me if you didn't work the Governor up about any of this yet. He has enough big stuff to worry about. Let's keep this between us for now. I'm on the case," Pack said.

"Roger, General. It's between us," Schnee assured him. "And one final point: Damon passed his physical with flying colors."

Strang had called, running words together quickly, said he needed to see Hackman ASAP. Now he was here, in Hackman's office, the door closed, pacing back and forth in front of Hackman's desk. "Billy, *stop!*" Hackman commanded, letting an easy smile come to life on his face. "Look at me, and sit down." Hackman sat straight in his swivel chair, shoulders back, still with the easy smile.

Strang sat down as he was told, and began to run his hands down his trouser legs.

"Now explain what it is has you so worked up. It can't be as bad as you're making out. Just take a breath and talk to me," Hackman said.

"You've met my intern, Bill Damon," Strang began. "Kid's like a thoroughbred itching to get out of the gate. Always wanting to scour the woods to find bad guys to write a citation on. I keep him secure but he doesn't appreciate it. I'm saying the boy doesn't have a lotta love for me. He can never say so, but that's what I think. So he gets a notice to go all the way to Helena for a physical exam. First time I've heard of such a thing. I speak to my Sergeant to question it, he says 'this is coming from the Governor's office, we can't ignore it, get your man over there.' Right off, I smell something fishy, like this isn't actually about a physical."

Hackman interrupted. "Well, did he get the damn physical or not?"

"Of course he did," Strang answered, "but he got a lot more, or maybe I oughta say we got a lot more. Damon's feeling special that he had a nice chunk of time with the Governor's Chief of Staff, who Damon called 'a really smart young guy.' At that point, Damon got quiet, acting coy and reserved like he's got me over a barrel, waiting for me to probe for details.

"That's it? I say. That's all it was he called you in for, coffee and doughnuts?"

"Let's get to the point, Strang," Hackman said. "So far you've told me nothing, and I have work to do."

"Unh-unh, Bob," Strang said, "you need to get the context of all this. You need to listen to how all this went down between me and Damon."

"All right, get to it, then," Hackman prodded.

"This punk Damon wanted me to pull it out of him," Strang said. "I did, not because I wanted to, but because I had to. Anyhow, Damon says this guy Schnee said the Governor just wanted to learn from someone in the field how the game warden system is working. Yeah, right, I was thinking, and I believe Damon doesn't believe that's true either. So I asked Damon what kinds of things they discussed, and he said Schnee was interested in what he and I view as the big problems in our sector, and whether we're making arrests in line with those big problems. Schnee was focusing on *me*, Bob. And that little shit Damon went on to tell him I have a close relationship with you. And who the hell knows for sure what else he might have told Schnee? This is not good, Bob, not good at all. Just put the pieces together. You told me Pack was down here asking you questions about the Upper Yaak, about how you're policing it. Pack and Dahl are bosom buddies. Dahl's Chief of Staff hammers my intern with questions about you and me, and I'm not supposed to be concerned?"

"You aren't thinking straight, Bill," Hackman said. He maintained his upright posture, chest outthrust, eyes unblinking, speech slow and low. "Have you read the newspapers, seen the news on TV? The Governor is absolutely consumed by the mussels problem. Pack can poke around all he wants, but all he hears from the Yaak is the sound of crickets. And all Dahl *wants* to hear from the Yaak is the sound of crickets.

"I don't think we need to take any counter-action at all, Bill, but if it would make you feel better, maybe you ought to inform your game warden bosses it's been nice training up Damon, but now he's ready to move on—you know, recommend he be assigned to the next available opening or given to another warden to broaden the young man's experience. What's the worst that could fall out of that? That you'd have to give up your Deputy's duty working for me? You don't need the money, and I could promote someone from within, a young riser like Tom Wilson. An added benefit would be that we see less of one another, get the bloodhounds off our scent. But fine with me if you elect to do nothing because, my friend, I've known people like Pack and Dahl, and although they succeed in fooling most of the people most of the time, I'm telling you they're not a fraction as smart as they make themselves out to be. They have nothing on us, believe that. Your outgoing President, Keith Rozan, isn't popular in our state, but he's one of the few who's seen through Pack, and hates the man for good cause. Wouldn't surprise me if the President puts Pack in his place before he, Rozan, leaves office in about a month. Rest easy, Strang. Sheriff Hackman has the situation under control," Hackman concluded, this time with a broad smile meant to reassure.

Hackman observed Strang trying to get himself together before he left. Strang even tried to produce a smile, but it was weak, and Hackman knew his erstwhile Deputy remained jittery.

The Sheriff hadn't let Strang in on the fact that Jack Schnee had called him as well, to ask about Strang's performance of duty. Hackman would not have wanted Strang to know what he told the Governor's man. It wasn't flattering.

Late in the afternoon of the day of Strang's visit, Hackman took a phone call from Strang. "It's Pack again. He wants to meet me on the ground in the Upper Yaak. Damned," Strang muttered.

"Hey, Billy, this is great news, you ought to be joyous," Hackman said.

"Are you crazy? This is the devil we were talking about this morning. He's not coming to tell me Dahl wants me to lead the FWP department. I don't see anything good coming from it." Strang was pent up again, and Hackman had to get him straight.

"I'm not crazy, Billy. I'm serious as a cardiac thrombosis. This is a half-full moment if there ever was one, my friend. Just look—you're a smart fellow, everyone says so, and you know it too. Just be calm and show him you're good at game-wardening. You nailed down details yet?"

"No," Strang said, "told him I'd have to review my schedule, that elk's in season and it's a busy time. He said, 'great, maybe I can go along with you on your checks.' I was thinking about seeing him in about a week or so."

"Well, there you go," Hackman said, "that's perfect. Couple pieces of advice. One, don't let Damon anywhere within the area code of you and Pack, so maybe send him to Libby for something. Two, maybe have an outfitter planted to ask a few technical questions, so Pack can see you know your stuff. And three, my friend, you've got me excited, so apprise me of the time and place of your meet so I'll know when to debrief you, which will be right afterward, I guarantee you. Good work."

"Really, you're saying good work? Feels to me like Pack is cinching the noose around my neck," Strang said.

Hackman hung up a minute later, thinking it wouldn't exactly be a noose.

Chapter Twenty

Pack's cabin wasn't easy to locate. Sheriff Hackman had imagined Pack's seclusion was total, that he and Tetu would be tucked into bed at this hour of 9 p.m. with the lights off. But he saw a different picture as he rolled past the cabin to a turnaround point higher up the hill. It was a bright evening, stars twinkling through the trees, a full moon illuminating the area a little too brightly for Hackman's purposes. Even at this hour the temperature was 40 degrees, the promised warming having arrived. The roads were melting. Hackman climbed out of his Lincoln County Police SUV, closing his door as quietly as he could. Looking toward Pack's cabin, he could see the wood smoke trailing and curling gently from the chimney. The inside was well lighted. More curiously, behind Pack's Jeep in the gravel driveway sat two other vehicles, one a plain-looking car the make and model of which he couldn't make out. The last vehicle in line was a police SUV Hackman recognized as belonging to Sheriff Joe Mollison.

Hackman ground his teeth together, flexing his jaw muscle, concluding he had come too far to turn back. Carrying a small tool bag, he made his way down the hill. A ditch ran beside the dirt road, in part to prevent Pack's property from flooding. Where the dirt road turned off onto Pack's gravel drive, a culvert supported vehicle traffic. When Hackman drew near the culvert, a small animal darted out, startling him. He could tell from the eyes and outline it was a red fox. Hackman regained control of himself and crept down the drive toward Pack's Jeep. He had a story ready, one he'd just conceived, should they step out to discover him. But he wanted to act quickly and be gone. He wore thin form-fitting gloves the better to handle his tools as well as the item he searched for. He got to the driver door and twisted the handle...it opened...huge relief. An interior light came on, so he had to be quick. Nothing in the front. He opened the rear door, passenger side, and found an object he was looking for. He handled it carefully, inserting it into his bag. These doors didn't make a racket when opened and closed, a very good thing, Hackman was thinking.

Hackman stayed low and began to scuttle away in the darkness up the road. As he was still quite near the drive, he heard Pack's garage door opening, light and voices spilling out. His outline would be easy to spot, so he more or less dove downward into the muddy ditch, landing on his stomach, then rolling onto his back. He heard them laughing and thanking one another for he knew not what. They talked for some minutes. Damn them, he thought, kill your talking and break it up, I'm freezing my ass off. He saw Pack change his expression and look up through the trees where Hackman's SUV sat. Five seconds tops, he thought, watching Pack through the slime. At last he heard the garage door shutting and an SUV engine backing out. Hackman sat up to peer over the edge of the ditch. Seeing Mollison's vehicle lights disappear down the road, a very cold Hackman pulled himself out of the slushy sucking mud for the now much tougher slog up the road to his vehicle. To hell with it, he thought, I couldn't care less about muddying up my vehicle. Get the heater cranked and be away from this stupid place. He drove in blackout mode until well past Pack's cabin. Then, despite his shivering, he felt the crappiness of this night to this point had been worthwhile. He would rest well when he got back to Libby. But on the way home the thought struck him that Mollison might be colluding with Pack.

There was an extremely important reason for the vehicles in Pack's drive. Mollison had called to find out if Pack was home. Pack answered the phone, which also answered Mollison's question. Mollison said, "Can I come up for a few minutes? I have a surprise for you."

"Sure, Sheriff, you're always welcome. What's the surprise?"

"Hang on a second, Simon," Mollison said. Pack could tell the Sheriff had covered the mouthpiece with his hand, and was fast-talking with someone in the background. "Sorry, Simon, guess it won't be a surprise, 'cause she wants to know if it's OK if she comes up."

Pack's heart skipped a beat. Was Keeley really nearby? Did she really intend to come to the cabin? Now? Right now? He had difficulty forming a response. "Yes, yes, please come."

The twenty minutes it took them to get there were the longest of Pack's life. All the mind-numbed Pack could think to say to Tetu was, "Ms. Eliopoulous is coming here, on the way now. The spare room's ready, isn't it? I suppose she'll stay the night, Tetu." Tetu watched in wonderment as he saw his Matai manifesting with absolute clarity the signs of love. Tetu watched as he observed Pack feel a sudden need to sit down. Matai's eyes looked straight ahead at nothing, as if his mind had been erased of conscious thought. But he did have a single thought: *I sent the letter to Greece. She couldn't have received it yet. She came without my asking her.*

When Tetu answered the door Mollison typically used, the side door, Pack remained glued to his sofa seat, eyes fixed on nothing. Presently, Mollison ushered Keeley in, finally rousing Pack. Keeley halted a few feet inside the door. Pack rose, nearly stumbling, then froze. They looked beseechingly at one another, then took small steps toward one another. Keeley licked her lips, smiling. Pack didn't pull his eyes away from hers. When they came close enough, Pack leaned into her and clinked his forehead against hers. "That, that right there," Pack said, "butting your head is what I have dreamed of for a long time." She laughed at that, saying, "I have too. I love the way you butt my head, Mister Pack." Then he hugged her close and stayed that way for an eternity.

Mollison and Tetu were opposite each other in the room, smiling, feeling like fifth wheels when Pack came back into the moment and gazed at them in embarrassment. Words weren't coming to Pack, so Mollison said, "Hey, looks like I made a good call in bringing this nice lady on over here, so now I'll just rest on my success and buzz on outta here! Lucky you, General, that you gave Ms. Eliopoulous my contact info. Sayonara."

"Wait a minute, Sheriff. I've barely acknowledged you and Tetu. Thanks for escorting Keel over, 'cause I doubt even with GPS she'd have found this place. And Tetu, come on over and give your old friend a welcoming hug." Tetu saw an opening to ask if he could bring out refreshments, but they shook him off. They then walked Joe Mollison out to his vehicle, where unknown to them Sheriff Bob Hackman had just looted Pack's Jeep. Chesty was in for the night, downstairs curled up in his bed. Good thing for Hackman the pit bull hadn't gone to the garage with the others.

Tetu said goodnight, and Pack and Keeley went to the sofa where they brought one another up to date until the sun broke the eastern sky. She told the full story about herself—all except about her money.

Chapter Twenty-One

Tetu had gotten the most sack time, and was the first out of bed. He wondered how Pack's talking with Ms. Eliopoulous might have changed their plans concerning all things Yaak, but he operated on the assumption they were still headed up today or tomorrow, so he began to load out the Jeep. He couldn't help but also wonder whether Chesty would go too, considering someone would presumably be at the cabin to care for him, and—as he was certain Pack would think of it—for Chesty to care for her. Tetu privately hoped Ms. Eliopoulous would never leave Pack and this cabin again.

Pack was the second up; a few hours were sufficient for him most of the time. When he walked into the kitchen, he observed Tetu bent over the coffeemaker, trying to make it do something it seemed to want not to do. "Morning, Tetu, or should I start calling you Buddha Ninja?" The giant was attired in black head to toe. Black shirt and jacket, black military rip-stop cargo pants, black boots. "Do you remember Johnny Cash?" Pack asked him.

"Of course, Matai, I do, and I also remember when Matai starts with this kind of question he always makes joke on Tetu, so Tetu will just lay back and let it happen. Go ahead."

"People called Mr. Cash 'The Man in Black' 'cause he dressed as you are. My question is if you know what they called his black shoes?"

"No, Matai, Tetu is stupid, and now begs you to tell him."

"OK, Mr. Stoopit, they called them Cashews, which also happened to be his favorite snack," Pack chortled. Pack was having a grand time, poking at his blood brother Tetu in this fashion. "Now go ahead, Tetu, and say it: 'Matai, this makes no sense to Tetu, and I think makes no sense to anyone else either.'" Now both of them were laughing, and Pack delivered a half-force gut shot to Tetu.

"Looking to Tetu Ms. Eliopoulous is making Matai happy man again. Is this meaning we will not go back to Yaak?" Tetu asked sportively.

Pack got back to his sober self, saying, "Nope, the truth is, Tetu, that Keeley has come here does make me happy. I have explained to her what we've been doing up there and our reasons for going back. Outside of you and me, she knows the full picture better than anyone. She understands we must go again. She will stay here with Chesty. Today I'll show her around this area, how to get around if she has to, take her to the grocery to stock her kitchen, and generally be sure she's in good shape before we head out. For your information I've also given Keeley the phone number to Georgann's store, and told her I'll try to use Georgann's phone to check in with her each day or every other day. I think we have a couple weeks stockage of wood, but I'd appreciate if you could add to it because we don't know for sure how long we'll be gone. Would you mind?"

"Very good, Matai. Tetu will chop and saw today, and be happy to. Keeley will have no worry about wood."

Keeley finally appeared, looking ready for the day. "Wow, gentlemen, that's a great mattress! Haven't slept like that in ages."

"Or could it be this western Montana mountain air?" Pack chimed in.

"There's that too. This is truly a wonderful setting, Simon. Within fifteen minutes of waking up I saw out my window three deer and two foxes running through the trees. It's heavenly," Keeley said.

"How about some coffee and toast before we go shopping?" Pack asked.

Tetu headed out into a day that seemed warm by last week's standards, and commenced his chopping.

They sat at the kitchen table sipping coffee and munching on the toast. "Simon," she said, avoiding his eyes, "I've always been truthful with you, and I think you know that. We covered a lot of ground in our talking last night, most of it personal. But I'm feeling a trace guilty this morning for leaving out an important piece of my story from the trip to Greece."

"OK, what's the big news? You get married to an old boyfriend or something?" Pack said airily.

"No joking for a minute, if you don't mind. See, Simon, I was wealthy when you first met me, but I'm quite wealthy now. To put a bit finer point on the matter, I have accounts now that total somewhere in the six to seven hundred million dollar range." She looked at him for a reaction.

The look he showed she would describe as nonplussed. "What?" he said. "Am I supposed to be elated or bothered or angry? How did you imagine I would take the news, and it is news to me, assuming this is not a joke?"

"I'm not sure. I know you pretty well. And it is assuredly not a joke. You almost never mention the topic of money, one way or the other. Further, I don't recall you expressing either disdain or admiration for people with money, and you do know many people who have loads of it, and you have lots of friends who have little of it. I suppose if I were to produce a scale with admiration on one end and disdain on the opposite end, I'd suspect your reaction would be closer to disdain than admiration. Let's just get it over with now. What do you think about my news?"

"Well, Keel, I think it doesn't affect me...."

Her head dropped, her mouth drooped. This wasn't the reaction she had hoped for. She *did* want it to affect him because she hoped he would see it as his money as well. She wanted him to speak with her as her partner, but all he'd said was 'it doesn't affect me.'

"Hold on now, I was just taking a moment to think. I wasn't finished," Pack said after the brief pause. "All I meant was that you're quite correct. I'm neutral about money. It doesn't make a person good or bad, competent or incompetent, loved or loathed. And I mean that your money is not my money, and would not be even if we were married. I myself do not want your money, but am not unhappy that you have it. I think that of all the people I know, I'd rather you possess—that...to me unfathomable--sum of money, than anyone else. You'll know how to handle it. Dear Keeley, please understand it doesn't make me think differently of you. Now, I ask if that answer disappoints you?"

She smiled broadly, looking as elegant and glamorous as ever, cocking her head to one side. "That answer, Mister Pack, is how I see you...

perfect." Then she popped out of her chair, swiftly donning a frown, jamming her hands on her hips, as if she wanted to provoke a spat, saying, "So if we're going out to buy groceries mainly for me, are you going to insist I use my money?"

"Oh, girl, let's just drop this subject, OK?" he asked with a genuine smile.

Chapter Twenty-Two

They were leaving for the Upper Yaak, not yet completely off the gravel drive when Tetu started in right away: "Tetu does not wish to get personal, Matai, but has big question to see if he has hole in his learning."

"Who has the hole, you or me?" Pack said.

"Me, Matai, maybe. Tetu saw you bump heads again with Miss Keeley before we left. I see you do this before. Is this like Eskimo kissing, something I need to teach Swan Threemoons?" Tetu was kidding, and Pack knew it, but both acted as if they were taking the question seriously.

"It's a Montana thing, Tetu. Montana men have done this from the beginning. See, kissing is forbidden in this state. I'm sure you've never seen a man kiss a woman in this state, and if he did, I'm also sure you saw the both of the scalawags arrested moments thereafter. Our lawmen won't stand for kissing, no sir, and that was my General Order Number One to the state police. But you're right in thinking the gentle head bump is the approved substitute for kissing. So I suggest you introduce Miss Threemoons to this custom forthwith."

When Pack had finished his foolish answer, Tetu began laughing, laughing hard, harder than Pack had ever seen him laugh. The big fellow couldn't get control, could hardly breathe so hard was he roaring with laughter.

"Come on, Tetu," Pack said, "it was funny, but it wasn't *that* funny. What in the world are you thinking? Let me in on it if it's that funny."

Tetu tried twice to get it out, but had to calm himself a little more before asking, "Is the gentle head bump also a substitute for all forms of love with woman, Matai?" He fairly spit out the final four words, continuing to burp with laughter.

After a staccato of his own laughter, Pack said, "Tetu, your future in comedy would be bright if you weren't so damn ugly."

They both remained in high spirits until they arrived at Georgann's general store. They would stop here first in order to make their camp purchases, in keeping with their personal interest in giving Georgann whatever business they could send her way. It wasn't Georgann, though, who greeted the two very large men. It was a bright-looking brown-eyed lady of around fifty, of medium height, satiny skin, almost unnaturally white teeth, and long black hair flecked with gray. Seeing their momentary surprise at finding someone else behind the counter, this new person said, "Hi, fellows, I'm Judith Buck. Georgann's told me about Governor Pack and his friend Tetu, and ordered me to treat you right. She loves you both, and Tom does too. From your looks, I think you expected Georgann, but she's down at her house looking after a problem. Can I help?"

"Just came in to say hi to her and Tom, and buy the supplies we'll need for several days of camping," Pack said. "We've heard good things about you also, and your mate Craig Wood. I was planning to get up your way in the very near future."

"You won't have to come up unless you want to, because Craig will be here shortly. I told Shane Goodfellow where to find him this morning, so Shane'll be hauling him in here any minute," Judith said.

"What's the problem with Georgann?" Pack asked.

"It's not Georgann, it's Tom, been real sick for two days I think. Craig's the Upper Valley's medicine man, so that's why we've called him. I say medicine man because I'm telling you I haven't seen a person or an animal that man can't heal. He's a human doc and a vet, and he's damned good at both, believe me. I think I look pretty healthy, and if you agree, I'd tell you it ain't all genes. Craig keeps me in good shape. Those woods out there are one big pharmacy to him. I wrote down what we've seen of Tom, and I'll bet he comes here with the stuff that'll fix the boy up," Judith said. She was proud to boast about Craig's facility in adapting the natural world to human ailments.

Pack knew Tetu was much concerned about the boy's welfare. At the moment the giant was kneading his forearms, an obvious signaling of his restlessness and anxiety. Had he been surrounded by four ill-intentioned criminals, Tetu would have been cold, calm and coiled to spring into action. But this news about the defenseless boy had unsettled him, somehow made him feel some of Tom's pain.

"How bad is it?" It was Tetu speaking for the first time, now directing his question to Judith.

"From what I see, pretty serious. Nosebleeds, bleeding gums, bloody stool, chills, trouble breathing. This isn't a common cold. When I came in yesterday, poor Georgann was sick with worry. I sent her back down there to be with him and I slept in the store last night. I should've called Tom yesterday afternoon, but Georgann hoped it would pass."

Tetu wanted to ask if he could go down, but backed off just as the words were about to stream out. He would sit with the boy after Craig Wood had treated him, he decided.

At that moment Craig appeared in the doorway toting a small black bag, followed by Shane Goodfellow. While standing in the doorway, the medicine man was all business in instructing Judith to bring down a bottle of hydrogen peroxide and to take some charcoal bricks out of a bag and grind them into a powder. Craig hurried on down the path to the house. Shane came in and shook the hands of both Pack and Tetu.

Judith had delivered the supplies Craig asked for, and now was back in the store. Three people came in over the next ten minutes and she rang them up without mentioning the reason for Georgann's absence.

"Your man's focused, Judith, didn't talk much coming down, but I can tell you he's convinced he has a good fix on the problem. I've never seen my buddy Craig stumped yet, so to all concerned, I'd say we shouldn't be thinking the boy's life is in danger. We'll see. Young Tom's in good hands," Shane said. Wanting to believe Goodfellow spoke the truth, Tetu's shoulders visibly relaxed.

Judith said, "Why don't we let Craig do his work while we all take a chair and have a much-needed cup of coffee or tea or anything else we have for sale?"

Pack said, "Judith, we'll pay separately for whatever we buy, but here's a donation to Georgann for whatever she wants to use it for." He handed here a thick wad of twenties. Tetu immediately fished in his pocket for a smaller donation himself.

"Thank you, Governor and Tetu, from both me and Georgann," Judith said. She found an envelope to tuck the bills into, then stuck it in her pocket. Patting her jeans, she added, "Safer here for the time being."

The little group talked congenially among themselves about inconsequential matters, but each knew the others' minds were trained on what was happening down below in the little house. The waiting game continued for two hours before Craig walked in the back door. "Can I join you ladies and gentlemen?" Craig asked casually. His calmness instantly imbued everyone else with the same feeling. "I'm going to stay here overnight, right here in this room, people, so Judith, you damn woman, you better make me a comfortable bedroll," he said with a smile and chuckle.

"OK, you're waiting for me to tell you what's going on, because you love this woman and son as I do, so let me get on it," Craig said. "Shane, ole buddy, while I'm talking, would you do us a big favor and scoot down to Rex Carnes at the Sportsman's Lodge and ask him about that plate of food he sent over last night? Who prepared it, who he gave it to, who delivered it, and what the meal he sent consisted of?" To the others, Craig said, "I know all of you in here by reputation, but not in the flesh till now. Nice to meet you."

Shane left and Craig continued. "I think Tom was poisoned. Not with just any poison, but with rat poison. The various types of rat poison kill the target by thinning its blood to a deadly level. It acts the same way in a person, which accounts for the nosebleeds, the bloody stool, and bleeding gums. No credit to me, 'cause this is just what I do, but if I'd gotten here tomorrow, it might've been too late. Let me explain my thoughts, which are probably incomplete, and then I invite anyone present to add or subtract from them. OK, Tom's a young boy, but old and experienced enough in rural living to know not to eat rat poison, if there had been any around. Georgann says she didn't put any out, and hasn't for many years. Two, when we're stressed we often don't think straight and the obvious eludes us. Georgie figured it was an illness, and didn't consider it might've been food at fault. Her eyes lit up when I asked what he'd eaten recently. Turns out, somebody brought her and the boy food last night, compliments of the Sportsman's Lodge. Didn't recognize him, but he seemed polite and kind, saying Rex Carnes sent it over as thanks for coming to his place for dinner last week." Pack and Tetu sat up straighter at this revelation.

Wood continued: "At that point, I believed my diagnosis was confirmed, so I went on with the counteraction plan. I put enough hydrogen peroxide to make him throw up everything in his stomach, then I made him drink a small glass of water heavily enriched with the powdered charcoal, intended to filter out the poison. That'll stop the bleeding, and when that happens, I'll begin a two-day diet of Vitamin K foods and my special herbal recipe I call butt root. Am I confident he'll be OK? You bet I am."

Shane Goodfellow had come in to hear Craig Wood's peroration. Now Craig turned to him. "Rex Carnes was shocked. Said he wished he'd been thoughtful enough to send them some food, but he did not. He did not give anyone any food to bring over here, and he questioned his kitchen about it, but they acted as shocked as Rex. That's it, Craig."

They sat in silence for quite some time. Finally, Pack spoke. "Maybe it would be best if we kept all this information close to our vest. Much as we place our faith in you, Craig, let's give it enough time to confirm your diagnosis. In the meantime, if we all agree, Tetu and I will visit Carnes to see who was in his restaurant night before last. We might stumble onto something there. Or maybe not. I know you trappers are busy right now, but is there a way we could compare notes in two days?"

Shane said, "We all want to know how Tom's doing, and to see what we can do for Georgann, so we'd return here anyway." Craig nodded yes to that, as did Judith. "OK, say four o'clock two days from now this group meets up here."

Pack and Tetu bought their supplies, paid Judith, and went back to their campsite, promising to check in tomorrow morning for an update on Tom's status. The medicine man and his crew remained right there in the store for their own beddown.

"Let's go see Rex Carnes, Tetu," Pack said.

Goodfellow had told Carnes Pack and Tetu were at the general store, so when Carnes saw them coming, he knew they would want a word with them. To speed things along, he simply waved them to his office. "I'll put my hand on a Bible right now and swear I had nothing to do with whatever has happened to that boy," Carnes said first thing.

"Nobody said you did, or thinks you did," Tetu said. "Matai has ideas you can help, though."

Carnes turned to Pack, the look imploring Pack to explain how he could assist. Pack listed each food item on the tray that had come to Georgann, and asked Carnes if he had served those things that night.

"This is a bad dream," Carnes said haltingly. He was actually turning paler before their eyes. "That was the special of the day. Somebody laced it, if it's really rat poison that's put Tom down. I guess Georgann didn't eat any, thank God, if she didn't get sick. How was the boy when you left? What does Craig say?"

They brought Carnes up to date, then Pack said, "I think we ought to review everyone who was in here. Bring out your receipts and let's look them over, see if anything comes to mind."

"No problem, I have them filed by date and they're time-stamped. Let me go get them."

They went over each tab together, looking at each one and asking Carnes whether he knew the diner(s). He'd had a full house that evening, many of them people staying at the lodge, and others coming for a nice hot meal from the area's five cold campgrounds. The ones he felt comfortable vouching for went into one stack. Before long they were working with three stacks...then they happened upon one that struck a chord with Pack. It was signed Ng Trang. He had purchased three meals.

"Who were Mr. Trang's guests?" Pack asked Carnes.

"He had only one, an unforgettable-looking lady, which is how I remember. I can point you to the two-top where they sat. And when I checked with them to see if the service was acceptable, I noticed she had barely touched her food, as if it wasn't to her taste," Carnes said.

"She was an exotic Asian woman, roughly mid-twenties, right?" Pack said.

"That's right," Carnes said. "You seen her before?"

"No," Pack said, and left it at that. Then he added, "Tetu, please take the Jeep and go to Georgann, ask her for the most detailed description she can provide of the guy who brought her the food. When she thinks she's finished, think of another question to ask."

Tetu was on his way before Pack had uttered the final syllable.

After the camp host had raised the name Ng Trang, Pack had leaned on Jack Schnee again. Schnee's readout was that Trang was the son of a Vietnam War refugee who resided in Los Angeles. The parents had obviously put great weight on school studies, because their son Ng had performed brilliantly and been awarded a scholarship to Berkeley. Schnee opined that Ng must have disgraced those parents, however, by leaving Berkeley after a semester. A motor home valued at one million dollars, give or take a hundred grand, as well as several more normal modes of transport, were registered to him in the state of Washington. Occupation listed as unknown. Was not registered to vote. Interestingly, Trang apparently was a big fan of camping, particularly in Montana, and more particularly in Yaak River Valley campgrounds. Pack didn't divulge this information to anyone, but he believed all signs were pointing toward Trang for the general run of crime in the Yaak.

Tetu, Pack discovered as a result of dispatching him to get the description from Georgann, might've succeeded as a sketch artist. He came back with both verbal and pictorial descriptions. Typical Tetu, doing every task more thoroughly than expected. It was nonetheless a futile effort, as Pack suspected it would be. Trang was too smart to send someone who hung out regularly in these environs. Whoever it was probably was now an asomatous being flying amid the throngs of a large West Coast city.

One other thing Tetu had said upon returning to Pack and Carnes: "Matai, would you mind being alone in camp tonight? Tetu would like to relieve Georgann and sit with Tom tonight." Pack agreed without hesitation, proud yet again of his younger companion.

Tetu did not sleep that night, but sat and watched Georgann sleeping on a pad at the foot of the bed. Tom would alternately kick his covers off and shiver from the cold, at which point Tetu would cover him again. Much of the time Tetu sat close enough to place a reassuring hand on Tom's arm. By morning he could see Tom was calmer and breathing more evenly. Georgann awoke as if gripped by panic, bolting upright, wide-eyed, forgetting Tetu was there. Before she could speak Tetu put a finger to his lips, shushing her. He smiled, to let her know Tom was improving, definitely improving. She got up slowly, Tetu guessing she was going to the bathroom. Once freshened up, she approached the seated American Samoan, the puissant Tetu, hugging him in a gentle thank you. Tetu gave her the seat and went back to the store. Shane, Craig, and Judith were in the chairs drinking coffee.

"Better go have a look, medicine man," Tetu said to Craig. "Tom looks better to Tetu. Not so restless now." Craig nodded unexpressively, picked up his black bag, and set off for the house below.

On the morning that Tetu left Tom's bedside, Pack walked down to the camp host's RV and knocked on the door. The man appeared, stepping out to greet Pack with "Governor, General, etc., I hope I have atoned for my earlier sin in not recognizing you. Where's your partner?"

"He's up at the general store taking care of some business," Pack said vaguely. "I was hoping you could help me locate Mr. Trang, the gentleman we discussed last time I was here. He was at the Sportsman's Lodge a couple days back, so I figured I'd run into him here at the camp."

"You missed him by two days, I'm afraid. He cleared out two days ago, early in the morning, him and that pretty lady. And I guess you remember that monster motor home he drove?"

"Yep," Pack answered, "couldn't easily forget that thing."

"Well, he didn't have it this time. Wanted to get more in line with the regular people, I guess. Driving a small RV this time. But who the hell knows, maybe he still has it parked down in Missoula or over in Spokane or anywhere."

"Was he here a full week?" Pack asked.

"Just one day," the host said. "I can't be sure. People can come and go without I notice. I did see one car come into the camp and leave a few minutes later. Could've been someone just looking around, then decided not to stay here, don't know."

"What time was that?" Pack asked.

"Oh, man, I can't say, my memory's not that great," said the host.

"This could be important, so give it another try. Can you associate what you were doing at the time with the car's coming and going?"

The man pondered this, and said at last, "Yeah, I think I can help you. The old lady and me were watching *Jeopardy* on the Missoula station, which I think comes on here at seven. Yeah, seven, because back home it comes on at seven-thirty, so sometimes I miss it here thinking it comes on at seven-thirty. Thanks, Governor, my brain needed that jumpstart, so yeah, the car was here sometime between seven and seven-thirty."

"And what kind of car was it, and the color maybe?" Pack prodded.

"Sorry, I've reached the limit of remembrance. We could be here till Kingdom Come and I wouldn't remember that. Unless a vehicle's really unusual, I don't care to notice. I'm just not a car guy, General."

When Pack checked with Rex Carnes to ascertain the time Trang and A'nh were in his restaurant, he was not surprised to learn the answer was between six-thirty and seven-thirty. And when he found out the time Georgann accepted the platter, he was not surprised to learn the time was around eight.

What was the point of targeting two people who were no threat to his business? Was the action intended to shut down Rex Carnes's lodge by propagating the claim that the tainted food came from his establishment? Was Trang sending a message to Tetu, and by extension Pack himself, to abandon interest in the lodge and just go home, stop nosing about in the Upper Yaak? Or maybe Trang's tentacles were so deep he somehow knew of Tetu's ineffable connection to the lad. Whatever Trang's motivation, Pack was determined to peel it back.

Pack was on the store phone talking with Keeley, at the moment telling her he was urging everyone around the area to spread the word that, incontrovertibly, Rex Carnes had nothing to do with the poisoning. Thanks to the near-otherworldly homespun healing talents of Craig Wood, Tom was out of the woods and would recover fully. He told her Tom didn't want to let Tetu out of his sight now, so tightly bound to the big man had he grown in a short period.

Not exactly switching topics, Keeley said, "What do you think of Tetu?"

"I think you know," Pack said, "but for some reason you want to hear me say it out loud. And I'd be happy to do just that, Keel. I'll start by saying Tetu Palaita and I have been through stormy weather together, and I can think of no one I'd rather have at my side in those situations. He's calm, tough, totally dependable, utterly loyal. I swear, the man views me as a demigod, and I guess I think of him the same way. Without trying, he's a giver, not a taker. His heart's bigger than he is. I've wondered times without number how this man came to appear in my life, and join me in so many important ventures. OK, he doesn't look like an angel, but that's kind of the way I see him, this Heaven-sent messenger who has so often guided me. Nobody has Pack's back like Mr. Palaita."

"OK, Simon, we've established what you think of Tetu. You like him, you admire him, and because you do, so do I. You know I'm getting to a point, so here it is: I think he has waited too long for his loan approval. You think he'll get it, but there's still a possibility he'll be turned down, you have admitted. Why don't I just give him the money? I won't even notice that amount of money taken out of my account. Don't you think he deserves it?"

"I don't know, Keeley," Pack said. "I believe we should tread lightly. The man has pride, and the offer of a gift could damage it. As I told you, the money is yours and you can do with it whatever you want. I'm just advising you to think it over, maybe conclude a zero-interest or low-interest loan would be better, let him fix the payback timeline. I appreciate your wanting to do this. That's nice of you, so thanks from me, and I'm sure from Tetu also. And here's another angle, Keel: we think more about how the offer ought to be presented, then if his loan package isn't done by say, New Year's day, you approach him with it. What do you say?"

"Suits me. I'll give the company until the first day of the new year. We also have the chance the present owner will lower the price if it's an all-cash deal," she said.

Ng Trang was still reveling in his overseas mission. He had been instructed to fly to Bahrain for the big meeting with the Arab bigwigs, which meant sheiks and princes and business billionaires. A few hours before his original flight, however, they deliberately rerouted him to Sarajevo. There, instead of meeting with the principals he was supposed to meet, he met with their gatekeepers. They let Trang know from the outset who was in charge of the impending arrangement.

They met in a heavily-guarded farmhouse in the open farm fields near the Sarajevo airport. They were all Muslims, and they made no attempt to conceal their disdain for the infidel Trang. Their research had told them Trang's allegiance was to power and money above all else. He had never manifested any allegiance to the country he lived in. He had, in fact, resented his parents' shucking of allegiance to the land of their birth. He was ashamed of the degree to which they had shirked the legacy of their proud ancestors and adopted the ways of the shallow Americans. Trang would, in his own fashion, follow the lead of his Americanized parents, which translated to taking as much of their filthy lucre as he could. He had made millions helping them numb their minds and bodies through pills and booze and hard drugs and women shipped from the Far East. Now, in this, his grandest undertaking, he would slash out at them all...these sloppy, licentious, sybaritic Americans of all stripes and colors, these rootless lost souls.

Neither did he enjoy the arrogant lot of Muslims in the farmhouse. They did, indeed, piss him off; their condescension was of the sort that he had killed other men for. He made the mistake of taking food with the wrong hand, an offense for which they severely upbraided him. And at one point he forgot—because his focus was entirely on the business proposition—and crossed his legs, causing the sole of one shoe to go on display. They all got quiet, staring at him with cross expressions, until one said in raised voice, "Mr. Trang, put your foot down, and never do that again. Do you understand me?" To have to swallow such an insult was hard for a man of Trang's temperament. At that moment he only hoped that after taking their money for this operation he might have the chance to inflict upon them a long lasting, soul-piercing pain.

They had made the deal with Trang because they wanted none of their own fingerprints on the operation. It would be Trang's job to assemble the resources required and have them on hand in four widely dispersed locations in America for execution on or about 19 January, slightly more than one month ahead. Hand-picked jihadists would actually execute the missions. It was a tall order with a tight time constraint, Trang's most challenging mission yet. In a sense he was going from grade school to college. The Upper Yaak would still be central to the plan he envisaged, but he had to clear all accounts with his present crew first. The price of failure would be his own death.

Trang's dinner with A'nh Tran at the Sportsman's Lodge had been self-celebratory. Trang's 'Last Supper', he hoped, in this place. After leaving the campground nearby, he would go undercover, with trips to the Philippines and Hong Kong and Canada on his immediate schedule. He had to recruit and employ the best in the business to get this job done. But first he had to brief everyone he had ever employed in his Yaak crime syndicate. He enticed them with the promise of a new job that would ensure a future free of money concerns. He told his top lieutenants in advance that security was of prime importance and that all weapons and phones had to be relinquished and stacked neatly before entering the outdoor amphitheater, such as it was. "Just like they do it in the corporate world," he told them, "taking all recording and commo devices away from the execs before they enter the boardroom." No exceptions. When they had all arrived, their total was seventy-six. Four females were among them.

Trang's people knew the routine. As the General about to speak to his troops, his people knew to be absolutely silent when he addressed them.

They took seats in a low section of the bowl, with Trang on higher ground opposite them. In this scooped-out area of the forest sound traveled well. Trang had paid Bill Strang a nice *pourboire* to blockade the key dirt roads leading here.

Trang smiled down at the assembly. "We have achieved much together. I want to say thank you in person. Now we are going forward on new, more exciting missions. The kinds of taskings you have accomplished are now in the past, to be replaced by bigger ones. Our new mission will be called Operation Aceldama, and I promise you will make it successful." At this point, Trang was just toying with his people, making fun of them by gambling not a one of them knew the meaning of Aceldama. If he or she did understand its meaning, he would most likely have felt his eyes bulge involuntarily. Recognition, though, failed to dawn for any of them. Trang continued, "For your patience with me and for your unwavering commitment to every venture you have set out to do, I have today a quite sizeable bonus for each and every one of you. As part of this bonus, I first have a big surprise for you. You ready for it?"

"Hell, yeah...oh, yeah, we're ready, bring it on, boss...." Only they weren't ready, and they really did not want it brought on.

Trang pressed a button at his side, and from the flanks of those in the lower bowl, there appeared two Humvees with .50 cal machineguns mounted. The rate of fire of this model was 1200 rounds a minute. Firing commenced as soon as they crested the rises, and within seconds the natural amphitheater became a natural Aceldama, a field of blood. No one escaped the carnage.

For their troubles, the Sovereign Citizens soldiers received the machineguns and the vehicles bearing them, as well as whatever they could salvage from the belongings of the dead. And they would claim all those expensive motorcycles as well. The Sov Cit leader was happy to have been promised more work and more payoff in the future. Now the cleanup began, and Ng Trang closed this chapter of his life.

Chapter Twenty-Three

Pack went alone for the linkup with Bill Strang. From a distance he could see Strang peering through his binos at someone or something hidden from Pack. Strang stood near his state-issued Fish, Wildlife and Parks (FWP) truck.

Pack dismounted and extended his hand to Strang. "Hey, Governor, how are ya?" Strang answered by way of accepting Pack's hand.

"I'm fine, and hope you are too," Pack said. "Guess I'm just a born information gatherer, which is why I'm talking with you."

"I don't believe that," Strang said bluntly. "Maybe that's part of it, but a man didn't function in your big jobs without making good sense of the information he gathered. So, it seems to me what you're really doing here is trying to make sense of information you've already collected and will maybe collect here. Aren't I right?"

"You are right. Word travels fast, it seems. You want me to cut to the chase, so here it is. I think, based upon random shards of evidence, most anecdotal, that a lot of criminal activity is happening in the Upper Yaak, and did right under my nose when I was Governor, and that irks hell out of me, Warden Strang. What do you think about that?"

Strang was thinking perhaps the opening he'd so meticulously planned might've sounded the wrong tone, and just might be having the effect of abrading Pack's sensibilities. So now he affected a more laid back demeanor, leaning back on his elbows atop the hood of his truck. Smiling wanly and in softer voice, he said, "Sorry, Governor, I'm sure I came across as defensive, when the truth is I have nothing to defend myself against. I'll lay it all out on the table. You know that I know you've already spoken with Sheriff Hackman, and that he says the nature of your questions concern him. He thinks you believe he hasn't policed this area as effectively as you'd like. And it makes sense to me that you probably have your suspicions about me too. Well, you needn't worry about me. I have a purely professional relationship with Bob Hackman, and I think we coordinate very well. He'll occasionally give me a lead, and I'll follow through to check it out. Most of the time those leads amount to nothing, but that doesn't matter to me, because maintaining that professional relationship means a lot to me, and I want to show him we're part of the same law enforcement team.

"The state has a budget, as you know as well as anyone, and there just aren't enough wardens. We have huge territories to cover. Mine is the biggest territory. I'm one man with around a million acres to cover, which is why I've argued successfully for a series of interns. I'm a peace officer, just like any other in the state. Only in addition to having the usual arrest authority I have to know a thousand hunting and fishing regulations, as well as be somewhat proficient as an animal biologist. And more than once I've had to walk into a hunting camp among a dozen armed men, all drunk, to inspect their kill and licenses, no backup, and I'll tell you it's always harrowing. Nothing easy about this job. A man's gotta love it, 'cause the pay leaves something to be desired."

"I'm not a pillow to cry on, Strang," Pack declared. "Many good people around would be happy to get any job. Your heart's not in what you're telling me anyway. You're trying to distract me from the question I asked, which in case you've lost track, was about the state of lawlessness up in this territory. By this time I have collected most of the puzzle pieces, and I'm starting to fit the jigsaw pieces together pretty well. I'll never stop the info gathering, but what I'm mainly doing now is preparing to act on the case I'm assembling. So if you don't want to talk, that's your prerogative for the moment, but there'll be a time soon when I imagine you'll wish you had."

"Are you still the Governor?" Strang asked rhetorically. "Oh, you're not? Then...are you an official of the law? If you're neither, I've finished this discussion. You can't railroad me, Simon Pack, ordinary citizen. You best remember I'm the one wearing the badge here." Then he added ominously, "And carrying the gun." He tried vainly to stare Pack down.

Pack grinned, shook his head slowly, and said, "You're a bigger fool than I thought, Strang. See you around." He ambled slowly to the Jeep and followed his own tracks back out the dense maze of rutty trails.

Sheriff Bob Hackman had observed the full exchange through his field glasses less than 300 meters away. Strang remained agitated, pacing around near his FWP truck, wondering what his next step should be. While Strang was still befuddledly fuming and pacing, Hackman appeared.

"What the hell, Hackman? You've watched the whole thing? Why didn't you tell me?" Strang observed absently and without comment that Hackman wore overshoes, a piece of apparel seldom seen in these parts.

"You did, remember? You told me when and where you were meeting him, and I said I'd see you afterward for a post mortem, or something like that," Hackman said.

"Yeah, I guess I did," Strang said. "That didn't go well, no matter how you look at it. The man as much as said he's got our situation figured out and now he's just finalizing his case against us."

Hackman interrupted. "*Us?* Did he mention my name? What did you say about me, Strang? Come on, man, out with it, damnit!"

"Hold your water. He didn't say your name. I just got the impression he's painted the picture pretty accurately and completely, which for damn sure includes you," Strang added.

"OK, Billy, we're both gettin' too worked up, in this Sheriff's opinion. Let me get a note pad. I want to make notes, carry 'em back to the office, develop some counters, just think this through with a level head." Hackman walked over to his Lincoln County SUV. He put his gloves on and reached under his seat for the object he sought, then while still bent over the seat, slid it under his right jacket sleeve. He went back over to Strang.

Strang was leaning against the bull bars of his truck, bent over, head in his hands. Hackman had intended to query Strang a bit deeper, but decided he couldn't pass up this inviting target. In one flick of the hand he released the telescoping mechanism on the titanium nightstick and clubbed the game warden in the sternocleidomastoid muscle of the neck; the flicking sound gave Strang a split-second warning, causing him to jump forward an inch, but no more. Strang tumbled forward hard. Hackman couldn't tell if life had left Strang, but he took no chances. Now that Strang was an inert target, he brought the nightstick down with brutal force on the back of his skull, almost dead center. Feeling and hearing the grisly crack, he could see the pronounced indentation. Strang was lifeless, he felt sure, but he would wait awhile to check his carotid pulse. He slid the extended part of the billy club back into its recessed holding compartment and looked around for a spot to drop the device, which was now about one foot in length. Amid the snow and mud there lay a clump of mountain grass some thirty feet away. In a horseshoe-throwing motion he tossed it directly into his target, congratulating himself. No sense dirtying up the crime scene. Before he checked again, Hackman strode back to his SUV, retrieved a premium cigar, bit off its cap, and fired it up. Big problem gone, he thought, as he made the first sweet puffs.

When Hackman got back to Libby, he called FWP for help in locating the intern, Bill Damon. Hackman was confident Strang would have dispatched the young man back to the HQ to avoid being anywhere in the vicinity during his meetup with Pack. Hackman was proved right when the person on the FWP end of the line said, "I'll connect you, but here's his extension for future reference." Hackman said thanks, but he didn't copy the number.

Damon's voice came on the line. Hackman said, "Hey, Bill, how ya' doin'? I'm Bob Hackman, Sheriff here in Lincoln County. You know how to reach Bill Strang? He told me he was meeting with ex-Governor Pack this morning, and I wanted to ask him how it went."

"Tell you what, Sheriff, we have radio contact, so if you'll give me a little while I'll walk over to the Ops Center and try to raise him for you. Any message for him?"

"Well, yeah, if he'll pass GPS coordinates I can meet him someplace up there. If he says he's too busy to stop in one place, tell him I can come over to your place to speak with him over the radio...if your people wouldn't object," Hackman said.

"No prob, Sheriff," Damon said. "I'll call you back at this number in one hour if I don't have information for you before that. Anything else?"

"Nope, that'll do it," Hackman said. "Incidentally, Bob has said great things about your eagerness to do a good job, young man. Hope to sit down and have a talk with you soon."

They cut the connection, with Damon thinking, "That's bullcrap, Hackman, and we both know it. This call doesn't pass the smell test. Strang never had a good word for me with anybody."

Damon called Hackman back after an hour of trying to bring Strang up on the radio. "Haven't reached him yet, but we're still trying. There are spots up there that even the radio can't penetrate. Give me a few more hours and I'll let you know more."

"OK, Bill, you fellows know what you're doing, but if it was one of my men and I couldn't reach him for hours, I'd think about sending out a search party."

"Well, Sheriff, it's only been an hour so far, but we'll keep your advice in mind as we go forward."

A search party wasn't required. The Forest Ranger, the laconic Ranklin Shiningfish, called it in to the Three Rivers District station in Troy sometime around mid-afternoon of the day Hackman called Damon. Acting on a tip from a tipsy Lucas Lincoln that he had heard loud and sustained gunfire deep in the woods, Shiningfish acted, in the process discovering Strang's body.

Ranklin Shiningfish wasn't merely laconic; he was a deep-dyed cynic and friend to few. He suspected the motives of everyone he met. At the same time, he was a shrewd assessor of character, a man able to size up a man or woman with the best of them. It was true that he didn't like most people. Misanthrope, an educated man might call him. It was unsurprising, then, that he trusted old Lucas Lincoln enough to check out his story, when most in a similar position of authority would have laughed him off as a foolish drunk. In Ranklin's judgment, Lucas might be a reprobate, but he wasn't a liar. He deserved the respect of a response to his request for information. Ranklin knew these forests weren't clean, and he detested his colleagues in law enforcement who failed to do the requisite cleaning up.

Although Shiningfish believed old man Lincoln had heard gunfire, he didn't believe it had occurred where he found Strang. It was clear Strang had been bludgeoned, not gunshot, and there were no shell casings in the vicinity. Shiningfish also knew to avoid tampering with the crime scene in any way. If he had discovered shell casings, he wouldn't have handled them. He went through his own chain of command to report his finding, delivering his typical nonjudgmental, sterile, dispassionate report. Just the facts, ma'am, was the Shiningfish way. His seniors had alerted the Lincoln County Sheriff. Shiningfish did receive assurance, however, that Hackman would send someone up there to secure the crime scene. Without security, the animals might have dragged the body off before morning.

Hackman was slightly disappointed he hadn't had the chance to arrive on the scene earlier, but once he received the information Strang had been found, an idea occurred to him he regarded as brilliant, to wit, call the FBI, given that the crime had taken place on federal land.

It was Saturday afternoon, still on the day of Strang's murder. Pack and Tetu were back at the camp, checking their tent and generally tightening up their place. "Let's get everything just as we'll want it when we bed down tonight. I'd like to just brush my teeth and hit the sack. We're going out tonight, part of our continuing mission, Tetu. You up for a wild Saturday night at the Armpit?" As they talked they got things ready and Pack lighted a fire and got the chairs set out.

"If Matai is ready, Tetu is ready. We are looking for the bad guys, right Matai?"

"Yeah, we'll leave camp early enough to go the store, say hi to our buddies, buy any small items we might need, and I can call Keeley to check in."

"Ask if Chesty misses Tetu," Tetu broke in, aware of the silliness of the comment as quickly as he made it.

"I'll do that, Tetu, for sure. We'll have a real story if Chesty answers that question. But back to our evening...after the store, we walk across the street and check in with Nick Surgeon, ask him to deputize us as bouncers. If there's trouble, we take the offenders outside and demand identification before we release them. We'll also—after I clear this with Nick—ban them from future appearances in the bar. Beyond that, I intend to attend church at this Reverend Dar's place tomorrow morning. Just to be safe I'm going to confirm the location of the church with Georgann."

"I've been thinking of asking you something very big to me, Matai."

"About the lodge, am I right?" Pack asked.

"Not at all, Matai. It is about Tom, but also very much concerns me and you."

"Fine, go ahead and ask," Pack said.

"You gave me this fetish," Tetu said, pulling it from his pocket. "It means so much to me. It is one of biggest gifts Tetu ever got. It came from your heart. Because it means so much to me and to you, I would like to pass it on to Tom. Would you think this is wrong, Matai?"

Pack sat silent in front of the crackling flames for a long while, just watching the embers spark and flare. Presently he said, in a voice so quiet Tetu had to strain to hear clearly, "Yes, indeed you can, Tetu, with my blessing, but consider this: each fetish represents a different aspiration or strength, and I'm thinking if you could wait a little longer, you could go through my little chest of fetishes to find one *you* think would fit your intention for Tom. You are most welcome to select any one you choose."

"No need to think about it, Matai. That is what I would like to do. Tetu thanks for the offer."

They brewed camp coffee and sat there placidly until it was time to head back up to higher ground.

Tom ran to give Tetu a low five as soon as they walked in the door of the general store. Tom was seven years old, and he was finding it an awkward age. His first instinct was to run to Tetu for a hug, but the man's immense stature made it awkward, and besides, he wasn't a little boy any longer. The truth was, he could run the store better than any city ten-year-old. Already there was little Georgann could do that Tom couldn't do almost as well. How many seven-year-olds could ring up tabs, run the cash register, and make change? And keep track of the stockage and place resupply orders?

It wasn't time to go over to the Armpit yet, so they just went directly to the rockers in the center of the room. Tetu tousled Tom's hair and asked him how he felt. Tom said he felt like his usual self. "Mom told me you sat by my bed that bad night, Mr. Tetu. You're a real friend, not just a big talker. Thanks, so when are you coming to the lodge? I still want to help down there when Mom doesn't need me as much. I like the way you talk. You're the coolest talker I know."

"Tetu thanks you, my new friend. He does not know when he will come, but soon he hopes. I guess when bankers and lawyers decide these things, takes them long time. If Tom and Tetu decide, it is done fast, right?"

"I've saved up almost all I've earned, Mr. Tetu, so if you need more money, I can help," Tom said.

Tetu didn't laugh about Tom's offer. He just said, "Thank you."

Pack and Georgann were conducting a side conversation between themselves. She said she had seen mostly her Yaak neighbors the past couple of days, except for those tourists from the West Coast who were obviously enroute to Glacier National Park.

"How do you mean? Can you be more specific?" Pack asked.

"Let me think...well, there've been rough guys coming in here for a long time. They usually don't talk, not even a hello, and never a smile. Just come in, get what they're looking for, and they're out the door. Most times they're on their motorcycles. It's those people I'm talking about who haven't been around. I can't recall a day at least a few don't come in, but so far none today or yesterday or the day before. Heck, that doesn't really mean anything, though, 'cause they'll probly come streaming in tomorrow."

Pack made his call to Keeley. All was calm at the cabin, and Chesty had begun to follow her around. The dog let her know his schedule for going out, and she said she was venturing a bit farther from the cabin each time they went out. She said the area around the cabin was fast becoming her favorite spot on earth. Mundane topics, but they enjoyed the chat, as always.

Simon signaled to Tetu it was time to adjourn to the Armpit, but Tetu asked if he could join him in a few minutes. He wanted to call Swan. "Just a short call, Matai," Tetu said.

Pack pushed open the door of the Armpit to see perhaps twenty people dressed in cowboy and cowgirl garb appearing to have a good time. From behind the bar Nick Surgeon barked above the crowd noise, "Ladies and gentlemen, Bouncer Number One has arrived, and Number Two no doubt is not far behind. So mind your manners tonight." A sharp-looking lady yelled back, "Only a handsome Governor's fit to be a bouncer in our place!" The normal catcalls followed.

Surgeon waved Pack to a seat at the bar. "Got something for you, General." He tossed over a sweatshirt. "3XL. Hope it's big enough. Normally we sell 'em, but if you're gonna be a bouncer, there's your payment." The sweatshirt was a black hoodie, with 'Montana's Armpit' emblazoned in white across a black background. Underneath was the drawing of a man sniffing his underarm with obvious displeasure, as judged by his facial expression. "OK, people," Surgeon called out again, "let's give the General our own salute," at which time, more or less in unison, each person present went into the underarm sniff pose. Which is when Tetu walked in, with various good-natured hooting calls about how unappealing the big man's pits must be. Tetu reacted with a sheepish grin.

Surgeon now waved Tetu over. Pointing toward Pack's new acquisition, Surgeon said, "Sorry, Tetu, but I don't have one that'll fit you, else I'd give you one too. So instead, here's one of our ball caps, fits any size, they say." Tetu stuck his bear paw out to shake Surgeon's hand in thanks.

By nine-thirty some thirty to forty more folks had come in, and there was no hint of trouble. Both Nick and his young wife were kept on their toes filling orders, which included lots of food orders. When there was a lull in his action, Nick stopped at Pack's barstool for a little chat. Pack opened with, "This bouncin's a pretty easy gig. Good pay, no work, shoulda been doin' this all my life."

"Seriously, General, I don't know what's going on, but have to think something is. The troublemakers seem to have vanished. I like it this way, back to how it used to be before they descended on us. People are having the kind of pretty innocent good times they had before those ruffians brought their hard edges with them. I'm pretty sure everyone in here now is a friend, somebody from twenty miles around."

About that time an old man walked in and took a table by himself. Catching Pack take a long look in the old man's direction, Nick said, "That's Lucas Lincoln. Good guy. Drinks too much, but he's a quiet drunk and wouldn't hurt anyone. I'm guessing he hasn't seen a doctor in his adult life, but the man's damn strong for his age. Everyone knows his age is 90, though to me he doesn't look it."

"Yeah," Pack said, "I heard the story about him and the prostitute. Did he ever work?"

"Oh, yeah," Nick said, "he was involved in lots of jobs, all having to do with the timber industry. He knows the Upper Yaak as well as anyone. Man's not afraid of anything. He wanders all over the Yaak, just walking with his stick, but no weapons, and I guess no animal's ever harmed him. Like they know he belongs there as much as they do.

"Everybody who lives around here knows Lucas by sight, and most have talked with him a few minutes here and there, but not many really know him, partly because he doesn't give them a chance. He's always walking, but he's the kind of man if you run across him in the woods—you know, you're the only two people out there—he'll pause for a word or two, then get on his way. But you know, General, we share the blame because I guess we shoulda pinned him down and made him truly be a part of the community. I sound like a barkeep, don't I?" Nick said, shaking his head.

"Interesting, Nick. Think I'll see if he'll tolerate my company for a few minutes," Pack said.

"Howdy, Mr. Lincoln, I'm Simon Pack. Wonder if I could join you for a beer and maybe a plate of food?"

Lucas pointed his hand toward an empty chair inviting Pack to sit. "I got friends," he said, apropos seemingly of nothing. Pack thought maybe he had come to sit with a man whose mind had mostly abandoned him. Then Lucas added, "Most people think I'm ornery, which I am. Others think I'm a drunk, which I sometimes am. Others think I'm a liar, which I ain't. All the people wearin' uniforms of the law of one kind or another don't like me very much, look for ways to harass me. That game warden Strang was all the time shooin' me away seemed like wherever I went. Told him I got as much right as anyone to be out there, not hurtin' anyone or anything, just trekkin' around takin' in God's natural cathedral. The County law come all the way up here to arrest me when I told them a woman friend stoled from me."

"Mr. Lincoln," Pack said, "I used to be Governor of Montana, and I was a Marine before that. For reasons that would take too long to explain, I believe what you've said, and I'm very interested in your story. Would you mind answering a few questions?"

Pack ordered them both beers and food.

Lincoln said, "I'll take your questions, but I don't promise to answer them."

"All right. Let's start with why you think this game warden was always shooing you off."

"Short answer is, he didn't want me to see what was goin' on in the direction I was headed," Lincoln said.

"Can you give me a 'such as' or an example, I mean?" Pack said.

"This happened more than once or twice, I can tell you that. See, I reckon I walk ten, fifteen miles most days, so I get around, and I don't need a map or a compass to tell me where to go. I know ever bend in the cricks and ever dip and ever rise. So, see, one time I see him up the trail, sittin' on the hood of his truck, readin' a book, like he's a lookout or something. I'm thinkin' something's goin' on back in there he don't want me to see, so I do what the man says and go back in the direction I come from.

Only what I really do is go hide in higher ground. I can't make out details of what I'm seein', but I can tell there's a bunch of guys with motorcycles parked back there listenin' to some small guy tell 'em what to do. Exactly what they're doin' I can't tell. So I wait a long time till they finish up. They all leave on the same trail the game warden's on, go right by him, and after they're gone, he gets in his truck and goes on his way too. What would you think?"

"I think you're telling me the truth, and I think he was acting as a lookout. What else have you got, Mr. Lincoln?"

"I can tell you a good man in a uniform, and that'd be the Kootenai, Ranger Ranklin Shiningfish. He's a lot like me, only he's in uniform. Nobody seems like likes him. He does his job, don't matter to him who's doin' the crime."

"Why do you bring him up? What made you think of him, given that we've been talking about something a little different?" Pack asked.

Their food and beer came, via Nick's pretty young wife, who cheerfully asked if there'd be anything else for the two nice gentlemen. Pack said, "There just might be. I'll flag you down, thanks." Pack looked on happily as he saw Lucas had zero deficiencies with respect to appetite as he shoveled the food in, and gulped the beer with gustatory delight.

Lucas paused to say, "OK, where were we? Oh, yeah, about Shiningfish. Answer is for simple reason the man took me serious when I told him what I heard."

"What was that?" Pack asked. "And when?"

"I lose track of time, don't wear a watch or look at calendars anymore, but I'd say five or six days ago I heard a lot of gunfire. A helluva lot of gunfire from big guns. Wasn't hunters, I promise you that. Lasted a minute, maybe less, but it was serious shootin'. I told Shiningfish the next day, and he said he'd look into it."

"Did you show him where to look?" Pack asked.

"Couldn't really. Way sound gets trapped out there in some spots and magnified in others makes it hard to judge direction it come from. Plus, I can't be sure how far away I was from where it come from."

"Could you take me to your location when you heard the shots?" Pack asked. "Probably not tomorrow but maybe Monday?"

"Yeah," Lucas said, and that was that. They agreed Pack would leave a message at the general store.

As Pack had told Strang, he thought he had collected most of the puzzle pieces, but had to fit them together correctly. He had also told Strang he would always be in the collection mode, and tonight proved the essentiality of that; the chat with the surprisingly loquacious Lucas Lincoln amounted to adding important new puzzle pieces. Pack thought of his present position this way: "I have a little velvet bag with lots of jigsaw pieces. In fact, I might have already collected almost all there are to collect. But I haven't actually solved the puzzle, which entails fitting these many-shaped forms together. It might be that in two or three days I can go back to the cabin and metaphorically dump out all the pieces and figure out the connection points."

Ever since Pack was a young man, he had a sense that cautioned him not to get ahead of the facts. But something told him there well could be a connection between the story Mr. Lincoln had related about loud sustained gunfire and the sudden absence of the alleged lawbreakers from Georgann's and Nick's establishments. Pack had no thread of connectivity at this point, though. The 'thread' was a flimsy filament, but he was already making plans to run down more facts.

He wasn't ready to present his suspicions to anyone, including Tetu, just yet. He asked Tetu to make runs down tomorrow morning to Shane Goodfellow and Rex Carnes, to ask them to keep their eyes out for the short-term pattern of the bad guys dropping out of the Yaak picture. For now, however, he was thinking about attending church in the deep woods tomorrow morning.

Sheriff Hackman had shared the news about Strang's murder with the FBI, but no one else except for those sent to secure the scene. Even the latter group was threatened with expulsion from the force if they leaked the story to anyone. The stoic Ranklin Shiningfish couldn't care less about telling anyone he'd discovered the body. He didn't care what anyone thought of him, and he wasn't looking for a pat on the back. So as Pack and Tetu set off for church, there had been no news release about the murder in the Yaak.

Reverend D'Artagnan Castor had considered standing outside the door to greet the churchcomers for the eleven o'clock service. But on second thought it was too cold for him, even as the temperatures remained twenty degrees above the seasonal average. He wore his best Sunday clothes, but his first attempt to don them over three layers of thermal underwear didn't work, so he broke down and wore the Michelin Man coat over his suit. Meanwhile, the fire had turned the wood stove cherry red.

When Pack steered the Jeep up to a makeshift parking area, he observed two men smoking pipes outside the church entrance. One looked to be a tribal member and the other was Lucas Lincoln. Pack shook hands with the Indian and embraced Lucas like an old friend. "See, I'm not drunk most of the time. My rep as a drunk is exaggerated, but I don't mind people thinkin' I'm crazy, or crazier'n I really am. But lettin' people think I'm crazier'n hell is crazy itself, I reckon, 'cause the mask don't serve me too well. Anyhow, I'm here to get churched up. Even ran a warsh rag over my face and under my armpits before comin'."

"Good for you, Lucas. What you told me about Shiningfish now makes me more sure he's a great judge of character," Pack said.

"I think he's comin' this mornin'. I told him I put this preacher on notice last Sunday he better show he gives a damn about these people comin' here," Lucas said, as the Indian nodded his head in agreement.

Then Nick and Lucy Surgeon could be seen chugging up the hill, and when they drew closer Pack saw two figures in the backseat. They turned out to be Georgann and Tom. Heck, Tetu was wondering if the church would have room for all these people. A couple of minutes before eleven all the outside chatters went in together. Dar was beaming and Moms was already anchored to the seat closest to the pulpit (and also to the stove).

Pack and Tetu sat in the rearmost seats in order not to block the view of anyone to their rear. They were disappointed that Ranklin Shiningfish did not show up.

It was an aimless worship service. Dar had no theme, no title for his sermon, and no bulletin, presumably because there was no established order of worship. He did try to lead the people in singing, and to his credit this week did have reprints of the hymns selected, perhaps designed to mollify Lucas Lincoln. The sermon, however—if that's what it was—was again centered on Dar himself. Over and over he spoke about how he feared the new Governor and President would not attend to the material needs of "the least of these." It was clear he viewed himself and his congregation as victims of an "uncaring and unfeeling government." Connections between his words and the Bible were next to impossible to discern. Pack made up his mind on a course of action. When Dar had muttered his parting prayer, Pack stood up and walked to the front before the congregants left.

"Ladies and gentlemen, for those who do not know me, I am Simon Pack. I have an earnest plea. I'd like to thank Preacher Castor for this service. The church is a place to think about our faith. Please have faith in me now as I ask you, and I hope more of your neighbors, to attend this same church next Sunday, which you know is Christmas Day. Our faith in this church will be rewarded, I feel sure, in remarkable ways none of us can now explain. Mr. Lincoln, let me be bold and ask if you will agree to return next Sunday. Will you?" Pack knew this was a gamble. If Lincoln said no, he'd had enough, most of the others would also, given the unsatisfying nature of this service. Pack waited, watching Lincoln purse his lips and appear to bite his tongue. Finally, he said, "I'll be here, God willing," at which Pack was greatly relieved. The people filed out. Pack handed the Jeep key to Tetu and said, "I'll be a while, so get in the Jeep if you want."

Moms was back with Dar. Pack said to Dar, "May we have a word alone?" Dar looked at her and said, "I'll be along shortly." She didn't like it, but she left.

Pack began, tone mild to commence, eyes fixed directly on Dar's, who seemed aware he had an ass-chewing coming. "You're going to sit there, you're not going to interrupt, and you're going to listen to what I say whether you like it or not, and I can pretty much promise you won't like it. I think you live up here in a vacuum, you seldom go out, you don't know your neighbors in the valley, you have no church chain of command checking on you, you receive a meager stipend, you feel sorry for yourself, you view the people who came here this morning as poor ignorant victims, and you're jealous of anyone who's ever succeeded at anything. Further, because you've isolated yourself, you don't know what people are saying about you. Very, very much to *their* credit, they don't badmouth you, although right about now I'll say you deserve it. They want this church to be a significant, meaningful part of their lives. They want to enter the House of God and be touched by God. But you don't take their wants and needs into account. Unlike you, these people are not generally oriented on the material. They aren't looking to the government to take care of them. Let that compute—these are self-reliant people. And if you think they're unintelligent, then you're the stupid one. They have so many smarts it's staggering, and if you think about it, they almost have to because they are so self-reliant. Not long ago I saw a man named Craig Wood. They call him the medicine man, and I think it'd be worth your time to find him and learn why they call him that. Remember the little boy sitting here with his mother this morning? His name's Tom, and he would be dead if Craig Wood hadn't saved him. You need to get to know the folks in this valley. They are fantastic people.

"I want a direct answer to this question: when is the last time someone in your church hierarchy visited you?"

"No one so far," Dar replied.

"That's what I thought. Sorry, Reverend, but that doesn't speak well of them. As of now, *I am* filling that void.

"Next question: why was this service without focus...no, I'll refine the question and ask why the service was positively desultory, that is, why did it follow no established method of worship, no liturgy?"

"Because I believe in free-form worship," Dar said.

"You better have a good memory, because I'm going to give you a to-do list, and if it isn't accomplished by next Sunday, I might see to it that no one ever again crosses the doorway into this church.

"Show us that you care enough to make this feel like a church. There were people here who, had you requested volunteers, would've happily made wreaths and brought flowers to brighten it. Make them a part of the church.

"I'm no saint, and maybe in God's eyes, not so great a person either, but I read the Bible daily searching for answers. I defy anyone to say it's an easy book to understand. It's pretty hard, but one of the purposes of a church is to foster understanding of the Bible through mutual discussion. How much mutual discussion of the Bible has there been since you opened the doors of this church?"

"None," Dar said, head hung low.

"I'm willing to stipulate that you've had proper training in theology. But it didn't show today. Stop feeling sorry for yourself and become the minister you were ordained to be. If you can't do it, resign your commission and leave.

"I don't want the excuse that you prefer free-form. No, sir, you'll come here next Sunday with a service that follows an observable structure, and you'll present the people who enter with a copy of the structure.

"You've got to engage with the people. I'm going to plant a seed I haven't discussed with anyone yet. Someday soon we'll have a new resident of Yaak, a lovely young Blackfoot girl who's going to marry the big fellow with me in the back. Her name is Swan Threemoons, and she is passionately committed to establish a lay ministry to help abused females of the Kootenai tribe. I can see you, her, and possibly your wife running that operation right out of this church. Now I want you to think about these things. I'll be back around midweek, I think, to check on your progress. You can, you must, and you will."

Simon Pack sat there for a while, unsure which decision the disconsolate preacher would reach. Pack figured if one of Dar's church elders had said what Pack had, he or she would now see this as the time to offer words of encouragement on the way out. Pack didn't. He just walked out at a normal pace.

Pack had penned many Fitness Reports on chaplains in the Marine Corps. He'd never had to go as far as he had with Dar, but if he had, he would've called it "the Wayward Chaplain Speech."

Chapter Twenty-Four

Events of the next few minutes caused Pack to reflect that he might miss several of the appointments he had pledged to keep this week: the leaving of a message for Lucas Lincoln at Georgann's and the inspection of Dar's bucking up being chief among them.

Waiting beside a black unmarked SUV were a man and woman dressed more nicely than the locals. Pack knew instantly they were government types, probably FBI. And he was right.

The morning began on an eerie note, as from the camp they saw a rare occurrence, winter lightning in the leaden, heavy, gray southern sky. It had continued to be a gray day for the minister, and probably for the churchgoers, and possibly now for Pack himself. Yes, it had been the birth of morning, yet it felt that the curtain of darkness was draping itself over the Upper Yaak, that night was coming on.

The FBI woman was courteous enough to refer to Pack as 'General.' "General Pack," she said, showing her cred pack, "which is your vehicle?"

"The black Jeep," Pack answered.

"General, we're investigating the murder of Mr. William Strang of the Montana Fish, Wildlife, and Parks Department. We're going to ask you to follow us to Kalispell for questioning, but before we do we are obliged to search your vehicle. We are empowered to search for a black telescoping titanium nightstick. Do you own an item fitting this description?"

"I do," Pack answered, "and I can tell you where I stow it." He described the stowage configuration under the rear of the driver's seat, as well as the specific container it was in.

They had prevented Tetu from getting in the vehicle since they arrived. The male agent held up the canister Pack had described. "Was this the container you said it was in?"

"That's the one," Pack said. The agent unzipped it and shook it downward in the open position, showing Pack it was empty. The two agents said nothing more. They removed every item, opened every compartment, searched every tiny space.

"Could you have left it at home, sir?" the female asked.

"No," Pack said. "I keep it in this Jeep at all times."

"Does Mr. Palaita have access to it?"

"Of course he does. We're partners. He has access to everything I possess," Pack said, getting more irritated the more this went on. "Don't you think it's about time you told me why you're looking for my baton?"

"No, sir," the male said. "We'll do further talking down in Kalispell, so follow us."

"Be happy to," Pack said, willing to let his consternation show by crossing his arms, "but first we're stopping by our campsite to gather our camp equipment. That we most affirmatively will do."

Reverend Dar had tracked the questioning and searching through a small window at the front of the church, but was not sure how he felt about seeing Pack as the object of legal scrutiny.

The FBI maintains ten small offices in Montana. In a city like Seoul, they'd be the equivalent of police boxes. They all fall under the governance of the Bureau's Field Office in Salt Lake City. These two agents worked out of the small office in Kalispell, an office responsible for Lincoln and Flathead counties.

Once they had cleared the camp and paid the host, Pack let loose. "Tetu, I'm royally pissed. You haven't seen me in this state very often, but I figure it's good for me to go to this place every so often. Listen to me. I wouldn't be surprised if they did attach a listening device in here somewhere, so if they did, I'm speaking to both you and them. You know I had that defense baton behind the seat. You've seen it. I haven't taken it out of the canister in a long time, probably since we inventoried our weapons before going up into the Michigan woods. I've been set up. They haven't said so explicitly, but it's clear that's the weapon used to kill Game

Warden Strang. It'll be interesting to learn when he was murdered. I figure it was right after I saw him, and that whoever did it knew when and where we were going to meet. I think I know who that was. The good news is you weren't with me, and you didn't know the linkup location. Having said that, if they want to question you, get a lawyer...I'll pay for the service. I don't want you sullied in any way by this. Also, if they arrest me—and who the hell knows, they might—I've got several tasks I'd like you to perform for me up in the Yaak." He went on to describe the meetings he had planned to have with Lucas Lincoln and Reverend Dar Castor. Tetu read back for clarity of intent, and Pack proclaimed him ready to accept the mission. He also asked Tetu to tell Keeley not to get overwrought, that it would work out, but that she could see him in Kalispell. When Tetu had performed his missions he should report back to Pack, then return to the cabin to assist Keeley and Chesty.

Pack could sense where Tetu was. Tetu Palaita had burrowed into his cold cavern, his ice world, the personal habitat in which he was most dangerous. His mind was surging with rage, a hatred seething inside, wanting to rip the limbs from any and all responsible for abusing Matai. He was once more the mute Tetu, offering nothing to whoever might be on the other end of a listening device.

None of the churchgoers, or even the agents who were at the church to take Pack in, were aware that an unseen world of activity was engaged in this same matter, and none of the activity seemed to have much to do with the deceased or his family, with the exception of Governor James Dahl. Some of what the world at large, and in miniature, did not know was transpiring behind the scenes included the following:

Governor James Dahl got the word from his FWP director that they had lost one of their game wardens, he of District 75, Bill Strang. It looked like a murder, the FWP man told Dahl. Dahl instantly recalled Pack having asked him to speak with Jack Schnee about a relatively minor matter having to do with a game warden. Dahl called in Schnee, who explained in full what he and Pack had been looking into. Dahl pressed Schnee for an opinion on the matter, and Schnee said his educated guess was that Strang had been involved in illicit activity, although it was far from provable. Schnee further surmised that Pack himself had been trying to establish the evidence that would hold up in court. Some hours later Dahl received the devastating news that his predecessor and mentor, Simon Pack, had been detained for questioning by the FBI. Although Dahl knew with unbridled certainty that Pack had not committed the murder, he also knew he had to take every precaution to appear unbiased and dispassionate. A hundred thoughts sought purchase in his mind as he tried to establish not just a next step, but a series of steps that would lead to a favorable outcome for Pack.

In the nation's capital, White House Senior Advisor Sharon Locke approached the President, Keith Rozan, with the news. After nearly eight years at the President's side, Locke felt she had earned the right to be slightly less formal and more independent in the Administration's final month. She entered the Oval Office, waiting until Rozan looked up before she said, "Well, he's not dead yet, but he's in FBI custody." As much as the President hated Pack, he had no doubt to whom she referred.

"Pack?" he said with sudden enthusiasm.

"The one, the only, the man who has..." She almost said 'defeated,' but caught herself in time, and finished the sentence with, "stood in your way for years."

"Give it to me, tell me what he did this time," Rozan said, placing his calling hand next to the phone bank, ready to call someone. He was clearly infused with special energy.

Locke ran through the story concisely until the President interrupted with, "Stand by and listen in." The President was enjoying Locke's news. He rolled his classic Mont Blanc fountain pen up and down the palms of both hands, the phone on speaker.

He got the FBI Director on the line almost immediately. "I hear you've detained Simon Pack out there in no-man's land. So listen up, here's how you're gonna play it. You've detained him for questioning, which means to me you suspect him of involvement in this murder, which it damn sure looks to be. If an invisible string connects him to it, it's still a string. I want him arrested. Good job." He had hung up before the Director could say anything.

"Sharon, get the Communications Director in here. We need some good pictures for the press. We'll get actual photos of karmic justice."

Until the President's decision to get mixed up in the situation, it had been close hold. Even though Mollison was Sheriff of Flathead County, he was one of the last to learn what happened to his friend Simon Pack. Coincidentally, the seat of Flathead County was Kalispell, where Pack was now in FBI detention.

Six years ago Mollison joined with an Arizona sheriff to found an organization called the Constitutional Sheriffs and Peace Officers Association (CSPOA). The group's aim was to support the US Constitution. It had more than 500 members nationwide, about one-sixth of the total sheriffs around the country, and most of them were from the western states. They believed the federal government had overreached in the areas of guns, taxes, and land management. The Arizona sheriff argued that for local sheriffs, the feds "are the greatest threat we face today." It was not a crackpot association. They had challenged the Brady Bill's mandate for local sheriffs to perform background checks on gun buyers. That case wound up in the US Supreme Court, where the Arizona Sheriff and Mollison won.

When commentators criticized Mollison for refusing to follow the orders of federal officials, Mollison retorted that the officer who arrested Rosa Parks said he was simply following orders. If an order violates the Constitution of the United States, he countered, it is by definition unlawful. As a onetime Marine himself, he also reminded them that the military rule is that you are subject to court-martial if you willingly follow an unlawful order. At the same time, CSPOA stressed their purpose was to put the feds on notice not to put them in a situation in which they were forced to choose between the Constitution and a fed order that contravened its provisions. Further, Mollison always emphasized the association's desire to avoid violence and confrontation except as a very last resort.

Most relevant to the instant matter of Pack's detention, the CSPOA members had voluntarily signed a declaration that they would not tolerate any federal agent who attempted to seize property or arrest someone in their counties *without their consent*. Joe Mollison resolved to embark immediately on two courses of action. (1) Write a summary of this case for dissemination to all CSPOA members. (2) Go to meet the FBI on their turf, and firmly state his belief that they had no right to arrest Pack without his permission. Mollison felt sure Pack's detention for this long signaled the FBI's intention to arrest him.

Mollison was on good terms with the FBI people in his town. Because of the ongoing meth problem, he had extensive contact with them. But as he traveled the short distance to their office, he knew this promised to be a head-butting encounter. "Good to see you, Joe," the chief of this FBI shop said in greeting Mollison. "What can we do for you?"

"You can tell me why you have the recently-departed Governor of this state in one of your back rooms, questioning him as if he is a murderer, without mentioning a word of it to me," Mollison said. "You are familiar with our organization, CSPOA, and you know our beliefs. We've even debated those beliefs a bit. Way I see it you've violated our covenant. So you should know not to be surprised to find a couple hundred sheriffs outside your door tomorrow morning, telling you you will not get past us if you try to arrest Simon Pack. We don't want violence but we're not averse to it if you push us."

"Calm down, Joe," the Bureau man said soothingly. "Make sure you have your facts straight. At least do that. Sit down and let's talk this through."

"I'll talk with you, but I'll also talk with the Governor. I'm on the outskirts of this case and only know you've charged the finest damn man I've ever known with murder. You can show me what you've got, that's the least *you* can do," Mollison said.

"Come on, Joe, you know I can't do that...but give me a little time, and I'll see if there's a little something I can dislodge for your eyes only.

Correct me if I'm wrong, Joe, but CSPOA says fed agents can't arrest someone in a CSPOA sheriff's county, is that right?"

"That's right," Mollison answered.

"Then I'm afraid you've lost your argument, Joe, because we took custody of Pack in Lincoln County, where Hackman's not a member of CSPOA," the FBI man said.

"Does he have a lawyer with him back there?" Mollison asked.

"He doesn't need one yet, Joe, because he hasn't been arrested."

"Couple things, then: One, you said he doesn't need one yet. I take that to mean he probably will need one. Two, your statement that he was detained for questioning over in Lincoln County means nothing to CSPOA. Our position is that you need my consent to arrest him, which—if it does take place—will happen in Flathead County. Three, I'm asking a direct question: will you arrest him?"

The FBI did a great job teaching their people in the field how to comport themselves with resolution, poise, and calmness around suspects and interviewees. This man, however, was sitting with another officer of the law, and he was squirming. Mollison could tell this man didn't want to answer, because the answer was 'yes,' he would arrest Pack. After a long pause in which the FBI man seemed to be holding his breath, he finally answered. "Joe, I'm in real bind. I'm not at all sure I would arrest him, but word has come down from the top...the very top...and don't ask me for a name, because I won't answer...ordering me to arrest him."

They looked placidly at one another, each thinking of ways they might work together on this. The FBI man's name was Juan Martino. Juan said, "Joe, I like you. We've gotten together at least once a week to hash out operations, and we've never had problems, have we?"

"None that comes to mind," Mollison said. "So, I agree, let's talk and brainstorm this thing, see if we can reach an accommodation."

"Believe me, Joe," Martino said, "I've already thought seriously about telling my boss in Salt Lake that if grounds don't exist to arrest, I'm not going to do it. I'd feel good doing that, but you know what? That would accomplish nothing. I guarantee that, Joe. He would replace me in a heartbeat with someone who'll do his bidding. He is that kind of man, no question. At the risk of immodesty, I'll claim you're better off dealing with me than whoever would replace me."

"I don't want trouble either, you know that, but I also won't have Governor Pack railroaded. Let's do some 'what if.' I'll start. When I get out of here, I'll call his gal friend and ask her to get the best lawyer she can find and get him here quick. He'll probably say your case won't stand up and he'll demand you release Pack. You say no, he's under arrest for the murder of the game warden. Meantime, the lawyer's investigators find evidence exculpating Pack, and the FBI looks bad. My group is outside demanding Pack's release also, and we tell you if you intend to move him to Salt Lake or wherever, we'll stop you. Also, there's the little matter of putting him in a jail, which happens to belong to me. He will not be welcome in my Flathead County Adult Detention Center, so you would be forced to transport him elsewhere. So there we are, our weapons against yours. Maybe Washington pressures Governor Dahl to deploy the National Guard to remove me and my sheriffs. Think Dahl's going to comply with that? I don't, but maybe I'm wrong, we'll see. At that point we have a big-time standoff, with the nation's eyes trained on little old Kalispell. Options aren't good, are they?"

"No, they're not," Martino said. "Best option is to find convincing evidence to clear Pack as quickly as possible. Aw, hell's bells, Sheriff, let's close the door. Maybe I can give you some ideas."

Tetu collected himself sufficiently well to update Keeley on Pack's disposition. She took it like a trouper. She was not the type to shriek, panic, or freeze into inaction. Quite the opposite, she focused her mind, and set off on a search for legal representation. Because she was still unfamiliar with this part of the state, she called the brightest person she knew, Wilkie Buffer. He told her not to fret, it wouldn't take him long to find the right person. Wilkie said no need for me to call you back; if you trust me, I'll have him phone you directly.

His name was Hawk Rawley, and he was as flamboyant as his name. He dressed in buckskins and bolo ties and, when outdoors, wore a huge Stetson. The legal world knew him as The Cowboy Lawyer. He happened to be undefeated in capital cases, and he took only the ones that garnered the greatest publicity. He told Keeley he was expensive, to which she replied, "would you like cash or check?" He promised he would be in Kalispell before nightfall, and Keeley told him she would meet him there, opening payment in hand.

Hawk Rawley looked every bit the Cowboy Lawyer. He was tall, early sixties, with weathered skin as if he were a rancher, and he was driven up to the FBI office in an expensive limo. He met Keeley in a waiting area, and asked how Simon was doing. "I don't know," she said, "they haven't allowed me back there to speak with him. You know, 'you're not his wife' so we can't give you special consideration,' and so on."

"Well, Missy, I'm going to fix things up. Just have a seat a while longer, and let me see him. Just remember this, sweetie: you've hired the best, and the Governor couldn't be in better hands."

Keeley sighed, but swallowed her instinct to chastise him for his chauvinism. "As long as he can do the job..." she thought.

After a time he came out. The Cowboy Lawyer looked like he'd been in a rodeo and the bull got the better of him. You could say it wasn't just his brow that was furrowed. His face was furrowed. He clearly did not have the good news Keeley anticipated. "This is gonna be harder than I thought, Missy. I'm fightin' politicians, not arguin' the law, 'pears to me. But not to fret. I've fought these bastards before, and I know how to beat 'em. Wanna stand beside me in a news conference in front of this historic old Courthouse around noon tomorrow?" Keeley did not answer, but considered that standing by Rawley in front of the media would be totally inappropriate.

Governor Jim Dahl knew Tetu as well as anyone except Pack. He had people trying to contact the big Samoan all day but had been told Tetu was on the go, doing tasks Pack had asked him to do. Late that night,

Tetu called the Governor back. He was using Georgann's phone in the general store. Dahl was interested in what Tetu knew about the charges, as well as in how Tetu was handling the entire matter. Tetu decided to go ahead and mix fact with opinion guided by his observations. He laid out Pack's reasons for insinuating himself into the goings-on in the Upper Yaak. He emphasized the point that Pack did want not to lay a problem at Dahl's feet that he believed he himself was responsible for. When Pack embarked on his Yaak mission, he was not sure a problem existed. It didn't take him long, however, to confirm his suspicions, as well as to establish there were crooked law officers abetting criminal activity. As he was closing in on the source of the problem, Tetu said, the game warden was murdered and it was pinned on Pack.

Dahl asked if Tetu could come down to Kalispell to meet him tomorrow morning, early. Tetu said resolutely, "Is hard to say no to my friend and teacher Governor Dahl, who Matai loves much, but Tetu has assignments from Matai that are important to Matai. He must finish doing what Matai asked. If Tetu has luck, he might get information that can help Matai."

"You're a good man, Tetu, a great friend to the General. I understand your position. But, listen, if you get any information, any, that you think might help him, call me at this number as soon as you can, any time of day or night, OK?" Dahl said.

The first thing Dahl did after sorting out his courses of action was to call a man then-General Pack had relied upon a couple of times for counsel in critical moments. His name was Charlie Ramstedt, and he was Deputy Director of the FBI. He had demonstrated he could be trusted to be honest and to maintain confidentiality. After the first few minutes of back and forth, it was evident that the arrest of Pack was a political decision. Dahl learned off the record that the FBI Director was mad as hell that he'd been ordered to arrest Pack and, because the President allowed no rebuttal, retort was not possible. The Director had told Ramstedt to look into the matter and report back to him. Ramstedt informed Dahl that no reasonable prosecutor would take this case, chiefly because it rested almost exclusively on the testimony of one man, Sheriff Bob Hackman of

Lincoln County. "Flimsy at best," Ramstedt had described the evidence against Pack. Dahl expressed his gratitude for Ramstedt's continuing support of the Dahl-Pack duo. Ramstedt concluded by saying, "I know you two are tight, and have been a long time. General Pack has been through enough tribulations for a platoon of men, but he'll make it through this trial too. With your support, Jim, if you catch my drift."

"I do indeed, Charlie. Once in a while, it's nice to have friends in high places. Thanks indeed."

Before Dahl took a command position in the Marine Corps for the first time, a wise old head told him, "Not everyone gets this chance. Take full advantage of it. Do it your way. You're a good man, so I can tell you to trust your instincts, and don't be afraid to act on them. When in command, by damn take command." Thus, after sitting alone with his thoughts for an hour, he recalled those words and resolved now, less than two months into his gubernatorial tenure, to take charge.

Dahl called in the Lieutenant Governor, told her she would assume his original schedule for the next day, and perhaps longer. She was slowly growing into her job, showing herself smart enough to process large volumes of information swiftly. She liked explicitly being placed in charge of the Helena operation. Meantime, Dahl was taking Jack Schnee with him to Kalispell.

Tetu Palaita was hard at work. He had run down Lucas Lincoln, with Georgann's help, and with Lincoln tucked in the Jeep, linked up with Ranklin Shiningfish as well. They made an odd team, one of them widely considered loony, and the other two looked upon as brooding and laconic. A psychologist, however, would have wanted to study the impact each had on the others. There was a quality of realness in each that communicated itself effortlessly, the result of which was instantaneous solidarity. Tetu told them his Matai had been charged, and that was wrong, and it was their duty to find out what was really going on, and who was responsible for Strang's death. Old Lucas was fully alert, acting as if he were the captain of a ship, making sure every detail was attended to.

Tetu found that no one had spoken to Shiningfish about the crime. Hackman's deputies had relieved him at the scene, but it was done wordlessly. Whether those Lincoln County guys analyzed the scene was unknown to the Ranger. Tetu asked Ranklin Shiningfish for details of what he had observed. "Not many vehicles venture into this area," Shiningfish said, "in winter especially. We had warmer weather than normal, so it was muddy. When I came by, I saw three sets of tracks into this location. One was Strang's FWP truck, which was still parked there. Besides his there were two others, both fresh and both about same age, I would say. I stayed away from those tracks, did not drive over them or in them. Parked over there," he said, pointing to firmer ground a bit higher up the hill. "I stopped because I saw FWP truck I know was Strang's, with driver door open, Strang out of sight at first. Just took a moment to see him lying face down at front of truck. Big gash in back of his head, like he had been leaning on truck hood, got hit from behind. Right off to side, in the mountain grass over there, I saw metal billyclub, the type that opens up by flipping it open. Able to see it because it was partly extended, and metal stuck out. First thought was why would killer leave it there. I think most people would take murder weapon with them, right?"

"Plain as day," Tetu said. "Leaving it intended to put blame on owner. Someone knew Matai was meeting game warden, then comes after and uses weapon he stole from Matai. Who knew Matai was meeting with game warden? Three tracks you said, one from game warden truck, one from Jeep there, and one from killer. After that another County sheriff truck comes. Where did it park?"

"I kept them back," the Ranger said. "Made them walk about fifty meters."

"Did you see them make prints of tire tracks?" Tetu asked.

"It was getting dark. Not while I was here," Shiningfish said.

Lucas spoke up. "I bet you woulda called for a tire print, though, right?" he asked, looking at Ranklin.

"Yes, but I fell down in not telling them what to do. If any of the Lincoln County cops went to the Academy, it does not show. I should not have counted on them to do the job right. My fault. Cannot see anything they have ever done for people up here," Ranklin said.

"You're way too nice," Lucas interjected. "They're assholes, enda story. Tell 'em they's a murder in progress it'll take 'em three days to show up. Call in someone pissin' in the woods they'll be up in two hours."

"Not a bad point," Ranklin said. "They got up here quick this time, did they not?"

Tetu said, "Ranger Shiningfish, we have cameras. We ask if they at least took pictures of tire marks, but even if they did we ought to take our own. You will say what you think order was they drove in. Also, we will make rough measures of track widths."

They took their photos and measurements. Before continuing to the next part of their operation in the field, they returned to Georgann's store so Tetu could call in his little team's initial findings to Governor Dahl.

The town of Kalispell has a population of about 22,000. This small-town seat of Flathead County was overnight becoming the center of attention in the entire United States of America. As had been the case for almost every day of the last five years, Simon Pack was a man whom the media simply could not ignore. History had found him, he had not looked to insert himself into it. His achievements had virtually reached the level of lore, yet the truth was the public appreciated him more for his calm demeanor, fixed values, and fearlessness before the country's business and political titans. When the national media heard Pack was about to be behind bars, they leapt on it with the vigor usually reserved for the most major stories in the nation's history. They were scrambling like fighter jets to an enemy attack. Getting a hotel room anywhere in the wider Bitterroot region was suddenly difficult.

Keeley Eliopoulous and Hawk Rawley already had theirs and they weren't letting them go.

Sheriff Joe Mollison had commitments from 200 CSPOA sheriffs to arrive for support. Roughly 75 were already on the ground.

The Governor and his party also had rooms. The Governor's party happened to be large. At the moment he was on the road in the midst of a large state police escort. Dahl intended to arrive at the FBI office at 0900. He had not called ahead to either the FBI or Sheriff Mollison. He had, however, taken a call enroute from Tetu Palaita, and he found it most useful.

Shiningfish and Lucas Lincoln were in the general store as Tetu called the Governor. When he hung up, Tetu looked at his new partners and told them, almost sheepishly, "Tetu had to decide. Governor wants Tetu to meet him in Kalispell with information we gathered, so Tetu thinks it time to go there. Thank you for helping Matai Pack. Tetu is most sorry to let Mr. Lincoln down, but he promises to go back into forest with you when he finishes in Kalispell. Would that be good?"

Shiningfish spoke up. "Tetu, I will take Lucas and we will search all day. If we do not find what we are looking for, you can help when you return."

Neither Tetu nor Lucas appeared to notice that Shiningfish had not yet employed a contraction in his speech. This Shiningfish was, you might say, seriously formal in his manner of speech.

The FBI office was ground zero. Mollison had his CSPOA sheriffs in a holding area a mile away, with Mollison briefing them on their tactical plan of operation at the FBI facility. He was planning to deploy his people at 1000 hours.

The media were there already, setting up cameras, notebooks in hand, staff printing notes on whiteboards as talking guides for on-air personalities, some here and there rehearsing their opening salvos of sound bites. They didn't know what was about to occur, but whatever it was promised to be exciting. There was sufficient buzz in the air from which a reasonable person could surmise that a serious conflict was about to be played out, and it was a conflict that involved nearly every level of the American government.

Hawk Rawley didn't know it, but his pledge to speak at high noon was likely to be upstaged.

Chapter Twenty-Five

Ng Trang was now winging his way out of the San Francisco Bay heading to the Far East. In the days between saying goodbye to the Yaak and boarding this flight, he was as mellow and satisfied as he ever allowed himself. The reason for that languid state of mind was secondarily because this mission promised the proverbial pot of gold at the end of the rainbow. Primarily, however, it was because he was able for the first time to understand, and to take stock of, the reasons he had become the international power player he was. He asked himself how many people would feel as serene as he when such pressures of time and performance had been applied. He loved to think deductively, from the general to the specific, and to make all the pieces coalesce into a work of living art.

To begin with, he saw himself back in Sarajevo. What a contrast! Those teaboys were speaking self-importantly on behalf of faceless wealthy oil tycoons who, but for their oil, would be teaboys themselves. They were all his intellectual inferiors. It was right and just that they should be separated from a sum of money that to them collectively was small beer stuff. Those men had thrown around terms the Americans had attached to age-old military concepts, but which they used--for example, 'asymmetric warfare'--as if they were original to them. They kept asking Ng if he understood what they were talking about. *Duh*...as the current American dismissal of stupid comments goes. *No, Aristotle and Plato, that's too hard a concept for me to comprehend.* Did they truly understand who and what they were getting when they hired me? You're damned straight this assignment will take world-class brains to pull off, but that's what you're getting. I have under a month left in which to make it happen.

Anyway, he was thinking, back to the deductive reasoning thing. I have to put together a team of experts, a task mostly done, and it's refreshing to be dealing from now on with people who survive by brains instead of brawn like that riffraff I employed in the Upper Yaak. And it's also comforting to know I was in the right place all along. That was no accident. Great men are regularly the beneficiaries of good fortune. See, I'll be using the Yaak again, and I'll sweeten the pot for Strang to make sure all the lawdogs look the other way. Been there, done that. I find Strang reprehensible, a smarmy little snot, but I don't have to like him. I pay him, he does the job, he keeps his mouth shut, and jimmy crack corn, the rest doesn't matter. A rule of this business is never to have personal relationships with the people working for you. Be prepared to kill everyone you meet. I'll tell him to work up a protection plan for those caves up near the border, the ones we've used before as cache sites.

They're paying me to terrorize Americans. That's not hard to do these days. People in America seem nervous most of the time. They get jittery if someone bruises their feelings. Snowflakes melt easily. They want asymmetrical warfare, with a resultant degree of terror out of all proportion to the numbers of people actually killed or wounded. They want what I will engineer to be on the tongues of everyone in the world within an hour after the events. I recommended the weapons, they agreed, and they will have competent operators at the several locations. They're jihadists, foolish young men and women ready for martyrdom. Go martyrs! I say, because if they're absolutely successful that would mean no one left to connect me.

They're giving me 10%, a nice sum itself, plus operating expenses up front with the balance to be transferred to my overseas account upon mission completion. There will be more jobs like this, they say, and while I ordinarily don't trust any of them, they're so out of their minds with hatred, so manifestly filled with a loathing unruly as a flood toward the infidel that I can believe them on this declaration.

Now here I am on a crappy Cebu Pacific jet heading toward the island of Cebu in the central Philippines to meet with more of them. When A'nh asked my reason for coming here, I told her, "It's surely not for the maize and chili peppers, babe." I'll take watercraft for the inter-island travel down to Basilan, then be met by the Abu Sayyaf jihadists who'll ferry me over to the Autonomous Region of Muslim Mindanao.

These Abu Sayyaf guys are good. I've done business with them at least a dozen times, and they always get what I want, and they've got excellent connections with the Chinese shipping agents in Vancouver. So, while this operation has several points where it could all unravel, none has yet, thanks primarily to these guys and their Chinese buddies on the other end of the sea lane. And they work cheap.

The flight attendant brought him Lumpia and rice and an ersatz wine, which he consumed before falling asleep.

Chapter Twenty-Six

Keeley was getting worked up. She left the hotel early, tired of sitting around waiting for Hawk Rawley to update her on his new plan. She got in her car and drove over past the Courthouse to the FBI facility. What she saw was startling, even for a lady with her savoir-faire and worldliness. There was a tangle of communications trucks and cars of all makes and models. She did not stop, just kept struggling her way through the clotted mess until she found an opening in the road. A mile away she saw Sheriff Joe Mollison speaking to a clump of other sheriffs. Should she risk interrupting him? She got out of her car and began walking in his direction, but was not eager to have him see her. Shielded from view, she listened in as Sheriff Joe expressed his passionate belief that this arrest of Simon Pack was illegal, and was the true reason for their association. He explained that they were going to the facility to show their resolve, not their weapons, which he ardently hoped would remain holstered. One sheriff raised his hand to ask what outcomes Joe and the Arizona sheriff were seeking, then he amended his question to ask what outcomes would be acceptable. The Arizona sheriff answered, saying only one outcome would be acceptable, and that would be to release Simon Pack under his own recognizance until they had convincing evidence he had committed the murder. That the FBI had not produced that evidence for the sheriff in the county of the arrest was all that was needed to decry the arrest. As the Arizona sheriff was speaking, Sheriff Joe's mobile rang.

"Sorry, Joe, for not informing you sooner, but I couldn't risk a leak. This is Governor Jim Dahl, and I'm coming to take General Pack out of FBI custody. I hope it doesn't get nasty. We're about 10 minutes from the destination. I have 80 state troopers who will escort me in. Since we spoke last, I've gotten more information on what happened up in the Yaak with that game warden, and there is no doubt they have the wrong man. This is a political witchhunt, Joe, which I suppose you've already figured out. I understand you have CSPOA on station, which is fine, but I'll ask you to go into backup mode. President Rozan told me to deploy the National Guard to assure you and your people didn't get him out. Last I checked the National Guard is under my direction, not the Federal government's, so...to put it gently...I declined his order. Let me do my thing at the FBI's place before you announce what I've told you, OK?"

"We had a great governor," Mollison said by way of reply, "and now we have another one. Good job, Governor. When this is all over, let's have a two big Governors and one lowly Sheriff confab down at the Sundance."

"It'll happen, Sheriff. See you later."

Attorney Rawley was still in his hotel room rehearsing the speech he would make on the Courthouse steps at noon. He was good and he knew it. Sure, he didn't get anywhere the evening before, but on the positive side it opened the door for him to speechify in public, far and away his favorite part of lawyering. He finally pronounced himself ready, and slowly donned his buckskins and custom boots, all the while gazing happily at his handsome damn self reflected in the full-length mirror. "The Hawk's 'bout to swoop down and swaller some mice for lunch today," he said, chuckling to himself.

Instantly upon hanging up Mollison called for deputies to clear the streets around the FBI building, not telling them it was so the Governor's motorcade wouldn't encounter a snarl there. On schedule, Dahl's cavalcade of state vehicles swarmed the street in front of the facility, troopers leaping out ahead of Dahl and shortly forming a cordon around him. Dahl's group walked up the short flight of steps and Dahl himself pressed the buzzer. When he got a reply, he said, "Governor James Dahl. Open your door." He could see the small camera capturing his progress all the way up the walkway.

Dahl got buzzed in and proceeded back to a young lady manning a desk. "I want to see the person in charge. Now."

In less than a minute, the person in charge appeared, announcing himself as Agent Juan Martino. Dahl got straight to the point. "I'm here to take General Simon Pack out of your control. It would be embarrassing to you for me to recount the reasons I'm taking him, and you know that, so I will refrain from going into that level of detail. If and when you actually develop a case, you can have him, provided you present that evidence to Sheriff Mollison first. Let's make this quick. Would you like us to go back and get him or would you prefer to hand him over out here?"

"We're all accountable," Agent Martino said, "and I'm accountable to the Special Agent in Charge in Salt Lake City. I'll have to discuss this with him."

"Your internal policies don't interest me at this moment," Dahl said. "I don't have time to argue. Get the General."

"This is unprecedented, Governor. You can't walk in and demand a prisoner be handed over to you. I'm trying to help you in reminding you that you might be accountable to the Salt Lake FBI chief as much as me. And think for a moment, this will involve the Attorney General of the United States in no time at all. And I would imagine the President as well. Sure you want to lock horns with them?"

"You don't know your history very well, Martino. General Pack and I already have locked horns with them, so notice, if you will, I'm not shaking."

Martino stared at the floor, locked in thought, and Dahl believed he knew what Martino was thinking. So Dahl took the initiative again, changing tack. "Listen, Agent Martino. Here's what I think: you're at the bottom of this organization right now—you probably are skilled in your duties, and have hopes of moving up, given your youth—but still, you understand you've been put in an untenable position. You know you're holding General Pack before you've even commenced a real investigation. When this is all over, Pack's going to be released anyway, and young Agent Martino will be left holding a sack of crap, to wit, no evidence that will stand up in a court of law, and you'll be the subject of a case study at Quantico about how not to make an arrest. Your peers will mock you, and you'll never advance, and maybe you'll even be relieved. But you're on the horns of a dilemma, which is like that of the captain of the ship who can't give up without a fight.

"Now look at my troopers here. They have hands on their still-holstered weapons. Believe me, we're taking Pack out of here, even if we must resort to force. I give you my *solemn...oath...as...a...Marine*, that's the truth. Now, I ask you, what is the way out of this dilemma? I think you know."

Martino chewed on the inside of his jaw and shuffled his feet, coming to a decision. "Yes, I do. I have to appear to have put up a fight. Arrest *me* for unlawful apprehension...but leave my team in place. I'll bring General Pack out."

Martino was gone just long enough, in Dahl's view, to brief his team on what was taking place. Then he appeared with General Simon Pack, who was looking as stolid, stoic, and determined as ever. After shaking Dahl's hand, Pack informed Dahl he would be back in touch shortly. Pack had spotted Keeley and sped toward her.

Then other storms loomed, as Dahl knew they would.

The chief of the Salt Lake FBI office had never encountered anything like this, but he thought intervening was above his pay grade. He batted it to Washington, where the still-piqued Director batted it to the Attorney General. The AG called Dahl's action "unconscionable," but she didn't want to be involved either, so with a month remaining in office, she batted it to the Office of the President. Rozan knew it would come down to this, so he prepared a statement. "I'm willing to give the Governor of Montana the benefit of the doubt. He's been in his position only weeks, really, and may have received bad legal advice from his own attorney general. I also am aware he has no legal training. He was just a military man, and so may well be out of his element at this point. Based on the solid evidence we had, Simon Pack should be behind bars. I, however, am a fair man, and generous...sometimes, I suppose, to a fault. I am therefore amenable to having the case against Mr. Pack re-examined by other legal experts. If, after that occurs, and the evidence is as strong as I am told it is, I will certainly have the man apprehended." The President did not desire to engage with the media on this matter. From the President's point of view,

Pack the Second, James Dahl, had temporarily gotten the measure of him.

Dahl phoned Charlie Ramstedt in Washington. As Dahl spoke, Ramstedt interrupted to say, "I appreciate what you're telling me, Governor, but I really think we should have the Director on the line."

The conversation paused until the Director could join the talk. Dahl said, "Your agent in Kalispell, Juan Martino, conducted himself professionally. In order to hand General Pack over, he had to be arrested. I had a wall of state troopers in his office. He resisted laudably, and insisted his people be immune from my action. You can be proud of him.

"At this point I want to go off the record. Will you give me your word we can do that?"

"Go ahead," the Director said. "You have my word."

"Your man admitted he had not been at liberty even to begin a proper investigation yet. I have more information about the crime than he does, I'm sorry to say. It is clear this is not how the FBI does business. This arrest had its origin in the White House, I believe, an educated opinion I do not expect you to confirm or deny. I would be no kind of leader if I allowed General Pack to languish behind bars even one minute longer. He is simply one of the best Americans we've seen in an exceedingly long time, but I understand that's not sufficient reason to demand his release. The fact is your agency lacks evidence strong enough to arrest him. The police forces in my state are quite eager to share the leads we have if you will pursue them with an eye toward genuine justice. Further, I'd like to request you reinstate Agent Martino into his position, and allow him to conduct the investigation. I am absolutely confident he will do a great job, and he will have no interference from anyone in the state. What say you, Director?"

"I say you're a helluva leader, Governor. I understand what you're doing here, and I respect it. There'll be heat on my end, and I might be fired in a day or two, but let me handle all that. Martino can go back to work without prejudice."

Dahl dispatched most of the troopers back to normal duty as he and Jack Schnee waited for Tetu to arrive. In surprisingly incisive fashion, Tetu explained to the Governor what he, Shiningfish, and Lucas Lincoln had found. Dahl captured the photos Tetu had shot as well as the tire track measurements. Dahl finally understood what a shoddy crime scene it had been. Had the site been taped off? Dahl asked, but of course the reply was negative.

Dahl was taking notes on everything Tetu related. He said, "Did the General meet with Strang that day?"

"Yes," Tetu said, "but Tetu did not go."

"And what else do you know about the General's relationship with Strang?" Dahl asked.

"Tetu cannot say with sureness. But I think he had idea Strang wasn't enforcing law as supposed to." Dahl glanced at Schnee, who nodded in affirmation.

Schnee decided to interject. "Boss," he said to Dahl, "I think our investigators need to speak with Bill Damon, Strang's intern, again. Where was he when the murder took place? If Strang was in an out-of-the-way setting, which he was, how did whoever killed him know where he would've been? I don't believe it was someone randomly wandering the woods or a hunter with whom he had a sudden set-to. Maybe Damon can help us."

"Also," Tetu picked up where he left off, "Matai told us he thought something was not right between Strang and Sheriff in Lincoln County. Where was Sheriff at that time? Maybe visit to Sheriff's office necessary."

The FBI would be back in the lead in the investigation, but Dahl had no doubt that the sufficiently-chastised Agent Juan Martino would henceforth tie in seamlessly with all elements of Montana law enforcement.

Dahl's phone buzzed. It was Pack, apologizing for his abrupt exit. He thanked Dahl, then told him that after a night at the cabin he had further business in the Upper Yaak, which he intended to pursue re-commencing tomorrow. Dahl passed on Mollison's hope that soon the three of them could get together at the Sundance.

Before signing off, Dahl admonished Pack: "Take care of yourself, General, and I don't think I've ever spoken those words with such gravity. You have to keep in mind there really are people who wish you harm."

Sheriff Bob Hackman had been watching the morning's events in Kalispell on TV. He saw how it ended, with Governor Dahl leading Pack out. And now he was worried. If Dahl had the chutzpah to walk in there and forcibly release Pack, he must not believe the evidence implicating Pack. Dahl was known to be a bold leader, yes, but he was also rational. Hackman's agitation called for two Tums, but he told himself to act as if he were just waking up from a nap. He walked over to the snack room hoping to get a sense of what his deputies thought of those events.

Acting uninterested in the news, he slowly drew himself a cup of coffee and pretended to be searching for a pack of sugar substitute. One of the cops there was officer Tom Wilson. No one was biting on Hackman's attempt to draw out their reactions, so Hackman threw it out there, "Whaddya think, gang? That was a helluva thing Dahl did, huh? Threw the FBI way up under the bus, didn't he?"

Wilson said, "We don't know, do we, Sheriff, what evidence they had to make the arrest? Maybe the Governor knew they had nothing, and he was simply stopping a miscarriage of justice."

"Listen, son," Hackman said, "those FBI boys are pro's. They operate by the rules, each time, every time. Nobody plays closer attention to the rules than them. My money says if they think Pack's guilty, he most likely is." Hackman did not appreciate Wilson walking out of the room without further comment. Hackman wouldn't stand for insolence.

"Wilson, get back in here," Hackman called out. "What you just did right there is a show of dis-damn-respect, and you'll damn well apologize." He said this in front of the three other officers present. Everyone, including Hackman, was uncomfortable at this turn in the proceedings.

"Gee, Sheriff," Wilson said, "no disrespect intended. I thought you asked a question, and I replied, and that's all there was to it."

Wilson had touched a nerve. Hackman said angrily, "All right, all of you, listen. I for one got no love for Simon Mister General Mister Governor Pack. I saw the bunch of you swooning over him when he came in here, as if he's some high-and-lordly Hollywood star. I had a good friend named Bill Strang, and I believe the bastard murdered him.

Let's get one damn thing straight, right now. I'm the boss here. Anyone here doubt that?"

Wilson noted the non-sequiturs in the Hackman tirade, but like his peers, kept still. Hearing no one come to his defense, Hackman stormed back to his own office, liberally sloshing coffee onto the carpet in his wake. One of the officers shrugged his shoulders and lifted his eyebrows in a show of befuddlement.

In his office, still fuming and somewhat fearful, Hackman's phone rang. It was Joe Mollison, who said succinctly, "We need to meet at the county line."

They got there about the same time. SUVs parked nose to nose, they met in the center. "What's this about, Joe? Still pissed I didn't join CSPOA?"

"You wish that's what this is about, Bob. But I'm actually kinda pleased you never joined. If you don't mind high-handed feds, you oughtn't be a member. And that's exactly what we saw with General Pack's arrest, high-handed feds. Nosir, this is about something different, and I think you know it. See, I'm not the simple-minded Sheriff next door, as seems to me you think I am. I've cogitated quite a bit on Strang's murder, and I believe you know who did it. Why didn't you step up and speak? It took place in your county, after all."

"Get serious, would ya? The FBI took the reins right off the bat. It was and is their investigation. On the other hand, I do have my suspicions," Hackman said.

"Did you express your suspicions to the FBI, then?" Mollison asked.

"They didn't seem interested, so I said nothing," Hackman responded. After Mollison had no quick comeback, Hackman said, "Strang told me many times about all the problems that intern gave him. Said the young man was lazy, just wanted to spend time in the headquarters where he could bootlick. Had a hard time with him. Also had poor relations with that Forest Ranger, Shiningfish, I think his name is. Could be either of them, or maybe he had a run-in with a hunter and it went sour."

"And which of those seems most likely to you?" Mollison said.

"I had to choose, I'd say it was that intern," Hackman said.

"Hmmm, that's interesting, Bob. Cause I don't think it's any one of those choices. I think it was you."

"Whoa, buddy, you treading on squishy ground now. You are out of your Flathead mind," Hackman said, beginning to pace around in small circles, his right hand gripping his Smith & Wesson. He halted suddenly, squinting hard at his fellow County lawman. "You better be damned cautious in making a wild-assed charge like that."

"OK, forget it, Bob. Don't want to get you all steamed up. I'll speak in a calm voice to say those feds you don't think are high-handed are now looking in your direction. I'm just giving you a heads-up."

Mollison's swift change of tone nonplussed Hackman. He didn't know whether to apologize to Mollison or kill him. He swiveled his head as a means of giving himself time to think. Before he could reply, Mollison said, "One final question, Bob. Did you nail down crime scene tape to preserve the murder site?"

"I'm finished talking, Joey," a crimson-faced Hackman said, stamping off to his cruiser. "And take that stupid Constitutional Sheriffs Association and stuff it up your anal cavity," he yelled childishly.

Mollison had accomplished his objective. Hackman had played his hand, which consisted of identifying fall guys. Now he could tell his story to the FBI. When Hackman said the intern was lazy, Mollison picked up on what he thought was an important tell: Hackman raised one eyebrow, tantamount to a direct admission he knew he was lying, but it was a lie too easily checked out, too late to retract.

As circumstances unfolded there was no immediate need for Hawk Rawley's services. Neither Rawley nor Keeley felt Pack was comfortably home free yet, though, so she kept him on retainer just in case. Rawley understood he wasn't the proximate reason Pack got freed, but he wouldn't mind if potential clients thought otherwise.

Chapter Twenty-Seven

Tetu had been in Kalispell on Monday, taking his findings to the authorities, but had missed going out with Lucas Lincoln at the agreed upon time. He spent Monday night at Pack's cabin with Pack and Keeley. Keeley pronounced that day as one of those memorably pleasant, big American days, like the Presidential Inauguration and the lunar landing and the completion of the transcontinental railroad or the Empire State Building. A grand day. So she planned to prepare a very special multi-course meal to celebrate the occasion. The basic meal would be chicken and herbal cornmeal dumplings, but it would also consist of a broad assortment of side dishes, as well as an eye-catching dessert tray. Pack and Tetu were allowed to set the table, but not much more. She ran the kitchen, and wanted this meal to be her work alone. Pack had always held, but never expressed, his idea that a woman highly skilled in the kitchen is usually an innately intelligent woman, quite creative, and an above-average problem-solver. And, he further thought, it also is rare to find such a woman without high character, although he had not assayed why that should be.

It was a meal he would recall into his dotage, as it turned out. To have shopped for all these wonderful—but some unusual—items must have meant she had already planned this meal. This wasn't a meal you put together with the things you had in the cupboard. As she went about her preparations, she asked the men seated at the table about what they had been doing, and of course she was especially interested in the details of Pack's confinement. It was a cheerful chat, with all three happy to talk.

Pack said, "Those FBI people were trying to figure a way out of the mess they recognized they were in. It was as if a huge sack of groceries had been dropped on them, pinning them to the floor. They weren't injured, but were flailing around, twisting back and forth, trying to crawl out from under it. That sack of groceries, obviously, was the orders they'd gotten from higher up in their chain. They just yet didn't have the experience to know how to handle it. A military person would've seen at the start he'd been issued an unlawful order, and would have protested it. The FBI guys were good people, I think, and might have protested, but first they had to get that sack of groceries off their collective chest. Dahl handled the situation perfectly. But all that aside, you can't overlook the fact that, to use my analogy, an unlawful order was issued somewhere up the chain. I'm not conspiratorial, but I'd be dumb not to believe the President was the one pulling the strings. I railed for years in the Marine Corps and at West Point about creating a professional environment in which you can decentralize decision authority, so this kind of thing gets under my skin wherever I see it. Was the President briefed on the details of what actually happened to that game warden? Almost assuredly not. Just as much to the point—and no callousness intended toward Strang's family, if he has one—but why is the President of the United States concerned about the murder of a single person out in Montana when there are thirty or forty a weekend in Chicago? One answer, actually an excuse, is because the murder happened on federal land. The real answer is because I was said to be the person of interest, and my name got his attention, so naturally he morphed me into the prime suspect. He has been out to nail me for five years and hasn't yet, but he still has another month in office, I have to remember that. The other side of the coin is that he's leaving the Presidency in a month, and won't have to pay for trying to destroy my life. That's just how it works. Enough of this. Can we change the topic, Keel, and let's enjoy being together with fine food? And drink," he concluded, starting to sip his Negroni.

When they had finished the main course, Pack couldn't resist: "Miss Keeley, that was real good, but...."

"But what?" she said in mock fury.

"Not a big thing, Miss Keeley, really, but those dumplings had a touch too much fennel," Pack said, not wanting to staunch a good laugh. Tetu grinned ear to ear.

"Know how I know you're lying?" Keeley asked. "Because you don't know fennel from a funnel."

Keeley and Chesty stayed back again as Pack and Tetu set out on the familiar drive to the Upper Yaak. Pack was giving solid consideration to tarrying in Libby a bit to confront Sheriff Bob Hackman. Pack was driving this trip, and pulled over well before Libby to make a call. He had noted Officer Tom Wilson's number in his phone Contacts list. He pressed the number, waited, and got lucky. "Officer Wilson, Simon Pack here. You on duty?"

"Go on in two hours, sir. What's up?"

"Wondering if we could get together, same place as last time. Shouldn't take long," Pack said.

"On the way, General," Wilson said, hanging up immediately.

Within fifteen minutes they had united, Tetu remaining in the Jeep as Pack met Wilson at the picnic table.

"Thanks for coming, Tom. I guess you're aware of the brouhaha in Kalispell over the weekend?"

"I know as much as I saw and heard through radio and television, General. Real sorry you had to go through that. What was the FBI thinking anyway?" Wilson said.

"Really, Officer, none of that stuff, in and of itself, matters very much now. Understand, though, in my opinion the FBI doesn't deserve the blame. I'm looking at where we are now, which is that someone killed the game warden, and apparently used one of my tools to do it. That device was stolen from my vehicle. Your men use a motor pool for official vehicles, correct?"

"Sure do, but there are provisos. One of the longest-running bitches on the force is who gets to drive their vehicles home and who doesn't. The Sheriff himself decides, and somewhere around half the force gets to take theirs home and half don't. Bitching comes in, as you'd figure, from what seems to be arbitrary selections. But I'm getting sidetracked. So again, yes we do have a motor pool."

"OK, for those who get to drive their vehicles home, how often do they have to check into the motor pool?"

"Since I'm in that group, I know. The answer is every fifth duty day. You take it in, the mileage gets recorded, mechanics do a walk-around inspection, check the oil and tires, and that's about it. Unless, of course, you've reached the mileage where a major service is due. Oh, yeah, and the car wash over there is available to us at all times."

"Do the car washes get recorded?" Pack asked.

"If so, I'm a violator of the policy, because I've never recorded my own."

"You went out on a limb for me before, Tom. Willing to have another go at it? And I must tell you up front the effort might amount to nothing. I know various agencies are working on Strang's murder, but I'd like to assist. A man working for the state of Montana was murdered, with my tool I think, and I want to find who did it. And for your information, it's true I did meet him up there the day he was killed. Someone came after me, killed him, and wanted to make it appear I'd done it. Where do we stand right now, before I think about going on?"

"I'll help," Officer Wilson said with finality, proffering his hand as he did so.

"OK, I'd like to find out whether Hackman washed his vehicle on the day of the murder, and if so, about what time that was. It was muddy in that part of the Yaak on that day. Also, I'd like to compare his mileage totals for that week with whatever sample size you can get. I'd further like to know if he was around here the night before the murder. That night, I opened the garage door to see Sheriff Mollison to his vehicle, and in the light of a full moon, thought for a moment I had caught a glint reflecting off a vehicle at the top of my hill, where there's a turnaround. That could've been Hackman's vehicle, I don't know, and if it was, it might've indicated that was the night he stole the murder weapon from my Jeep." Pack settled an even gaze on Wilson.

"I'll do my best, General. I'll probably need a cover story or two to shake some of that info loose, but...I'll work on it, and hope I succeed.

One other thing: yesterday four or five of us were in the coffee room when he said Governor Dahl threw the FBI under the bus. He asked what we thought of that. I said maybe Dahl knew they didn't have necessary proof you'd done it, so he took ballsy action. The Sheriff went ballistic, accusing all of us of mooning over you when you visited our station. The man was super pissed, wow, you should've witnessed the scene. Angrily called you something along the lines of Mister Simon General Mister Governor Pack. Said we treated you like a movie star. His jealousy showed through to all of us."

"Got it," Pack said. "You ever see Strang's intern, Bill Damon, come into your offices?"

"No, sir, but I've overheard Strang telling the Sheriff that Damon was a bigger headache than any intern he'd ever had."

"Thanks, Tom. Expect to see investigators over here soon. If I have any influence, I'll ask them to speak to a few of you. Don't want Hackman to get any ideas by seeing them zero in on you."

Lucas Lincoln had experienced a personality makeover, although he might not have recognized it. He was enjoying this team thing; these fellows, Shiningfish and Tetu, treated him as an equal. They didn't treat him as a pet or as a cute old man known for his ignominious choices, and they didn't pander to him and they weren't constantly making references to his age. He was nothing more or less than a valuable member of the team, and they shared a mission. He hadn't sat in a vehicle as much in twenty-five or thirty years. He sat up in his seat, he paid attention, his mind was focused, and he wasn't thinking about the bottle. He couldn't wait to roll out of bed to go out to work with the team.

It was Tuesday morning. Pack and Tetu were leaving the cabin to return to the Upper Yaak, a fact Tetu had called in to Shiningfish. At ten this morning the four of them would link up at the general store to try again to find the source of the heavy gunfire Lincoln claimed to have heard.

When all arrived at the store, the first thing Pack noticed was the glint in Lucas's eyes. Gone was the dullness; the man was alert, ready to get to the field to prove he had heard explosions that presaged something bad. Shiningfish felt comfortable meeting Pack for the first time. If Pack was a hero to Tetu, Shiningfish had no reservations about accepting him into his confidence.

Lincoln rode with Shiningfish, their vehicle taking the lead, with Lincoln navigating the party to the location where he had heard the shots. They dismounted once on site. Pack suggested that they all first agree on the location of true north. From that point, Pack would walk the northwest sector, Tetu the southwest, Shiningfish the northeast, and Lincoln the southeast. All the terrain looked rough, so no one had an easier or tougher sector to negotiate. Each man had a whistle, and each would report at the top of every hour. Pack had taken his wristwatch off and handed it to Lincoln. One short blast meant all well, but nothing found. Two long blasts meant the individual was in trouble and needed help, and three long blasts indicated success, and the others ought to join that whistler. They would be prepared to stay out until six p.m. if necessary.

The hours dragged on, nothing heard but the hourly single short blast, times four. Finally, about fifteen past the hour in midafternoon, they heard three long blasts coming from the northeast sector. Shiningfish climbed to the nearest high ground so that he could guide the others to his location. Despite the thirty-something temperature, they were all sweating from their exertions. It took close to two hours for them all to reassemble. Shiningfish was keeping quiet until all four were on site. "I almost passed by until I saw the trees, a case of not seeing the trees for the forest." He pointed, first to his left front, then to his right front. "I will take you there, but this position gives better perspective before we go there. You will see big trees on both sides chewed up by large caliber ammunition, and even some saplings buzzed to the ground. What were they firing at? I will take you there, you look and tell us what you think."

They walked around the upper rim of a bowl-shaped area below. Shiningfish swept his hand across a span that looked to be fifteen meters wide. "What you see here is same as you will see on other side of the rim. Look around, then state your conclusions."

As Tetu and Lincoln walked away to have a closer look, Pack spoke softly to Shiningfish. "It's clear, isn't it? The firing came from both sides. They were firing down into the bowl, judging from the way the bark is ripped from the trees up here. The ripping is upward. What we are looking at are ricochets. They were shooting at something down there. I wonder how experienced the firers were, because from the looks of it, they're damn lucky not to have killed each other. The dummies were essentially firing into one another. And it's easy to see where the motorcycles were parked up there. Those cycle gangs are particular about parking with military precision, which they did. Somebody had to have brought enough trucks to carry those bikes out of here. Where did they go? What do you say, Ranklin?"

"I believe you are right. But there is more. If you go down closer, you will see that ground down there has been tampered with. Someone has tried to camouflage it with brush, but they did a poor job. I think what we have down there is a large, hastily-constructed mass grave."

Tetu and Lincoln came back, and they looked ashen. They had reached conclusions similar, if not identical, to Pack's and Ranklin's. Pack said, "Mr. Lincoln, you've given the proof. You did a great job. We shouldn't take another step. We need a big forensics team up here ASAP. Ranklin, you have a radio in your truck, right? Can you call this in? And tell them to contact both the FBI and Governor's offices. We'll stay in place until we've made a proper handoff. They need to begin tonight, so remind them to bring spotlights."

It was one in the morning on Wednesday before the forensics specialists arrived. Pack told Shiningfish and Lincoln to go on home and get some rest. He and Tetu were staying in place until the team had some answers.

As the sun broke through to herald a bright day, Pack espied a familiar face down below. It was Agent Juan Martino, at the moment on his hands and knees in the muddy earth. The yellow tape was now in place, so Pack was not free to make his way down to Martino. Within minutes everyone on site was wearing a surgical facemask that had just been distributed.

Official photographers were snapping pictures. What they were uncovering was ugly. Nobody had to tell that to him. Pack walked around amid the vehicles until he found one he was sure belonged to the Kalispell FBI chief. He would wait there until Martino came back up.

The sun was considerably higher in the sky before Martino came up the hill. For the first time he saw Pack. "This was carnage on a scale few in the Bureau have ever witnessed," the agent said. "It's truly gruesome. My people are saying it sure looks like a machinegun job, probably fifty caliber. These people were sitting there, didn't know what hit them. It was a slaughter. It'll be a while before we know how many," the young agent said, shaking his head.

Pack said, "For a few days I've been afraid something on this scale had occurred."

"What do you mean?" Martino asked.

"A member of our group who found this place yesterday told us he had heard loud sustained gunfire last week. Then the people at the commercial places in Yaak were all saying the roughnecks that have been around a couple years suddenly disappeared. Simple logic, really."

"Any ideas about who did it?" the agent asked.

"I'm getting out of the conjecture business for a few days at least, if you don't mind, so I'd like to leave that to you. In the meantime, I'd make sure your cordon is large enough to include evidence of vehicles that may have come in and out of this bowl. Second, I'd police up any shell casings you can find. Third, we know that some kind of dirt mover was required to make that burial pit, so who in this valley has that kind of equipment? Fourth, I wouldn't be surprised if the killers themselves didn't wound or kill each other in the crossfire, so there's that to check as well. Just my first hack at amateur analysis. Fifth, find the motorcycles. That many is worth a lot of money. You're better qualified than I at this, Agent Martino. And if you don't my saying at a time like this, it's good to see you got back on your feet so quickly and are on the ground leading your people. Says a lot for you."

"Thanks, General, but I'm more proud of those people down there. The forensics guys are a makeshift team, and they've been hard at it for two, two and a half days, at the Strang site and now here. Had to borrow from several agencies, including Governor Dahl, who's been generous in sending us talent. I can't pull this many people together so quickly from in-house resources.

"I'm not able to speak freely yet, but we think we have our man in the Strang murder. The circumstantial case against him is already strong, and growing stronger," Martino concluded.

"An officer of the law, I presume?" Pack said.

"How did you know?" Martino said, genuinely perplexed, but also wishing he hadn't made the admission.

They had come in asking for 500 gallons of diesel, Georgann said. Couple guys in a Ford 350 she noticed had a Sovereign Citizens decal on their back window. They brought the container with them. Pretty much cleared out her supply of diesel, she said.

"Lots of things run on diesel, you know that, Georgann, and 500 gallons really isn't that much if you have lots of equipment," Pack said.

"You're right. I don't know...thing is, they don't come around here that much. I'm told there are as many SC members across the border as on the US side. I think they'd rather buy in Canada than down here. Probably closer for them to go to Canada too," Georgann said. "Still, I don't know why I mentioned that random thing. Not important." Still contemplating her reason for bringing this up, she said, "I think it gets back to the fact I don't know these SC people, and it's rare to see them down here. The other reason, I guess, is that so many weird and bad things have happened in the Upper Yaak recently. I find myself getting nervous about strangers around after what happened to Tom, then the game warden, then this unbelievable massacre. I gotta ask myself if this is where I want to raise my boy. On the other hand, I don't have the money to move, so I'll just have to toughen up and be ready for whatever happens."

"G," Pack said in the friendliest, most confident voice he could muster, "It'd be irresponsible of me to give you a false sense of security. I definitely don't know for sure the potential threats not just you, but all of you," he said, swirling his arm in a complete circle, "could face. On the other hand, let's examine what we do know. Just a few days back, we had gangbangers passing through your store, the lodge, and Nick's bar. Since the massacre, none of the people fitting the description of those gangbangers has been spotted. The rational conclusion is that the people found in the mass grave are the same ones who came through your store. Whether they'll be replaced is open to question, I suppose, but if I were wagering, I'd bet they're gone for keeps. Maybe, just maybe, conditions can return to the normal of a few years ago. But even if I'm wrong about all this, you have some good men and women who're willing and able to protect you and Tom."

"General, you sure have a way of piecing bits of information together. All I can do is shake my head in respect...I could even say awe and not be exaggerating," Georgann said. "It's nice to have you on our side."

Tetu had been on out the slope down to the house throwing a new football he'd bought for Tom. He saw Pack waving him up, so he said to Tom, "Got to go, buddy. We throw again when Tetu comes back, OK?"

"Thanks, Mr. Tetu. This is my first real-sized football. I love it."

Next time, Tetu thought, maybe Tetu will tell Tom that General Pack was one of best football players ever. See what he thinks about that.

They were going back to Reverend Dar Castor's church, just as Pack had pledged. He didn't look forward to it, and frankly had little hope the preacher would've gotten his ministry more organized, but was doing this because he sincerely thought it was important to the health of the valley.

He pulled in to park in the same spot remembered as the piece of ground from which the FBI apprehended him. He opened the front door and saw no Dar. Instead, there were three women at work. Two were Kootenai and one was Judith Buck. "How ya doin', Governor?" Judith asked. She introduced him to the two demure tribal ladies to whom Pack communicated his instantaneous respect by making a slight bow and shaking their hands softly. They returned his smile.

"Just got started this morning," Judith said, "but we're lookin' to have this place full of light, if not grace, by the end of the day. You got the preacher's attention. He told Craig if he'd had someone in his church talk to him like that when he was a young'un, he'd have had a different preacher path. He might have smarted over the ass-lashing you gave him, but from the sound of it, he appreciated it. Anyhow, he asked for help, and almost everyone in the valley volunteered for something. Craig's out there somewhere, pulling wires around, getting a generator connected to give us good lighting. Someone else is driving all the way down to Troy to pick up hymnals they've agreed to loan us. We'll have us a real church soon enough. And you know what, Governor? If the Rev doesn't pick up his game, we're still gonna have a church. We already decided we'll run it ourselves if need be. Take Craig, for instance. He's not just your medicine man, but he can preach if you want him to. And you know what else? I'll bet Mr. Lucas Lincoln can teach us a lot also. And there aren't any better woodcarvers than the Salish-Kootenai, so they're working on getting us a proper set of altarpieces. Don't you think it's odd, even awful, that his church sent him up here with nothing? If they don't care, why should we? But you've reminded us we should care, and we're going to."

"Good, real nice, ladies. Proud of you. So what's the Reverend Dar doing now, do you know?" Pack said.

"I do believe he's down at his house workin' up a sermon," Judith said. Then, tentatively, she added, "We'll see."

Pack announced his intention to go down to the house to check in on Dar. Tetu told Pack he would follow in a few minutes. He wanted time to speak with the tribal ladies about Swan's intentions.

They used a card table as their kitchen table. This hut stunk, it was overheated, and it screamed poverty. It was Pack's first time in Dar's place, and he experienced dual feelings of anger and sadness. Dar had answered the door. "Good morning, Governor, come in. I can offer coffee. Moms is making me prouder than I've ever been of her. She took the vehicle—which we got started with the help of several fine tribal members—and set off into what for her is the virtual unknown to meet some of the neighbors we have, distant as most of them are. It's a huge step for her. She's left me here alone to work on the Christmas sermon."

Pack said the first things that came into his mind. "Mmmm. This isn't the easiest environment to work in, I know, but think of this: your faith is being tested. What did Joseph do when taken prisoner? He kept the faith, and after years passed, Pharaoh put him in charge of all of Egypt. And what of Daniel, subjected to one trial after another? And what of Moses, who began the exodus, in charge of leading three million people out of Egypt, which he did with no knowledge of where he was being led? Many times the three million lost confidence in their leader, and in their anger wanted to kill him. And what of Paul, the ineffably brilliant Paul, who was beaten many times, chained and imprisoned, and shipwrecked? It was a matter of faith for all of them. They did not lead cosseted lives. They were put in not merely tough, but dire, circumstances, and they overcame. They hurt physically. Was the faith of these men always strong? No, occasionally they lacked sufficient faith, but their God saw them through. Throughout the Bible there are many cases of backsliding among believers. No person is immune from reversion to old habits and patterns of living. If you want to leave a spiritual imprint on this part of America, I believe you can. It is a matter at this point of your faith and your personal determination. I do not know whether you will discover in yourself the right stuff or not, but I can see you are struggling against your environment, and that is a fine start. In my professional opinion, this is one of the few truly crucial moments you'll face in this life. In the military we take a young officer in training, and after a while we throw him into what seems to be a hopeless situation, and say to him 'OK, Lieutenant, what do you do now? The lives of your men are on the line.' With appropriate modification, that's you right now. It's time to see what Dar Castor has got. You've got three-and-a-butt days to get your shit together, preacher. I will leave you to your work."

Pack left, on the one hand still resentful that Dar's home base church had thrown him out here and forgotten about him, and on the other gripped by a determination not to sympathize with a man who had been demonstrably weak and lazy. His seniors themselves weren't worthy churchmen, and they deserved excoriation. Pack thought maybe someday he would get around to giving Dar's pompous church leaders a piece of his mind. Right now, though, that task was not a priority.

Pack was thinking 'next step' on his Yaak mission as he trudged up to the Jeep outside the church. He had to wait a while before Tetu came out wearing a broad smile.

Chapter Twenty-Eight

A'nh Tranh was more than a pretty face, more than elegance personified. Ng Trang latched onto her at Berkeley because from the first time he heard her speak he had an open view to the workings of her mind. She was a senior, he but a freshman. He belonged to the Asian-American Student Society, as did she. Occasionally, they socialized, typically in a bar, and Ng always angled to sit at her table. Many among them were studying math and sciences, and they liked to show their brilliance in these subjects by holding forth on some thorny problems their professors had assigned. Through Ng's eyes, the eximious A'nh looked to be a teenager, which indeed, even as a senior, she happened to be. She was actually a couple of months younger than Trang, having obviously been passed through some years of her prior education. A'nh let her fellow members prattle on, declaiming their erudition in their subjects. They would sit back, satisfied they had created the favorable impression of themselves they hoped for, then cobra-like, A'nh would rise up to spit poison at their arguments with her charming brand of venomous attack. How did this porcelain young woman know so much, Trang wondered, with so few years on earth? Even doctoral candidates in the hard sciences marveled at her knowledge. Yet she never appeared stressed and never expressed animus toward those whose arguments she obliterated. Trang observed that highly intelligent men of any background were malleable in her fingers; they were most eager to do favors for her.

She liked the way Ng Trang treated her. He was different. He could see through to her core. "He knows who I am," she thought. And what he thought was that the academic life wasn't for her. She eschewed the idea of a stale, uninteresting life in a lab. She wanted to become the renegade she imagined herself to be. And when Trang told her of his plan to leave school, she jumped at the chance to go with him. Cooking meth was child's play for her. If she identified a weakness in the process, which she indeed had, that cooker was history. A'nh Tranh was his quality control expert. She possessed similar abilities relative to any organizational process, as with the logistics issues they confronted.

And this A'nh Tranh wasn't interested in parchments attesting to her knowledge. She was so placidly confident in her understanding of abstruse technical knowledge she felt no impulse to defend her unwillingness to mount a PhD certificate on her wall. More important than a degree was her natural inclination to continue to stay abreast of the latest developments across the spectrum of sciences. She had always kept wicked-looking textbooks in Trang's RV and she loved commenting on scientific articles she found on the Internet.

A'nh Tranh's mind was a force multiplier for Trang. From the moment the Muslims in Sarajevo disclosed their reason for hiring him, Trang had to suppress a smile as he thought of A'nh. "She is my real weapon," he thought. "They want four things, I'll hand off two, maybe three, to A'nh, and she'll have them figured out by the time I get back from the Philippines. No way could I accomplish this assignment in such a short time without her."

He told her he was going to the Philippines to acquire the materials for a dirty bomb. Several such radiological weapons would explode somewhere. Within days, three other areas of the nation would be struck with different kinds of mass terror weapons. He wanted one area hit with a waterborne pathogen, one with a chemical weapon, and the last with plain old rifles, the easy-to-get kind like AKs and M-16s. He wanted them all cached in his favored caverns in the northernmost Yaak Valley no later than 16 January. A'nh would coordinate the shipments from the port of Vancouver across the border to the Yaak hideout, and would schedule the transshipment drivers to arrive in the Yaak at the last moment. Further, A'nh assured Trang she would take full responsibility for securing the waterborne pathogens and the chemical delivery systems by the appointed time. Ng Trang would plan the radiological weapon delivery and detonation, and he already had all the rifles required. Trang was feeling confident, and already thinking of life on an island with his exotic woman.

Chapter Twenty-Nine

Pack had a message waiting at the general store. Georgann read the note herself, "He knows me, ma'am. My name is Martino and I'm with the FBI. Here's my number. Please ask him to phone me soonest. Thank you."

"Thanks, Georgann. You really are the old-time telephone operator, and just as dependable. You guys doing OK?"

"Couldn't be better, General. I'm over that bluesy feeling I had the other day. It's a new day. Tom won't let go of that football Tetu gave him. Carries it with it everywhere he goes, like he's Mr. Bigshot now. How much longer you think before Tetu gets on up here?"

"What is this, Thursday before Christmas?" Pack was thinking of his commitment to Keeley to consider buying the lodge for him if the first day of the new year came and went. "I expect it won't be much longer. I'm thinking in terms of under a month, Georgann."

She pushed the old corded phone over the counter to Pack. "OK, make your call. He made it sound pretty important."

Pack pressed the numbers to reach Martino, and the answer came at once. "Hey, General, thanks for the callback. Look, I have a problem with us being not on a secure line. What's the chance of a sitdown with you here in my office? General subject is new information concerning the scene where I last saw you."

"I'll be there. How about five this afternoon?" Pack said.

"I'll ring you in myself. Until then, adios."

Tetu was somewhere outside with Tom again. Pack said, "Gotta go, G. Hope to see you again in a day or two."

He found Pack and Tom throwing the football just like before. Pack called to them, "Sorry, Tom, we have to move out quickly, but we'll see you again soon. Nice football, by the way."

He and Tetu got back in the Jeep, Pack telling him, "I've got to go to Kalispell to see Martino. Has new info on the mass murder. So we need to get back to Pete Creek to clear out of the campground."

"I have an idea, Matai. Let me go in and call Ranklin. He has invited me to visit him and his family, and this is good time to do. If he says is good, then you can take me to campground, and he can pick Tetu up there. And Tetu will clear, and Matai can go quick. OK?"

"OK with me if you're sure it's not just an excuse to leave me alone with Keeley tonight. And what if I can't get back tomorrow?"

"That's why Tetu breaks camp. If I can't stay more time at Ranklin's house, I come back here and set up camp again. No problem, Matai. Now I will call."

Ranklin seemed happy to have Tetu as his guest. Pack dropped Tetu off at the camp, then got back on the road toward Kalispell.

Pack had to drive directly to Kalispell to make it by five. They went into Martino's office, Martino behind his desk and Pack in a soft chair in front of the desk. "You were a General and the Governor, so you understand the danger of speaking confidentially. But absolutely everyone in the FBI, especially Deputy Director Ramstedt, says your word is inviolable. I'm asking, Governor, if I may speak with you in absolute confidentiality?"

Pack did not answer immediately. He was thinking ahead. There might be someone else with whom he should share some of what Martino would tell him. "With one possible reservation, and that would be Governor Dahl. If I should think he could help us, I will pledge to run the request by you first. If you can't do that, I suggest you tell me nothing."

Martino pulled the trigger in a flash. "That works for me. First, we're ready to indict Hackman over in Lincoln County. You knew he did it early on, didn't you? Also can tell you the things you had Officer Tom Wilson, Hackman's young deputy, working on, rooted out some good stuff for the case, so thanks."

"Yeah, I pretty much knew it from the start. Then the other day, an image popped into my head I hadn't consciously thought of. I remember seeing a vehicle parked at the turnaround spot up the hill from my cabin. I'm sure now that's the night he got into my Jeep and stole the baton. That was his SUV up the hill. Mollison, Tetu, and I must've come close to nailing him in the act of theft. It all added up."

"OK," Martino said, "that's pretty much old news, not the reason I asked you to come down. I'm able now to put proper attention on the mass murder. Incidentally, I expect that will be all over the news tomorrow. We're releasing some of that information tomorrow morning. Anyway, the bullets turned out to be fifty cal, as we thought. We got enough tire prints to identify the types of vehicles that no doubt were involved. Our supposition is that the machineguns were fired from Humvee platforms, probably an old Army Humvee, not a commercial model. It looks as if they simply dumped dirt over the bodies, after which they attempted to cover the grave with undergrowth. If that was the case, what we have is seventy-six human beings sitting on the side of the bowl, amphitheater style, listening to someone up the hill in front of them speaking to them. At some point, he or she called in the firepower and unleashed it on the defenseless people. Couple more points at this stage of my explanation: one, we now know none of these bodies had personal belongings on them. Nothing except their clothing. We'll identify all the bodies in time, but all a reasonable person has to do is look at them to see they were hard cases. Every one probably has a rap sheet. So why weren't they carrying iron? These guys don't leave home without their weapons. Their belongings are somewhere, probably in a container, which we can match up with the DNA of the bodies if we find them. Second, we found some footprints in the area from which we figure the speaker was located."

"Small feet, right?" Pack said.

"All right, I'll admit one more time I'm surprised. Why do you say that, what do you know we don't...yet?"

"I believe when this is all done, you'll find the speaker was a man named Ng Trang, probably the same guy who had a boy named Tom rat poisoned," Pack said.

"I'll be damned," Martino said. "Never heard of that case either."

"You wouldn't," Pack said. "The locals up here have learned to take care of their own issues. Hackman didn't give them the time of day."

"OK, General, you know this state better than I, so can you offer any thoughts on what I've brought up?" Martino said.

"Not really," Pack said, "except we both know some of the things to do is find the Humvees, identify the bodies and see who they were tied in with, find their personal belongings and find Ng Trang. And one other thing I've saved for last, and it's a point about which I'm on sandy shifting soil, and that's the Sovereign Citizen's group. I know you remember the Montana Freemen, how they grew from anti-government soreheads to genuinely dangerous radicals. There have been signs the Sovereign Citizens group is heading the same direction. Not long ago one of them shot a Missoula cop in the head. I have a feeling they're connected in some fashion but, I say again, it's just an intuition. And if they didn't do this mass execution, they might know who did. They have a compound up there maybe you want to visit.

"I'm ready to tell you I'd like to speak with Governor Dahl about visiting the Sovereign Citizen guy who killed the cop. He's in the State Prison. And you say?" Pack asked.

"If you think it'll help. You've done a lot already. Good luck with the Governor."

Pack went home that night, the first time alone with Keeley in a long time. He walked in, gave her a peck on the cheek and a hug, saying, "Let's go out. Over in Whitefish there's a great place called Stillwater Fish House. You like fish, so I'm sure you'll enjoy it. Let me get a shower, and you get dressed up. OK?"

Keeley said, "If you like it, I will. Sure, let's go have a good time."

Pack got his first warm shower in a few days. In five minutes he was ready.

They climbed the dozen steps to the front door. Pack had reservations, so the greeter at the front escorted them to their table. She had called Pack, "Governor." When they sat, Pack said, "This isn't the fanciest place you've ever been, but it does exude good taste, don't you agree?"

"I do, Simon, it's very appealing," Keeley said.

"It's more expensive than most restaurants in Montana, yes, but it's one of my favorites because I see the best of America here. In my opinion, it's how America was intended to operate. Attention to detail. Precision. Look around. If you'd been here as often as I you would learn that the wait staff is cross-trained. The manager can give a head nod if one area is overloaded and someone will peel off and help out in another area. For example, I've seen that kind of head nod, and a person who was serving tables minutes ago is now in the kitchen delicately shaping a cut of meat or dessert. Everyone can see the full operation in that well-lighted kitchen there." He pointed to the area that occupied the left wing of the place, the kitchen. Slanted plate glass shielded the sound from the restaurant, but every guest could observe the care with which each dish was being prepared. "And note that the staff is in virtually perpetual motion, rarely speaking with their colleagues. The food is wonderful, but I think the big reason I come here is because I love seeing such manifest commitment to quality.

"And we can talk and eat and drink all to ourselves. They don't hover over the table asking every few minutes how we find the service. They know the service is good. They keep an eye on the table from a distance. So...after that buildup, the meal better be super, right?"

"Hey, I love it already, regardless of anything that will follow," Keeley said. "But I do have a question."

"Sure, fire away," Simon said.

"If this place pays such close attention to detail," she said gravely, "why does the Health Department frequently shut it down?" She saw Simon blanch, then relax. "Got you for part of a second, didn't I? Giving you a taste of yourself."

"You know, Keel, for a woman of means, you are low maintenance. You know what's important in life. I respect that," Pack said.

"OK," Keeley said, "I've seen you operate for what, four years? And I know what I think's important to you. But how would you express what's important to you?"

"That's easy," Pack said, letting the reply linger, refusing to elaborate.

"All right then, explain," Keeley said.

"Listen carefully, kid. Money. Money is the most damn important thing in this life. If you don't have good finances, you got nada. Health…overrated. Friends…overrated. Everything besides money…overrated," Pack said.

"You're a coward," Keeley said, looking placid, sounding disappointed, speaking evenly. "I ask you a serious question, and you blow it off with a flip answer. What are you afraid of exposing about yourself?"

"You just don't understand, do you woman? I just told you money is value numero uno in this life and if I married you it would be for your money, got that?" Pack said.

"Be serious, man, please," Keeley said.

"Really, Keeley, if you see how I live, why must you ask what I think is important?"

"So, then…why would you marry me?" Keeley countered. It just came out, surprising both.

This was the first time *marriage* had been spoken, and seemed to stun each of them for a moment. They both looked at their laps and removed their hands from the table. They did not speak for thirty seconds. Then Keeley said, very softly, "May I amend my last sentence?"

"No, you may not," Pack said slowly. "I'm touched by your words, and I'd prefer to let them stand. I would marry you because I love you."

The server did not catch the topic of their conversation, else she probably would have delayed coming to ask for their order. But come she did. Pack ordered Miso Butterfish with roasted vegetables, and Keeley selected the Butternut Scallops with Jasmine rice and an Edamame salad. He ordered a Bonterra Chardonnay and she a Shooting Star Riesling. Before the young lady got away, Pack added, "And I'd like two orders of Alaskan King Crab to take home."

They got back to the cabin late that night, but Pack carried through with an idea he'd had since speaking with Martino in Kalispell. He called Jim Dahl at home. He explained what he wanted to do, and admitted it was risky. For him to pull this off would require Dahl's intervention. Dahl agreed Pack's plan was worth a try, so he took the extraordinary measure of calling his Department of Corrections chief at that late hour. Within forty-five minutes Dahl called Pack back with the go-ahead. He had greased the skids for Pack, with Tetu, to see the prisoner at four o'clock tomorrow afternoon. Pack got a number for Shiningfish's home, and spoke directly with Tetu. Tetu worked out a ride down, and after an early start from the Yaak, would be at Pack's cabin by nine in the morning.

The Montana State Prison sits three-and-a-half miles west of the town of Deer Lodge, population three thousand, down in Powell County. It is three hundred miles south of Yaak, situated between Missoula and Anaconda to the north and Butte to the south. Inside the prison at this moment sat Ted "Yukon" Phillips, cold-blooded killer of Missoula police officer Cody Wilcox. Yukon Phillips was about to have two visitors, and no one had told him about that.

At just after four o'clock, Phillips's cell clanged open remotely. Phillips was the lone occupant, not only of his cell, but of the entire block. He jumped back a little at the clanging of the sliding cell door, and his eyes widened at seeing six hundred fifteen pounds of muscle, sinew, and beef stride into his space.

"Where the damn guards?" Phillips barked. "And who the hell are you people?"

Pack and Tetu crowded up to within a foot of the prisoner. "Do you know who I am?" Pack asked.

"The hell I oughta care?" Phillips said.

"See, Teddy Bear, ordinarily I wouldn't care, but in this case I think you should. I was the Governor, Teddy Bear, until just a couple months ago. And the Governor now worked for me for many years. You could say he's simpatico with me. Lets me do pretty much what I want. Even ordered the cameras shut off and the guards out. He told me last night he couldn't be responsible for your safety if you attacked me or my friend Tetu. See, Teddy Bear, he was trying to look out for the safety of me, that would be his friend. Now it's the time in our show where Mr. Tetu puts on a funny little demonstration for the audience, which would be you. So, as Mr. Tetu's friend, Teddy Bear, I'm gonna expect some applause when he finishes, OK? Ready, Tetu?"

Tetu said nothing, but reached inside his jacket and drew out a juicy red Fiji apple the size of a softball. Tetu held it between thumb and forefinger of his left hand and displayed it at various angles before the prisoner. He then extended his right arm straight out and squeezed the apple, crushing it into juice that would fill a cup. He let the juice fall onto the squirming Phillips's head. Tetu glowered at Phillips, the minatory countenance sincere enough to pierce Phillips's patina of bravado.

"Look, Teddy Bear, the door's open…there's your chance. Go ahead, make a run for it if you like," Pack said.

Phillips was thinking of just that, wanting desperately to flee back into the arms of the guards and away from these two hulking maniacs. Seeing the inner workings of Phillips's mind, Pack stepped back and motioned Tetu to do the same. They had made a path for Phillips.

Phillips did it. He bolted for the door and ran down the short hallway, where he began banging on the next door. Pack and Tetu followed him slowly and deliberately until they came to him. Each of them grasped an arm and pushed his head forward, frog-marching him back to the cell. At the entrance they flung him roughly across the space until he tripped over the toilet.

"What do you people want?" Phillips shrieked.

"We want information, and if we don't get it, Tetu's going to do to your face what he did to that apple, Teddy Bear. We came a long way, and mark it down, this won't be a wasted trip."

The shuddering prisoner looked at them beseechingly, as if saying, "Don't hurt me."

"I want to know everything about the Sovereign Citizens compound. If I don't get it, I can't be responsible for what the neurotic, myopic, psychotic Tetu will do to you. On a much grander scale, I can't be responsible for seeing the Sov Cit compound looking the way Ruby Ridge and Koresh's compound ended up, and for that matter, busted the way the Montana

Freemen were. So tell me how many are inside, where the weapons are, where you have the big equipment, name of the man in charge, for starters. The entire lot of them'll be toast if you don't spit out everything I want to know. It's like this: this Governor is willing to reduce the place to a cinder and throw the lot of them in jail. We have enough charges against them to keep them imprisoned for life, every man, woman, and child up there. Of course, it's highly possible none will live to see a jail. Best way for you to help out your brothers and sisters and children is to tell us what we want to know.

"You committed a heinous crime, and you'll pay for it. But you're one individual, not the entire Sovereign Citizens organization. We won't harm anyone who hasn't actually committed a crime. You have my word on that, and you won't find any better word than mine. On the other hand, if you won't talk with us, there's that matter of the apple and your face I mentioned."

"You keep my name out of it," Phillips said.

"We never saw you," Pack said.

It was easier than Pack suspected. They didn't have to hurt the guy. The man's heart, such as he had, remained with his comrades in the compound. He sang like the proverbial canary.

Before they left, Phillips said again, "Remember you promised my name stays out of this."

In fact, Pack had been truthful. As far as he was concerned, the Sovereign Citizens people who had a beef against an overbearing government could still hold onto their beliefs in their little cluster of a compound. The legal analogy Pack relied upon was the search warrant permitting a search for specific objects. Most important at the moment, to Pack, was learning whether they had Humvees, dirt movers, and many motorcycles on their property. Phillips had given them solid information, Pack opined, as he had studied Phillips answering the questions.

Chapter Thirty

It was a breezy gray day, clouds thickening by the hour, and the locals didn't need a detailed meteorological report to tell them colder weather and heavy snow were imminent. Craig Wood and his trapping partner Shane Goodfellow were out in the willowwacks checking wolf traps when in the distance they glimpsed what appeared to be two military vehicles. "Let's go have a look," Shane said, "to see if the Army has come to settle all these conflicts up here."

"Pretty nice camo job," Craig said. They had to pull apart a wall of limbs and sod to get to the vehicles, which took more time than they cared to spend on a workday, but they had got this far and figured they should carry through with it. "I'll be damned, look at this."

"Suppose we could claim this as our own?" Shane joked.

"You know I think we've run upon something important," Craig said. "This might be related to that mass murder. Whadda you think?"

"Oh, yeah," Shane answered. "I'm sure of it. I know just enough about military weapons to recognize those are fifty caliber machineguns we're looking at. We shouldn't go any further. Let's hustle through the traps and get back to Georgann's where we can call it in."

"Who we gonna call? No way I'm calling Lincoln County. Is the General still around here?" Craig said.

"Let's find out. If not, let's call Joe Mollison over in Flathead, he'll know how to contact the right people," Shane said.

"Nope, the Governor and Tetu haven't been around since yesterday afternoon," Georgann said. They took off in a hurry. You can check to see if they're still at Pete Creek, but I don't think you'll find them there. Governor Pack called out to Tom that he'd see us again soon."

Shane and Craig couldn't risk anyone knowing what they'd found, so they didn't explain why they were looking for Pack. Craig said, "Georgann, mind if I use your phone to make a quick call to Sheriff Mollison down in Kalispell?"

"Course not, Craig. You have the gall to ask me that after what you did for Tom? You have a lifetime pass on our phone." Then she laughed, "Sorry, Craig, wish I could make it more special, but everyone else in the valley seems to have a lifetime pass too."

Georgann found some shelves to stock as far away from the phone as she could get in the little store in order to afford Craig a modicum of privacy. In short order, Joe Mollison was on the line. "Sheriff, this is Craig Wood up in Yaak. Shane Goodfellow and I were checking traps an hour ago when we ran across something both of us are dang sure had something to do with all those bodies found up here. We don't want to call Lincoln County. You know who to call, so how about calling back at this number as soon as you can? We got work to do, but we'll stay here until you call back. We can coordinate meeting whoever comes up here at the store to take them there."

"So I guess you're asking for crime scene techs, is that it?" Mollison asked.

"I think so, Joe. Shane and I ripped away a lot of camouflage, but we didn't touch the vehicles."

"Ah, so it's vehicles. Any bodies?" Mollison said.

"We didn't see any, but it's possible 'cause we couldn't see everything," Craig said.

"OK, Craig, FYI I'm notifying the FBI, who is headed up by a man named Juan Martino. Don't know if he'll be with them or not. Stand by for my callback."

"Thanks, Sheriff," Craig said, and hung up. He looked outside and watched huge snowflakes starting to fall. They were the sticking kind.

Juan Martino had so many thoughts rattling around inside his brain. Only days ago he was the weak link in all the FBI, an outpost agent teetering on the brink of losing his job. Not only that, he would be remembered throughout the Bureau as the former agent out in Montana now become laughingstock. Then the next day he had received plaudits from high up his chain. From zero to hero faster than zero to sixty. But he had also become one of the most overworked agents. He had a number of drug cases working, he had the Strang murder, and now he had the biggest mass murder outside of 9/11. He could witness his key subordinates being overworked to the point Martino saw it as a problem demanding redress. He had appealed to his boss in Salt Lake and gotten the latter to cough up a few people to help through this crisis period. His boss had no choice, in that national attention was now on the Yaak. Reporters were breathily speaking on air about this 'national tragedy' wherever you turned the dial. Martino shook his head each time he caught snippets of the reporting, thinking "a tragedy is an act of nature, an event beyond the normal control of man." What happened in the outdoor amphitheater was not a tragedy, but murder, plain and simple. But Martino couldn't take time to be a media critic; he had to keep his eyes on his own responsibilities. Right now, he didn't much care his people were overworked. Heck, they all were. He had to take those techs who had had precious little rest and order them to this latest site in the Yaak. And he also didn't care they already hated that unfriendly landscape. By and large, they were office people, and preferred the comforts of the office. Martino was thinking if they thought it was cold up there a few days ago, wait until they go up this time. It'll be cold as the old witch's teat, and they'll be trundling through snow, maybe a lot of it. He gave them their marching orders: get up to the general store and meet two fellows named Shane Goodfellow and Craig Wood. I'll be right behind you, after I clear about a hundred queries for information from my higher ups in the Bureau. When an important event transpires, everyone up the chain wants to feel attached to it, so their questions swiftly go from small snowballs to avalanche. "But," he said to himself wryly, "that's why I'm paid the incalculably *grande* bucks."

The past week had been only a respite from winter's wrath. Pack had once been in the city of Sarajevo, Bosnia-Herzegovina, when seventy-two inches snow fell in seventy-two hours. Only a couple of main roads in the city connected to the airport got plowed. The snowfall was so pervasive and blinding that Pack's taxi driver, a lifelong resident of Sarajevo, got lost going to the airport. They wound up stranded in a snowbank. It looked to Pack right now, driving north out of the State Prison, that the western area of the state was headed for the same fate. If it's this bad here, he thought as concentrated on the driving, what must it be like in the Upper Yaak. It was already dark. He wouldn't make it back up there tonight, nor did he want to. He had to make it to the FBI office in Kalispell.

He pressed the buzzer, and the duty officer let Pack and Tetu in. Pack said, "I thought with your big workload right now I might find Agent Martino here. Is he?"

"No, sir, he left a couple of hours ago for a return to the Yaak. Something big, he thinks," the duty officer said.

"OK, then, I have to ask you: I need to call the Governor on a secure line, so can I use yours? It's relevant to your biggest case, so I'm sure Agent Martino wouldn't have a problem."

The duty officer wasn't totally sure what to do, but since Pack said it was relevant to their biggest case, he thought his boss would say yes. "Yes, sir, you may use the phone in the boss's office. I'm not sure how to say this to a former Governor, but would you mind not disturbing anything on his desk?"

"Not to worry. Leave the door open if you want. The only thing I'm interested in is the secure line," Pack assured him.

When Jim Dahl got on the line, he said, "Before you tell me what you've got, let me ask if you're up to date on what we found within about eight miles of that general store you always call from?"

"Nope, been out of the loop all day," Pack said.

"Well," Dahl said, "it's interesting if not exciting. Two trappers up there found two Humvees, US Army retired, bought at auction legally. But they had mounted fifty cals that weren't bought at auction. They contained lots of prints, a good thing indeed if we find matches. Appears they had to ditch them there because—and this is wild—they were out of gas, at least one of them was, and the other had maybe ten miles of remaining fuel. Could've been empty because bullet holes had riddled the undercarriage and one the vehicles had blood stains. I understand the weather over there's wreaking havoc with the towaway, but in any case the FBI intends to have them hauled out tonight to their graveyard where they can work them over more. What does that tell you?"

"Tells me we have the killing agents. Those idiots hit themselves in a crossfire, just as we suspected. They weren't experienced fifty cal gunners. Weapon was too powerful for them, they let it rise on them after initially aiming into the bowl. Got the job done, but at a cost to themselves. Sounds like one of them was hit. By the way, I think this explains why some guy was down at the general store asking for diesel the other day. It was the nearest place. Do we know yet who bought the vehicles?"

"Yeah, some farmer in Oregon, never been in trouble. He sold them at a nice profit to some guys who paid cash, no paper trail. The buyers weren't interested in paper titles, and the farmer didn't see a reason to insist they get them. So, what did you get out of talking to the cop killer?"

"He's been in the hole most of the time down there, so what he told me can only be depended upon to be accurate before we nabbed him. But remember, he was on the loose for nearly two months after the murder. Continuing, he says there are about a hundred fifty total in the compound. Of those about fifty are males, and of those maybe five are capable of murder. As you might expect, those five are the ones in charge. They have a rank system just like the military, they wear military clothing, and a few are former military. They do military-like training, but it's all pretty simple, squad-level stuff such as marksmanship, fire and maneuver, close order drill, and some demolition skills. They have commercial walkie-talkies and a supply of batteries to last into eternity. For the demo training, they have det cord and C-4. Every individual, including the kids, that's all hundred twenty-five or so, has his or her own weapon. He claims those weapons weren't stolen, but bought legitimately, and they consist of everything from small .38 caliber handguns to 12-gauge shotguns to AK-47s. They don't do much shopping for anything in America, but save their bigger trips for across the border into Canada. In fact, a small percentage of those living in the compound are Canadian. I doubt you've forgotten, but the guy's name is Ted "Yukon" Phillips. He has a wife, brother, sister, and children inside, and if the man has allegiance to anything at this point, it's them. Seems genuinely repentant after having time to stew in his own juices, and doesn't want them hurt.

"How do they support themselves? He describes it as almost like a church's source of income. The hundred and fifty in the compound receive donations from, he says, *two to three hundred thousand* outside believers. They have a name for the compound, 'Shining Earth.' It's harder to get into Shining Earth than into the most prestigious universities. Each year tens of thousands apply, but only a handful are accepted. Moreover, he says, the unscrupulous leaders of Shining Earth don't want many coming in because it means they keep more money. How much pours in annually? Phillips doesn't know for sure, but said he's sure it's well into the millions. So you see, these people aren't poor. It's a clever racket. I wonder whether they keep the cash on site or in a bank, probably Canadian? But for now that discussion's a red herring. More to the point, he described the layout of the place, from which I drew a sketch he says is about right.

"Seems to me, Jim, that with the Humvees being found, what we need foremost from Shining Earth is the guys who committed the amphitheater murders. Maybe more important is why they did it. It doesn't make sense to me. It was stupid of them to do this, really out of their lane. I've been thinking the man who employed all those victims was one Ng Trang. I'm still having a hard time letting go of that idea."

Dahl had listened intently, taken plenty of notes, but interrupted now. "Why do you think it was this guy Trang?"

"Very long story," Pack answered, "but in a sense I've been following him ever sense I migrated to the Upper Yaak. All arrows have pointed toward him. Has heretofore spent time in a luxury RV shifting from one campground to another, has had visitors occasionally who fit the profile of those murdered; a dependable eyewitness, looking from some distance, saw a small figure talking—that is, someone fitting Trang's general description—to an assembly of motorcyclists in the woods; the small footprints lifted from the area Martino believes the leader was talking from in the amphitheater; the connection to the poisoning of the son of the general store owner, and there's likely more that aren't coming to mind right now."

"Your instincts have always been excellent, General...the empirical evidence is there, but...I was about to say 'what if you're wrong' but my instincts also say you're right. But if you are right, what's the connection to the Sovereign Citizens guys? Why do they suddenly jump into the picture when they haven't been in it before?"

"Believe me, Jim, I've pondered on that a great deal, and what I conclude is two things. One, Trang outfoxed the Sov Cit people and wanted it to appear they've been behind the Yaak criminal enterprises all along, so he bought them off to do the killing. Two, Trang is transitioning. He wanted to remove his fingerprints from the meth making, the gunrunning, the flesh trade, the booze business, all of it, to do something else. I don't doubt he was making serious money from his base in the Yaak, so why would he shut it down now? He's a young man, he has lavish tastes judging only from his RV, and people who get a taste of that kind of money typically want more. So I'm down to two primary possibilities: he's either retiring, which I find unlikely, or he's into a new line of work that promises a bigger payoff than he was into before. Therefore, what we need to get from the Sov Cit is what has happened to Ng Trang, and what is he up to now?"

Dahl took charge from that point. He brought in his staff, principally including his Division of Criminal Investigation chief, for a videoconference with Agent Martino. They sorted out who would do what, when, and how. They ended with a plan. What remained to be seen was whether the Sovereigns would resist. Both Dahl and Martino were inclined to think they would fight, because if word got out that Shining Earth had collapsed from law enforcement pressures, their funding would likely dry up. If you removed their fuel, anger at the government, they couldn't continue to function. Unless they could be persuaded way, way under the radar.

Chapter Thirty-One

"My Jeep can go damn near anywhere," Pack said to Governor Dahl. "I'll even ante up for a scraper to be safe. Jimbo, I think you're making a mistake. You and Martino. If you go big against those people, we won't get the information we're after. This needs to be low-key. I'll go up there as an emissary of Phillips, ostensibly to speak with his family, but I'll get around to talking to the commanders, or however the hell we'll refer to them, and I'll give them their choices, similar to the way I dealt with Phillips. I'll pledge to them if they hand over the idiots, their compound can stay intact, their people will remain safe, and their donors will be none the wiser. But should I fail, their existence is in grave danger. Think about it. You know I'm right."

"General, I owe more to you than to anyone alive. I can't risk having your blood on my hands. No, it's a risk I won't take," Dahl said.

"If you owe me so much, Jim, then grant me this chance. I'll sign a statement beforehand saying I bucked the system and contravened your plan. Besides, my blood's no more important than theirs in the final analysis."

"That comment about signing a statement is ridiculous. Nope, if you do this thing you'll do it under my authority. Call you back in a few. Bye for now," Dahl said abruptly and hung up on his mentor.

Dahl wasn't long in calling back. "General, sorry for hanging up like that, but I had to think. You are one stubborn man, know that? Of course you do, it's one of your hallmarks, and always has been. You win, and I have to say it's not just because I'm giving in. It's more because you have the stronger argument. Now I have to get back to Martino to see if we can delay this joint operation. I'll call you back again, but we can't say your mission is a total go until Martino has called off the FBI. Are we good?"

"We're good, Jim. Appreciate it. One more thing: I need a good radio, one with long battery life and enough power that I can talk from up there if I need to," Pack said.

Dahl said, "If you'll remain in place there for an hour, say, I'll talk with Martino about having his people there issue you one. Failing that, I'll have one delivered to your cabin, but let me try the FBI first."

The duty officer soon issued Pack a sturdy Motorola emergency radio, and a second as backup, along with a paper showing operating frequencies and call signs. Pack had been given the green light, and felt he was at last ready to go. First stop: his cabin, to drop off Tetu, who would not be happy to hear he wasn't invited on this trip.

Pack withheld the news until they were within a few miles of his cabin. "Good friend, Mr. Tetu, dependable ally, I have to leave tomorrow for the Sovereign Citizens compound. I wish you could go, but you can't. Has to be a one-man deal. Has to be. You stay with Keeley and Chesty. And listen carefully: you *cannot* tell Keeley exactly where I'm going. Upper Yaak's fine to say, but no more specific than that. I'm going to be fine, but if everything should go south and I'm not back in three days, I want you to take care of Chesty. I don't give a shit where I'm buried, or if I'm buried at all. The animals have to eat too."

"Matai," Tetu said, "I will do all you ask, but please do not speak like this. Nothing happens to Matai, my model Warrior." Tetu reached across the seat and patted Pack's arm.

The day before, on Good Friday, Kjell Johnson's publicist had gotten him appearances on three of the most-watched cable news shows. Johnson had jealously observed the prodigious public interest in the various stories of murder and intrigue in this strange-sounding place called "the Yaak" and he was being left out of it. Good golly Miss Molly, how badly he wanted in on it. Wasn't he the acknowledged chronicler of the Yaak, wasn't that how he had made his bones, achieved fame…at least among the literati? Wouldn't fresh exposure to the public sell more of his books? Why weren't the cameras seeking him out at this critical hour in the history of the place? That abysmal state of affairs had to be corrected posthaste, so here he was, in one of those three television studios, holding forth thus:

"I am Kjell Johnson, and I am weary. I believe passionately it's entirely fair to say I've given my life to the Yaak. I've certainly written more about it than anyone alive. I've brought public attention to this important environmental cause. I've probably raised more money for preservation of the Yaak than anyone. I've fought my heart out for the people of the Yaak for decades. And now," he said, pausing dramatically for a drink of water, apparently fighting back tears, "my heart is ravaged. I am feeling as if the possibilities I had dreamed of now are nothing more than a mirage. I appealed to the people in that small community of the Upper Yaak, but they ignored me. But you know what? They ignored *themselves*. I have come to the sad conclusion that their souls are dead. They have showed me they do not care for their land as much as I. I have tried to stick an electric prod in their rears, but even that has no effect. They just waddle along from day to day, afraid to step away from their comfort zones, I guess. Those who have heard of the Yaak believe those people to be among the last frontiersmen of America, but I have to report that that impression is false. They might as well be accountants going to their offices in the leafy business parks. I even made a very special plea to a new minister up there, asking him to get off his duff and mobilize the Valley on behalf of unity among the disparate groups, but to this moment I have not heard back from him. But they didn't heed my calls to work out their anger in a civilized discussion, and you see what happened. Eighty-two, that's eighty-two, people are dead within around two months, using the FBI's count, that we know about since I began my entreaties. I am not proud to say I was the prophet whose foretelling regrettably has come true. Who knows how long the bloodletting will continue? The people up there are turning my land into a killing field."

Kjell Johnson stopped in a ritzy bar favored by journalists after the final television interview. He felt he had upheld his reputation and satisfied his publishers. Now he would quaff some fine liquor and get a cab to his opulent hotel room. As he drank, he looked around to find someone who recognized him, the Lord of the Yaak.

Simon Pack got an early start on Christmas morning. He felt guilty that he would miss the service at Dar's church; he would try to find a way to atone as soon as he could. As quickly as he left, Tetu asked Keeley if he could borrow her car. He informed her that Matai had devoted considerable effort into making Dar's church a spiritual center for the people up there, and now Tetu felt obligated to stand in for the boss.

"Sure, Simon got the chains hooked up, so I guess we can make it. And I said 'we.' I'd like to see this church for myself," Keeley said. "I want to go to church on Christmas, Tetu. Simon said we could do the gifts when this Yaak business is done, and in case you haven't noticed, there are a few to open with your name on them."

"Then we both will go," Tetu said.

Keeley's car covered the ground much more slowly than Pack's Jeep. The roads were nearly impassable, but not officially blocked. They arrived at Georgann's store by ten a.m. With the off-road driving in front of them, they would be lucky to make it by eleven. Georgann and Tom were inside. Tom ran to Tetu, hugging his leg. "You're my Christmas present, Tetu," he said, and meaning it. "Seems like a long time since I saw you."

"Same for me, Tom. Makes Tetu happy to see you."

Keeley was introducing herself to Georgann. "Oh my," Georgann said, "you are as lovely and beautiful as the Governor said."

"Simon Pack said that? You sure he wasn't out of his head? He never says anything like that in my presence. But what he does like to speak of around me is how good you and Tom have been to him and Tetu, and I can see what he means," Keeley said.

Tetu said, "Sorry for Tetu interrupting, but we must go. You can go with us," Tetu said to Georgann and Tom.

"I'm so sorry to tell you, Tetu, but there won't be the Christmas service we've looked forward to, and that many have helped make possible. Word has gotten through the grapevine, I think, that the dirt road up there is absolutely impassable. Shane has a Ford 350, and he couldn't make it. Some of that snow is six feet deep. Can't even see where the road is supposed to be. I feel bad for everybody, including Reverend Dar. We'd be there if any way existed, but for now it doesn't. I figure God made the snow, so he'll understand. Maybe it was for a reason."

"In that case," Keeley said, "I have an idea. Is the Sportsman's Lodge open? If it is, let me take all of us for their Christmas dinner. I've heard a lot of chuntering between you and Simon about the place, Tetu, and if you're going to own it, I don't want to miss this chance to see it. We can just sit here and get to know one another better until it opens. Deal?"

Georgann was certain it was open because the Lodge guests needed a place to eat, and the proprietor was in business to offer it. After the huge meal, Keeley was sleepy, but in her drowsiness had made the decision to buy the place. They were back in the cabin by nightfall. There had been many questions about Pack's whereabouts, but Tetu had given no indication.

Chapter Thirty-Two

Ng Trang was accustomed to doing business in the Philippines. He liked it there, in part because he fit in so seamlessly. The Philippines Island group consists of more than seven thousand islands and islets, making centralized governance almost impossible. It is a mélange of cultures from all over Asia. More than one hundred million people live there, and Westerners generally think of it as poverty-stricken. It has poverty like all countries, including America, but it is easy to overlook the fact that it is the thirty-third largest economy in the world. That ranking would be considerably higher if not for the bustling underground economy. Trang early in life saw the advantages the Philippines afforded: Wild West mode of living outside the largest cities; a geographical position that had easy connections with the Asian Tiger economies; a potent Islamist Supremacist threat in Abu Sayyaf; and countless wheeler-dealers eager to turn a buck.

So now the camorra he was part of sat in the rear of a Thai restaurant that had been cleared of patrons until the meeting had concluded. Including Trang, there were eight men at the table. Two sucked on hookah pipes, and all the others, except Trang, puffed nonstop on strong-smelling cigarettes. Trang idly mused about what the hookahs contained—honey or hashish, or something in between. Their expressions bespoke hashish.

The man in charge looked about forty, but with the way some of these people abused their bodies, Trang thought, he might be twenty-one. Or fifty-five. The leader held up his hand, and all the chattering stopped instantly. "Mr. Trang," he said, "everyone around the table is conversant in English." Trang knew he could not underestimate this man; his English was precise and elegant, not at all in keeping with his untidy countenance. "You have stated that time is short, Mr. Trang, so let's go to the essence of your proposal. What do you want, when do you require it, and how much are you offering for our services?"

"Thank you, sir," Trang said. "First, the timing. I need these materials in my possession on the other end on 15 January, which is twenty-three days from today. The *Asian Lily* sails from the Port of Davao on 28 December. That's eighteen days of sail time. What you're shipping will be inside a casket I have already selected. It will be lined with four inches of lead. I want it designated for shipment to an address in Vancouver I will give you. That address is a funeral home. It will appear to be an ornate casket for a Chinese-Canadian dignitary in that city. As long as you handle the materials to be packed in the casket with normal precautions you would employ in handling a glass bowl, your handlers will be unharmed."

"So you have the lead-lined casket now?" the leader asked.

"I do," Trang said, "and I will explain in due time how you marry up with the casket."

"Continue, Mr. Trang."

"I want two objects, four of each if you can acquire them, but I will be satisfied with three each. There is much road construction all over the Philippines, because of course I have checked. At most of these sites you will find devices called density gauges...all transportation departments have them. They're roughly the size of those little robotic home vacuum cleaners. Nuclear density gauges are also used in the petroleum and mining industries, for your information. Some contain cesium, some radium, both of which are excellent materials for making dirty bombs. If you care, these gauges are used to measure the density and moisture content in roads. In other words, they measure compaction. My point in telling you so much about what they're used for is to convince you that if handled with common sense, they are no threat.

"The second type of item is Cobalt-60, a synthetic radioactive isotope of cobalt produced in nuclear reactors." He watched as nearly *en masse* the attendees pushed their backs up against their seats, in effect saying, "No, no, stop, we can't get anything related to a nuclear weapon."

"I see I alarmed you. You don't need to understand where it comes from, but just where you can get it. Fast food places use carbon-60 rods to irradiate their red meat, which is probably the easiest source for you. And I won't go into detail, but there are lots of uses for them in hospitals, including for sterilizing medical equipment and for treating cancer patients."

"This not a problem, Mr. Trang," the chief of the camorra said. He gazed at the others, who nodded 'yes, this can be done'. Then he added, "Of course it *can* be done, but will we do it? That entirely depends on what you have for us."

"I am empowered by some of the most powerful Muslim men on earth," Trang lied, "to extend to you an offer of half a million dollars, US."

"NO!" this man who handled English with such facility, said angrily, smashing the side of his clenched fist on the tabletop. "We are not street dogs begging for a bone. We are businessmen to be treated with respect. We demand seven hundred fifty thousand plus shipping costs. And we want half once the cargo has been loaded. Now we are wasting time. We have not much time left in which to put this package together. Make your answer."

Trang made a show of running his hands through his hair, mussing it terribly, and generally making a convincing show of the anguish he was experiencing. Inside his head he was exultant, giving himself high grades for a negotiation well and swiftly accomplished. Then, without speaking, he slowly pushed his hand toward the Abu Sayyaf man. The deal was done, only minor details requiring clarification.

A'nh had taught Trang about the commercial activity abounding in the Deep Web. He was aware the odds he could purchase these items through that platform were in his favor. He knew of sites that allowed prospective buyers to bid on uranium, for example. Working through the Deep Web, however, would in the instant case take much more time than he had, even had he been able to buy them. So he departed the Philippines for Vancouver feeling he had accomplished his first objective.

A'nh Tran had used her own phony passport to cross the border. The crossing went without incident, as it usually does for beautiful women. She was in Vancouver at their safe house, waiting for Ng Trang to return. She was happy with the progress report she had for him.

Chapter Thirty-Three

The most recent snowstorm had intensified, the vehicle radio saying it was already the worst in forty years. Pack's Jeep was getting a hard workout, the engine frequently groaning plaintively, at points almost refusing to move forward against the mounting drift. Most of the drive it labored in low four-wheel drive. In the whiteout, Pack had to pause often to recalibrate his heading. As the day was about to reach the gloaming, Pack saw the first open area in many miles. He estimated the distance across the blank space at two hundred meters. He knew that at this position he was within one mile or so of the northern border of America.

He felt certain the Sovereign Citizens compound sat on the other side of the open area. It just made sense. They would clear fields of fire. He pondered whether this area was natural or cleared by man. At that moment he got the answer: *THUMP!* "Damnit to hell," he cursed, He had bottomed his front end out on a stump. He got out, took his tanker's breaker bar and leveraged it off with a mighty heave upward and back. Before trying to continue, he had to identify some road or two-track. After a few minutes, he found, in the lessening light, what he discerned to be the path he had taken out of the woods. He squinted, letting the image of the path settle in his mind before he got back in the Jeep. Presently he could discern through the snowflakes the outline of a group of connected buildings that looked like a prison or a combat outpost in a military zone. He knew that in fact it was a cannery abandoned in the 1940s. The Sov Cits had made such extensive modifications to the place, however, that it didn't matter what it used to be. The buildings were enclosed inside a chain link fence topped with razor wire. Turrets sat atop the fence at the two corners he could see, and he knew there would be two on the far side as well. Those turrets probably were manned by sentries, but from this perspective he couldn't tell. At last he reached the main gate, which consisted of hydraulically controlled heavy wooden doors the thickness of larch trunks. The two-sided door opened outward. Cameras and speaker boxes rested atop the fence on either side of the door.

Pack got out and looked up toward a camera. Before he could speak, a voice said, "State your business."

"I want a parley with your commander, Eustace Mikel. My name is Simon Pack. I am alone. I just visited with Yukon Phillips, and he had a message he wanted me to deliver."

"Stand by," the voice intoned authoritatively.

Pack knew they would want to make him wait, and they did. After long minutes passed, the doors swung outward, slowly, and the voice commanded Pack to enter. He had memorized the layout Phillips had given, and was confident he knew where he would be led. On the inside, the snow had been removed from the traffic lanes. A uniformed figure walked ahead of the Jeep, showing him the way.

The guard said, "We obey military protocol here, Mister, so knock hard two times and wait to be instructed to enter." Another armed guard entered behind Pack and shut the door. He stood at parade rest with his rifle at this side. Pack thought that part about obeying military protocol was rich, given his own background in the real military. These were play soldiers.

Eustace Mikel's office looked like a hunting lodge. Two bearskin rugs spread across a wood floor. Big game heads decked the walls. His desk was massive, a mahogany piece that must've weighed half a ton. Behind his desk chair, some six feet back, was a broad fireplace, currently ablaze, with a stack of wood on either side. Five large comfortable chairs sat to the front of the desk. Credenzas on either side of the desk lay empty. Pack doubted much paperwork was associated with Mikel's duties. What, if they follow military protocol, does Mikel administer courts-martials?

Mikel said, "If my dumbass guard had known he was talking with the Governor, I'm sure he would have been more polite. Sorry about that. Have a seat. And welcome to Shining Earth, home of the most hospitable society on earth."

Pack sat. "What brings you up here? I heard you on the speaker, but why should I be interested in anything Phillips said? Probably wasn't the truth anyway," Mikel said.

"You won't know until you hear what he said, will you?" Pack said.

"Fair enough. So get to it," Mikel said.

"He has admitted to what he did in Missoula. He has taken responsibility for what he did, and he expects to die at the hands of a government whose authority you claim not to recognize."

"Again, I ask you why I ought to care?" Mikel said.

"Because he still has allegiance to this outfit also. He cares about the people inside your fence. I can assure you he loves most of the people here," Pack said.

"OK, I'll bite. Why are you saying 'most of the people'?"

"Because he was forced to admit also that there are some here who are willing to commit egregious violations of US law. He named those few people. I reminded him how badly Ruby Ridge and the Koresh compound turned out. The same can, and well might, happen here. I have spoken with both Governor Dahl and the FBI within the past forty-eight hours, and I promise you they will obliterate this compound, not happily, but they absolutely will, if you refuse to cooperate with them," Pack said. "And Phillips does not want that to happen here, because he loves the people here and still believes in the premises upon which it was founded."

"Phillips was low-level. He didn't know what was going on beyond what he was told to do," Mikel said.

"On that we'll disagree," Pack said. "He gave us sufficiently detailed information that we can have—and might already have—a warrant to search every inch of this place. They were ready to mount a military-style operation when I intervened and argued that I might be able to effect a peaceful outcome."

"So you're trying to be the big hero again. The big Simon Pack, the man who can't keep his face out of the news. Did you ever consider, Pack, that the President who hates you is still in office? He would never allow such an operation to occur. Besides, there are no grounds for invading our sovereign compound."

"Oh, there are grounds, I can tell you that," Pack countered. "With respect to the President, let's assume you're right. How much longer is left in his term? Not even a month, so you would only be staying your execution, and probably everyone else inside this place. If this is really Shining Earth, make it shine, and let the feds come in to search. Peacefully.

"So, Commander Mikel, your choice is stark: either allow a search of Shining Earth or see another unnecessary slaughter of many innocents," Pack concluded.

Mikel made direct eye contact with the armed guard, saying, "Take Simon Pack to his room."

"Who says I'm staying?" Pack said.

"Oh, you're staying, sir. You will be well treated. Enjoy your accommodations."

The armed guard in Mikel's office was his son, his most trusted agent. Nothing said between him and Pack would get out. Now Mikel was thinking of the value of his own life vis-à-vis everyone else in Shining Earth. He was guessing Phillips had fingered him as one of the few "willing to commit egregious violations of US law." If so, why should he open this compound to the feds? That might be signing his own death warrant.

Chapter Thirty-Four

Ng Trang had deliberately not canceled his return ticket to San Francisco. Although he traveled with a fake passport, he was unwilling to risk giving his identity away through a facial recognition camera, so he ticketed himself through to Vancouver, where he would oversee the offload of the casket from a safe position at the port.

A'nh Tran said, "This will be the most spectacular act of asymmetric warfare ever conducted on American soil, Ng. I have everything under control except for one significant one. During your absence, the game warden was murdered. They're charging the Sheriff in Lincoln County."

Ng Trang looked worried, and he was in fact. "Where is that Sheriff now? Is he in jail yet?"

"I do not know, Ng. Is it that important?" she asked.

"Most important, A'nh. He was working with the game warden, taking our money just as Strang was. Now do you see?" Trang said.

"Of course he is a threat to us. What do you want to do?" she said.

"I can't listen to what you want to tell me until I get this resolved. Give me an hour alone," Trang said.

Sheriff Bob Hackman's attorney was fighting the good fight, Trang was highly pleased to learn. His man was not behind bars yet, but he would be soon. Trang had to act quickly, and he did. The game warden's absence created a second problem, too—someone to guarantee safe passage out of the Yaak storage site. He would have to depend upon the Sovereigns to take over Strang's responsibilities.

Trang came back to the door of his office in the safe house to wave A'nh in. "Sorry, babe. I know you're eager to explain what you've got, but the news about the Sheriff was potentially huge. If I don't get that cleaned up, none of the rest of it will matter. He'll point the finger at us, and the Yaak will be saturated with lawmen."

"What are you going to do?" A'nh asked.

"Not to worry, my sweet. He won't be alive tomorrow morning. I'd stake my life on it. A good man has the job."

"How will he do it?" she asked.

"Poisoning, but not rat poison this time," Trang said. "Now let's hear what you have."

"The conventional weapons, rifles and rocket launchers, are the easiest, and ready to drive into the cave when you give the order. Ten small vehicles will drive them to New York. You have the site in Buffalo where we hand them over, and at that point, it's the jihadists' job.

"I've figured out the waterborne threat. Once water comes out of a reservoir, it gets treated again with chlorine. Chlorine can kill most any pathogens known. My problem was to create a tailored pathogen resistant to chlorine. Today we have genome editing techniques to enable us to do just that. Most scientists, either out of personal fear or fear of being sanctioned by the government, claim yes, it's possible to create new life forms, new deadly viruses, through genome editing, but it would take an extremely high level of scientific knowledge—and years—to succeed. But, Ng, your baby was able to do it in a week. I feel like if there were fairness is the academic world, I should receive this year's Nobel. What I've done is that significant. I did all the groundwork, all the chemical equations, enough to fill two chalkboards, then I gave it to a Professor friend at Cal Tech. He produced the new stuff, and was so excited he could barely speak. It doesn't even have a name yet. Our deal is that in a year he can write up his findings in a science journal and take full credit for the creation. He has tested this new creation many times in the lab, demonstrating conclusively chlorine cannot destroy these bacteria. Now what we have to do is first, get the fifty gallons he has promised, and decide upon the date we dump it into the Tennessee River, and where, given the river flow rate at this time of year, it will have an effect on the city of Huntsville, Alabama, on or about 19 January. Huntsville's water goes through a pumping station that—and these people have data showing they're quite precise about how many gallons get sucked in on specific days of the year—in mid-January it takes in about forty million gallons a day. Fifty gallons of my creation will taint that amount of water thoroughly. Now for the *coup de gras*: each of these organisms is less than 1.0 micron in size. That's important because any object 1.4 microns or larger the filtration captures."

"You are a genius, A'nh, and I love my genius," Ng Trang said, "but we aren't going to do this your way. Too much risk of dilution, regardless of where you dump it in the river. I want you to locate an access to the pump inlets, and dump it there. I think this job is not one we can delegate. I think you personally need to go there, find the inlet access point and hose it into the water yourself. Look at the calendar and tell me when you need to leave. Use a rental vehicle under an alias."

"Thank you, Ng, thank you for reminding me to remain who I am, which is someone poised and not susceptible to the common frailty of excitement. Excitement has clouded my thinking. What you say is correct, and what I should have thought of. I will do this job myself in the manner you describe."

"That is settled, then," Trang said. "Please tell me the chemical terror we will inflict."

"We have an ideal target in Lexington, Kentucky. The explosion should be timed with an event happening in that city on the nineteenth of January. That event is a basketball game three blocks away in Rupp Arena between the Universities of Kansas and Kentucky. Twenty-four thousand will attend. I have read it is the game of the day in the nation. The game will get nationwide attention. Two blocks off the main street there is a small industrial business that contains three five thousand gallon tanks filled with liquid chlorine. Each tank is double wall polyurethane. This store owner has chosen the cheaper option. These less-secure tanks cost about $7,500 each, as opposed to titanium alloy tanks that go for $75,000 each. They are in the storage yard at the back of the concrete block office building. The whole business is circled by a chain link fence.

This business has the kind of security designed to keep the curious out, but not the determined. A dog seems to be its main external security after normal operating hours, which it will be, as the game begins at seven p.m. To achieve the biggest cloud we should use thermite grenades strapped to each tank.

"Anyone within a hundred yards will die quickly. Their lungs will essentially melt and they will drown to death. Those within a cloud radius of at least twelve city blocks will require hospitalization, and most breathing the vapors will suffer permanent damage. Chlorine explosions have been shown to be highly effective as weapons of terror. Homeland Security experts are on record as saying it is one of the weapons of terror they fear most."

"OK, here's where we go from here: I need you to make sure you've addressed all details. For example, before hitting the chlorine tanks, cut the electric power first and maybe conduct a diversion at the front of the building so that if police come, they will go to the front. Every detail, A'nh. Second, I must travel to Kansas City for a meeting on the 10th of January with the Islamist in charge of the jihadists who are ready for martyrdom. It is the final rehearsal, so I must cover all of these details with him. I want detailed briefing books. Where everyone involved must be and when. You must write out every action and precaution to be taken. Am I clear, A'nh?"

"As you are always, Ng. I will not let you down."

"Third, I must get the casket with the guts of the dirty bomb to the Yaak storage site, but as I wait for the ship to arrive, I must get over to the Yaak to speak with that man Mikel to be sure the cache, and our exit out, will be secure. I will leave within twenty-four hours."

"In that case," A'nh said, "let us make big love to remember. Right now."

Chapter Thirty-Five

The people in the Yaak River Valley were feeling tetchy and dyspeptic right now. Just a few had watched the televised interviews with Kjell Johnson, but they spread the word swiftly. Most who came into the general store let Georgann see their most irascible natures. The store's proprietress observed that some would hang around a full half day just for the chance to vent to one of their neighbors. What they had taken from the famous author's comments could be summarized as, "If those dummies up in the Yaak had listened to me, none of the mayhem of the last month would have occurred." As they saw it, Johnson had shat upon their benighted Lilliputian population. Nick Surgeon heard the same plaints night after night now over in his bar. Some said, in their own manner of speaking, that Johnson had effectively accused them of being murderers. Johnson had never been one of them, and now he had shown that to the world. They hoped to have no further contact with him.

Simon Pack was locked in a lightless room. He had one woolen blanket for warmth against the bitter cold. An earthen jar was there for his toilet needs. He had no water or food. Around noon on his first full day at Shining Earth, three armed guards cracked on his thick wood door, and ordered him to come out.

His face was stubbled for lack of a shave, and his close-cut hair stuck out at odd angles. The bright sunlight momentarily blinded him. Pack grinned at them as if he had enjoyed a night at the Ritz. "How are you boys today?" he asked rhetorically. They did not answer. Two were mere boys, teenagers from the look of it, and the third Pack estimated was in his forties. One of the teens poked his rifle into Pack's back, nudging him forward, as the second teen motioned for Pack to follow the older one.

They walked him to a large warm room that was their mess hall. All ate on the same schedule, it seemed. Many of them turned to see Pack. Pack was unable to tell if any recognized him.

Everyone had bread, meat, and vegetables, along with beverages unidentifiable in opaque containers. Presently a woman brought him a cup of water and a bowl of soup that turned out to be broth. "Are you going to join me?" Pack quipped. "I'm sure it's excellent." They weren't going to speak.

He finished ladling out the broth in a couple of minutes. The guards stayed with their sign language and directed him toward the office of Eustace Mikel, who today wore the eagle insignia of a Colonel in the US Army and Marine Corps. "Stand before my desk, Mister Pack," Mikel commanded him.

Instead, Pack stepped forward and sat once more in one of the comfortable chairs. "I like this chair better," Pack said. "And your boy can drop his rifle. I'm not going to hurt either of you."

Mikel smiled. "Just remember, Mister Pack, with a nod of my head he'll blow the back of your head to Kingdom Come. Don't try to be a tough guy here. Or a smartass. I don't care for your attitude. What are my choices in the matter you came to discuss?"

"As I said, you can prevent the spillage of any blood simply by allowing law enforcement agents to search this compound. You and I can accomplish that with a phone call. That shouldn't take long at all. Let's say they're looking for a couple of Humvees," Pack said, knowing they had been found, not inside Shining Earth, "and they find them. They will seize them and be on their way, I suppose."

Mikel fixed his gaze on Pack. "That's a lie, and a pathetic attempt to pull one over on me. I thought you were some kind of professional, but you come in here and insult my intelligence. I need a written guarantee they will not arrest me."

"Why would they try to arrest you if you've done nothing wrong?" Pack said. "There's strong evidence that at least two men inside these walls killed something like eighty bikers in the forest south of here. Maybe you knew nothing about that. If you didn't, the agents seize those people and they go home. End of story," Pack countered. "They might ask you some questions, but so what, assuming your innocence?"

"I have a different idea, Mister Pack. How about we call these people you regard as legitimate lawmen, and I tell them to back off or I'll kill you? Doesn't that sound good?" Mikel said.

"That *is* an option," Pack said, "but it will mean not only my death, but the deaths of everyone else in here too. Do you want your son to die to save you?"

Pack had struck a nerve. Mikel reddened, and looked up quickly to determine how his son had accepted that. Mikel just as quickly turned back to Pack.

"Mister Pack, you fail to comprehend the loyalty my people have to the organization first, and to me second. There is no one in America's phony military that understands as well as my people do what true allegiance to a cause means. We are willing to die for our cause."

Pack sensed that Mikel was a coward. He did not want to die. So Pack called his bluff. "All right then, why prolong this standoff any longer? Let's call my contact and tell him to go ahead with plans to storm this place? We'll all die and go to Valhalla."

"Rennie," Mikel said to his son, a younger-looking carbon copy of the senior Mikel, "get the other guards and return this man to his room."

Another miserable night awaited Simon Pack, a man being held captive in the state of which just two months ago he was the chief executive.

Chapter Thirty-Six

Keeley had kept an eye on Tetu, and the big fellow was in cloudland. He didn't know what to do with himself, seemed at loose ends. This was the start of day four of Pack's absence, and Keeley had had enough.

"Enough, Tetu. Where is Simon? I want to know exactly where he is, and what he's doing. You're nervous, and you don't get nervous unless something is very wrong. Tell me what's going on."

"Matai did not want you to worry. That was big thing to him. Now it is fourth day and Tetu is thinking what to do. Tetu believed he would be back."

"He is doing something risky, maybe dangerous, then, right?"

"That's right, ma'am. Maybe you can give advice to Tetu. I believe he has gone to where Sovereigns Citizens live in camp near Canada border. He thinks they were involved with the big killing field," Tetu said. "But what does Tetu do? Who does he talk to?"

Keeley took a calmer tone. "Tetu, sit down, please, and let's talk openly." Tetu sat. "OK, Tetu, I am getting extremely concerned. Let's start by calling Sheriff Mollison. He'll have ideas."

Mollison could sense the tension in Keeley's voice, and told her he'd be right over. Forty minutes later he walked in, a happy Chesty charging up to nuzzle his powerful head into an unsuspecting Mollison's crotch. "Whoa there, boy!" Mollison said to the dog, as Tetu tugged him back.

They sat at the kitchen table. Keeley asked Tetu to explain everything he knew to the Sheriff. The most important part was something Keeley was hearing for the first time, namely, that Pack had asked the various police agencies to back off what would invariably turn into an armed confrontation with Shining Earth until he had a chance to negotiate with them. Mollison listened patiently, nodding affirmatively every now and then, keeping his powder dry until Tetu had finished.

"Well," the Sheriff drawled, "I think we have to honor the General's request to hold off the militia for a while longer. He told you three days, Tetu, so it's time to act. I'd like to get a flyover of the compound to see if we can spot the black Jeep. Can't ask the FBI for help...maybe I can get the Governor to help. Mind if I go downstairs and call Governor Dahl in a minute? And I also need to call my office. Stand by. Be right back."

Mollison came back. "All right, here's what I've got: the Governor was tied up, but his Chief of Staff said he'll speak with his boss as quickly as possible to discuss getting eyes on the compound. Second, I told my people to fill out a leave form for me, 'cause I'm taking a few days off. I'm going up to Yaak, have a chat with Georgann and anyone else who's around. You're welcome to go with me, and don't ask—no dogs named Chesty allowed." He saw the disappointment written on Tetu's face. "Just joking, guys. Chesty can go too. We might be back tonight, but we might not as well, so go get together some things for a few days. My vehicle's big, and we'll have the radios if we need them when we get out of cell range. I'm going to do the same, so give me an hour and a half to two hours. See you soon."

On the way to his house, the Sheriff took a call from the Governor. Dahl told Mollison he had no reservations about answering any request from Mollison. He just needed to hear Joe Mollison say it was mission essential, because he needed a damn good reason to put a chopper up in this weather. "Yes, sir,' Mollison said, "I'd like to be wrong, but if the General's still there after three days, I think he could be in danger. There could be, and likely are, others up there like the guy Yukon Phillips in Deer Lodge lockup. That said, I don't need to tell you nobody's better in a situation like that than General Pack. I know he asked you to keep state and FBI forces from closing in there until he had a chance to settle things, so I'd like to say I respect what the General wanted, and hope you will also. For a while longer. I'm leaving for Yaak in an hour or so. Keeley and Tetu are joining me. We aren't going to the compound, but I just want to get a sense of what the locals know. If I get any serious intel, I'll pass it to your Chief."

"No, Sheriff, as long as the pot is boiling, I want you to call me directly. Can't say how long my influence with the FBI will hold, but for now it's good," Dahl said. "I'm the fulcrum point for all the law enforcement intervention in this case, for the time being anyway."

The mansuetude of the slow-dropping snowflakes contrasted with the disquietude inside Mollison's official vehicle. Mollison gave primary attention to driving in the foul conditions, and Tetu and Keeley didn't feel like talking. Mollison did, however, remind them of the statement he'd made to Dahl about nobody being better able to handle the situation than Pack. Still, each of them was embracing the thought of Pack being treated maliciously, roughly, perhaps even brutally. Keeley didn't know if she wanted Pack's Jeep to be seen or not seen inside the compound.

While Keeley was upstairs getting her gear packed for the trip, Tetu snuck downstairs and placed two calls. The first was brief, expressing clumsily his endearments to Swan Threemoons. He told his love he hoped they were together, finally and for good, very soon. The second was to Shiningfish. He asked if the Forest Ranger could free himself to meet them at the general store later in the afternoon. Ranklin was happy for Tetu's call, and said God willing he would be there.

Mollison had met Georgann many times, and greeted her with a strong embrace. She was equally excited to see her favorite Sheriff. Tetu looked around, but saw Ranklin hadn't made it yet. "How's Tom?" Mollison asked.

"Been a few years since you saw him, so you'll see he's sprouted up like a weed. He's a good boy, helps me in so many ways. And you'd be proud how polite he is. See that big guy over there, the one you brought up here? Tom adores that man, let me tell you that. He brings Tom stuff... well, I'm sorry, Sheriff Joe, this is about Tom, not Tetu, so forgive me for getting carried away. Short answer is I'm proud of my boy."

"He's a good boy because you're a fine woman, Georgie," the Sheriff said. "So how about bringing me up to speed on how you folks are dealing with the aftermath of the bad things that've occurred around here. I ask as a private citizen, not officially. You know I have no jurisdiction up here any more."

The Sheriff had gotten so wrapped up seeing Georgann again that he he'd failed to introduce Keeley, who was off to the side listening in. So Georgann said, "Keeley, it's good to see you again. What can I get you to drink? Take anything that's to your liking from a drink case. Come on over here and listen in. And where's the Governor?"

Keeley gave a short reply, hoping Georgann would continue with an answer to the Sheriff.

Making eye contact with Keeley, Georgann said, animatedly waving her hands, "People are real upset with Kjell Johnson for saying us boobs up here are to blame for all the trouble we've seen. That's the big thing, I guess. Another thing is just a rumor, but since it was a couple of our guys who found those Humvees—by accident—it might just be true. They're saying those vehicles were used in the mass shooting. They probably got stashed about eight miles from here because the fuel tank got shot up. Connected with that is a Sovereign Citizens guy coming in here trying to buy diesel. If they were on the way back to their camp up on the border, they got stranded because they ran out of fuel. Probably didn't realize that when they came here, right? Anyway, people around here are putting the pieces together and saying it looks to them like the Sovereigns had something to do with those murders. Those are the big things, but they're negative. On the positive side, while we didn't want to see all those bikers murdered, things have definitely returned to the old normal since then. Nowadays, the people coming here, to the bar across the street, and to the Sportsman's Lodge, are pretty much the typical clientele of several years ago. What else you want to know?"

Tetu had secreted himself and gone down to the house in search of Tom. He had brought Chesty out of the Sheriff's SUV and taken him down to see Tom. Tom and Tetu came in inconspicuously and sat talking quietly in the wicker rockers. A few more minutes passed before Ranklin Shiningfish appeared. In his kindest voice, Tetu told Tom he had to talk some business with the forest ranger, and asked Tom again to take good care of Chesty until their business was done. Tom felt like a grownup being asked to take charge of Tetu's prize, Chesty.

Georgann could see that something of a formal meeting was taking shape. She gave Tom some chores to do back at the house, kissed him, and told him she loved him. Tom left, leaving the adults in the room. They all sat in the chairs for the talk. Sheriff Mollison condensed the material information he's gleaned from Tetu, and asked for their opinion. Before they could reply, the general store's phone rang; Georgann summoned Mollison. "His Jeep's inside," was Dahl's simple message. So Mollison apprised the group of that fact also.

The stalwart Forest Ranger spoke up. "Respectfully, Joe, you need now to leave us. Maybe go to the Lodge and get a room. We will call if we need you. What I am going to say are things you should not hear. I am putting myself in bad position too, but am ready to do it. I have thought already about doing something like I will propose. Please go."

The Sheriff studied the stoic Kootenai, just looking at him evenly, and said at last, "I believe I know what you're thinking, and I think I would do the same thing. Just be careful, Ranklin. You too, Tetu. I'll be at the Lodge if you really need me. May God be with you boys." At that, Mollison put on his coat and departed.

Ranklin spoke once Mollison was gone: "We, citizens of the Yaak, got to take care of this ourselves. If this had happened to our ancestors in this valley, would they have sat around and waited for someone else to take care of the problem? I say we round up a posse and get the General out. Sovereign Citizens are bad people. We will not storm the place. We will order them to let him go. If they do not, we will go in and take him. I drive near Shining Earth often. Let us get the men together, Tetu, and use this as our place to organize, if Georgann agrees."

Georgann nodded agreement; she was a full citizen of this Yaak Valley community, a pioneer woman in her heart, and she stood by upholding its honor, and for that matter would do anything else asked of her. "If he needs rescuing, brothers and sisters, we'll be more than happy to unleash hell on those Sovereigns if that's what they want. It'll be their choice."

Within hours the most hardcore of the Yaak men formed up at the store. Tetu would get a headcount before they left their staging area, once they got to that point, but for now they just paid attention to names and faces. Crowded inside were Ranklin and five Kootenai braves he brought with him; Craig Wood; Shane Goodfellow; Nick Surgeon; and the Lodge owner. And Tetu himself, of course. And Lucas Lincoln—all had tried to dissuade him from taking part in the upcoming activity that would be both strenuous and dangerous—but the old gentleman would not be dissuaded. He said, "I'd as soon die this way as down in my shack. Let a man have some nobility at the last, wouldya?" Everyone had reservations about allowing Lucas to go, but nobody except Nick Surgeon voiced them. Nick said, "Think it over, Lucas. This won't be easy physically, and none us wants to see you get hurt. From what Ranklin says, you singlehandedly led the law to the mass grave, so don't you think you've done enough?"

"I damn sure don't," Lucas said. "I ain't never joined in anything to actually help this Yaak community in my life, so I see this as my chance. I'm ready to join you." Tetu and Ranklin, in particular, wanted to stand behind Lucas because they had witnessed how much this endeavor meant to him. Even they, though, couldn't avoid the thought that having a nonagenarian in the mix was a bad idea. In the end, Lucas Lincoln's stubbornness won out.

Tetu had personally gone to Dar Castor to get him involved, but he wouldn't leave the cozy confines of his hut. "I'm not a killer," he said piously, his tone seemingly castigating the morality of Tetu and the others. "So you're willing to let my beloved Matai, a good man if ever there was one...die?" Tetu had countered. At that point Dar closed the door on Tetu. One other person wasn't in the posse—Kjell Johnson. They didn't know where he was today, and had no interest in finding out.

These men were all hardened outdoorsmen, and required minimal direction. So Ranklin just asked them to bring their strongest weapons and as much ammo as they could carry. Wear white, if you've got it, and tape your equipment down to stymie the rattling. Gloves thin enough to get good trigger pull. They would reconvene at the store at 2200 hours, and commence the slow drive to a staging area in the woods just south of the open area approaching the compound. There they would review their final plan of advance toward Shining Earth. They would cross the

Line of Departure at 0200 hours, or two a.m.. What remained was the call to Eustace Mikel, which task Tetu and Ranklin assured them they would take as their responsibility. Just go home now, and get yourselves ready, Ranklin instructed them.

When everyone had cleared out, Tetu opined to Ranklin that the call to the Sovereign's compound might better be left to Sheriff Mollison, who had said he would help. The call, after all, was a noncombatant role, so the Sheriff wouldn't be implicated in the extra-legal activity to follow.

They went to Sheriff Joe's room, and asked him the favor. There were two chairs in the Lodge's room, so they sat while Mollison made a few notes before placing the call. Shortly, the two visitors listened as Mollison spoke with Mikel.

"Eustace, we've met several times. This is Sheriff Joe Mollison, and I'm calling as a friend of General Simon Pack. I want to speak with him. I'll hold while you get him to this phone."

"I'm afraid he's indisposed, Mollison. You won't be speaking with him," Mikel said.

"Listen to me, Mikel. I have nothing to do with running an operation against you people, but I've been in on the talks, and I'm telling you if you don't send him out immediately, in good health, untouched, you will have about two days before a large force of feds descends on your place with evil intent. There's a chance all of you die. Do you understand? Call me within the hour when you've released him and his vehicle."

"Go to hell, Mollison," Mikel said, clicking off.

Mollison turned to Tetu and Ranklin. "Add another man to your posse, boys. I'm going with you. Who knows what they've done to Pack? And I'll be wearing a radio if we need it."

Simon Pack was dangerously cold. The bed was a few slats protruding from a wall. No mattress, no pillow. Just the musty woolen blanket. Dirt floor. He stood up several times a night to do calisthenics and pushups in order to keep his body temperature from falling to a deadly level. They fed him one time a day, nothing more than the gruel at lunch, but they had placed a jug of water in a thermal container in his cell.

Today at lunch in the mess hall, with the guards hovering behind him, he saw at the far end of the hall, in the section reserved for officers, Eustace Mikel enter with another man. He was a smallish Asian man. Pack didn't have to wonder; he knew it was Ng Trang. Pack could see them leaning into one another across the meal table, heads nearly touching. They were intense about whatever they were discussing. He had to his satisfaction thus established some degree of collusion between Mikel and Trang. He had to find out the subject of their collusion.

Following the trek back to his cell after lunch, Pack thought about how to get the information he sought. Back inside his pitch-black cell, he kept coming back to the same conclusion: the key to everything going on here was Mikel's son. He was the interior guard for every meeting held in his father's office, and was therefore privy, as the senior Mikel's only trusted agent, to every decision contemplated and reached. Pack needed an excuse to speak alone with the young man.

Chapter Thirty-Seven

When the men left the store, Georgann glimpsed Keeley sitting in a wicker with her head in her hands. Georgann approached Keeley slowly. She extended her two hands toward Pack's woman until Keeley took them and looked up. "Thanks, Georgie. I'll be fine in a moment. Maybe we should pray, if you wouldn't mind." Keeley delivered a short prayer for the safekeeping of everyone involved, including the people inside Shining Earth.

Georgann said, "Let's close this place up and go on down to the house. I've got some ice cream. Don't they say it's good comfort food? And check up on Chesty and Tom."

They made the slippery walk down the slope. When they entered the small home, they found Tom, arms wrapped around Chesty, crying into the dog's fur.

Keeley was the first to Tom. She sat on the floor beside him and pulled him to her. "We're all worried, buddy, about our very close friends who have gone out there to save General Pack. They are great people, all of them. I wish I'd been in your place growing up, among all these wonderfully strong people. Now, listen, Tommy: they'll come back with him. I've never been around people I feeler safer with. Tetu and Pack want you to be strong. See, you have two women here who're caring for you, but you can also care for us. And Chesty, well...you have to assure him Tetu's going to be fine. He was a heroic soldier, Tetu was, did you know that?"

Tom looked up, very interested in that. "He's never said anything about that. Really, he was a soldier?"

"Oh, yeah, my friend Pack was a General, and knows soldiers, and he says Tetu was a genuine hero. He got hurt badly in the process of saving some of his fellow soldiers. So badly was he hurt that he was what is called 'medically retired.' But because of people like you, and because of

Chesty, he has regained most of his former strength. Tetu is a strong man. Now it's time for us to be strong as our way of honoring him."

"I see what you mean, ma'am," Tom said. He brushed off the tears, got to his feet and asked his mom what he could do to help.

In the staging area less than a quarter mile from Shining Earth, Ranklin—the man never heard to speak using a contraction--had the posse huddled around him. He was going over the final checks before crossing the Line of Departure (LD). "I believe our odds are excellent. Tetu says there are about one hundred twenty-five inside. Figure forty are children unable to fight, and I am playing the numbers on the low side. That leaves eighty-five, of which we assume women are, say, forty-two. That leaves forty-three fighting-age men, at most. On the other side, there are twelve of us, but we have the advantage of surprise, and we will be hitting them when they are least alert. Craig is going to stay at Sheriff Mollison's vehicle to run our aid station. With all the medical supplies everyone contributed, Craig has some good material to work with. Let us hope we do not need him.

"We operate in pairs. Maintain ten to fifteen meters between yourselves. I will take our Kootenai braves and skirt around the woodline to the west and cover what I expect will be the three turrets on the north side. Tetu, your six men will orient on the three turrets to the front, on the south side. You are all experienced marksmen and hunters, so I do not need to tell you when to fire. One last thing, and it is important: the Sovereigns have cut down trees to make this open area. There are stumps all over the place. Move carefully through the snow so you are not felled by them. Once we get to the fence, we will breach it to get inside. Tetu is carrying one bolt cutter and I will have the other. Any questions or additions?"

"Suggestion over here, Ranklin," former paratrooper Nick Surgeon said. "Once we're inside, friendly fire will be a problem. You assigned us each a number, so let's communicate by calling out our numbers."

"Right, big point, Nick. Everyone hear that? Use your numbers to let the others know it is you....All right, everyone in the right frame of mind?"

"Let's do it, boys," Lucas Lincoln said. "We can do it. We're gonna get him out."

The snowfall had stopped. Ranklin left with his Kootenai force and moved as swiftly as they could around the woodline. Tetu gave Ranklin's men fifteen minutes head start before he led the main body across the LD, precisely at two a.m. They were cold, but their bodies warmed quickly with the hard labor of plodding through the snow and ice. A few lights were on inside the compound, producing an eerie dim halo above it. The halo was just enough to make the guard turrets clearly distinguishable. Fortunate, because they had no night scopes, and the Sovereigns most likely did.

Joe Mollison told Mikel the feds were coming in about two days. He hoped that would have the effect of causing Mikel to rest his best men until then. Can't keep the A Team on highest alert indefinitely. That would probably mean he had the rookies on duty tonight. But what the hell, that was just conjecture, Mollison thought to himself as he trudged along. Still, that's what I would do if I were in his position and intended to fight to the death.

After a hundred meters, halfway to the objective, they were sweating heavily. The adrenaline flowed, preventing them from being as weary as they might be under other circumstances. Nonetheless, although their bodies were stoked, their minds were semi-numbed, as if they were mowing ten acres of grass.

Mollison had surmised correctly. Had he been able to pierce the darkness with his eyes, he would have discovered two men per turret, most of them teenagers. And most were somnolent, the remainder asleep. They had never been in this situation before.

Within seventy-five meters of the objective, a man on the left flank of Tetu's squad barked, in calliopean voice, a piercing cry of pain, trying futilely to swallow it. He had fallen into a hole, twisting and wrenching a leg swiftly and violently, in a fashion reminiscent of a bear trap. The man saw white light for a second, the indescribable sudden pain literally blinding him. The moans continued to come, at first low but then progressively greater in volume as he lost physical control. As the man poured out his anguished yawps, the boys in the turrets awakened, startled badly by the putative attack. A hail of gunfire ripped out of the turrets toward the sound. Maybe they could see the downed man, maybe not. In any case, Tetu yelled for suppressive fire as he lumbered through the snow toward the victim. It was number seven, Lucas Lincoln. Bullets flew all around the field as the boys fired at new targets.

When Tetu got to Lincoln, he got as low to the ground as he could. He could see Lucas was drifting rapidly into shock. He got to the source of Lucas's pain and saw he could not throw him over his shoulder in a fireman's carry. His only choice was to lift the old gentleman into a cradle. "Stay with me, Lincoln," he whispered many times. Lincoln weighed no more than one forty, but even that was difficult for the mighty Tetu in the deep snow. Craig Wood had heard the firing, and came forward to the edge of the woods. He met Tetu there, and took Lucas in his arms as tenderly as he could. Craig carried the old man back to the Sheriff's vehicle, where he laid him in the cargo compartment and turned the heater on before setting to work on him.

When Craig got a good, well-lighted look at the misshapen, tortured leg, he knew the first—and perhaps only—priority was to relieve his pain. He had no morphine, but he had some natural powders he had used a few times on himself, and they worked to relieve his own highest pain levels. He administered twice that dosage to Lucas. The pain had caused Lucas's body to tighten into total tautness, but now Craig saw him beginning to relax, his breathing deepening. Craig knew then the sedative was having its calming effect.

He reset the bone as best he could, but feared his best effort was not enough to save the man. Allowing Lucas to participate in the mission had been a bad idea.

Tetu raced back to the front, all need for silence evaporated. He was in furious roar, exhorting his men forward. The Sovereigns in the turret were fleeing after hearing several of their own had taken a bullet. Their discipline and will to resist had wilted.

Then...less than fifty meters from the fence, something big happened.

When Eustace Mikel heard the first shot fired, by one of his own men, he bolted from his bed, threw on his boots, and made for his safe. He drew out a laundry bag, and grabbed his bug-out-bag on the way out his door. At the same time, the officers—including his son—were running to his office seeking directions. He yelled his rehearsed reply, "I'm going to Trang at the caves. He promised reinforcements. I'll lead them back. Now man your posts!"

Pack also heard all the commotion, the yelling and screaming by women and small children. He began to yell himself to the accompaniment of his hard thrashing and kicking into the door of his cell. A woman, probably without comprehending who he was, lifted the wooden bar holding the door in place. She was frightened witless. Pack told her he could save all of them, but needed to speak with Mikel's son immediately. "Bring him here as fast as you can," Pack said, both urgently and calmly. "I don't want anyone else to be hurt." The panicked woman just stared at Pack. Pack grasped her shoulder gently. "This is the most important thing you'll ever do for your children," he urged her. "Go now, and bring Mikel's son here immediately. Please." She left, Pack hoped, to coax young Mikel to come to him.

He did arrive, looking quite shaken, some two minutes later. He did not ask why Pack was out of his cell, or how, which Pack took to be a good thing. Although he kept his rifle trained on Pack's gut, he appeared at some level to be asking for help. He was fighting back tears, not so much from fear, it would turn out, but more from anger.

Pack said, "Son, these are hard men coming for you. Your father will not listen to reason. You can be the savior of your people. If you do not choose the right action, right this minute, there is a good chance everyone in Shining Earth will die. Do you want to be responsible for that?"

"He's gone," the boy said.

"What are you saying?" Pack asked. "Who has gone?"

"My dad said he was going to get reinforcements, but I think he lied. His safe was open, and he took all the money. It supported us all. I think my daddy deserted us. He's been planning a big operation with Trang about blowing America up, supposed to make a lot of money. Now the going gets tough here, and he bugs out, leaving us here to die. He wasn't the commander, after all. Commanders don't desert their troops in crisis." Rennie Mikel kept the gun pointed at Pack's midsection, trying to retain his resolve.

"OK, look, son," Pack said, "we don't have much time. You need to get me out of here. I give you my word I will stop the shooting. We can deal another day with the search warrant, and I'll deal with you, the person who's now in charge. Where did your dad go?"

"To the caves, he said, three miles west of here. That's where Trang was, and maybe still is. Or maybe he's just using the cave as a hideout. Damned traitor!"

"I'll need a snowmobile. Get me one and let's put an end to this," Pack said.

The boy dropped the barrel of his rifle and said, "Follow me."

He led Pack down two flights of stairs and into a cavernous storage room, in which Pack saw long rows of motorcycles when the lights flicked on. They picked out the best snowmobile and lugged it down a long underground tunnel. "Wait," Pack said, "I'll need another one to pull behind me. Rope it to this one. Got another man I might take with me." Rennie Mikel did as Pack asked. A door opened. The young man said, "This is the west side. Go three miles straight ahead. Don't kill him, please. I want him to answer before these people in the compound. And stop all the shooting before people die."

Pack hit the throttle and zoomed straight out into the zone of fire, turning south into the force of locals friendly to him. He was yelling his name. "This is Pack! Cease fire!"

Some of the Kootenai braves to the north, then some of Tetu's men to the south, were firing on his vehicle. Pack stopped it, and raised his hands. The waxing crescent moon was full enough at this hour to limn his shape. The friendly fire stopped. Then, quickly, the fire from Shining Earth stopped as well. Young Mikel had gotten to them, it seemed. He heard Tetu boom out, "Matai, is it you?"

"Yes, Tetu, I am safe, thank God and your men. Pull them back. You did great!" To as many as could hear, he added, "Hold your fire. I'm driving to where Tetu is."

"Tetu," Pack said, "First, do you have casualties?"

"One, not by gunfire. Lucas Lincoln. He is back with Craig Wood. Will go now to check condition."

Pack thought for a moment, of this man Lucas he had grown oddly and strongly attached to. "Craig will take good care of him.

"Who's left in charge?" Pack demanded authoritatively.

"Ranklin Shiningfish," Tetu said.

"Untie these machines, get on the second one, and lead me to him. It's easy enough to start up and drive," Pack said.

Once they got to the northern side, they sped directly to Shiningfish. Pack wasted no time in saying, "Ranklin, I'm taking Tetu with me. I need you to do a couple of things. One, call Mikel's son, name's Rennie, when you can and retrieve my Jeep. Two, give me your weapon, and get a backup for me too off one of the others. Tell the people who came here I'll thank them later. Get these people warm and dry. Love you, brother." Shiningfish did as Pack wished, and Pack and Tetu were gone into the western woods.

Pack would have liked all these men to accompany him to the caves, but they were exhausted, and he didn't have time or energy to brief them. And they were on foot—it would take them too long to get to the cave even if they knew the location. Besides, he had no plan himself. Beyond, that is, seeing what malicious activity was brewing in the caves. Moreover, he had no inkling of how much time he had.

As the men trod back to the staging area, they felt they had accomplished their mission. No one except Lucas had gotten hurt; lucky for them the Sovereigns' training had not netted much in the way of accuracy. No one knew how many rounds had been fired, but it was hundreds, estimated on the low side. As the men filed back, Shiningfish took a head count to be sure everyone had returned safely. Finally, Shiningfish himself became the last man to reach the vehicles that had brought them to the staging area.

There was no joy in the air, no celebration at the General's release. Some of the men stood in statuary silence, alone in their thoughts, despite what should have been an irresistible urge to seek the warmth of a vehicle heater. Shiningfish sensed instantly what had happened.

Craig Wood sat stonily on the tailgate, one hand touching the body of Lucas Lincoln. The strange, often dilatory old man had died a harsh death. Craig had covered his leg with a blanket. His bones, no longer strong, snapped like a sparrow's leg in a man's fingers. The evil compound fracture was a gruesome sight. Whatever his shortcomings in his earlier life, Lucas in death was bringing all present to an identical conclusion, in their own form of the thought: Lucas Lincoln died a noble death. He gave his life for a man he did not really know, but whom he intuited was worthy. Several of the men wept freely and unabashedly.

Chapter Thirty-Eight

By now the national media had gotten leaked information about Pack's kidnapping by the Sovereign Citizens. Who had let the information get out would never be known. The press was immediately taken back to the 1993 siege of the Branch Davidian compound in Waco. It was a spectacular storyline with spectacular video to go with it. There were differences, to be sure. Although the press was held at bay in Waco, they were able to get long-range standoff shots, given the relatively flat terrain. The Yaak terrain would not permit clear standoff shots; the press's only hope was from the air.

The President didn't want to be seen as impotent in the final days of his presidency. He was fed up. "Shut them down," he told his Attorney General. "Exterminate them if it comes to that." When the AG demurred, reminding the President there was a hostage inside, and that hostage happened to be the popular Simon Pack, the President said, "Sorry, Nancy, he's nothing more than collateral damage at this point. I cannot permit these lawless vigilantes to go unpunished." Secretly, he was much pleased to rid the country of this man who had been anathema to his administration.

President Rozan, however, was unaware that a few citizens of the Yaak had already dealt with the issue of the Sovereign Citizens.

Immediately after the odd operation, Sheriff Mollison, remembering Governor Dahl's injunction to use himself as the fulcrum point, radioed the Governor to tell him what had occurred, and to ask that he plead for the FBI to speak with the junior Mikel, who seemed inclined to allow a peaceful search of the compound. Dahl was elated that Pack got out safely. He promised to pass Mollison's plea to the FBI.

With the Before Morning Nautical Twilight now in effect, Pack picked up the trail of Mikel's snowmobile and followed it through a byzantine series of turns. He intended to stop a hundred or so meters short of the cave entrance to surveil it before going in. He slowed when he began to see the snow machine's tracks winding to a conclusion, leading into a hole in the mountainside. These snowmobiles, fortunately, ran with little noise, like a small Honda generator. Pack thought it unlikely that the sybaritic Mikel would be laying in ambush outside on the remote chance someone had tracked him here. No, Pack figured he would be inside seeking whatever comforts the cave had available. If Mikel's son had been right, his father would be in there with Ng Trang, who would whisk Mikel away to safety. And, Pack thought further, Trang probably has a protection detail with him. Pack would be cautious about entering before he had a clearer idea of who was inside. And now Pack observed another factor that complicated his planning: there were tire tracks out of the cave that extended a short way south before "U-ing" back north. The tracks were wide enough to belong to a truck or trucks. Clearly, it was an immense cave.

Pack whispered to Tetu to sweep around the exterior of the cave to identify any security Trang may have out. Pack would wait for Tetu to return before attempting to enter the mouth of the cave. If the kid Rennie was correct, there likely would be a security force, but a small one. Considering the operations they were planning were several weeks away, the heavy security wouldn't arrive until later.

Pack was running on adrenaline. He took stock of his situation: this was his fourth day with no quality sleep. He was dangerously frigid, and now was soaked to the bare skin. He needed to warm up or he would soon become physically unable to continue. He decided then that his plan to conduct a lengthy surveillance was no good. He would have to go in sooner than he wanted. He hoped the recon wouldn't take Tetu long.

Ten minutes later Pack heard a sound he had heard before, one he knew to be a rifle stock on bone. A rifle shot followed. One of the cave guards had spun around a moment too late. The big man had gotten too close to him. To Pack's front maybe thirty meters another man with a rifle ran across his field of view. Ran, that is, as swiftly as the snowy conditions would permit. He was headed in the direction of Tetu. Pack took careful aim. He fired to wound the man. The round struck the guard in the right shoulder, which Pack presumed was his firing shoulder. He fell into the snow like a turkey from the sky, yelling in pain.

Ten minutes passed, then fifteen. Presently, Tetu returned to Pack. He carried an extra rifle and its ammunition. “He will survive, Matai. I tied him securely to a tree.” Pack motioned for Tetu to sit. He whispered, “Let’s see if anyone else is guarding the cave. I’m awfully cold and tired, as much as you, but let’s wait another fifteen minutes.” Meanwhile, the felled man in the snow continued his pleas for aid. Nobody came. “Tetu, you overwatch me from here. If I call, it means you need to come in.”

Pack strapped the ammo belt around his waist. One of the rifles had a sling, which he loosened in order to strap it across his chest. He carried the second at the ready, pointed at the cave entrance. Only a few feet were illuminated by the ambient light. Not wanting to walk into an ambush, he fired three bursts of three rounds each across the width of the entrance. Sort of a one-man reconnaissance by force. One shot came back at him, then another. Both were wide by several feet. The echo inside gave no clue as to precisely where the firer was. Either the opposing shooter couldn’t see him or he was a poor marksman.

Pack dove inside, trying to get inside the cone of darkness as quickly as he could. Now that he was in a dry place, he could wait for the shooter to make the next move. It wasn’t long before he heard a rustling and a grunt some distance deeper in the darkness. He fired a round in that direction, rolling and low-crawling ahead. In reply, he heard a “Shit!”. Now Pack was thinking there was only one man ahead of him, and it sounded like a frightened man. He noticed it was surprisingly warm in here, suggesting a vent system and probably lights and heating as well. If this were a planning and operations center, it would have lights.

Another round cracked out, a disconcerting series of *whizzes* sounding as it ricocheted around the walls. Pack returned the fire, not with one round, but with another burst of three from the semi-automatic. Two more rounds followed from the opposing shooter, and again Pack returned the fire. “Stop!” the man screamed. Pack recognized the voice as Mikel’s.

"Give it up, Mikel," Pack said in a strong voice. "You're a play soldier and I'm a Marine. I'm bound to kill you if you don't give yourself up. Decide how you want it."

In response, Mikel fired two more rounds blindly. One came the closest yet to Pack, maybe inches away. Pack rolled again, then low-crawled in another advance on Mikel. From his new position Pack returned the fire once more, but this time, he got an agonized shriek in reply. "Help me, Pack, damn you. I'm hit bad. Help me, damnit!"

"Turn on the lights and let me see you," Pack called back, hoping he was correct about there being lights.

"I can't walk...light switch is on left side about five feet inside the mouth of the cave," Mikel moaned.

Pack crawled his way back, and after a half-minute of feeling found the lights. As he flicked them on, he hit the deck again out of abundant caution. Mikel had told the truth. He lay about fifty feet back with his rifle at his side. What appeared to be a laundry bag sat on the other side. "Reach down and throw your rifle away from you, holding it barrel first," Pack ordered him.

Pack had caught him with a round in the center of the thigh, and it had gone all the way through. It was definitely bad. He could rip clothing off himself or Mikel to make a tourniquet, but he asked Mikel where he could get something better to tie it off. "In the back," Mikel said. "Hurry!"

"Is anyone else back there, Mikel? 'cause if there is, I'll kill you with my hands by ripping your leg off."

"Nobody, I swear, just get something. I think I'm going to pass out."

Pack called Tetu in, assigning him to cover Mikel while he went deeper into the cave.

Pack walked rearward until he came to a fork. He took the right fork, from which he saw that both forks merged into the same huge open space. There was a backhoe, several trucks of various sizes, supplies of all sorts, a medicine chest, a vast cache of weapons and explosives, as well as a mapboard and multiple ringed notebook binders. From the medicine chest he drew out compresses, rubbing alcohol, hydrogen peroxide, and a bottle of aspirin. He returned to Mikel, cleaned the wound, and applied and tied the compresses and tourniquet. He then gave him a handful of aspirin with a bottle of water to wash them down. Mikel's eyes bobbled in his head, his eyelids beginning to close. Pack slapped him wickedly across the face.

Mikel moaned more. Pack said, "That slap's for your son, the one you'll remember you deserted. And I have one for each of the other one hundred twenty-four you left to die. Keep your eyes open, Mikel, or I'll leave you here to die."

"Get me out of here, to a doctor," Mikel moaned weakly, his head drooping. Pack walloped him again.

"I'll take you out when you've answered my questions," Pack said. "First, what were you and Trang up to?"

"I was giving security to operation coming up." He was nearing incoherency. Pack's hand whiplashed Mikel's face again.

"That's three, Mikel," Pack said. "Only a hundred twenty-two to go. Where is Trang and what is the operation?" He had to keep Mikel conscious for another minute at least.

"Vancouver, to get casket. Going to bring terror to America," Mikel said. His head lolled again, and Pack slapped him, hard, a fourth time.

"What kind of terror, where?" Pack prodded.

"Dirty bomb, chlorine explosion, other stuff," said a flagging Mikel.

Pack gripped the area of the wound. Mikel cried out in agony. "I'll do it until you answer, so where?"

"Las Vegas, Lexington…the one in Kentucky, someplace in Alabama, Buffalo."

Pack slapped him a fifth time. "When?"

"Couple more weeks. One's already started."

Pack ripped at his bad leg. More agonized screaming. "The woman left, going toward Alabama."

"A'nh Tran?" Pack said.

"Oh, Lord, yes...it's A'nh, don't touch my leg again," Mikel begged.

"When did she leave and what was she going to do?" Pack said, raising his hand as if to grip the leg.

"Poison water supply."

"What part of Alabama?"

Pack ripped the leg once more, Mikel crying out in pain. "Northern part, can't think of name. Name some, and I'll answer."

"Montgomery, Huntsville, Tuscaloosa?" Before Pack could continue, Mikel screamed, "Huntsville, damnit, now stop!"

Another slap. "When did she leave, I asked you."

"This morning, few hours ago, same time Trang left."

Pack attached a splint to Mikel's leg. He seized Mikel's moneybag and stuffed five ringed binders into it. Then he went outside and tied the two snowmobiles together, one behind the other. He returned to Mikel, who was now a dead weight after passing out. He hoisted the Sovereign over his shoulder and cinched him down on the snow machine.

Tetu disarmed the man Pack had wounded in the shoulder, and cinched him onto the machine with the Mikel.

Following their own tracks in, they passed within a couple hundred meters of the Sovereign compound, before turning south. The nearest place on the way back to Georgann's store was Reverend D'Artagnan's house, where Pack dismounted to look into the fuel tank. Because of pulling the extra load, he was near empty, as he suspected. He got off his machine and went up to Dar's door.

"I'm gonna need your vehicle," Pack said curtly.

"That's my only car," Dar said. "That's life and death to me."

"Listen, preacher, I haven't slept or eaten in four days, and I'm not in a good mood. Two men on the snowmobiles out there don't have long to live. I won't argue. Hand over your keys."

The minister went inside to retrieve them. He said to Pack, "I could have you arrested for this, you know?"

Pack looked him in the eye, grinned, and said, "Make the call, Rev. Better hope I don't wreck your vehicle."

Back at the store, several members of the posse lay asleep, uncovered, on the center of the floor. They were Shane and Craig and Nick. Georgann sat on her high stool awaiting customers. The women of the men on the floor sat quietly in the wicker chairs. Keeley was pacing the floor, worried sick about Pack and Tetu, who had not returned, going on nine hours after the other men had come back. Tom and Chesty were down at the house, Tom preferring to let the returnees sleep undisturbed.

Then a vehicle Georgann recognized as the minister's pulled up. She waited for him to come in. Instead, she glanced out the front window to see Pack with a man draped across his shoulder. "It's the General!" she screamed out. Then Tetu crossed her view with yet another man across his shoulder. The sleepers roused, uncertain for an instant where they were, and Keeley ran toward the door. As she reached the door, Pack said thanks, and deposited a comatose Mikel across the countertop. Tetu set the second man on the floor beside the counter.

"Call Lincoln County for two ambulances," he said wearily. "One for here and another for the cave. I'll explain to them where it is." Georgann was on it.

Keeley fell into his arms. "Simon, the good Lord has answered my prayers. I am so happy to see you. Sit down, dear man, and let me get you and Tetu something to eat and drink."

"I must look miserable," Pack said, "and I am."

"You're more handsome than I've ever seen a man, that's what you are," Keeley said anxiously.

"If you'll get us food, Keel, I'll get my calls out of the way while you're away," Pack said. "Then we can get caught up."

Tetu said nothing, just solemnly embraced everyone else in the store. Craig set to work again, doing his best for the wounded until the ambulance got there.

His speech cadence slowed to 33 rpm from fatigue, Pack patiently explained to Governor Dahl most of what he had unearthed from Mikel. He told Dahl there were things he could not say over an unsecure line. Dahl understood it was information of great import. Pack asked for a face-to-face, at his cabin, with the FBI man from Kalispell. Dahl said, consider it done, but that he was coming as well. He was dispatching a

Montana National Guard company of infantry posthaste to secure the caves until relieved by federal forces. He also explained that Sheriff Mollison had been a vital conduit of information in Pack's absence, to which Pack said, "Well, then, let's invite Joe too. Sounds like he deserves it."

When Keeley returned with a plate of food and hot coffee, Pack was sound asleep in one of the wickers. The laundry bag rested on the floor beside him. Now it was Tetu's turn to look on. Keeley gently grasped his arm. "Simon, if you don't want to eat, that's OK, but I'm taking you to a proper bed down at the Lodge." She got him up and to her car. Pack carried the bag as if it were the tablet of stone upon which the Ten Commandments were engraved.

Rex Carnes said he was sold out, but without question Pack would take his own bed. Pack insisted that he not be allowed to sleep past four in the morning. Then he added, "Keel, I'd like you to review the notebooks in that bag, and only if you get a chance count the money. Don't let anything in the bag out of your sight."

As Pack slept, Keeley went to work. Her eyes widened as she pored over the contents of the binder containing formulae written in A'nh's hand. After reading enough, she got up and asked Rex if she could use his computer.

Keeley stayed up all night. Pack had gone to sleep in the daylight, and now it was four in the morning. She had accomplished two things: one, she had lapped up the information in the notebook with all the formulae, and now understood it. Two, she had spoken with Rex Carnes and told him she was tired of waiting, and was going to write him a check on the spot to buy the Lodge in Tetu's name. He accepted the offer. Lawyers and bankers be damned at this point. She would tell Tetu when they got back to the cabin, at a more appropriate time.

She woke Pack up, saying, "Simon, you can use this bathroom. Shower, and here's toothpaste and a toothbrush I bought at the store. Hustle up. We have to be at the cabin by nine. I'll tell you more when we're driving. By the way, we got your Jeep back. I'm riding with you, and Tetu and Chesty can go in my car. Georgann said she'll make sure Dar gets his vehicle back. And the bag's contents are intact."

"My, my, aren't you Miss Efficiency?" Pack said with a smile. Pack's way of complimenting Keeley.

Once on the road, Pack said, "Don't keep me in suspense, woman. Seems to me you have something inside you want to get out."

"First, Simon, I bought the Lodge for Tetu, so I don't want to hear any more about it. It's done."

He reached across and patted her shoulder saying, "I guessed you would, and I won't say anything more. It's OK. Have you told Tetu?"

"Not yet. In a day or two we'll tell him it's a wedding gift."

"That's great, Keel. Really, truly great. I'm happy for him, and proud of you."

"Second, I found proof positive we're made for each other, Simon. When have you ever heard of an immunobiology degree having any utility in the real world? I'm guessing never. But last night I found a use. The woman, A'nh, is definitely brilliant, if misguided. She has developed a way to defeat the chlorination cleansing process in a water plant. This newly developed pathogen will kill quite a number of people, almost surely, and will put maybe hundreds of thousands in the hospital. Whether anyone can recover is in my mind an open question. From the correspondence with a Cal Tech professor she leaves behind, she claims to have fifty gallons of the liquid. I searched for information about where the water supply for Huntsville originates, and it is the Tennessee River. Now, where would she deposit this stuff? If she goes too far upstream of the water plant, she runs a big risk of dilution, so she isn't going to do that. It would be nearer to the plant, possibly even—to be sure it's undiluted—in the inlet intake source. We can study a local map to determine which location is most likely."

"I just added another vital player—no, the most vital player—to the meeting this morning. Keel, what you've done is fabulous. People who will never know to thank you, we hope, are going to wish they could've thanked you. I think you've abbreviated the FBI's investigative process in this case by a whole bunch. You've saved a lot of lives, I think. Thanks, buddy."

"You're welcome," she said softly. "And do you know that was the nicest appellation you've ever handed me?"

"What was that?" Pack asked.

"Buddy. What's stronger than 'buddy'? Nothing, to me."

"Well, in that case I'll call you 'Possum Face'," Pack said, chuckling, and tapping her on the shoulder.

Around Pack's kitchen table sat Keeley, Tetu, Pack himself, James Dahl, Agent Juan Martino, and Sheriff Mollison. Dahl's security detail waited in the open garage. Keeley had coffee and pastries for everyone inside and in the garage.

The meeting lasted three hours. Juan Martino was humbled, grateful that these other people had done so much legwork and, he had to admit, to the folks of the Yaak who preserved their reputations, and saved a good man in the process. He was equally grateful for being able to search Shining Earth without bloodshed. He had interrupted the conference several times to make calls to his people on matters of high urgency. One way or another they would nab Ng Trang, either at the Port of Vancouver or once he re-entered America. The FBI is particularly expert at catching someone on the run, especially someone who doesn't know she's being looked for. They would pin A'nh Tran down, probably well before she got to Alabama. And when the jihadists showed up in Lexington, Kentucky, they would not be greeted by anyone except FBI and local police.

Epilogue

Simon Pack and his little family, such as it was, for the time being including Swan Threemoons, had one final vital trip to the Yaak. Since there was no person *recognized* as a minister in the area, the locals gathered to speak their own prayers for the soul of Lucas Lincoln. Ranklin Shiningfish's words summed up the spirit of everyone else's. "My friends, Mr. Lucas Lincoln taught me about the true meaning of the biblical injunction to love your neighbor. He was ignored, shunned, and mocked by many of us, yet he may be the greatest among us. Only in the waning days of his life did we accept him. He was at the bottom of a barrel full of lies. We allowed him to lend meaning to our lives, and in return he died on our behalf. He was born in this Yaak Valley, and in it he happily died. I guess he never traveled to foreign lands, never supped at a finely laid table, never wore a fine suit. He is a part of every tree, leaf, and beautiful flower in this lovely place, no matter where we place him. Every animal in this vast land was his friend, better friends than we were, and could be they are mourning. I have met no person, not even among my own tribe, who had such powerful force in my life in such a short time. Why did everyone not see the goodness in this man? We let his rough appearance deceive us, let the devil play tricks with our own souls. Every human being, my friends, has something life-instructing to give. We have to discover what it is, and encourage it to come out. I am proud," Ranklin intoned, his voice breaking and rising, "to say unto the far hills that Lucas Lincoln was my friend, and I am evermore grateful that is so. God rest his gentle soul."

And then someone said the Aaronic blessing: "May the Lord bless you and keep you. May the Lord smile on you and be gracious to you. May the Lord show you his favor and give you his peace." They interred Lucas Lincoln.

Pack had thought a good deal about the decision—made in his absence—to let Lucas Lincoln join the posse. Specifically, he thought about the many comments he'd heard averring that it was a poor decision. After thinking the matter through, Pack concluded he did not agree with the prevailing opinion. He reviewed the chain of cause and effect: (1) Against the wishes of most, Lucas goes on the mission. (2) Lucas suffers an injury that ultimately proved to be fatal. Said injury alerts Shining Earth sentries to commence firing. (3) The firing begun by Shining Earth creates panic and havoc inside, thus further creating the conditions that led to Pack's door being opened. Additionally, the sudden gunshots were the immediate cause of Eustace Mikel's desertion. (4) Mikel's obvious desertion provoked Rennie Mikel to release Pack, on the promise that the assault on the compound would cease. (5) Pack's pursuit of Mikel led him to uncover the plot to rain terror on the four corners of America. No, sir, Pack concluded, Lucas's position on the posse had been fortuitous. Maybe the old man even knew that from the start. It was a good decision. He had saved Simon Pack and he had saved nearly all the residents of Shining Earth, as well as hundreds of thousands in other areas of the country Trang had targeted.

Montana's last death penalty was administered in 2006. Ted "Yukon" Phillips broke that streak in 2017. Eustace Mikel would be confined to a wheelchair for life, which would extend no more than a year into the future. He and three fellow Sovereign Citizens would follow Yukon Phillips in receiving a swift death penalty. The federal cases against Ng Trang and A'nh Tran promised to drag on for years, showing the value of being able to afford a high-priced legal defense.

Governor Dahl permitted a few people to stay at Shining Earth, but they were subject to monthly inspections for an indeterminate period, and gave their oath to provide for themselves through honest work. Young Rennie Mikel was cooperative; he was not the zealot his father had been in earlier years. He had witnessed his father grow slack the longer he enjoyed the privileges of his position. In fact, the genuine zealots remaining after Eustace Mikel's betrayal left Shining Earth voluntarily, and resolved to establish a new radical community in another section of the Yaak.

The amiable Nick Surgeon at Montana's Armpit saloon had no more need for muscle in the bar, except for the occasional special event when a significant number of outsiders were expected.

Sheriff Bob Hackman never made it to trial. He dropped dead walking across the street in the company of his lawyer. An autopsy revealed poisoning by cyanide.

The amount of money the FBI seized from Eustace Mikel went undisclosed. It is now the property of the US Government.

Shane Goodfellow had tons of backorders on the products he and Craig Wood had trapped, hunted, tanned, and carved. He was thinking about buying Craig a new truck...if Craig would have it.

Wilkie Buffer's University of Montana system was finalizing plans for a three-way exchange of teachers with the United States Military Academy and Hillsdale College. West Point's connection would lead it to siphon off some of the rich football talent in North Dakota and Montana.

Craig Wood's and Judith Buck's series on a nature channel vaulted to the number one show on cable. Craig was besieged by autograph seekers when he tried to go through the Denver Airport after being summoned for a production meeting by his network. Neither he nor Judith materially altered their mode of living.

Young Tom worked for Tetu whenever his mother could spare him. He adored Tetu and loved Chesty as if he were his own. Georgann's store continued to be the heartbeat of the valley, and she remained the beloved caretaker of her people. Tetu arranged a small ceremony to present Tom with an eagle fetish (heavenly spirits), the one he had intended to present Lucas Lincoln.

Kjell Johnson charged off on another crusade. He made a big splash with his new book about the aquatic invasive species outbreak, and how the state should've seen it coming.

Pack's pilot, Paul Fardink, was slow in recovering, but he did in full. He is scheduled for a fishing outing with Pack and Governor Dahl in the coming summer. He has told Governor Dahl, however, he thinks he will pass on flying for at least four years.

President Keith Rozan had missed another opportunity to bring down Simon Pack. Rozan seemingly had everything a man could want as a twice-elected President. His life was full; he'd probably had fifteen or twenty thousand meetings during his eight years, but the one he remembered most bitterly was with Simon Pack in the Oval. How he wanted to destroy the man who had stood in his way on big issues! The outgoing President wasn't going away, he knew, just to a new life, and he therefore might still have a chance to get at Pack.

No one in the valley darkened the door of Reverend D'Artagnan Castor's church ever again. His denomination, perhaps at the instigation of a member of the community, recalled him, presumably to Georgia, but the Yaakers neither knew nor seemed to care. Turning his back on Pack twice—among other reasons—was the death knell for his service in the Upper Yaak.

But the building Dar had used as a church did become the spiritual center of the valley that Pack had envisaged. The minister was the genuinely and thoroughly Christian Swan Threemoons, and she led a Bible-based church. The membership roll grew rapidly, quickly outgrowing the small wooden church. Her ministry to abused girls and women of the Kootenai tribe was paying rich dividends. Tetu was proud of her in the extreme. As was Chesty, it seemed, as he sat respectfully beside her as she preached at each Sunday service. Relations between the Kootenai and the white residents spilled over into a number of non-church-related activities.

Tetu had occasional misfires with respect to his Lodge responsibilities, but he learned not to make the same mistakes, and the outdoorsmen who frequented the place loved him. The reservations list for his Lodge was thick for twelve months out. But nothing mattered more than the wedding he was planning with Miss Swan Threemoons. It would take place in Tetu's Sportsman's Lodge. The gift from Keeley had been refused. He promised to repay her. The most he would accede to her wishes was in accepting a lower-cost loan than he could get at any bank. His devotion to Matai Pack continued to be solid as granite. He and Swan would visit Keeley and Pack often.

Governor Dahl had faced big challenges in his first few months in office, but he had handled them all with relative aplomb and great understanding. At this early time, the citizens of the Treasure State gave him their unqualified stamp of approval. He was altogether happy to be where he was. He had scheduled a summer fishing trip with General Pack.

Simon Pack and Keeley Eliopoulous were still thinking about making it official. They viewed themselves as two people meshed in every critical like and dislike. They were considering the possibility of a honeymoon to Greece.

There was peace in the valley again.

One evening not long after the culminating events in the Yaak, Pack slipped out of the cabin without telling Keeley or Tetu. It was just for a walk up and down the dirt road near his house. He wanted to be alone in the bracing night air for long enough to let his mind convert all the discrete events of the many Yaak experiences into a short motion picture. First, his brain had been bruised, literally, then figuratively, as he caught sight of all his shortcomings as Governor. The picture went from gloomy to cloudy to ominous. He had feared darkness for the people of the Upper Yaak Valley. Now he could permit himself the makings of a small smile: "It's not dark yet," he was at last able to say.

Author's Note

This is a work of fiction. No character is in the whole a real person.

Similarly, no single place is precisely as I have portrayed it. I think impressionistically more than literally, and what I have described is the Yaak as seen through my own eyes, in person. I have great affection for the people and places of that wonderful piece of American earth. I hope this book conveys that love of the people and place.

Lincoln and Flathead counties actually split in 1909, not the more recent date I suggested.

I am absolutely certain the Lincoln County Sheriff's Department, led by Sheriff Roby Bowe, and the District Game Warden, are highly competent and professional, but making you otherwise helped in the telling of my story. Nothing more. Please accept my gratitude for your indulgence. Further, I've met a few Montana lawmen and unreservedly admire them. One of them is a former Marine who's a fine friend.

Special thanks to Mark Levin, whose excellent book, *The Liberty Amendments: Restoring the American Republic*, I used as the basis for the Constitutional Convention Pack led to restore federalism and limited government.

A few of the characters are named after my friends and relatives. If I've offended any of you...tough. Live with it; I love you all.

The most astonishing aspect of writing this stuff, to me, is how the story and characters develop on their own. I marvel at where they come from. I feel these characters as personal acquaintances, especially Lucas Lincoln, for whom I feel a special kinship, one beyond the boundary of author and fictional character. Whether this book is liked or loathed, it pleases me that when I struck the final period keystroke, the words that popped into my head were, "I want to be frozen in this moment." This last phrase meant to me that for the time it took to write this book, I was in a strong sense living in the Upper Yaak, and I hated to leave it.

In the end this book is a letter to my family and friends.

Thank you.

John M. Vermillion
6 February 2017

76381060R00160

Made in the USA
Columbia, SC
03 September 2017